In this Sign

AN HISTORICAL NOVEL

Lt Col (ret) the Reverend
LYMAN R COLEMAN

Published by

GENERAL STORE
GSPH PUBLISHING HOUSE

499 O'Brien Road, Box 415
Renfrew, Ontario, Canada K7V 4A6
Telephone (613) 432-7697 or 1-800-465-6072

ISBN 1-897113-04-8
Printed and bound in Canada

Cover Photo: Author conducts field service for 1 RCR, Germany, 1964.
Used with permission from
The Royal Canadian Regiment.

Author Photo: Used with permission from the
Canadian Department of National Defence

Cover design and layout: Custom Printers, Renfrew, Ontario

Library and Archives Canada Cataloguing in Publication

Coleman, Lyman R., 1930–
In this sign / Lyman R. Coleman.

ISBN 1-897113-11-0

I. Title.

PS8605 O445I6 2005 C813'.6 C2004-906711-7

I dedicate this story to...

Friends and loved ones

Foreword

Lyman Coleman is that somewhat rare combination of compassionate clergyman, enthusiastic soldier and romantic novelist. In the book you are about to read (and enjoy), you will find he has a good grasp of the realities of life in all three areas.

His fictional hero is a wartime chaplain who experiences all the horrors of the battlefield and all the problems that army chaplains face in their dual role as army officers exposed to combat, and as those who minister the gospel to as diverse a "congregation" (in those days 100 percent male) as one can imagine. Many of his "flock" had been separated from their wives and children for several years. Domestic upsets, homesickness and the inability to adjust to military discipline, plus the prospect of mutilation or violent death, were matters that were all brought to the chaplains' ears.

Added to this was the fact that he himself suffered from at least some of these worries. He, too, walked in the shadow of the Valley of Death, and yet he also had to set an example as an officer and champion of the Faith. In the midst of killing, he had to instill a sense of brotherly love toward captured and wounded enemy soldiers, and at the same time encourage the more reluctant soldiers to fight bravely against the enemies of their King and Country.

He comforted the wounded and the dying of each side, and buried each side's dead. He had to fit into the army's concept of the proper relationship between officer and other rank, and yet had to let down some of the barriers to fulfill his role as the Christian friend of all, despite their rank. It was a role exceedingly difficult to carry out, but the "padres," as we called them, of the Royal Canadian Army Chaplain Corps, in almost every case, carried it out magnificently whether in barracks or in action, for they were men doubly dedicated—to their King and Country, and to God. In Coleman's fictional padre, Ralph Russell, we find these qualities.

Coleman spent twenty-eight years of his life as a military chaplain and thereby gained a profound knowledge of his fellow man. He ended his military career as a lieutenant colonel and senior Protestant army chaplain. His service, on account of his age, was post-Second World War, but he acquainted himself with the wartime organization, equipment and customs of those times so that his writing rings true in the ears of the knowledgeable reader. As to his abilities as a romantic novelist, these will be discovered as the reader progresses from page to page. Coleman is above all a realist. He entertains. His characters live in the minds of the reader, for he paints them in vivid colours that portray human beings in both their strengths and weaknesses. Perhaps the best school for would-be novelists should be a few years as both a clergyman and a soldier. In that way they would get to understand people—which, after all, is the required art of a writer who has a message to give through his fiction. In any event, our author in point—Lyman Coleman—confirms that opinion.

Colonel Strome Galloway
OStJ, ED, CD
Sometime Colonel of the Regiment
The RCR

Chapter 1

Ralph Russell had been given a special gift: the ability to speak with people at whatever level he found them. When he reached out to them, they were aware that the man was totally with them. It registered on his face. It mattered not if it were an adult or a child, Ralph was there for them. Little children especially loved him, for he would sink to his haunches, smile engagingly, and immediately launch into conversation with them. Soon he would have even the shyest child in stitches of laughter. The man was a natural communicator and leader.

He had been raised as the son of an Anglican clergyman. His father was his shining example, and Ralph admired the man for his devotion and dedication to his ministry. In his late teens, Ralph made the decision to follow in his father's footsteps. He entered the four-year Bachelor of Arts program at the University of Toronto, and after completing his undergraduate degree, he became a student at Wycliffe College. In the halls of higher learning, Ralph hit his stride. He found that the freedom to pursue his own goals was both challenging and exciting. In the field of athletics he moved from the team sports he had excelled at as a teenager to develop individual skills. He found boxing a rigorous form of recreation that gave him both the thrill of competition and an opportunity to become physically robust. His social life and personality blossomed simultaneously. The female students were drawn to his shyness and boyish good looks, and he was physically stimulated by their attention. He dated but never became serious over one girl. Rather, he backed off from intense intimate involvement, as he believed purity of heart and body was an essential part of his calling. It was a promise made to himself that he would find difficult to keep.

Ralph graduated in 1937 with his Licentiate in Theology at twenty-five years of age. Two months later he was ordained as a deacon and asked his bishop to place him in a difficult parish where he could prove his worth, for deep down he was still beset with doubts as to his calling.

The Bishop of Ontario assigned him to the northernmost community of his diocese. It was called the Highland Parish, considered by most clergy as an arduous and widespread mission station. It consisted of three churches in three hamlets, each separated by several miles. The area was rugged country on the height of land between the Ottawa Valley and the eastern basin of Lake Ontario. Once the region was part of an ancient mountain range, but now, after several ice ages, the high peaks were ground down. All that remained was a land of rocky outcroppings and hog-backed hills, filled with lakes and streams and covered in a patchwork of evergreen and hardwood forests.

A great timbering industry had sprouted in the mid 1800s that drew strong, hearty men with their families into the highlands to settle and work the bush. The people who came first were English, Irish and Scottish. These were followed a few years later by hard-working Germans. They penetrated this unfriendly terrain by hauling their scanty household goods on sturdy wagons. When they arrived they found a handful of aboriginal people who had garnered a living at the headwaters of the Mississippi River since the earliest of times.

The families of English origin were storeowners, teachers, clergy and one busy doctor whose practice covered a wide expanse of the difficult territory. The Irish and Scots laboured for the timber companies, felling trees—primarily pine—in the virgin forests. The fallen trees were hauled to the riverbanks with teams of horses, where the logs awaited the spring spate to carry them downstream to waiting sawmills.

The German families were mainly farmers. It was their goal to find what marginal tillable land was available to homestead. They raised hay to feed the horses that drew the logs. In time, their stout sons joined the forest crews and, along with the French Canadians, they became adept at riding and guiding the logs down the swollen streams each April. It was a dangerous job, but paid well.

There was plenty of food in the forests, with deer and bear providing the most obvious meat source. The lakes teemed with fish. Large migrant flocks of geese and ducks blanketed the waterways in the fall. The streams supported beaver, mink, otter and other fur-bearing animals. It followed, then, that the pioneers of this country became ardent hunters, fishermen and trappers. They were skilled at improvisation, as ready money was only available for essential commodities such as flour and salt and other necessary items such as rifles, knives, axes, traps and fishing gear.

Their women were equally strong and imaginative. They worked long hours, bore many children, prepared meals for their families, made their own bread and pastry, sewed clothes and quilts, preserved fruits and berries for the winter months, and filled the root cellars with vegetables from their gardens. They smoked or canned the game and waterfowl for future consumption. As their children grew older, they, in turn, were allotted daily chores to share in the family workload.

The religious background of the people varied. The Irish came from Protestant or Roman Catholic backgrounds. The Scots were Presbyterian or Methodist. The German settlers were either Lutheran or Roman Catholic. However, in 1890, the Church of England congregation became the largest church of the area, when a Lutheran pastor was no longer available, prompting the Lutherans to join the Anglicans. The community as a whole was devoted to their respective congregations. They were a conscientious people, and they saw the handiwork of God's creation all about them. Even in hard times, when others would tend to curse God for whatever calamities they faced, the highland families clung to their faith with the sure and certain hope that the Good Lord would see them through.

It was here in the midst of these God-fearing people that Ralph began his ministry. While the logging industry still employed many, a budding tourist industry was developing. Improved access to the area encouraged "outsiders" to venture in for a fishing holiday, or to join the annual hunting season for waterfowl and deer in the fall. Cottages and lodges were being built on the sparkling lakes, which provided an income for carpenters and other tradesmen, while women and girls were hired to do kitchen work and cleaning. So, although the Depression years of the 1930s meant there was not much money, most had a roof over their head and food on the table.

It was love at first sight for Ralph, and the feeling was soon reciprocated for the young clergyman. His intense blue eyes quickly caught everyone's attention. His brown wavy hair drew envious looks from the fairer sex, while the men sensed a kindred spirit in his wiry frame; Ralph quickly adapted to the local lifestyle, and just as quickly the community accepted him.

It was haying season when he arrived in June, and as he made his first visits about the parish, he did not hesitate to strip off his clerics, grab a pitchfork, and help toss the cocks of hay onto the waiting wagon. He learned to carry a set of coveralls in the trunk of his car in case he needed them.

"Soft hands, Parson? Better get a pair of leather gloves if ya plan to fork hay like that," said Charlie Watkins, a farmer in the south end of the parish. He smiled with his eyes as he watched Ralph heft a cock of hay and lift it high onto the load.

"You're right, Mister Watkins. My hands are pretty good, but I'm not used to this kind of work," replied Ralph.

"You run back to the house and have Greta get you a pair of mine. Don't want to be blamed for blistering your hands now, do I?"

The next day Ralph purchased a pair of his own at Ostler's store in Plevna.

Visiting the farms, he was always made welcome to share meals. Over the breaking of bread he was instantly caught up in the conversations buzzing around him. It was a valuable learning experience for Ralph, and he grew to know the more intimate face of his parish.

Often the men would invite him to go fishing with them. They knew from his conversations that he enjoyed the sport. "I know this little speckled-trout lake back in the bush. No one ever seems to go there. Reverend, how about you and me wetting a line after the haying is over? Oh, there'll be blackflies, but you'll soon get used to them! The trout bite best when the wee beasties are the thickest."

Ralph rarely missed an opportunity to accept an invitation. He would trudge through the bush to those "little-known" fishing holes, and as he went, he would study the countryside. He would marvel at the lore that would pour forth from a companion as they trudged along a trail leading toward a lake. He listened eagerly to the stories about those who had pioneered the area.

"Those growed-up fields over there were part of the old Bonnie farm. They homesteaded here in the 1880s. Could never make a go of it. Soil full of stones. Every year they would bust their ploughs tryin' to turn the ground. See the big rows of stone piled up to separate their fields? Took it for forty years then moved to Alberta after the Great War. Never heard from them since."

A good deal of male conversation centred on hunting, and some of the stories were a bit far-fetched. The men often sought to see how gullible Ralph was, to see if he would swallow a tale, hook, line and sinker. They would watch their story play over his face until it was time to reel him in. Ralph didn't mind the leg pulling. It was all in good fun, and he stored these memories away in a diary. But many of the hunting legends were of keen immediate interest. He learned much from the telling and even though he had never shot a deer, he looked forward to the fall when he knew someone would eventually come by and say, "Going hunting tomorrow. Want to come?"

Ralph wasn't sure he could shoot an animal, but it's the way of things in this country, one of his fishing companions explained. "The Good Lord put the deer here to harvest. Many people woulda starved hereabouts if it weren't for them critters. Besides, there ain't nothin' better than a venison steak sizzlin' in a pan o' butter."

In the back of Ralph's mind there would always be that nagging doubt. All creatures great and small were gifts of God. Where did one draw the line between the beef of the fields and the game of the forest? In the face of it, he had been strongly imprinted with his maternal grandfather's innate skills as a hunter and woodsman. Grandpa Robert had been a government timber cruiser along the Ottawa River. In fact, he had worked the highland watershed area, including that part in which Ralph's parish lay. His grandparents had homesteaded a tract of land southwest of Pembroke in Alice Township, where they had raised a large family of twelve children. Ralph's mother and her twin were the youngest.

It soon came time for Ralph's first hunt. Two older members of his congregation, Ernest and Art, took him out into the bush. Art placed him on a rocky knoll above a beaver dam while Ernest circled away with the dogs.

Ralph had taken an immediate liking to Ernest in particular, a slight man with a small hump to his back, who lived in a log cabin in the woods. He, too, was a bachelor. He lived a quiet existence on the pioneer farm his German forebears had staked out on the Old North Road in 1875. He kept a couple of dairy cows and a team of horses that he used for logging his woodlot and ploughing his garden. The man enjoyed growing a variety of vegetables, particularly potatoes, which thrived in the sandy soil. He also raised honeybees. Ernest had a droll sense of humour that was reflected in the sparkle in his eyes and his ready chuckle. The man was well-read and always on top of current affairs. His quiet voice was respected in local politics and he accepted leadership roles in his church congregation.

Art was roughly the same age, but that's where the similarity ended. Art was a stump of a man, square of stature, rather pudgy, with a full, round face. His smile, rarely seen, was forced. He was easily riled and seemed to wear a perpetual frown. He had a vile tongue in his head and showed little respect for whoever might be within listening distance. He was sharp in his business dealings and renowned for his tight purse strings. Art was never seen without the stub of an old cigar clenched between his teeth, and frequently punctuated his conversations with a gob of brown saliva from the free side of his mouth.

Art laid out the description of the watch. "The main runway crosses below the dam. See there on the bank where the deer have been coming out of the water?" He aimed a stream of tobacco juice in the general direction. "They've got it muddied up a bit. See where I mean?"

Ralph nodded, trying hard to keep his bile down.

"A nice buck has selected this spot as his territory. Look over there where he's rubbed his antlers against that small tree?" Another stream of tobacco juice. "You can see he's a good one by how high the rub was made. And just under that hemlock, he's scrapped the ground, and pissed in the middle of it, then stamped his print in the centre. Oh, yeah, he's a nice one!"

Ralph went over to the hemlock. He could smell a musky odour.

"What's that smell?"

"That's the buck's way of letting any does in the area know he's nearby, and when their mating time comes, they'll know where to find him. The does have scent glands, too, and if they don't belong to another harem, the younger bucks search for their 'bouquet' and try to mate with them before the dominant male can get to them."

"Fascinating," mumbled Ralph, mostly to himself.

"Now make damn sure to watch all around you, Reverend. The old bucks like to sneak about, and if they see or smell you first, they're gone! And remember to stay still. Don't wander around. Plant your feet and swivel your head around slow like. Put your back against that big tree and don't move. The dogs should start over there." Tobacco juice arched in the direction of an oak ridge rising beyond the beaver pond. "You stay put till Ernest comes out to you. I'll be at the far end of the flood where another good runway crosses the little stream. From where you are here, you can shoot in any direction, but remember: the dogger is coming toward you from over yonder hill. Know what you're damn well shooting at before you squeeze the trigger." A large gob of spit ended the lesson as Art hefted his rifle and walked to the right at a swift but quiet pace. He soon disappeared from sight. Ralph peered around expecting a deer to jump up at any minute.

Soon his arms ached from holding the gun at the half ready. After thirty minutes he leaned the rifle against the tree beside him, took a cigarette from his pack of Players, tapped the end against his thumbnail and lit it. The pull on the fag seemed to steady him. It was a brisk frosty morning and he had raised a sweat on the way into the watch. Now he was feeling chilly and began to shiver. He wanted to jump up and down to warm himself, but he remembered Art's instructions.

Across the beaver dam, on the opposite slope of the oak ridge, Ralph heard the sharp yip of Ernest's beagle pup as it caught fresh scent on the frozen ground. In a few moments it was sounding a clarion peal, as it headed directly for Ralph's watch. Fully alert, the young hunter strained to spot the deer, when, all of a sudden, he saw it clear the crest and come leaping down the slope in his direction.

For a moment Ralph was mesmerized by the fine buck bounding toward him with its long white tail flashing against the darker background of the forest floor. When the animal struck the flooded seep at the foot of the dam, water and mud flew in every direction. Ralph remembered his instructions, and in a fluid, intuitive movement, brought the rifle to his shoulder, drew in a breath, took aim and fired. He fully expected to see the magnificent animal drop in its tracks. But it was not to be. With a gigantic leap the buck cleared the ditch and swiftly changed direction. Ralph fired two more hurried shots at the moving target before the deer disappeared from sight over a slight rise. Ralph stood there shaking. Now he knew what the men meant when they talked about "buck fever."

A shout from his right heralded Art's fast approach. "Did you get him?" he barked.

"I guess I missed," Ralph groaned.

At this moment King, the beagle, with Spot, the second hound, trailing, splashed across the muddy ditch to the track the deer had taken. He began to squeal stridently as if to say, "You missed! You missed! You missed!"

"Come with me," shouted Art on the run, "I think you may have hit that goddamn deer. Sounds like the dog's on a blood trail."

With a surge of hope, Ralph plunged after the other hunter, and when they had mounted the rise where the animal had last been seen, they came to an abrupt stop. For there, below in a small depression, lay the ten-point buck. It had been struck with the first shot, sucked in air, and had run another forty yards before falling dead. The last two shots had fired wide.

"Wow! That ol' bugger's a beauty! Congratulations, Rev!" shouted Art as he pumped Ralph's hand.

Within minutes, Ernest joined the pair, and with a teasing grin said, "I thought you had missed him when I heard those last two quick shots."

"To be honest, I did, too," replied Ralph with a blush.

"Now you've got your own good story to stretch," continued Ernest.

"I don't think it needs stretching," the young cleric suggested. "I think it's good enough as it stands." He was right.

This became the first of many adventures Ralph shared with Ernest in the highlands and the start of a whole new education: experiencing nature in the wilderness, appreciating the art of survival, and learning the skills of a woodsman.

News quickly spread throughout the community that the Anglican minister had bagged his first deer. Men gathered at the general store in the village later in the afternoon to witness the weighing-in of the 225-pound buck and to welcome Ralph into the fraternity of local hunters.

"That was some shot," one man remarked as he examined where the round had hit. "He must be a dead-eye dick!"

"That's about right," declared Ernest wearing an impish grin. "For his first deer, it couldn't have been better!"

That winter the new minister was the talk of the logging camps. Even though Ralph didn't stretch the story of the buck, Ernest, with a great twinkle in his eye, added a little more every time he repeated it. By February, he had the animal "weighing close to 260 pounds," a near-record size for a highland's whitetail deer.

Ralph took advantage of the snow-packed roads and frozen lakes to visit the logging camps where he was taught the use of the double-bladed axe and learned how to handle one end of a crosscut saw like a regular. He was always invited to share in the cookhouse meals, where he thoroughly enjoyed a good visit with the men. In no time at all, he was fully accepted as "one of us," an amazing feat in itself for an "outsider."

One day he met an old-timer who cooked for one of the gangs. "How do, preacher! Hear your grandaddy was Robby Armstrong from up Pembroke way. That right?"

"That's right," replied Ralph.

The old man settled into what Ralph quickly realized was a "story-telling" pose. His right hand, gnarled and red from long hours in dishwater, stroked his grizzled chin. He sucked on his squeaky old corncob pipe. He was a short, whizzled up, elderly man who had once been a stocky faller.

"Knew him back in the 1890s," he began in the Ottawa Valley twang so common among Ralph's parishioners. "Used to come to these parts timber cruisin'. Strong as an ox, and wiry too. Stood about six-two. Never cussed. Never touched hard liquor, but always stayed at the tavern in Ompah where they rented out a couple of rooms over the taproom. The men would come in from the woods on the weekend and booze it up, and when they got drunk, they'd have some real dandy brawls outside. It was a regular sideshow. The villagers would gather on the knoll beside the tavern and cheer them on.

"I remember one day when a burly drunk thought he was king of the bush and challenged your granddaddy to a fight. Robby said he'd have none of it, but the boozer kept at him, pushin' and teasin' him. Finally ol' Robby had enough. He said to the guy, 'If yer so durn strong, I'll challenge you to somethin'. Come in the tavern an' we'll have a competition.' Well, sir, in they go an' stand in the middle of the barroom floor. Both were wearin' cork boots, you know, the kind with metal cleats on the bottom, an' Robby says to the drunk, 'Here's what we're gonna do. From a standin' position we'll flip up in the air an' plant our cork boots in the ceiling. Whoever can do it the most times will be declared the best man, and the loser will buy drinks for the house. Agreed?' The drunk grinned a toothless smile and cried 'Yer on!'

"It was a sport in which he was well accomplished. The tavern had a seven-foot ceiling of soft pine planks, already well scored from countless other similar contests. They flipped a coin and yer granddaddy won, so he was first off the mark. Up into the air he somersaulted, clunk, into the wood went his imprint an' down he came to the floor in perfect balance with his feet together. A great cheer went up. The so-called 'King of the Bush' was next, and he, too, was successful. Another cheer erupted from his cronies who were betting on the side. The competition went on for twenty-two strenuous jumps until finally the drunk sunk to the floor in a heap on his last try. The crowd roared. Yer granddaddy said nothing, simply turned, nodded his head, and went up to his room. Nothing needed to be said, and besides, he was a quiet man who didn't need to boast.

"Someday, if you like, Reverend, I'll take you over to the old place, they call it a hotel now, an' show you exactly where yer grandaddy's cork boot marks still can be seen in the ceiling. He carved the date and his initials, R.A., right on the spot."

Ralph was tickled with the story and replied, "I'd like that." He told his mother about it some time later to her great delight.

"That preacher's some guy," the loggers agreed as Ralph left the camp. "A real down-to-earth fella." They grew to respect and admire the outgoing, versatile, young cleric.

In time, Ralph drew the younger crowd into his church, many of whom had begun to slip away from attending church prior to his arrival. He started square dances for the young people in the parish hall, and would join in the fun. It became a social event for old and young alike. Several of the local belles took a shine to him, but he treated them all with the same casual courtesy. This pleased the boys, for they saw no threat in him as a contender for their women. In that department he was still an "outsider."

Ralph's three congregations began to grow significantly as the young people joined in with their families. Ralph stressed the sacramental aspects of his church, and the worshippers responded with enthusiasm. He was a good preacher, too, and kept his sermons short. He limited himself to fifteen minutes to make his point, for he knew a couple of the older men would begin to nod off and snore if he took longer.

However, the introduction of dancing at the Anglican Church Hall raised the ire of the two Methodist mission ladies who conducted services for that denomination. They fumed and fussed over the gall of the young minister for starting "that devil-serving activity" and vowed to some day fetch him his comeuppance.

"Why the gall of that young puppy. And he calls himself a pastor. Just leading the youngsters into sin," sniffed Miss Martin.

"Should be rode outta town. No way to set an example," tsked Miss Clegg in a most unchristian-like manner.

"Well, we'll just bide our time. One of these days he's really going to bite off more than he can chew!"

Although the two old maids were narrow in their views, they were in fact devout in their own way and led their little charge as best they could.

The grip of winter began to recede in late March and the daytime temperatures began to creep above the freezing mark. It was the last

Sunday of the month that Ernest asked Ralph if he would be interested in watching the way maple syrup was made.

"You can even pitch in if you like, and I'll share some of the syrup with you. I don't have a fancy evaporator like some of the large operators. I just use a pair of old iron kettles, is all. I picked them up for next to nothing after I came home from the war in nineteen. I only make what I can use for myself, give some to my sister and brother in the village, and if the run is good, I'll make a few extra gallons to sell to the tourists in the summer."

"I'd like to help," Ralph answered with enthusiasm.

"Well, come out t' the house tomorrow and you can help me tap. We're about to get the perfect temperatures for the first real run."

"What is the best time?" Ralph asked.

"When you get a daytime high of forty degrees Fahrenheit and an overnight of twenty-five, the sap really pours, especially if the sun's bright and there's no wind. The radio weather reports are forecasting this for the next few days."

"What time should I come out?"

"Come out for breakfast at seven, and we'll tap after we eat."

"I'll be there," answered Ralph with a grin.

The next morning they had a hearty meal of fried potatoes and slab bacon and fresh eggs from the chicken coop. Slices of Ernest's homemade bread were toasted over the glowing coals of the wood fire in the kitchen stove and spread with farm-churned butter. A pot of hot coffee rounded out the offering.

Before Ralph arrived, Ernest had the horses harnessed in their stalls, ready to hitch to the farm sleigh when breakfast was over. He had placed two hundred tin pails with flat bottoms in the box of the sleigh, each of which would hold about a gallon-and-a-half of the sweet maple sap. His tools consisted of a hammer, a brace and bit, and a basket of cast-iron spoils. Ready for a full day's work, the two men, with the team and sleigh, headed out to the stand of hard maples behind the farm buildings.

"Hep, Tom," cried Ernest to his lead horse while flicking the reins. "Get along there, Lucy!" to the mare. A gathering trail was made between the trees, and as they came into the maple grove, Ernest would stop the horses, alight from the sleigh, pick up his brace and bit, and drill a hole for the spoil. It was Ralph's job to follow behind and tap the spoil into the small opening where the sap was already beginning to flow. He would then hang a bucket from the hook at the spoil's underside. It took them two hours to complete the job, and as they went along, they could hear "tink, tink" as the sap dropped to the bottom of the tin pails.

"Sounds like music, don't it?" remarked Ernest, smiling broadly. "I love this time of year when everything begins to come awake again."

"What do we do now?" asked Ralph with the eagerness of a convert.

"The first thing is to scour out the old iron kettles with sand and water until they are free of any dirt, and rinse them well. Don't want any grit in the syrup. When they are stored away between seasons, the dust and spider webs accumulate."

"Right!" said Ralph, "I'll get a couple of pails of water from the well."

When the cleaning was finished, Ernest went on to explain. "I use two kettles over the six-foot firepit yonder. You see where the two hollow pipes are anchored in cement along the edge? I have cranes that fit inside them to swivel out over the fire. On the extended end you see a bit of a crook and the kettles are hung in place from that. When the first has been filled with sap, it's swung over the hottest part of the fire. I let it boil down until about three-quarters of the liquid has evaporated, then I ladle it into the second kettle, and swing that one over the pit where the fire is a little less intense. It still boils, but slowly there. The first kettle is refilled with sap until it, too, is ready to be transferred. This is repeated until I have the quality of syrup that I like in the second kettle."

"How do you know when it has turned to syrup?"

"I'll show you when the time comes, but the simple answer is as the sap in the second kettle continues to bubble, I keep stirring it. This is called 'finishing off.' From time to time, I dip out a ladleful, and slowly return the sap into the container. As it runs over the lip of the dipper, I watch for a sheeting effect that occurs when the sap has thickened into syrup. This is a very tricky stage, for if you wait too long, the liquid begins to crystallize, and then it will quickly become maple sugar."

"What kind of wood is best for boiling down?"

"I use mainly windfalls of oak, maple, ash, whatever's around. But for a fast, hot fire, I burn split dry poplar or hemlock. The hardwoods leave a heap of ashes, but the latter turns pretty much to dust."

"How many gallons of sap do you need to gather to make a gallon of syrup?"

"That depends on the sweetness of the sap," replied Ernest. "In my sugar bush it's generally about thirty-five to one. That's a pretty good average."

Ernest worked his sugar bush for two weeks that spring, and Ralph slipped out to help him for a couple of hours every afternoon. The syrup would be ready to be "taken off" about two when it was strained through woolen bags into a twenty-gallon stainless-steel milk can. This done, the men would gather the day's run and store some in the kettles while the remainder would be left in the wooden barrels mounted on the horse-drawn gathering sled where it would be ready for the next day's boiling down. When the season ended, they had made sixteen gallons. Ernest offered Ralph half of the product, but the cleric declined.

"I'd be happy with two gallons, one for me and one for my parents." It was agreed.

In his second year in the parish, Ralph's stature continued to grow and was reinforced by his faithful ministry to his flock in particular, and the community as a whole. He was on first-name basis with the other clergy of the region, and offered to work with them any way he could. Most viewed this ecumenical approach as a generous form of Christian outreach, and esteemed him as a fine leader until one Saturday, when Ralph celebrated a marriage in his church. After the service, he was invited to the bride's home for a country-style reception, where beer and stronger drinks flowed freely. Ralph was no teetotaller, but neither did he drink excessively. He would sip on a beer or nurse a rye and ginger in his hand for an hour.

However, on this particular day, the two Methodist ladies, who were also members of the Women's Christian Temperance Union, were among the wedding guests, and saw Ralph appear to stumble and spill his glass. What they hadn't seen was the slap on the back delivered by one of the lads in the wedding party the moment before. The Misses Martin and Clegg promptly left the reception and returned to their manse to make several phone calls, including one to the diocesan bishop, alluding to the fact that the Anglican minister had been seen drunk. Furthermore they passed on a story that Ralph had had a wild affair while at university. On top of that, he was leading the area young people into sinful ways by sponsoring wild dances.

As it happened, a deanery meeting for the regional Anglican clergy was scheduled for the following Monday in the Highland Parish with Ralph as host. The bishop arrived with the rural dean and requested Ralph to meet with them privately prior to the main gathering.

"Your parish seems to be growing," began the bishop. "The reports I am getting are most promising."

"Thank you, my Lord, it's a wonderful place to begin a ministry. The people are the salt of the earth. A man couldn't ask for better congregations," remarked Ralph.

"However," continued the bishop, "I received a call over the weekend that you had been observed dancing in a drunken state. Is there a problem?"

"Why no, my Lord, I'm sure you have been misinformed."

"How then do you explain the call?"

"I have no idea what it's all about. I had a wedding on Saturday and went to the reception. Drinks were offered, but I only had two during the whole time, and I certainly wasn't inebriated. The bride's family will attest to that. It was a very sociable affair."

"I believe you, Ralph, but you must be careful. As a clergyman, you are always under scrutiny. You are expected to set an example. Some busybodies can't wait to find fault with a young priest's background and behaviour. So do be careful. Your first years of ministry are very important as they set you up for God's work in the future."

"Yes, my Lord, thank you for understanding," answered a thoughtful Ralph.

"The caller also suggested that there were some pretty wild dances being held in the parish hall. What's that all about?"

"No such things, sir. The young people needed a place to get together and the parish vestry agreed with me that since our hall was the only place in the entire area that could accommodate them we should offer a supervised environment. This is done with parental support and quite often the older generation is invited to the square dances as well. It's an occasion that everyone enjoys," answered Ralph.

"It seems that the caller was set on malicious intentions. I won't comment on what else was said. Now, let's go meet the clergy," concluded the bishop with a tone suggesting the matter was resolved to his satisfaction, if not the Misses Martin and Clegg's.

Ralph took his work seriously. He was diligent in every way to bring the services of his church to his people. He was non-judgmental and treated all in a kindly manner, even those who appeared to be undeserving. Sometimes, in retrospect, this had a humorous side.

Ralph made weekly visits to an invalid whose wife, Gertie, was a regular harridan. She would harangue and berate her "useless" husband in front of the clergyman to the point where the man blushed fiercely and held back tears. He gave her no argument and suffered her onslaughts in silence. When he was alone with Ralph, he would simply say, "She's a good woman at heart. Her life has not been easy raising a family of twelve. The kids are a handful and won't listen to her. She takes her anger and frustration out on me. I've learned to accept it for what it is."

A few months later the man died. Ralph conducted the funeral service and as the casket was lowered into the ground, Gertie leapt upon it and cried, "You can't leave me, Dan, I won't let you!" Her whipping boy was no more.

Ralph was speechless.

"Don't worry, Reverend," one of the older sons offered. "Watch this!" He took a shovel full of earth and threw it on his mother who literally rose from the grave, calling her son unmentionable names. Then, with her hat askew, she strode down the hill to an awaiting car.

Ralph could only shake his head and roll his eyes.

Another character in the parish was "Pickles" Petrie, whose lineage included Algonquin blood. He had married Eunice, a hard-working girl of German descent, and lived on the shores of Turtle Creek. Her family belonged to Ralph's parish, and she with her teenage children frequently attended church.

The husband had acquired the nickname Pickles when, as a young lad, he borrowed things without permission, which invariably landed him in a "pickle." However, after his marriage to Eunice he settled down and became an energetic rough carpenter and successful trapper and guide. The couple raised three boys, Fredrick, Gunter and Alfred, and a girl, Marta. In time he built on his waterfront property four small cabins that he rented to outdoorsmen; his enterprising wife, well known for her mouth-watering cakes and pies, provided substantial homecooking for the sportsmen. Pickles and Eunice worked well together as a team building up their small enterprise; that is, until Pickles began to hit the bottle. He was unable to hold his liquor and, in time, became the local drunk.

One September day, at the opening of waterfowl season, four American hunters sought Pickles out to guide them for the weekend. Since he was broke and "dry," he agreed, and moved the men into two of the cabins. That evening after their dinner in the Petrie home, they invited Pickles over and proceeded to pour him hefty ryes. A plan was made for the morning. Pickles was to place the men in duck blinds downstream from the campsite where wild rice grew. It was a great feeding ground for waterfowl. The hunters turned in early, but made the mistake of offering the last of the rye to Pickles to take home with him to consume "at his leisure." Little did they know that his "leisure" would be the rest of the night! He finished the bottle between the cabin and his house and lay down under a tree only to fall into a drunken stupor. His wife found him there at three a.m., cussing in his sleep, so she roused him, poured some black coffee into him, woke up the men in the cabins, and told them to be down at the dock in half an hour.

Pickles, somewhat in a fog, managed to get the men set up in their blinds, told them he would be a couple of hundred yards downstream and would come back for them after the shoot. Once in position, he lay down in the bottom of his canoe and fell asleep. First light came and the ducks began to rise. As they flew over the Americans' blinds, the hunters deemed them to be just out of range, and the main flock was gone in a matter of minutes. For an hour nothing moved, and then a single mallard flying high above passed over their heads going downstream. As it made its way over Pickles' blind, he fired a single shot, and the duck plummeted down to splash in the water beside his canoe. The Americans were astounded. How could the man have possibly hit a duck flying that high?

"Hey, that was some shot you made, Pickles—unbelievable shooting. How did you ever do it?"

Pickles shook his aching head and blurted, "With a flock like that flying over . . . how could I miss?"

Ralph never missed an opportunity to visit the Petrie family when in the area. Eunice always had a cup of tea and a delicious piece of pie waiting. Besides that, Pickles, when sober, had some pretty hilarious stories to tell about his adventures. At heart he was a very kind man and would go out of his way to help someone down on his luck.

The first two years of ministry passed quickly for Ralph. He was not only a pastor to his people, but took time to learn from them as well. They were good, hard-working, honest people who enjoyed the young priest's openness. The relationships shared and the bonds that were forged would be treasured for a lifetime.

Chapter 2

At the beginning of his third year in the parish, war was declared in Europe. Hitler launched his armies against his weaker neighbours before Britain and France responded in kind. The Second World War was underway.

The young men of the Great Pine Ridge Country, as the highlands were also known, were keen to sign up, and prepared to leave their back woods communities to join the North County Highland Regiment. Ralph felt left out as the men of his parish rushed to enlist, so he approached his bishop to seek permission to volunteer as chaplain to the NCHR. The bishop opposed this move. He told Ralph that he was too young and too sensitive to face the realities of war.

"I know all about it," stated the bishop with a sigh. "I was a chaplain with the Canadians at the Somme and at Vimy Ridge. I was with the boys in their bloody, mud-filled trenches. I saw the rats feeding on the bodies. I still have nightmares that wake me up at night in a cold sweat. In them, I see the fog of poisonous gas creeping toward me. I know you, Ralph, and I don't think you have the experience yet to deal with the horrors of war. Besides, I know for a fact that the Principal Chaplain is looking for clergy who served in the First War."

"Then I will resign my parish and join as a regular soldier," countered Ralph. "I must be with these men. I know them, and I know I can help them in times of suffering and stress." When the bishop still looked doubtful, Ralph continued. "I feel called to do this."

The bishop sighed again. "Don't be impetuous, Ralph. Give this more thought and I will contact the Principal Chaplain in Ottawa and seek his direction for the recruitment of chaplains.

The senior cleric called the Principal Chaplain after Ralph left the bishop's office.

"George, this is John Lyons in Kingston. How is everything going with you these days? Busy, I'm sure."

"Well, hello, John. You're right. Things are rather hectic these days with the sudden urgency of an expanding military," answered Wells.

"I thought it would be, and that's precisely why I am calling. Within the last few days I've had a number of my clergy request permission to join the chaplaincy. I need some guidance."

"My first choice is to bring in some of our former chaplains from the Great War. They're experienced and know precisely what is expected of them. Anyone younger would have to be trained, and at this point, the only training they would receive would be on the job!"

"But would the former chaplains be willing to join?" asked Lyons. "Most of them are over fifty and few are in top physical shape."

"I know what you are saying," began Wells, "but I feel strongly that experienced men must prevail over younger priests." Wells paused. "But to be honest with you, unit commanders are requesting chaplains of an age more compatible with the troops. They see older men as a liability in action, due to their physical limitations. I am going to have to give this more serious thought. In the meantime, use your own discretion, particularly where the militia is concerned. The majority of these formations have recently acquired younger COs with convincing ideas of their own. They must be heard," stated Wells.

"Right you are, George. I'll deal with my men accordingly."

The following day, Ralph took Fredrick and Gunter Petrie and Johnny MacDonald, three of the lads from his parish, to the NCHR recruiting station. He used the opportunity to inquire more deeply into the Regiment's need for a chaplain. While debating whom he should see, a hand was clapped on his back and he turned to see the friendly face of Scot Morrison, the lumber baron of the Great Pine Ridge area. He was wearing a uniform.

"Well, Reverend Russell, what are you doing here? Come to join up, I hope? I need a man of your calibre as my regimental chaplain. My padre is a little long in the tooth . . . getting old for the business at hand."

Taking a second look, Ralph saw the lieutenant-colonel insignia on the man's shoulders. Then he remembered that Morrison was a member of the militia and the commanding officer of the NCHR. Morrison was a tall, slightly built man sporting a trimmed, full mustache. His deep bass voice resonated as he spoke with ready laughter or steely determination, as the situation warranted. He had no patience with slackers.

Ralph replied to the colonel's question. "That's precisely what I came to inquire about—a chaplaincy. But I have a problem. My bishop doesn't want me to go. He says I'm too inexperienced."

"I want a chaplain who is young and strong," countered Morrison. "I know you and your reputation. You'd fit the bill perfectly. Let me speak with the powers-that-be in Ottawa. I am acquainted with Bishop Wells, the Principal Chaplain, and I'll call your bishop for an appointment to see him. We need young clergy who can keep up with these youngsters," he said as he pointed to a group waiting to be processed.

"I'd appreciate that Mr. Morrison . . . er, Colonel."

Colonel Morrison stood for a while musing over the encounter as he saw Ralph mingling with several recruits. He noted the immediate rapport the young priest had with the men. "He is just what I need to replace Padre Wright. I admire and respect him, but he has reached an age where he should stand down. The battlefield is no place for a man in his fifties. Now Russell on the other hand would be a perfect replacement. He is vigorous and keen to be with these young men. Look how they group around him—I must have him even if it means going to the Commanding General to pull strings!"

The following week, the senior cleric gave his priest grudging permission to apply for a chaplaincy, but not before sharing a few cautionary tales from the trenches of the Great War.

"It was most difficult to look into the faces of those dying men, their intestines rolling out in your hand as you cradled them before death. They called out pitifully for their mother or wife. It was even worse if you knew them by name, as you will—for many of the boys of the NCHR will come from the highlands, and your parish in particular. Your task will be daunting, and you will want to scream to the heavens for the boy's pain . . . and yours. You will feel that somehow you have failed them. I know, Ralph, I was there."

As he drove home, Ralph pondered the bishop's words and a well of doubt began to flood up within him. He began to wonder if he had done the right thing to sign up. Perhaps the role should rightfully fall on older, more experienced shoulders. Would he let the men down? Would he run like a coward when the shells began to fall? The great fear of the unknown engulfed him—doubts, doubts, and more doubts! He thought of the families who would be back home and knew it would fall upon him to write a letter to them regarding their son's sacrifice. How would he do this? He even had problems dealing with the death of the elderly in his parish. His emotions ran deep and surfaced quickly.

Within the month, Ralph was called to active duty. The NCHR was assembling its various companies in Brockville, Ontario, and it was there that Ralph joined the regiment on the 9th of October.

Prior to his departure from the highland parish, the three congregations came together to bid him a solemn farewell. Each of the churchwardens said a few words expressing for all their appreciation for Ralph's ministry among them.

Ernest, warden for Holy Trinity, summed it up best, "We'll sorely miss you, as both our priest and our friend. However, we give thanks to the Almighty that you will be with our boys as they step into the unknown. Their need will be greater than ours."

The transition to military life was relatively easy. Ralph was in top physical condition and excelled in the rigorous training. Every day he worked out with a different group of men. He had the gift of putting names to faces, and had made a vow to himself to learn the first name of every man in the battalion. Those he had known before welcomed him into their midst and informed others that the padre was a good sort. "He may wear the rank of an officer, but underneath those three captain's pips, he's a great guy, someone you can really talk to."

A few of the officers disapproved of Ralph's familiarity with the other ranks and brought it to the Commanding Officer's attention. But he saw this as an asset. "Let him minister as he sees fit," Lieutenant Colonel Morrison ordered. "After all, he has the care of their souls. Believe me, the day will come when the men under your command will benefit from this chaplain, as I am sure you will, too. My fear is that he will take his responsibility too much to heart. He is, as his bishop said, a very sensitive and caring man."

The NCHR concentrated on basic infantry training through the late fall of 1939. Many were given leave in early November, and the men used this opportunity to visit their families, or to go hunting one last time before going overseas. Ralph spent the first few days with his parents at

Pakenham, Ontario, where his father was parish rector. His mother, famous for her home baking, immediately set about to add a few pounds to her son's slim frame.

"Military life seems to suit you, Ralph." His father had noted his boy's fitness.

"That may be so," agreed his mother, "but he needs a little more reserve added to his ribs, and I intend to send him away with some!"

He let his parents pamper him for a few days, as he felt it would be some time before he would be home again.

"I'm going to slip over to my old parish for a final visit," Ralph told them. "Ernest has invited me to hunt with him, and I want to store up some of the 'essence of the highlands.' Like Mom says, I need a little bit extra of the good stuff to take with me."

His parents were aware of the special friendship that had developed between Ralph and Ernest. The old-timer had introduced the young priest to the lore of the woodlands: how to "tickle" a trout; how to track deer; how to travel the forest so you would know how to find your way out. This was brought home to them when their son began referring to his friend as "my father of the bush."

"The way you describe Ernest, he must be very much like my father," remarked Ralph's mother. "He, too, loved the rhythm of nature, and could slip through the forest without making a sound. You may remember the stories I used to tell you about him when you were small—how he was taught the ways of the woods by an Indian family. He loved to hunt and fish with them."

She was right. The two older men could have been brothers.

Ernest had a number of tame hives, but his great delight was to search the woods for wild honey trees. On any given summer day, he would watch the clover in his hay fields for any sign of bees flying toward the woods. When the worker bees returned for more nectar, he would sprinkle a little flour on them, then watch them fly back to their cache of honey. He would follow the "ghost" bees until they disappeared from sight, waiting a few minutes until he caught sight of the "ghost" bees, until eventually he found the tree where the sweet treasure was stored. He would then mark the tree and store the location in his memory until it was due to be felled, sometime after a light snowfall when the air was heavy with frost.

As it happened, Ralph arrived at Ernest's cabin two days before the opening of hunting season. The weather had turned suddenly cold, dropping to a few degrees below freezing, and an inch of snow had fallen the night before.

"How do," cried Ernest as Ralph alighted from his car. "Looks like conditions are goin' to be prime for the hunt. No problem trackin' the deer on this white blanket!"

"I saw some nice prints crossing the road just beyond the bridge," replied Ralph. "Looks like there's a nice buck in the neighbourhood."

"I've had my eye on that one. He's been feeding on the last windfalls from the old apple tree. Put my flashlight on him three nights ago—an eight-pointer!" announced Ernest. "And I saw the track of that old grey-muzzled rascal down by the spring. He must be eight years old by now, sixteen points or better, and I'll bet he's tougher than shoe leather.

"There's a few around, all right. We'll get a better idea when we go into the woods tomorrow morning. In the meantime, I want t' cut me a bee tree."

"Hey, that's great," replied Ralph, "but what will you do with the honey when we're hunting?"

"Oh, I've got a couple of old milk cans to store it in. You know—the ones I strain the maple syrup into. It'll keep in the woodshed forever. I'll can it up after the hunt's over."

"Is there much of a market for it," asked Ralph?

"You bet. Lots of people favour the flavour of wild honey." The friends chuckled companionably.

The two men spent the evening getting Ralph caught up on local events. A new clergyman had been appointed to the parish, and Ernest reported "the new preacher" to be nicely settled in. "He's not an outdoorsman like you, but he seems to be a nice enough fella. He's a book person. You know what I mean? Always got his nose in some book. I glanced at one on his desk the other day and couldn't make heads or tails of it. Hope he doesn't start preaching the way those books read, or he won't last long up here. People like a practical parson like you, Ralph—one who speaks their language." Ernest still blushed slightly when he called Ralph by his first name. When Ralph was in charge of the parish, everyone had called him Mr. Russell or Reverend Russell. Now they were simply friends, and the cleric insisted Ernest should call him by his Christian name.

It was still dark the next morning when Ernest roused his guest from slumber.

"I always thought soldiers were wide awake this time of day. Why, I remember in the last war they used to haul us out at four a.m., and we'd have our shave and clean-up done, boots polished, long before this. That is, if we weren't in the trenches up to our you-know-what in slimy mud. Then they'd just have us stand to and wait for shells to fly." Ernest sighed. "It was a dirty war."

After a hearty breakfast of porridge, toast, bacon and eggs, the two men hitched the horses to Ernest's old sleigh and loaded the milk cans and tools needed to fell the tree. The horses puffed out miniature clouds on the frosty air while their shod hooves crunched in the snow.

"Perfect mornin' for it," declared Ernest as they pulled up to the marked tree. "You ready to swing the axe? We'll notch it first, then finish off with the crosscut."

"Ready when you are," came the reply.

And the work began. It took half an hour to bring the hollow maple down with a mighty crash, sending snow flying in every direction. A swarm of bees erupted from their restricted nest, only to fall helplessly to the ground as they hit the freezing air. Ernest selected a spot a few inches below the bees' entrance hole, placed the crosscut saw against the trunk, and began to draw it across the bark.

"Grab the other handle and we'll be into the 'honey pot' before you know it!"

The trunk was cut in three places, each piece about two feet in length. In the hollow areas the honeycombs clung to the wood and dripped with golden brown honey. Using a broad knife and a tin dipper, Ernest scooped the viscous substance into the waiting pails. Finally he was satisfied that he had garnered all he could.

"The rest in the bottom is just bee-bread. We'll leave that for the bear cubs denned up in the limestone cave down by Mud Creek. They'll have it cleaned up in no time. Give them sweet dreams for their winter sleep . . . heh, heh."

Since the day was still young, they decided to strain the honey. It took the rest of the afternoon and part of the next morning to complete the job. It was a sticky business.

In the evening as they sat around Ernest's wood-fired kitchen range, their thoughts inevitably turned to the hunt ahead. A pack of cigarettes was passed around and both men lit up. Ralph had brought a bottle of rye and he poured out a shot for each of them to sip. Then a plan was tentatively made for the runs that would be made the next morning, the first day of the deer season. Ernest removed a piece of stationery from a pad and began to sketch out the lay of the land.

"How would you like to do some of the dogging this year, Ralph?"

"Hey, I'd like to do that!" his young friend eagerly replied.

"Well then, take a look at this rough map. It's important to know where you are at any given time, and where you've already been. No sense taking the dogs to a place that you've already run out. Notice how I've marked the points of the compass in the top right-hand corner? You take this with you when we run out the corner down by Mud Creek. See how the stream takes a ninety-degree bend here at this point," indicated the old-timer as he pointed to the sketch. "Here it flows from the west until it reaches the bend where it turns south. There's a main runway crossing here. It comes off the maple ridge that lays to the northeast. See here, I've made round circles indicating hardwood. Now in the cup of the bend, to the southwest, I have made little triangles. These show you where the evergreen swamp lies, mostly hemlock, spruce and a few pines. There's also a large grove of white cedar in the centre. The deer have them nibbled up as high as they can reach. It's one of their winter feeding areas. The main runway, after it crosses the stream, heads down through the evergreens, skirts the stand of cedar and comes out down by the bears' den. See? I show it here as a cave in the side of the hill. Notice how I indicate a hill. These contour lines come closer together to indicate how steep it is." Ernest looked at Ralph. "I suppose this is as clear as mud?"

"I think I get the hang of it," Ralph nodded slowly. "If I lay my compass on the map, and align it with your north-bearing point, it would certainly give me a rough heading."

"Right! Now in the mornin' you'll take the dogs right from the house, past the spot where we cut the bee tree. Keep going in a westerly direction into the prevailing wind. When they start, deer always fancy to run into the wind. Our line of watches will be in the hardwoods west of Mud Creek. You just keep coming through and you'll come out to one of us."

"Sounds like a plan to me," responded Ralph.

The ensuing days were devoted to hunting. Art and three others joined them, and each day they would move to one of the other men's bush lot. Their dogs were trained to hunt deer. Ernest's beagle, King, was a ripsnorter. He had a great tongue and let you know at any given moment the status of the hunt. You could tell when he was cold-trailing and when he was onto a scent. You definitely knew when it became hot. Two other dogs were used—a blue-tick named Spot and a female black and tan called Queenie. All three dogs were great hunters, and together they made the bush ring. It was a thrill for the men to hear a race, especially one that finished with a shot from a watch.

At the end of the hunt, the men butchered three bucks and a dry doe. One was the deer from the apple tree, but "old grey muzzle" escaped to live another year. Ralph saw him just beyond the bridge as he was leaving by the North Road. The buck stood regally just inside the treeline and nodded his heavily antlered head as the car drove by, as if to imply, "See you when you get back!"

In Pakenham, Ralph spent the last night of his leave with his parents before returning to his unit in Brockville. The first soldier he met brightly informed him that the regiment would be boarding a troop train within forty-eight hours. Strict security was imposed in the camp. The men were not allowed to leave the site, nor were any private phone calls to be made. Their destination was not revealed. Those returning from leave were instructed to ensure their kit was in order.

Ralph was requested to attend the Battalion Orders Group. It was here he learned that the NCHR was moving to Camp Valcartier near Quebec City and from there they would embark for England as a part of the First Canadian Division. This information was privileged and was not to be transmitted in any way, shape or form.

Later, in the company lines, rumours were rampant. As Ralph "visited" his way through the groups of men, he heard twenty different tales of scuttlebutt. A number of the highland men approached him. "Hey, Padre, what's the word?"

He shrugged his shoulders, "Anybody's guess. No doubt we'll hear soon enough."

And they did.

A battalion parade was called the next morning. The pipe band led the companies as they formed up, and Ralph felt a little awkward as he marched on with the other officers. He had not yet found the rhythm of the movement and found that he had to skip a pace to keep in step. He blushed with embarrassment. The commanding officer, Lieutenant Colonel Scot Morrison, addressed his men.

"Today, we take the first step on a journey into battle. At 1400 hours, the NCHR will entrain for Camp Valcartier. We will embark for overseas from Quebec City as a part of the First Canadian Division. I want you to keep in mind that in the days ahead you will hear many rumours. They've certainly been flying around this camp in the last twenty-four hours. Do not take them to heart. Do not spread them. We are going to war and any idle gossip can only do us harm.

"You belong to a proud regiment. It has earned its colours honourably on the field of battle by men such as you. Your training to date has been sparse, but there is every indication that you are fast learners. Listen well to your instructors. Many of them are veterans from the trenches of France, another generation ago. They will share their knowledge and experiences with you.

"You will be given lectures at the platoon and company level during the crossing. When we arrive at our destination you will immediately begin intensive field training, some of it under live fire. The hours will be long and hard, but at the end of it all, you will be ready to face the Hun. Remember our Regimental motto? 'AYE, READY.' In closing, I call upon our regimental padre to lead us in prayer."

Ralph, forewarned of this request, stepped up to the dais, while Regimental Sergeant Major Fred Hume gave the order to remove headdress.

"Let us bow our heads in prayer," Ralph began.

"Lord, we stand before you as men who are about to set out on a great crusade. We come from the hill counties of Eastern Ontario where we leave our loved ones in Your gracious keeping. We know not what lies before us, only that You, the Good Shepherd, are with us every step of the way. Give us the strength to face our foe with courage, and with the determination to carry on until the end when the kingdoms of this world become the Kingdom of our God.

"Let us repeat together, and always hold in our hearts, the psalm that has become known as 'The Soldiers' Psalm'—The Lord is my shepherd . . ."

It was the first time that Ralph had used the Twenty-Third Psalm with the men of his regiment. While he served with them, it would form a part of every worship service he conducted.

In the middle of the assembled troops, the pipe band skirled out the notes of John Newton's hymn, "Amazing Grace," as a closing hymn. The normally raucous screech of the bagpipes was somewhat subdued, as Pipe Major Will Farley led his pipes and drums in an emotional rendition.

The journey along the shores of the mighty St. Lawrence River took six hours. Many of the men had never travelled outside of Ontario, let alone the country. Indeed many had never wandered out of the highlands. The Great Depression had left them homebound, and there had never been enough money for gas, even if one had access to an auto.

A few were becoming nervous of this new adventure. A handful were plain homesick, especially the very young who had been encouraged to join up by older friends "for the excitement of it all." Ralph, ever attune to the men's changing moods, quickly picked up on the homesickness as he made his way along the length of the troop train, stopping here and there to give a cheerful greeting to those with long faces. He made a mental note of the more vulnerable individuals and planned to draw them out at every opportunity as they made their adjustments to a new and very different way of life.

Others were enthralled with the majesty of the river valley. Long, narrow farms settled under the seigneury system stretched back from the river's edge to hardwood forests. There, only a few bleached leaves twisted in the breeze, desperately trying to hold onto what had been, like some of the yearning men on the onrushing train. Periodically, great waterfalls plunged from the higher ground, while smaller streams meandered to the St. Lawrence. How different it was from the highlands.

At Quebec City, the train left the main line and was shunted out to Camp Valcartier. The first leg of the regiment's journey was completed.

It was late evening when the troops disembarked from the train somewhere on a siding within the sprawling military camp. A march along a road lit by occasional lampposts took them to a tented encampment where they were allocated space by platoons in company lines. Many fell asleep as soon as they bedded down. Others talked softly far into the night.

A bugle call sounded reveille at five in the morning.

"All right now, you lads. Up and at it," barked the NCOs. "No more sleepin' in for you lazy bastards!"

The men were flushed out of canvas and ordered to the wash racks and latrines. After ablutions, they were formed up and marched to a field kitchen area for a breakfast of scrambled powdered eggs, tepid fried potatoes, and two slices of dried-out cold toast with a glutinous portion of lukewarm porridge on the side. The meal nearly started a riot. The CO, eating in a mess tent nearby, stepped outside to see what the fuss was about. The RSM came forward and briefed him on the situation.

"It's the food, sir. The men can't abide it."

"Well, we'll have to see about that, won't we, Mr. Hume."

"That we will, sir, but it won't help the moment. Would you mind, sir, if I took my mess tins over there and ate with the men?"

"Fine idea, Mr. Hume, I'll join you."

The two most respected men of the regiment sauntered over to the noisy area, entered the kitchen tent, and presented their eating ware. The cooks came to attention and anxiously looked to the RSM.

"Well, get on with it," he ordered. "The CO can't stand around all day!"

The kitchen staff in a flush served the two men. Together they made their way outside and began to eat their food.

"Coffee's a little thin, don't you think, Mr. Hume?"

" 'Tis, sir, thinner than . . . than . . ."

"Right, Mr. Hume, and these vittles are a mite on the chilly side," he remarked as he spooned some porridge into his mouth. "Would you have the sergeant cook join us? I'd like his opinion as well."

The senior cook made his way to where the CO stood. He bobbed his head and rubbed his hands on his apron. A deep hush had settled over the groups of soldiers standing about.

"Morning, Sergeant Cuddy! Seems the men don't particularly care for your breakfast offering. I hope this is not an example of how you are going to feed the regiment. The food's not bad—it's just the way you've prepared it. Not up to standard. Might have to put up with it under battle conditions, but surely not in the tent lines. Do I make myself clear?"

"Yes, sir, perfectly clear, sir. I'll see it's done better, SIR!"

The CO handed the cook his mess tins, smiled a steely smile, and turned to leave with the RSM. A cheer broke out from the assembled men. The CO stopped, turned, and faced them.

"Men, we are at war. Sometimes things will not be as we would like, but like it or not, we have a job to do. So let's get on with it, and be sure you are up to the mark—or it will be more than the cook who hears from me!"

Ralph stood outside the officers' mess tent with an admiring look on his face. What had just happened was a sample of the decisive manner in which Lieutenant Colonel Morrison intended to lead. He, too, had a duty to perform, sometimes under adverse conditions, but do it he would. And in the doing, his men's well being would be high on his priority list.

The regiment's stay at Camp Valcartier was short. In mid-December, a few weeks after their arrival, a warning order was issued for their departure. The First Canadian Division made ready to embark for England, and the NCHR, along with the Hastings and Prince Edward Regiment—"the Hastie Pees,"—was the first unit to board the waiting ships.

Ralph's unit boarded the HMT *Ormonde*. She was a well-appointed ship of the Cunard Line. Her luxurious cabins had been re-fitted, each with six bunks for the officers. Meanwhile the men were crammed below decks to sleep in hammocks in any space available, and they soon began to gripe. It was their way of letting off steam. They envied the officers, who had received spacious accommodations and a commodious lounge for their mess. Rank had its privileges. Therefore it fell to the RSM to settle the men, and Mr. Hume was up to the task. He spoke to them in their mess hall and laid down the law in no uncertain terms. His words were sharp and crisp and his eyes shone with intensity.

"There are times when I think of you as a bunch of backwoods hicks without any grey matter at all. You skulk around and whine like a pack of hound pups lookin' for mother's milk. You are supposed to be soldiers, but it is obvious you don't know what that means yet! As you get to know me, you will find that I am a man of few words. When I speak I expect your brains to stand at attention. I am not given to profanity, so if ever I am driven to use that kind of language, you will know I am extremely unhappy, for want of a better word, and you will know it even more so by the actions that follow the words. If I have call to speak with you directly, I expect you to look me in the eye. I will brook no sullen or insolent glances. When I say something, I say what I mean, and mean what I say.

"Your behaviour at breakfast the other day was degrading. If ever the commanding officer feels it necessary to stand before you in that way again, you will have to answer to me, and I will mete out the necessary punishment. The sergeants and other NCOs will answer to me personally. I tolerate no nonsense. Do I make myself CLEAR?"

There was no doubt in any man's mind as to the RSM's position. However, they would learn in time that he was a fair but firm man.

As he made his rounds, his eyes missed nothing. He was a man of rigid bearing. His dress was impeccable. His moustache was precisely waxed. The company sergeant majors emulated his example and respected him as the top soldier of the regiment. They listened to his counsel and learned.

The HMT *Ormonde* picked up her escort off Anticosti Island. There had been reports of German U-boat action east of Newfoundland, and the Navy, ever on the alert for possible incursions, began its perimeter manoeuvres around the small, fast-moving convoy that consisted of the troopships and several transatlantic freighters, heavily laden with munitions and war material.

The North Atlantic was a wilderness of rough seas cloaked with a steel grey mantle of scudding clouds. Seasickness meant few men moved about the decks, and along the passageways the air became foul with the smell of vomit. The men of the NCHR were in no way born sailors. Some were sick from the time they stepped aboard, their faces turning to a green-grey pallor. Some thought their innards would be brought up on the next dry heave, while others expected they would surely die. They were a pathetic-looking lot. Ralph was not to be left out. But after two days at sea, he found his sea legs and regained his appetite.

The morning of the fourth day at sea, the RSM, not all that well himself, let it be known that a cabin inspection would take place at 1000 hours. On hearing this there were loud howls of complaint from the men, but by the time the check was made, some semblance of order had manifested itself below decks. The men, gaunt and ailing, stood by their bunks with their kit laid out on the mattresses. The RSM did not dally in his rounds, and the men put up as brave a front as they could muster. Mr. Hume's countenance did not alter as he made his way from place to place. He looked each man in the eye, gave a slight nod of his head, and moved on to the next. Later that day many of the men stood to for the evening meal. Somehow they began to feel a little better as they pulled themselves together. A ghost of a smile appeared on the RSM's face as he glanced in at the diners.

Two days later most members of the regiment had become accustomed to the motion of the ship and began to move about. Some played cards while others read. Two hours in the morning and afternoon were set apart for lectures on the art of warfare. Mess tables were set aside to permit calisthenics—one company was brave enough to work out on a wind-protected deck.

That night the ship's company was awakened by the sound of depth charges and the whoop of escort warning sirens filling the heavy air. A general alert was given on the troopship, and the men scrambled to don their life preservers and put into practice their lifeboat drills. All lights aboard the vessel were dimmed for blackout, which only added to the soldiers' fears.

"Stay in place until you receive orders to move. Check your life preservers to ensure they are properly secured. Section commanders make a head count and advise your men as to the procedure for abandoning ship," shouted the NCOs.

Each taut face was attentive in the murky, low light. The occasional explosion of underwater munitions—too close for their liking—vibrated along the length of the ship. The quiet, when it came, was almost unnerving. Anxious glances were exchanged. Then, from somewhere out of the depths of their apprehension, someone cracked a joke, and the tension dissipated. Small talk resumed, and soon relaxed into noisy chatter. The all-clear sounded, and the men shouted, "Hurrah for the Navy!"

It was a chilling experience that became an "instant" war story, and one that would be told many times over with as many embellishments as there were men to tell it.

Two British destroyers joined the convoy mid-Atlantic. The high swells had receded. Soldiers lining the rails cheered as the warships came within hailing distance, while sailors on the attending ships waved back. The meeting of soldiers and sailors would not always be as cheerful, as the army men would soon find out once ashore. Inter-service rivalry would spur on many donnybrooks, especially among the rowdier elements in the forces, prompted by a rude remark in a pub or when a man made eyes at another chap's girl.

It was a foggy morning when the convoy made port in Southampton. The dampness penetrated to the bone, and the soldiers donned layers of clothing to protect against the chill. It was winter, and a foreshadowing of the unpleasant days ahead.

Military lorries awaited them at dockside, and the NCHR moved off to Aldershot, some fifty miles distant, by way of Winchester. Ralph noted the spires of the great cathedral as the road convoy passed through the town. He recalled its history and knew he would visit in the near future to absorb some of its fascinating antiquity.

As he bumped along the narrow English roads, a light rain fell and his thoughts turned homeward. This countryside was quite different to the highlands. It would take some getting used to. The damp air suddenly reached his bones and he shivered. He realized the chill was not just the weather but the unknown future that lay ahead.

Chapter 3

Aldershot was the principal base of the British Army, encompassing a vast area around the garrison town, and the NCHR, with other elements of the 1st Canadian Division, was assigned space in Barossa Barracks. It was a cold, damp winter, the worst in forty years, and the quarters were inadequately heated. The next few months would be a difficult period for the troops. They would miss their cosy Canadian homes, hearty meals and the ability to come and go as they pleased. Griping, a favourite pastime of soldiers, generated a fair bit of heat itself.

Occasionally, Ralph would walk through the barracks, often to deliver messages from home—sometimes good news, sometimes bad. But even then, there was the odd man who mouthed off because he saw the padre as an officer who was invading their privacy. Such was the case with Private Joe Martin, a boy from Ralph's former highland parish.

In January 1940, a message had come in from Canada to inform Private Martin that his father had passed away. The adjutant called Ralph in and asked him to deliver the death notice to the soldier. It was early evening when the padre went to Martin's quarters. Men were lounging around in small groups, shooting the bull or playing cards. Some wore greatcoats against the chill, while others draped their shoulders with grey army blankets. The room was thick with tobacco smoke. Ralph stood at the doorway and called out to one of the lads that he knew, and asked if he would fetch Martin. At the sound of the padre's voice, several of the men sent sour looks his way, and one even grumbled, "What's he doing here?"

When Martin came out, Ralph suggested that he get some warmer clothes on, that he wanted to speak to him in privacy. The room became silent as the soldier donned his greatcoat and followed the padre out of the barracks. They made their way to the small office that Ralph had been allocated near the men's quarters—an area readily accessible to them.

"What's up, Padre?" asked Martin.

"Come on in, Joe, it's a little warmer in the office. I'm lucky to have a small coal fireplace and it makes it more comfortable for a talk."

"Am I in trouble, Padre?"

"No Joe, but I have some bad news for you."

"Oh God, what's happened?"

"Your dad's had a heart attack, son."

The boy looked stricken, "But he's all right, isn't he?"

"I'm afraid not, Joe. They couldn't revive him. It was quick, so he didn't suffer. At least that's something to be thankful for."

Martin heaved a great sob and tried to hold back the tears. He and his dad had been very close, more like buddies than father and son.

"Let it out, Joe," counselled Ralph. "We're here by ourselves, and I know how close you were to him. He was a great guy. He used to brag about you all the time and tell everyone what a great shot you were. 'Even as a kid,' he would say, 'Joe could hit a partridge in the eye with a .22 at thirty paces.'"

With those words, the young soldier released his emotions.

Shortly, he said, "You mustn't think much of me, Padre, with all this crying. I'm not one for blubbering. I can hold my own."

"I know you can, Joe. Someday, with your courage, you'll make him even prouder. You're a good soldier. I've watched you. You've got a lot of your old man in you. Remember how he was gassed in the last war? How he came back and fought the sickness in his lungs? Some said Tom Martin would never hunt again. But he fooled them. No way was it going to get him down. He was a man with guts, and he's passed that quality down to you. I know he has."

Ralph put an arm around the lad and gave him a pat on the back. "You stay here as long as you want, Joe. I know you'll want to be alone for a while. I'll come back later and we'll talk if you want."

"Thanks, sir." There was a pause, followed by a shy question. "Could we have a prayer together? My dad would like that. He always said that if you get down in the dumps, say a little prayer, and the Good Lord would be there for you."

Ralph never forced "religion" on any man. Instead, he preferred to wait for them to indicate a need for a few words. It happened aboard ship on the way over, and he knew that somewhere down the line, when things got tough, it would happen more often. Most of the lads came from God-fearing stock, and had been brought up to say their prayers. They knew when the time was right. Ralph could tell by the men's demeanour how seriously they were involved in worship. Some were opposed to attending formal services, and would do anything to get out of it. Deep down, Ralph understood them, and it bothered him that compulsory church parades were a source of aggravation to them. But, that was the army, and those were the orders. He would try to talk to the objectors individually on the side.

"I know you hate being forced to attend the services. That it goes against your grain for whatever reason, good or bad. If I had my way, I'd make them all voluntary. But I don't have my way, even though I've made my feelings known to the powers that be. I'm told, as you are told, 'Get on with your job, Padre. It's a mainstay of discipline!'" More often than not, those men were placated to some degree by Ralph's personal interest in them. They didn't dislike him so much as they disliked the system.

Throughout the winter, the men of the 1st Division were drilled and manoeuvred until they came in from the cold, wet to the skin and disgruntled. They had difficulty drying their sopped clothing and frequently had to climb back into damp battledress. Many came down with colds and flu-like symptoms. The NCHR medical officer, Captain Sandy Jones, attending a 1st Brigade Mess function, casually complained to a senior officer that the conditions the men were training under were reprehensible. He, too, was basically told to get on with his job.

"Doc," as he was dubbed, was a country boy who had been raised on a poor farm north of Highway No. 7 in Frontenac County. His parents had scrimped and saved to find enough money to put him through medical school. Fortunately, he had been able to find summer employment to help pay for these expenses. In winter, he also worked as a waiter in a Toronto restaurant close to the university. No one ever knew how he endured the long hours of work and gruelling study. During that period he had no time for a social life, even if he had wanted one, and became rather introverted—a bit of a loner living in a shabby room near the campus. This hardship added a certain amount of depth to his character.

Sandy was a good-looking, barrel-chested man, six feet tall, with black hair and black eyes. He suffered fools lightly, and when his medical opinions were ignored or criticized by those outside of his profession, his mood changed quickly, revealing a hot temper beneath his normally quiet and reflective nature. He and Ralph became fast friends almost immediately, and worked well together as a team.

After receiving his comeuppance for his complaint against general health conditions, Doc later stormed into Ralph's tiny office fuming like a volcano ready to erupt.

"I've never in my life been so pissed off with another human being as I am right now! You won't believe what I've just been told!"

"Whoa, sit down before you blow a gasket, Sandy," urged Ralph. "What's the fuss?"

"I was just unofficially talking to one of the staff officers from Brigade about the wet conditions the men are training under—being marched here and there, getting drenched and unable to get their clothing dried properly before another exercise. You'd think they'd let them have a break in between to get their kit ready. But no, orders are orders, come hell or high water. Why you'd think they were being trained for the Great War all over again—digging trenches and marching in the pouring rain. Didn't they learn from the sickness caused by the last time?" On and on he ranted, his face scarlet, until finally he subsided.

Ralph waited patiently, knowing that the outburst would help relieve Sandy's pent-up feelings.

The incident tickled the padre's funny bone, and Ralph first grinned, and then laughed aloud.

"What's so funny?" bellowed the MO.

"Sorry, Sandy, but right at this moment you're so out of character, I just can't help myself," chortled Ralph, a bit out of character himself. "You're always so cool, calm, and collected."

The MO blushed and slouched against the doorframe. A moment later, he too was giggling. "Sorry Ralph, I didn't mean to take my frustration out on you. But really, some people are so bloody insensitive and incompetent!"

"I know what you mean. I've been up that road, too! Hey, why don't you slip up to the Field Ambulance and speak with the CO. He seems to be a knowledgeable chap—should be, too, with all the ribbons he wears."

"You're right, he's a great guy. I'd serve with him any day. Why don't you come up with me, and we'll see what his mess has to offer for dinner. The change will do us both good. What do you say?

The break was rewarding. They were treated to a fine meal with drinks before dinner and a fine wine served with the meal. Sandy's talk with his senior officer was beneficial, and on his strong recommendation to the brigade commander, wet-weather marches were scaled back. The men were appreciative, but they never learned to whom they should be grateful.

The next morning a note appeared on the padre's desk. It was a memo from Sandy Jones.

To: NCHR Chap (P)
From: NCHR MO
0700 hrs 21 Jan 40
1) Thanks.
2) I want you to know how much I admire your tolerance and your sense of humour.
3) After talking with you yesterday, you brought everything into perspective.
4) If it weren't for you, I wouldn't have enjoyed the malt whiskey and fine wine at the Field Ambulance mess.
5) Let's do it again!
Signed: Captain JR (Sandy) Jones

On a wet February day in the village of Bewdleigh, a community close to Aldershot, the vicar of the parish, the Reverend Paul Gwenn, sat at lunch with his daughter Erin and her husband. It was a rare pleasure in recent months to have Lieutenant Michael Ross on a visit to the vicarage. He was an armoured corps officer who, with his regiment of Lancers in the 1st British Armoured Division, was stationed on the Continent as a part of the British Expeditionary Force. It was placed there to thwart the German army's advance toward the Channel ports. He had been granted a short leave, as his troop of tanks, now in reserve, had been on high alert for over a month trying to anticipate the direction of the enemy spearhead.

Michael was a man of medium height and a proud military bearing. His uniform fit him like a glove. Even in the turret of his tank he was the model soldier in every way, with his brown hair slicked straight back and his trim, thin moustache. He came from an upperclass background and obtained an undergraduate degree from Oxford before attending the military college at Sandhurst, from which he graduated at the top of his class. He had met Erin during their university days at Oxford, fallen in love with her, and in the spring of 1939, had married her in her father's church of St. Tristan's, Bewdleigh. Erin was an attractive young woman of medium height, with long black hair usually worn high in the pompadour style of the day. Her flashing blue eyes and flawless white skin were in vivid contrast to her dark tresses. She had a stunning figure, quickly noted by every male she encountered. She was a beauty as her mother before her. Her father adored her and was ever commenting on the likeness between his recently deceased wife and that of his daughter.

When Michael's regiment crossed the Channel with the British Forces following the outbreak of war, Erin returned to the vicarage. Her father's health had failed noticeably after the death of his wife. He had wanted to retire, but there were no clergy to take his place. Most of the younger clerics had made their way into the British Forces. Therefore, the bishop had urged him to stay the course, declaring that Britain needed every man, young or old, to do his duty. Paul Gwenn was made of stern stuff, and putting on a brave face over a weak heart, agreed to stay on.

Slightly built, with finely chiselled features, Reverend Gwenn had been a swift runner in his younger years and had captained his cricket eleven. He was usually strategically placed in the cross-country game of hare and hounds, and won renown for his teams on many occasions. Now, at the relatively young age of fifty-five, his physical stamina drained, he found himself on the horns of a dilemma: "Can I soldier on?" He knew he would give it his best try.

The conversation around the dinner table inevitably turned to the war. Michael, ever the optimist, declared, "We will stop them at the Somme!"

"That was a deadly place in the last war," declared the vicar. He had been an infantry captain at the Second Battle of the Somme in March of 1918, when the Germans threw their might against Amiens in an attempt to break through the Allied lines. They were unsuccessful, but at a horrifying cost of 200,000 casualties to the British and French forces, not to mention the 180,000 Germans that were either killed or wounded. When these losses were added to those that occurred in the First Battle of the Somme in 1916, over one-and-a-half million men were either dead or mutilated. Paul Gwenn had been one of the badly wounded. At first he was given up for dead, but was found later half-buried in a mud-filled trench among the corpses of his men. In a military hospital several months later, he dedicated the rest of his life to the service of God, "for I have been in hell and now I will devote my life to help prevent others from going there!" He had been awarded the Military Cross for his fierce and sustained leadership in his last action

"Ah, yes," Michael observed with confidence, "that was then. Now we have greater mobility, and provided the Allies hold firm, we will stop them!"

"Maybe that's my greatest concern. Holland and Belgium are the weak sisters of the Alliance, and I fear France may fold if the Germans threaten Paris." The vicar posed this as a dire omen.

"Squire Pride says that a Canadian unit will take over Bewdleigh Park come spring. He's offered the manor for their headquarters," commented Erin, changing the topic diplomatically. "Already an advance party is looking the area over. Apparently the men will be bivouacked in tents. I do hope the weather improves soon. It's been such an unhealthy winter."

"Those Colonial boys shouldn't have any problems. They're mostly farm boys or backwoodsmen anyway. Probably not up to much as soldiers, I would guess," huffed Michael.

"What a boorish thing to say," teased Erin. It was the one thing she found irritating about her new husband. He had that snobbish upperclass attitude toward anyone not born to England's gentry.

"Yes, be charitable, my son," chided the vicar. "These young men have come to our aid. We're fortunate to have them with us in these desperate times. I've met a few of their officers, and they appear to be fine men. I personally welcome them, and remember it was 'those Colonial boys' who turned the tide for us at Vimy in the last war."

Michael nodded, but the expression on his face stated more clearly than words that his opinion of the Canadians would not change.

"All right, lads, what's it going to be today?" ventured Ralph.

In a lecture room, the men of C Company had gathered for a bull session. As the dreary winter months dragged on, the CO had asked the padre if he would gather the men of NCHR to hold monthly discussions aimed at bolstering their morale. The session, simply called "The Padre," was blocked into weekly company training schedules.

Initially, it had been a daunting proposal, and Ralph felt a little insecure about implementing it. In the back of his mind he was somewhat uncomfortable with the idea of imposing "religious" instruction on the men, who may not all be in tune with Christian teachings. "Protestants" was a general term that was often loosely used in Canadian units. It could mean members of a Christian church other than

Roman Catholic, or in its widest usage, it could be construed to mean everyone who was not RC. This latter lumping together would include mainline churches, nonconformists, Jews, Muslims, agnostics, atheists, or any form of sectarianism one could imagine.

Ralph struck on the concept of developing the program in a way that would give great leeway for topics to be discussed. He based his approach on an army pamphlet that had been circulated among the officers entitled, "Techniques for Conducting a Discussion Group," which emphasized focusing on a specific interest, stimulating thought, provoking discussion, and pooling opinions. The aim was to get everyone thinking, encourage the inarticulate, control any that were talkative or obsessive, restate and clarify views offered, and, finally, summarize and consolidate. Ralph encouraged both religious and secular themes, which would allow the men to get things off their chests, explore avenues of social behaviour, deal with anxieties within the group, and show them that they did not stand alone with their concerns or fears. If his invitation to open a debate was not taken up, he would throw in a subject of his own to get the ball rolling.

If he felt intimidated at the beginning, his mind was soon set at ease, for the men of the highlands loved to talk and enjoyed wrestling with concepts and ideas as they applied to their daily life. Occasionally, Ralph had to redirect a topic that had the potential of getting out of hand. Not that he would stop the debate, rather he would invite another soldier to offer his point of view on the subject. These lively sessions sometimes developed into a genuine debating society with one team opposing the premises of another.

"I'd like your views on catching the clap, Padre!" called a voice at the back. The men in the room broke up with laughter.

"What makes you think our chaplain is an authority in that field?" More laughter.

"Actually, I regard that as a valid subject," said Ralph, leaning back in his chair. "According to the MO there has been an increase in the number of cases of VD in the last month." More smothered hooting.

"There's some pretty fancy girls in this town, Padre. You'd be surprised how willing they are!"

"Howling hormones! Now that's the problem as I sees it," added another voice.

"You should know, Murphy, you've been to the Doc a couple of times!"

"All right, lads, let's keep the conversation at a decent level. How many of you know what 'the clap' actually is? Is it a matter of just getting treatment or can it affect your health in other ways?" asked Ralph.

A chorus of voices broke out with a variety of responses.

"I'll tell you what," offered Ralph. "How about I invite the MO to our next Padre's Session and offer him the floor? I'm sure he'd give us the low-down on venereal disease. It's really a serious problem. You can get very sick from some forms, and it could even render you sterile or impotent."

"Yeah, and yer dick could fall off," sniggered a skeptic.

"Well, what do you say, lads, shall we ask him to join us?" asked Ralph.

"Whatever you say, Padre, it could be hilarious," offered one.

"Or it could be something we should know," suggested another.

As the group fell into platoons outside the building, their company commander, Major Jock MacPherson, ambled by. He was a rotund man in his early forties, not always turned out as neatly as he should be, in spite of the hours his batman put into maintaining his officer's kit. His thick reddish-brown hair sat like a mat on the top of his head, his eyebrows were thick, and he sported a red walrus-like moustache, which obviously tickled his nose as he was always scratching or picking at it. He walked around with a pipe hanging from the corner of his mouth, and he had the disgusting habit of spitting gobs at inappropriate times. Once the RSM saw him hawk at the side of the Parade Square and immediately approached him.

"Mornin', sir!"

"Morning Mr. Hume."

"Begging your pardon, sir, that was a mighty poor example you just set beside my Parade Square, sir."

"Indeed, Mr. Hume," said the major with a surly look, "as long as it wasn't on your Parade Square. I'll spit where I like." He turned his back and walked rudely away. The RSM glared at the man's back, and, as those who had witnessed the scene later said, "if looks could kill . . ." In the NCHR, the Parade Square was the RSM's hallowed domain. Any soldier caught crossing it casually would be on the fast track to extra duties.

Ralph came forward as Major MacPherson watched his company form up.

"Well, Padre, did your 'Black Protestants' behave today? Sounded like a goddam free-for-all to me," blurted MacPherson in his peculiar attempt at crude humour.

"We had a good session together, thank you." Ralph refused to be intimidated by this impolite officer. He knew his reputation only too well. The major had joined the regiment in 1934 as a subaltern. His appointment was based on political largess through an uncle who was an MP. This family influence was in place at the outbreak of war, and the same man brought political pressure to bear on the Minister of National Defence to have MacPherson raised to the rank of major. He was without friend in the regiment, with the exception of a few "toadies" who fell in with his whims. MacPherson was also a devout Roman Catholic who viewed members of other faiths as heretics, and openly berated their religious beliefs. In short, he was a bigot.

Ralph turned to leave. He could only take the man for a bit at a time before his own angry thoughts began to rise. He promised himself that he would not allow the major to provoke him, as MacPherson would see it as some kind of personal triumph. The padre made his way over to the medical inspection room where Sandy, the MO, sat with his feet up on his desk smoking a cigarette and drinking a cup of tea.

"How's things today, Padre?" he inquired.

"Can't complain too much, Doc, just a little miffed with the OC of C Company."

"What's the old bugger done now?" asked Sandy as he blew a series of smoke rings.

"Oh, just up to his usual nonsense. He'd be a perfect candidate to sit as a member of the Inquisition."

"Sit down, relax, and have a 'cuppa,' as the Brits say. Here, have a smoke." Two more rings floated upward. "Corporal Smith, bring the padre some tea."

"Right, sir," responded a voice from the orderly room.

Ralph continued, "Just had a Padre's Session with MacPherson's company, and the idea came to me that I should invite you to give a lecture on VD. The boys have agreed. Even with all their bravado, I think this is a good opportunity to give them the big picture. It was just the other day, wasn't it, when you indicated the problem was on the rise."

"Hey, that's a great idea!" Sandy snubbed his cigarette. "Those lads can get into real trouble when they down too many good English brews. When do you want me to come?"

' "Let's plan a series for each company during April. That'll give you time to get some notes lined up, and maybe a film or some slides on the subject. As they say, 'a picture is worth a thousand words.'"

It was planned accordingly, and by the end of April the entire regiment would be made aware of the perils of 'the pox.' Most of the companies' NCOs had asked to sit in on the sessions.

For some men the lecture would make a difference, especially those that had resolved to remain faithful to their wives and sweethearts, but for others, they couldn't care less and would have to learn the hard way.

The idea of a series of educational lectures, apart from the Padre's Sessions, appealed to Ralph, and he ran it past the CO.

"Sir, I know you're concerned about the morale of the men since coming to England. They've had to deal with some pretty rough conditions these past few months, weather being what it is. They don't have much to do with their free time, and as you are well aware, a bored man can easily get into trouble. One of the things that have come out of my Padre's Sessions is the fact that many of the lads would like to acquire more knowledge about the U.K., and this region in particular. Would you agree if I were to approach some of the local people to see if they would give talks on the area? There are some great historical sites nearby, and I'd certainly like to take those interested on a tour of Winchester Cathedral and old Sarum. There's also pre-historic Stonehenge. Most of the men have passed these places on their way to Salisbury Plain for field training, and a number have asked me if I know anything about them. So I know the interest is there. The New Forest is close by, too, where they could see herds of protected deer. Many of the lads are hunters who would enjoy watching deer, even if they couldn't hunt them."

"You may be onto something, Padre. Let me run it past my O Group tomorrow morning. Personally, I think it's a marvellous idea," observed Colonel Morrison.

The CO's O Group consisted of the battalion second-in-command or 2IC, the company commanders, the adjutant, the RSM, the MO, the padre, and other designated officers who might have input. When Ralph's suggestion was raised, an open discussion was held to assess its merits. Everyone, with the exception of Major MacPherson, was in total accord.

"Sounds like a lot of Protestant propaganda to me! I trust the men will be made aware that those lovely old cathedrals are stolen Catholic properties!" he snorted, as he rubbed a finger beneath his nose.

"Major MacPherson, you are totally out of line. Please keep your snide remarks to yourself," remarked the CO, glaring at the company commander.

"If you say so, sir," he replied with an insulting smirk directed toward Ralph.

"I do say so, sir, and I would like you to remain behind after this meeting is over!"

Later in the day, a red-faced MacPherson accosted Ralph in the officers' mess.

"Russell," the major snarled with his face pressed against Ralph's, "you've made me a laughing stock. One of these days I'll make you sorry. So be warned."

"If you're a laughing stock, Major, you've only yourself to blame."

"Oh ho, feeling cocky are you. Tut, tut, Padre, that's no way for a clergyman to act!"

"You're a damned bigot, MacPherson, and if you continue to squawk like a ruptured bagpipe, you'll be the sorry one!"

MacPherson bristled and pushed Ralph backwards. "If you didn't have your collar on, I'd beat the shit out of you here and now."

Ralph stepped back, grasped his clerical collar, and ripped it from his neck. "All right, Major, here's your chance. Now put up, or shut up!"

At that moment Captain Barry Hutchings, the quartermaster, entered the mess. Major MacPherson snapped his mouth shut, turned on his heel and departed.

The QM was a squat, heavily muscled man with penetrating eyes, known for his skill in diplomacy and mediation. Barry noted Ralph's flushed condition, and the fact that his clerical collar was removed, "What was that all about?" he asked.

"That obnoxious bag of wind pushed me too far this time," panted Ralph, "but he's not man enough to be called out, the bastard."

"Now, now, Padre, that's no way for you to talk," chuckled the QM. "Don't let him get you down. He's all talk and no guts. Everybody knows that. Here, let me buy you a drink."

The incident passed with no further reference until the following Saturday, when the NCHR was celebrating its regimental birthday. The event included a sports day, and a variety of team events were held with inter-company competitions. Individual stands included boxing matches that would determine the best pugilists in the regiment. These would go on to brigade, and then to the divisional finals.

Ralph had done some boxing as a lightweight while attending U of T. HQ Company had no contender for that weight, so Ralph volunteered. His first match was against a Private Mutt Duffy, a Catholic boy from the highland region who belonged to A Company. Mutt was a cocky youngster with a flailing roughhouse style, and Ralph had no difficulty figuring out the man's weakness. The padre danced around his opponent's vulnerable right side and watched for the precise opening when he could crouch and bring a right uppercut to the private's exposed chin. The man went down with a thud and sat on the canvas shaking his head.

"Hey, Padre, take it easy on the kid!" shouted the crowd. Ralph dipped his head in acknowledgement.

In the second round, the two men sparred without either scoring any serious points, but at the opening of the third, Duffy, with a flurry of wild round-about punches, closed on Ralph and caught him square on the side of his head. The padre saw stars, and when the soldier made his move to finish his opponent, Ralph ducked and came up with the same right that he had used in the first round. Duffy went down again. The crowd roared. The referee looked into the soldier's glassy eyes and called the match.

MacPherson sprung from his seat at ringside screaming obscenities and shouting, "Foul blow! Foul blow! What the hell's wrong with you, Ref? You're so goddam blind you should be in an institution."

Major Jim Browne, officer commanding B Company, was also a man of strong opinions. He was sitting beside MacPherson. Where the latter was rather dumpy, the former was tall and slender with a touch of grey at his temples. Browne was a skilled strategist and had a natural instinct for making the right decisions in field operations. His tactics employed in the "advance to contact" deployment proved successful nine times out of ten. He was well respected by the officers and men of his company. The two men were fiercely competitive in every aspect of their work with the Scotsman generally ending up as the underdog. Browne couldn't resist any opportunity to give MacPherson a good dig.

"What do you think, Jock, do you suppose he'd could do that to all the Catholic boys if you lined them up?"

"Let him try," was MacPherson's sharp retort digging at the itch in a nostril.

"Well how about you and the padre having a go-about?" said Browne, humour flashing in his eyes.

"Don't tempt me."

"Good, let me see if I can arrange it," offered Browne, and he left a sputtering MacPherson at ringside.

The commanding officer would not hear of it. "You're just trying to make trouble, Jim, and that's something we don't need. Besides, that right of the padre's is dynamite. I think Major MacPherson got the message!"

Ralph moved on to the regimental semi-finals, where his opponent won the match on points. But the padre gained a victory in his own right, for the men of the NCHR recognized a man who was willing to fight with the best of them.

All through the day Ralph was beset with an excess of blasphemy and foul language. It seemed that the majority of the troops had adopted a full vocabulary of four-letter words, not unusual for soldiers in the field. But this special regimental day, the beer flowed freely and the men's tongues became well-laced with profanity. By late afternoon, the padre had had enough of their obscenities and went to his quarters with his head ringing. Normally, he blocked out the coarse language often heard in barracks and in the field when men were isolated from their families. It was something that seemed to become natural to them, viewed by many as a manly conversation.

A formal dinner was held in the officers' mess that the evening. The chatter was loud and raucous during pre-dinner drinks. Many of the younger officers had over-indulged in the free draft beer that had flowed all afternoon, and some were drunk and could barely stand. It didn't bode well for a two-hour meal where they were not allowed to leave the table. The first part of the dinner proceeded with some decorum, but as the meal wore on, the commanding officer was prompted to comment loudly on the unruly behaviour of several subalterns.

"Major Browne, note carefully the names of those who are displaying conduct unbecoming an officer," he ordered the mess president. "They are an embarrassment to the regiment. They shall be given extra orderly officer duties to atone for their rude and ungentlemanly conduct."

The CO's remarks had little effect, however, and the evening degenerated into a near debacle until he declared the function ended and suggested that everyone turn in before "I place the lot of you on charge!"

Needless to say, there were some very large heads throughout the camp the following morning. The men howled at the thought of a formal church parade, and the NCOs became thunderous, with colourful orders emanating from the Parade Square. At ten o'clock the regiment formed up on three sides of a square, and the pipes and drums marched on the colours. The drums were piled at the open side and the padre took up his position beside them facing the regiment.

The Drumhead Service was a formal event. Prayers were given for the regiment and for the fallen of previous conflicts. Families were remembered. There were prayers for courage, for a final victory, for the king and Allies. Then, the padre began what everyone expected to be his sermon. "You will be pleased to hear that I do not intend to preach a sermon this morning. However, I do want to say a few well-chosen words, which I feel, must be said. These should be prefaced with a text of some sort, so I have selected this—Jesus H. f—ing Christ!"

There was a dead silence in the ranks. The listlessness of the previous moment was frozen in time. Every eye swung in unison to the chaplain's face. Ralph paused and slowly looked over the ranks of men before him. The CO appeared to be on the verge of apoplexy. The ramrod RSM rolled his eyes skyward.

"You see," continued Ralph, "I can use those words and a lot of others, too. Yesterday, the air was blue wherever I went. Perhaps four-letter words are easier to say. But is our means of communicating to each other so poor that we have to use the lowest common denominator of our language to get our points across? Do we seriously believe that this kind of talk is manly? How many of you would converse with your families in this manner? I'm sure your mothers, wives and sweethearts would be pleased to overhear your conversations. You know that I am not a prude, but when I hear blasphemy on this scale I feel sick.

"We are preparing for battle. I would hope that when we invoke the name of God and his Son that it would be in a more prayerful manner. Lord only knows, we will need his protection." Ralph paused to allow his remarks to sink in. "Let me conclude with this little story. It may seem somewhat sacrilegious to you, but it makes a point. A foul-mouthed drunk who had no consideration for other people's sensitivities was cruising down the road at top speed on his motorcycle when he hit a bump, careened off, and hit a telephone pole. As he lay dying in the ditch, he turned his head to heaven and asked, 'Why me, Lord?' Just then a large thumb came down from the clouds to squash him into the ground as if he were a bug, and he heard a loud voice say, 'BECAUSE SOMETIMES YOU PISS ME OFF!'" A chuckle floated across the crowd. Ralph smiled.

"Rather an insipid little story, isn't it? Not at all in good taste? But think about it. If we alienate God by our deeds and actions, if we curse Him, and degrade our fellows by the things we do and say, where does that leave us when we seriously call upon His Name? When we look to the man beside us for his support under fire? I know you are decent men. I know where you come from. I know your language gets forceful at times, but for the love of God, think about what comes out of your mouth. These words are not only for you, I must also direct them toward myself. I have had to bite my tongue on several occasions in the last few days as well. What we say speaks volumes about who we are. Amen."

Immediately following the Drumhead Service, Colonel Morrison drew Ralph aside.

"Padre, I don't quite know what to say. When you announced your text, I thought I'd fall through the Parade Square, and then I wondered if I should have a chat with your senior chaplain. I really thought you had lost your wits—gone batty. But as I listened, I had to agree with what you were saying, particularly about blasphemy. However, I have to tell you this: there's no way in h . . . ah, heck, you'll ever put an end to a soldier cussing and swearing. It seems to come with the first issue of his uniform. It's his way of letting off steam and frustration, and then it becomes second nature to him. You know the expression, 'He swears like a trooper.' Well, that saying goes back to ancient history."

"I apologize if I have offended anyone, sir, but at the time it seemed like the right thing to do. I guess with all the 'blue' air at the sports meet yesterday, and then the foul language around the table at the mess dinner, I simply short-circuited. I had to get it out of my craw. It won't happen again."

"Well, be that as it may, I believe you have made your point. I've just heard several officers say, 'That padre sure makes a fellow think.' And you know, I wouldn't doubt that's the talk of all ranks right at this moment. Don't know how long it will last, but you certainly made an impression."

Easter Sunday, on the 24th of March, 1940, dawned in the spring mists of a bright English morning. Ralph conducted an Easter Service in a large drill hall with the regiment on parade, and he had managed to put together a choir of sorts from volunteers he had drawn on from his Padre's Sessions. The voices were strong but untrained. They did, however, provide a basis for the uplifting Easter hymns, and although the small portable organ wheezed out the tunes rather harshly, it was better than nothing at all. During his sermon, Ralph apologized for the language he had used at the Drumhead Service two weeks prior, but not for the message the words were meant to convey. "I know in your hearts that you are fine men through and through, but I will always ask you not to use God's name carelessly. I have no doubt you'll find need to call upon Him with deep sincerity in the dark days ahead. You will see Him then . . . as our strength and hope."

In the next weeks, Ralph made arrangements with several prominent people in the civilian community to present lectures to the regiment. A variety of topics were offered, and they included an outline of local history from ancient times to the present, by Sir Cedric Hardy. He was a jovial history buff who incorporated a great deal of British wit in his talks. At first the men found it difficult to follow his sense of humour, but when they caught on, it brought the house down. Hardy was adept at bringing out the native colloquialisms and translating them into language understandable to the troops. The presentation was hilarious. The historical meat he placed before them was made more palatable by the simple fact that he was able to laugh at himself and his fellow countrymen. It was a feat not often seen among the conservative English.

Hardy put Ralph onto a cleric in a nearby parish, who was a skilled lecturer on the Norman period, when so many of the square-towered churches were built in England.

"If you wish, I will call Paul Gwenn and arrange a meeting with him. He's not in the best of health, but if he agrees to speak, he will be a gem for your series."

"Thank you, Sir Cedric, I would appreciate that."

It was two days later that Ralph received a call directly from Paul Gwenn, Vicar of Bewdleigh, and was invited for tea, Friday next. Ralph was given a jeep and driver to make the short journey, and he arrived at the vicarage at four o'clock sharp. He was about to knock, when a stunning young woman dressed in soft pastels opened the door. Ralph stood for a moment with his mouth open. He had never seen such graceful beauty. He found it difficult to form words, but finally blurted out: "Are you the vicar's wife?"

Her smile was warm and inviting. "No, I'm his daughter, Erin," she said, and held the door ajar for Ralph to enter. "You must be Padre Russell. My father's expecting you. Please come in. Let me take your hat and coat. I'll fetch us some tea."

"Ah, Padre Russell," said a voice coming from the study. "Please come in. How good it is to meet you. I understand that your regiment will be moving into Bewdleigh Park next month. I do hope the weather straightens up before you are required to go under canvas. I remember well what it was like in the last war, in the wet and the mud. Wouldn't wish that on anyone!"

By now Ralph had gained his wits, but he still savoured the soft scent the woman had left in the hallway.

"Thank you for receiving me, sir, you are most kind."

"Not at all! Not at all! I understand you are an Anglican priest as well?" remarked the vicar. He was short in stature, standing about five-foot three inches, with thin grey hair that barely covered his head. There was an unhealthy pallor to his face, but his voice was strong and mellow.

"Yes, sir, I am."

"Where is your home in Canada?"

"Not far from Ottawa. In fact, my last parish was eighty miles west of our capital."

"That may not be far in Canada, but here in England, even twenty miles is considered a fair distance," the vicar remarked. "Why, over here, most people never get more than twenty miles from home in their lifetime, although when a war is on things do tend to change. I just can't imagine a country three thousand miles wide!"

"When I go home," replied Ralph, "I'd like to travel by train from Ottawa to Vancouver. It takes five days, but I'm told the scenery is spectacular."

"Ye gads, five days, is it? Ah, Erin, my dear, we are indeed ready for tea. Please join us."

Ralph watched the lissome movement of the young woman as she set the tea service on a small table in front of the two men. It took a concerted effort not to stare at her.

"What do you take in your tea, Padre?" she asked.

"Just as it comes, please."

The three people exchanged pleasantries for several minutes, and then the vicar began to question Ralph concerning the request for his services. When he had determined the purpose of the lectures, which was "to enlighten the Canadian troops on the Norman Period," he indicated that he would be delighted to share his knowledge. It was agreed that the presentations would take place after the regiment took up residence in the Park.

"Could I offer you the use of St. Tristan's while you are with us? We could arrange appropriate times for your services that wouldn't interfere with the regular services."

"That is very generous of you, sir, I will speak to Colonel Morrison about your kind invitation. If he agrees, I will, in turn, offer you any assistance I may be able to provide."

"I would be most grateful for that, my health is not the best these days."

"Indeed," remarked Erin, her engaging smile spreading across her face, "my father would appreciate that. Thank you, Padre."

Ralph bade the vicar farewell, and as he took leave of Erin, she extended her hand to him. It was soft, but the grip was firm. He felt a sudden rush—feelings like he had never experienced before. He was reluctant to release it until he saw the wedding band on her left hand. The bubble of his illusion burst. Embarrassed, he blushed, and made his way quickly to the waiting vehicle.

He was totally distracted on the way back to camp. Reflections came flooding back of the time he broke his vow of chastity. It had happened in his last year of theology. Barbara Hunter was organist at St. Mark's Church where Ralph was student assistant. She was short, petite, with snapping black eyes and straight brown hair that just touched her shoulders. She was not particularly pretty, but she gave off a certain aura that drew the attention of many males.

In addition to playing the organ, Barbara was also the choir director, and part of her duties was to train the clergy in plainsong that was used at sung services. After practice, when the choir had departed, she would have Ralph sit beside her on the organ bench and would teach him the chants. He learned quickly, and when several weeks had passed, she announced that he had become her favourite pupil.

"I have composed a piece of music for you," she remarked before launching into a soft, rather sad rhapsody that gradually became playful, then, more and more lively, until it reached an explosive climax. "That is how you make me feel," she said and dropped her hand from the keyboard to his lap and stoked the inside of his leg.

Without thought, the gates of passion burst inside Ralph. He took Barbara in his arms and crushed his lips against hers. She moaned and melted against him.

"Let's go to the choir room," she groaned, pulling him from the organ bench. They staggered, clutching at each other, until they had reached the darkened room where they collapsed on a couch. For Ralph, the act was over before it had begun, but Barbara was not to be denied. Stripping off the remainder of her clothes she encouraged him with wild movements to keep going. He obliged. She climaxed like her rhapsody, with an explosion of feeling and a piercing cry. Ralph panicked, thinking he had hurt her.

"Are you all right?" he shouted.

A voice called out from the depths of the parish hall. "Who's in there?"

It was the rector who, seeing the lights still on, had come to check on the building.

Ralph was about to answer when Barbara covered his mouth with her hand.

"Shhh," she whispered.

The rector walked toward the choir room, but seeing it in darkness, turned and left the hall, turning out the lights as he went.

"That was close," said Barbara, giggling, as she began to dress herself. Ralph sat on the couch shaking, feeling the shock of guilt rising up in him. Barbara sensed his alarm and tried to calm him, but he could not face her. He put on his trousers and slunk from the hall.

In the depths of despair he sought solace on bended knee in the church. He honestly believed he had performed a deed that went against all his training. Ralph spent the night in the church, and in the morning when the rector came to read his morning office, he found an exhausted, pale, young man waiting for him.

It took several weeks of gentle counselling before the rector convinced Ralph that he need not abandon his studies toward Holy Orders, but rather he should use the experience to strengthen his moral integrity.

"In the years ahead you will encounter many who will be lured from what might be called the straight and narrow way. Your experience, even though I cannot condone your behaviour, can be a touchstone for you. Use it to temper your counsel to those who fall. A wise priest weighs all the factors, and reaches conclusions that will redeem the sinner rather than condemn him. Remember that things in life are rarely black and white. The human spirit bears the patina of many shades of grey. You are not a perfect man, Ralph, even though you strive to be one. In the entire history of mankind there was only One who could claim that distinction, and He was stretched on a cross. In the beginning, Adam was meant to be God's 'perfect man' but he fell. We theologians call it 'original sin.'

"You are young and full of zeal. You strive diligently to achieve high ideals and goals, and now you have stumbled. So what are you going to do about this reality? Throw in the towel, or turn the experience into something positive? This folly has humbled you, and perhaps you needed that. Now you will understand the importance of tolerance. You will have a deeper perspective when dealing with other people's failings."

Ralph emerged from these sessions a stronger, wiser man. He also had a clearer understanding of the frailty of man. Meeting Erin, and being instantly attracted to her, had reminded him of his own weaknesses, and what that might lead to.

The NCHR spread its canvas in Bewdleigh Park during the latter part of April 1940. The weather had broken to the degree that the constant rain and heavy clouds of winter gave way to overcast skies and occasional light showers. The temperature increased by a few degrees, and spring flowers bloomed in profusion among the trees and vistas of the Park. The regimental companies were allocated specific areas where they erected their tents. Ralph was set up near the regimental aid post, or the RAP, a short distance from the MO's, a location that was readily accessible to any soldier who might wish a private conversation with his chaplain. The park was a pleasant place, and the men were under strict orders to keep it that way.

The village of Bewdleigh offered several pubs for the entertainment of off-duty personnel. These establishments were quite different from the drinking holes back home where one section of a hotel beer parlour would be designated as "ladies and escorts," while a separate area would be for "men only." The British pub was used more as a family meeting place where neighbours would gather for a pint of an evening. Normally, the soldiers were welcomed, provided they didn't try to take over. Regimental regulations laid down guidelines for the men's behaviour, and the unit's military police strictly enforced these directions. The officers and senior NCOs were cautioned to watch for trouble and to stop it before it got out of hand.

As a whole, the men of the highlands had no difficulty with this code of conduct. They were a shy breed where strangers were concerned, but in a military unit such as this, where men were drawn from a variety of locales within Eastern Ontario, there could always be found a few of the more rowdy types who invariably led others astray, especially after several pints. It happened one evening a week after the NCHR set up their tented homes in Bewdleigh Park.

Paul Gwenn, the vicar, invited Ralph to the Royal Swan, a rather quiet pub on the village green. The vicar's doctor had suggested that a daily pint of stout would be good for his health, so he made it a custom to stroll across the green of an evening to partake of this tonic. It also gave him the opportunity to visit with some of the folk of his parish in an informal manner.

At eight o'clock, the two parsons met at the pub where the vicar took his usual seat. After exchanging greetings, Ralph began, "I have presented your offer concerning the use of the parish church to my commanding officer. He was mightily pleased and extends his personal thanks. He has asked me to invite you to our officers' mess for lunch tomorrow if you are free."

"I'd be delighted to join you," the vicar replied. "I'm looking forward to meeting Colonel Morrison. I have already spoken to the churchwardens and vestry council about sharing our facilities with you. All are in agreement, as I thought they would be. Would nine o'clock on Sunday mornings be helpful to you? I have an early Eucharist at eight o'clock. You're welcome to share that with me, and invite any of your Anglican soldiers to come as well. You could just follow on with your Divine Worship for all the denominations afterwards," suggested the vicar. "Our principal service takes place at eleven."

"That would be great, sir. I'll make the necessary arrangements. I wanted the services to be voluntary, but the CO felt there should be a parade. I don't believe in 'driving' men to church. It goes against the grain. But, the senior officers up the line don't see it that way. They seem to want religion instilled in the men. Good for their discipline, they say."

"Well, I hope they set the example themselves then," observed the vicar with a side glance.

"I told the CO," Ralph continued, "that it would be impossible to cram a regimental church parade into St. Tristan's. The seating capacity is far too limited. I believe two hundred would fill it, would it not?"

"Quite right, Padre," the vicar confirmed. "We've managed twenty or so over that figure on high feasts such as Christmas and Easter by placing chairs in the Baptistery and along the back. But that makes for over crowding. Not comfortable at all!"

"That's what I figured, so he has agreed to compromise. Only one company will be required to parade to church each Sunday, and for the remainder, it will be voluntary. I always have my Anglican Eucharist each Sunday morning at the same time as yours, and normally get twenty-five or so out. I'm sure they would be pleased to join with your people at that hour, and in that way, I can be of greater help to you," Ralph suggested.

"Ah, you are so kind. I do appreciate your offer. I know Erin will be pleased, too. She's become so protective of me recently and the girl has enough to worry about with her husband in Belgium with his Lancers. He's commander of a tank troop, and they're in a very delicate situation at the moment. Hitler is amassing his troops on the Belgian border. They are expected to make for the Channel ports any day now!"

"She's a very attractive young woman. Her husband is a very lucky fellow," said Ralph shyly.

"So much like her mother," sighed the vicar wistfully. "How I miss her."

In one corner near the bar, a group of soldiers was singing loudly, accompanied by a local lady on the piano. She was a mature woman, who seemed to enjoy pub life to its fullest, and was frequently rewarded for her musical renditions with drinks, gin being her favourite.

"Well," remarked the vicar, "your lads are certainly in good voice tonight."

"They seemed to have found someone who can play the songs they like," answered Ralph.

"Rosie was a music-hall entertainer before she fell into the bottle. She has the knack of playing a piano in any state, poor thing. But she is a very accomplished pianist with a wide repertoire. Ask her to play anything, from opera to the latest stage tunes, and it's at her fingertips. She's had several husbands. Current one is on the continent with our forces. Not a bad chap, Bertie! He keeps Rosie on the straight and narrow when he's around," smiled the vicar somewhat sadly, "But when he's not . . ."

The clergymen sipped on their stout.

The music became louder and more boisterous, to such a degree that the Irish barkeep approached the soldiers' table. "I'd ask ye to keep the noise down a wee bit. It's a little too early in the evening for a hullabaloo. We still have some of the family crowd in," he said, nodding to a corner where several elderly folk sat quietly sipping their evening drink. They were his regulars, and he didn't want them to feel displaced.

"F—k off," snarled Corporal Mac McNutty from Perth, who was well into the suds. "We're just getting started."

"Oh, for God's sake, Mac, watch your tongue or you'll have us picked up," complained Private Tim O'Neil, one of the group.

McNutty pushed his chair back and grabbed O'Neil by his battledress tunic, shoving him against the wall. O'Neil swung and clipped the corporal on the chin, knocking him backward over an empty table with a crash.

Ralph jumped to his feet to intervene, but before he could get between the men, Sergeant Walter Fender from B Company, who had been drinking a pint of bitter at the bar, stood over them. He was a giant of a man with a great waxed mustache.

"Hear now," he said, "we'll have none of that! If you can't behave yourselves, out you go." He placed his balled fists on his hips and stared the offenders down.

"As you say, Sergeant," muttered the corporal, cowering away from the burly man.

To the group Fender said, "I believe the gentleman from the bar asked you to pipe down. If you want to sing your bloody lungs out, maybe you'd like to join the Padre's choir." Grinning, he jerked his thumb in Ralph's direction. "What do you think, Padre, would they suit your purpose?"

"Well, Sergeant, we could at least give them a tryout," suggested Ralph, also grinning.

Turning to the vicar, Ralph said, "This has given me an idea. As you know, men away from home can become bored and fractious. Their energies need to be channelled. I think I'll try to get a bunch of them together and put on a show. It would be great if we could get some of the town's people to join in. It'd help break the ice between the civilians and our men, too. What do you think, sir?"

The vicar looked amused. "Might be just the thing. I know Erin would be tickled to help out. She has a gift for organization, and loves to sing. In the university, she belonged to a student Gilbert and Sullivan group."

"Oh, do you think she would? That would be grand if she could get the support of a few local girls to take part as well. How about Rosie? Do you think I could approach her? Her skills would give a tremendous boost!"

"Why don't you ask her?" suggested the vicar.

"Well, I will, but first let me run the idea past my CO, and if you'd find out if Erin is willing to assist, perhaps we could draw up a plan," concluded Ralph.

"It would be just the thing to distract her. She has been feeling quite low since her husband's last leave. Yes, I'm sure I can persuade her to agree," stated Gwenn thoughtfully.

It was settled, and the two clergymen went their separate ways, agreeing to meet again the following day for lunch at the officers' mess.

Colonel Morrison sat back in his chair smoking his pipe. It was mid-afternoon, and he had just dealt with some paper work. His thoughts drifted back to the luncheon he had hosted for the vicar of Bewdleigh. Ralph had briefed the CO on Paul Gwenn's background and record from the last war. Morrison mused, "Amazing how a man can come through a cauldron of fire and be so galvanized in his faith while others are mentally maimed by a similar fate."

"Captain Barnett," he called to his adjutant, "would you call the padre? I'd like to see him if he's available."

"Right, sir!"

Mike Barnett, the adjutant, was a bright officer in his late twenties. Some of his peers called him "Shiny" as he was always turned out totally "spit and polish." While his responsibilities included carefully screening those who would call unnecessarily on the CO's time, in the mess, he was a convivial comrade and well liked by his fellow officers.

Ralph received the message and proceeded to the CO's office.

"I'm very impressed with the vicar," began Morrison. "I think you've found yourself a fine friend. I dare say even padres need someone to talk to from time to time. Quite self-effacing where his stories from the trenches were concerned. Amazing experiences!"

"He's a sound man with a modern approach to ministry," remarked Ralph. "He's certainly not stuck back in the Middle Ages like a lot of Church of England clergy appear to be in these parts. He's open and forward-looking where his parish is concerned. Very close to his parishioners."

"It's generous of him to share the parish church with us. Please proceed with any arrangements you wish to make, and if I can be of assistance in any way, remember, my door is always open to you."

"Thank you, sir, I will."

"I have given your idea of an amateur show for the troops considerable thought, and I like it. It's important to develop a strong bond with the local folk. Reduces friction and makes for a happier sojourn all around. Although our language, and in many cases our roots, are the same, nevertheless, our attitudes and approach to life can vary dramatically. I would welcome a healthy interaction with the community. Keep me informed, and good luck with it!"

Over the next few weeks, with Erin and Rosie's enthusiastic support, an amateur stage show was organized. They decided to present a country theme, using the Ontario highlands as a background for the plot. Julia Pride, Erin's closest friend, eagerly offered to help. She was a petite young woman with flashing blue eyes, a trim figure and her blonde hair cut in a pageboy. She was a knockout.

Ralph asked for volunteers from his Padre's Sessions, and several men with good voices came forward. Four fiddlers, two guitarists, and a drummer were found to add instrumental depth for the musical score arranged by Rosie, while eight young ladies from the community also joined the group. All sang well, and they quickly learned the steps to three square dances.

Arrangements were made with the local theatre to stage two performances in mid-May. The theatre could seat six hundred people, but the anticipated crowd was over one thousand, so two nights were necessary. The cast agreed to a third night if the show proved even more popular than hoped for.

By opening night, the village was a-buzz. Free tickets were made available at stores on the High Street and were colour-coded for the event—red the first night and blue the second. If a third performance were required, it would be first come, first served. Civilians and military alike eagerly sought admittance. The whole community came together in a jolly mood and, for a moment, the war was almost forgotten.

First-night front-row seats were reserved for the senior officers of the NCHR, along with the mayor and councillors of the village. Ralph acted as master of ceremonies.

"Honoured guests, people of Bewdleigh, and members of the regiment," he welcomed them. "It gives me great pleasure to offer you a couple of hours of musical entertainment. You might say that this production is an international effort proudly starring the young people of England and Canada. I want to thank them from the start for their efforts. I also take this opportunity to express my gratitude to Erin Ross and Rosie O'Reilly for putting the show together and let us not forget those behind the scenes. Let's hear it for the stage crew—for their work on sets, lighting, and costumes. It has been a co-operative effort that I hope will bring us all closer together. Special thanks, also, to Mr. Thompson, for the use of the theatre. The NCHR will not be here for too much longer, as you know we have a job to do." Cheers from the audience. "While we are here,

I'd like to think we could have a jolly good time together. So, on with the show!"

The curtain parted to reveal a summer setting in the Ontario highlands. Trees and shrubs, rocks and steep slopes had been painted onto the backdrop. A sprightly rendition of fiddle music introduced the dancers who formed a ring on centre stage, while a man in bib overalls appeared to one side and began to call a square dance. Before long, all in the audience were tapping their feet to the music.

Included in the entertainment were several ballads and a comedy monologue between two soldiers depicting life in the back country—their one-liners spiked with Ottawa Valley inflections. A fiddle competition drew a team of tap dancers onto the stage, which was followed by two more square dances and a community singalong. The lights dimmed for the finale. A pale moon shone, and two people walked to centre stage from opposite sides with their arms reaching out to the other, the man in uniform and the woman in a smock. They sang a poignant ballad depicting separated lovers. The curtain fell, and silence filled the theatre, until the quick strains of fiddle music called all the players to dance again. They filled the stage to wild applause.

The evening was a resounding success. The second and third nights were equally well received and the long-reaching results brought a generous response from the local people, who went out of their way to make the soldiers feel welcome. They opened their homes and their hearts and genuine bonds were formed that would last for years to come.

The training schedule increased in tempo following the show. The war on the Continent was heating up, so more physical demands were placed on the troops in an attempt to harden them for the task ahead. They underwent strenuous route marches and dug trenches in the chalky ground on Salisbury Plain. Many ended up with blisters on both hands and feet, some serious enough to warrant medical attention. The MO advised a rest period to allow the bodies to heal.

That didn't last long. On the morning of the 23rd of May, the NCHR was ordered to pick up its canvas and kit and proceed in convoy to Dover, where it boarded the SS *Canterbury* along with the Royal Canadian Regiment. At last, thought the troops, we're off to battle. It was almost a festive affair as the high-spirited Canadians mingled together on board ship. To their chagrin, the "Dash-to-Dover," as it became known, turned out to be a curtailed deployment. Higher-ups reassessed the situation on the Continent and felt that the commitment of Canadian troops would be suicidal, as the British Expeditionary Forces were retreating quickly toward Dunkirk. The following day, an about turn was ordered, and the Canadian force returned to its various camps in and about Aldershot. They remained on high alert, however, for it was anticipated that the Germans would immediately invade England. The Canadians were poised to move in any direction at a moment's notice.

On their return to Bewdleigh, the NCHR again pitched tents in the Park. It was Friday evening when Ralph went to see the vicar to brief him on what had happened and to discuss the Sunday services. Erin promptly answered his knock at the vicarage door. She appeared distraught.

"Ralph, it's good to see you. In the confusion of your unit's departure I didn't get a chance to say goodbye. Sorry!"

"Good to see you too, Erin. You look upset."

"I'm afraid I've received unpleasant news. Word has come through that Michael's Lancers are in a fierce fight against a Panzer regiment. Our forces are in disarray and are falling back from the front. I do hope he's all right." Ralph led her toward her father's den fully expecting to see the vicar come forward.

"Is your father here, Erin?"

"That's more bad news. Yesterday he suffered a mild angina attack. He's in hospital."

"Here," said Ralph, "sit down. Can I get you anything—a cup of tea from the kitchen, perhaps?"

"I'll be all right in a moment," she sniffed, dabbing a handkerchief at her eyes.

"I'll look after the Sunday services, provided we're not ordered out again," Ralph offered.

"Oh, that will relieve my father," Erin sighed. "He's such a worrywart, and so easily distressed these days."

"I'm so sorry to see you so worried. Things are rather piling up on you. I wish I could be of more assistance," Ralph paused. "I'll slip over to the hospital and see your father. Are you sure you're all right?"

"I'll be fine," said Erin in a low voice, her head bowed.

Ralph wasn't so sure. "I'll drop back after I see him."

"That would be a comfort," Erin hesitated, "providing I'm not taking you away from your duties."

"The adjutant will know where to reach me if I'm needed. Why don't you stretch out and rest for a while? I promise, I'll be back soon," said Ralph as he inched toward the door.

The vicar was dozing when Ralph arrived at his bedside.

"Now this is an easy way to draw attention," Ralph teased.

The vicar brightened and smiled wanly. "You're back, my boy! That must have been a short war?" he teased in turn.

"I wish that were the end of it, sir, but I'm afraid it's just heating up."

"Ah yes, bad stuff." The vicar looked reflective for a moment before changing the subject. "You've seen Erin, I gather? Poor girl, I'm afraid her Michael may be in for it. He's right in the thick of it, you know. God help him!"

"The news is not good at all," remarked Ralph. "We were turned back before we even got across. Your army is making for the beaches of Dunkirk. It will be a massive evacuation—and terribly confusing. May the Good Lord be with them all!"

"Could we pray for them, Ralph?" The two men bowed their heads.

The vicar spoke. "Lord our hearts are heavy with the news of the battles in France and Belgium. We know that you are with our soldiers as they fight a rear action toward the beaches. Many will be killed. We ask that their sacrifice will not be in vain. Bear them up, O Lord, to your heavenly keeping where they will toil no more, and where they will receive their reward for their battle against evil. We pray for the wounded. Grant that they may be returned to their families. Our cause is righteous, Lord, we will fight the depraved dictator to the end. We know that the final victory will be ours. Thanks be to God. Amen."

The two men remained silent for several moments, as they communed with the Almighty. Before he left the sickroom, Ralph placed a hand on the vicar's shoulder and said, "Rest comfortably and get your strength back. I'll look after the services on Sunday unless duty calls. I'll slip over to see Erin now before I return to camp."

"Assure her that I am fine," asked the vicar.

"I will, and you take care," answered Ralph.

Erin was at the door before Ralph could knock. She had been watching for him.

"How is he?" she asked.

"Seems to be resting easily. I spoke with the matron, and she affirmed that he was responding well to treatment. She indicated that it was a minor seizure, but considering his overall condition, he requires constant monitoring."

"Thank you, Ralph. It was kind of you to take time to visit." They walked into the parlour together. "I'm sure you must be tired after your mad dash. You need your rest, too!"

There was a sharp knock at the front door and Erin hastened to respond. There she found a runner from the telegraph office holding a message in his hand.

"Is the vicar home, ma'am?" asked the young man.

"No, I'm sorry he's not," Erin replied.

"This telegram's for you, ma'am, but I think it may be bad news."

Ralph overheard the conversation and promptly came to Erin's side.

"I'm Padre Russell," he said to the man. "Can I help you?"

"Oh, sir, I'm glad you're here!" He passed the envelope to Ralph and walked away.

"May I open it for you?" asked Ralph sounding calmer than he felt.

"Please do," answered Erin nervously.

Ralph opened the telegram and scanned the first line. He took a deep breath before reading, "The War Office regrets to inform you . . ." He looked compassionately at Erin.

"Oh, no! Please no!" she cried. Suddenly, her body stiffened, and she burst into tears. Ralph reached for her, and tenderly took her by the shoulders, and looked into her eyes. She fell against him—her face contorted with pain and disbelief. She tried to speak, but the words wouldn't form, then she uttered one word, "Michael."

Ralph eased her into a comfortable chair and went down on his haunches beside her, grasping her hand. No words were spoken as the minutes passed. Erin's heaving sobs slowly abated, but her grip began to tighten in Ralph's hand, as if she needed the assurance of another living being beside her. She looked at him through eyes, still flooding with tears, and tried to compose herself.

"Let it come, Erin. Believe me, it will help release the tension. I know how devastated you must feel."

"How can you know?" she cried in sudden burst of anger that was so alien to her nature. "You're a man. Men start wars and get themselves killed, and women are left with no husbands, and no father for unborn children."

Ralph was startled, "Are you pregnant, Erin?"

A silent calm came over her. She placed both her hands over her abdomen, and with eyes downcast, nodded.

"Michael didn't know. I conceived while he was on his last leave. We didn't plan on this. We had decided to wait until the war was over before we had children. Nature didn't see it that way. I didn't write him with the news, as I wanted to see his face when I told him. I'm in my third month."

The sobbing began again. Ralph moved up to sit on the arm of the easy chair so as to relieve his cramping legs. She was grateful for his presence. After an hour slipped by, Ralph knew that Erin had regained a degree of composure.

"I must be going," Ralph said, "but before I leave, let me call someone to come stay with you."

"Thank you. Julia is my best friend. She was maid of honour at our wedding," Erin started to cry again. "I know she would come."

Ralph put in the call, and a man answered. Ralph asked for Julia.

"May I ask who is calling?"

"Yes, it's Padre Russell. I am at the vicarage. I'm afraid Erin has received some terrible news. Her husband has been killed in action. Erin shouldn't be left alone tonight. Would Julia come to be with her?" Ralph couldn't believe how matter-of-fact he sounded. Would he ever get used to delivering this kind of news?

"I'm sure she will. Will you wait until she gets there?" responded the man, obviously Julia's father, the Squire.

"I'll be here." Ralph hung up the receiver.

Within minutes, Julia arrived and took Erin into her arms, the two of them crying.

"I'll leave now," said Ralph and turned to leave. Erin put her hand on his arm.

"Thank you for being here, Ralph. You were a godsend," sighed Erin through her sobs. Ralph never felt so helpless before in his life.

"I'll check back in the morning," he offered, "after I see your father. I'll break the news to him then, not before—both of you need a night's rest."

"He will be terribly upset, but I'm sure you're right—the morning would be best," Erin answered.

"Good night, then." Ralph left.

It was an uneasy, restless night for Erin. Memories flooded her head as she tossed until the early morning hours. About five a.m., she arose for a drink of water, but when she returned, she sat on the edge of the bed, and wept. She wrapped her arms about herself and rocked in an attempt to control the new wave of sobs and convulsions that racked her body. The crosscurrents of feelings experienced over the last hours were overwhelming—first her father's illness, and then the shattering news of her husband's death.

Julia, who was sleeping in the next room, heard her friend stirring. She went in to her without speaking, sat on Erin's bed and held her hand until she slipped into a shallow sleep.

Erin's dreams were chaotic. Her subconscious was a tangle of horrific images that left her gasping for breath. As the first glimmer of dawn broke, she awoke and felt totally drained. Life had lost its meaning. Then, her hand strayed to her stomach. A baby, she thought—a tiny spark of warmth began to stir within her.

In Bewdleigh Park, the military camp also stirred. Soldiers began their morning routines. Ralph shaved and dressed in readiness for the new day. He knew it would not be routine for him. His involvement with the Gwenn family had changed all that, and he didn't look forward to the day ahead.

Chapter 4

On the morning of the 25th of May, the NCHR was notified that the regiment would move when transport could be made available. As the vehicles arrived, the coaches and buses were herded into the transport compound while the unit's stores and supplies were loaded on a variety of civilian trucks and lorries, large and small, as few military vehicles were available. The general staff of the 1st Division, under the command of Major General A. G. L. McNaughton, had to requisition all non-military conveyances. In the Park, the regiment was readied for the road.

Ralph and his new batman, Private Joe Jankowski, were busy. Jankowski came from the village of Wilno located on the northeastern slopes of the highlands. He had been born in Poland and his family had later emigrated to Canada. At age thirty-nine, he was an older soldier, somewhat overweight and partially bald. His peers had nicknamed him "Gramps." He took no offence at this, as he knew he could hold his own, and as "the old guy," the men often deferred to him. He was quiet and efficient by nature—a scrounger *extraordinaire,* which was an admirable trait in the military. However, beneath his calm exterior, he had an infectious, droll sense of humour that would erupt spontaneously. When he was designated as Ralph's batman, he was aware of the padre's confrontations with the opinionated Major MacPherson.

"Sir, I want it clear from the start that I'm not a bigoted 'Mick.' I will look after your needs as if you were my own priest. You can count on that!"

"I don't doubt that Gramps—or would you rather I didn't call you that?" asked Ralph.

"Don't mind at all, sir. It'd seem strange for anyone to call me anything else. At least when someone asks for Gramps, they'll know who they're looking for. Fact is, I do have a grandchild. I was married young and so was my daughter."

"Right, Gramps it is!"

Together, the men set about the task of reorganizing the padre's baggage in preparation for another move. In a barrack box, Gramps packed all of Ralph's clothing, including his clerical robes. He wanted his officer to have handy all the items he would require in a field operation: Ralph's personal communion kit (a departing gift from his parents); a Union Jack to use as an altar cover, or in the event of a funeral, a pall; a small, wooden, altar cross; and other Divine Service accessories. A satchel held the few resource books Ralph required for sermon preparation and chaplain's periods. In Ralph's kit bag were three blankets, a poncho, a gas cape, a great coat, an extra pair of boots, and spare socks.

He carried a small pack that contained his mess tins, knife, fork, spoon and cup, a water sterilizing kit, a shaving kit and towel, sweater, scarf, and his "housewife" containing needle and thread. A package of emergency rations was placed on the bottom.

Gramps laid out Ralph's steel helmet and carefully cleaned web gear. A gas mask was attached to the web by a strap, so the only thing the padre would have to do would be to slip the gear over his shoulders and cinch the belt.

The organizing completed, Ralph made his way to the hospital to visit three soldiers. They had been slightly injured in an accident that had occurred during troop disembarkation from the SS *Canterbury*. The MO thought it best to have them thoroughly examined before returning them to the regiment. Ralph saw that all were physically fit. Only one required a sling to support a sprained wrist.

In another room down the hall, Ralph stopped in to see the vicar. He was sitting dressed ready to be discharged. Yet despite his impending release, he looked haggard.

"Ah, Ralph," he said as the padre entered the chamber, "you are obviously poised to leave us again."

"Afraid so. We could get the call at any time, although we're still short of transport."

"Thank you for being there for Erin last night. A terrible shock for both of us! She was here earlier with the news. She's such a brick—solid as a rock. But still, losing a mate is never easy. Poor thing! I should have been there to comfort her instead of being incarcerated in this place," he said with a renewed show of strength. "I told the doctor that I wanted to go home immediately, with or without his permission. Erin will be here shortly with the Austin."

"Do you think that's wise?" asked Ralph with concern.

"I'll be all right," the vicar reassured him. "I promised Erin I would pace myself. If I'm with her, it will help keep her from dwelling on her husband's death. Mind you, that will take some doing, but if I have to, I can be a pretty good actor." The two men smiled.

"I don't think it will take much acting to get her attention," Ralph remarked. "By the way, I may not be here tomorrow to take the Eucharist for you. We'll have to play that by ear."

"Right. Not to worry. If worst comes to worst, dear old Canon Carter will mumble through the service for me. He's ninety-three now—an amazing old codger."

At that moment Erin entered the room, her face a portrait of anxiety. A sad smile broke the lines of worry when she saw Ralph. She bent to kiss her father on his forehead.

"I'm not so sure about all this," she said. "The doctor really wants you to stay for at least a day or two more."

"Rubbish!" the vicar exclaimed with conviction. "I want to be home. He can see me there just as well!"

Ralph helped Erin walk the vicar to his car. She slipped in behind the wheel.

"Can I give you a lift to the Park?" she asked. "It's on the way."

"That would be fine, but take me with you," Ralph suggested, "and I'll help get your father settled. Then I'll check back with the unit."

Ralph telephoned the adjutant from the vicarage and learned that it would take another twenty-four hours before all transport was in place.

"It appears I'll be here for the Eucharist after all. We're on hold for another day."

Erin smiled, "Oh, that is welcome news. Now, Father," she said turning to the older man, "I want you right into bed. If you think the matron at the hospital was on your tail, wait till you see what I have in store for you."

The vicar gave Ralph a side-glance and winked.

Galahad, Erin's cat, usually called "Galley," rubbed a welcome against the vicar's leg. He was a grey puss with a white bib and underbelly, but what made him distinctive were his white paws, each with six toes. The cat's intelligent green eyes took in everything at a glance, and if he sensed motion he would dash off to investigate, his big feet thumping the floor.

He was an independent character, quick to indicate his fondness or distain for someone, and would twitch his tail in anticipation or displeasure. Galley would show his acceptance of you by kneading his forepaws into your lap, stomach or shoulder.

"I'll be off, then," said Ralph. "I'll drop by in the morning with your communion, Vicar."

"I'll come to the Eucharist," indicated Erin. "Thank you, Ralph, for your continued kindness."

"You take care. I hope you're able to get some rest yourself. You look exhausted."

Later that evening in the officers' mess, Ralph was talking with some of the younger officers when one of them, Lieutenant Tom Nugent, called him aside.

"Padre, do you suppose there's any chance I could meet that cute little blonde from the variety show? What was her name? Julia something-or-other? Rather a knockout, don't you think?"

"Julia Pride, do you mean? She's the Squire's daughter. And yes, she's a lovely girl. But I'm not so sure I should introduce her to a rascal like you, Tom," answered Ralph with a chuckle. The lieutenant was a dashing young man with a flashing white smile, who had a reputation with the girls. He was also a bit vain, and had an obsession about his wavy hair. Tom was often seen glancing at his reflection and running a comb through his locks.

"Oh, I promise to be on my best behaviour," Lieutenant Nugent assured the padre. "She seems like the kind of girl a fellow could write home about."

"Well, let me put it this way. She usually attends the eight o'clock Eucharist in the parish church. Now, if you happened to be there tomorrow . . ."

Sunday morning the Park was active with personnel moving about in anticipation of their departure, and church attendance was noted as voluntary in Part Two Orders. Only a handful of Anglican soldiers appeared for the Eucharist, but one of them was Lieutenant Nugent. As always he was spotless and well groomed. He had taken a pew just in front of the Pride family where he could see Julia from the corner of his eye. Ralph smiled ever so slightly and shook his head almost imperceptibly, as he turned to enter the sanctuary. Nugent grinned and ran a hand across his hair. The service lasted for half an hour, and at its conclusion, Ralph walked to the back of the church to greet the worshippers. He saw Erin hold back, and nodded toward her. As the Pride family made their way out, Ralph observed that Julia had lagged behind her parents and was talking to Nugent. When they all came to where Ralph was standing, he spoke to the squire and his wife, then turned to Julia and Tom.

"Ah, I see you've met one of our officers, Julia. Lieutenant Nugent, I'd like to introduce you to Squire and Mrs. Pride, Julia's parents."

Greetings were exchanged. Julia's mother watched the young couple with acute interest, and turning to her husband, said, "John, why don't we have the young man for lunch?"

"Jolly good idea. Would you join us, Lieutenant?"

"Normally I'd be delighted, sir, but I really must join my platoon. We're having a company inspection in an hour. Perhaps I could come another time?"

"By all means," replied the squire. "We'd be delighted to see you." The Prides left the church, but Julia and Tom lingered in the churchyard.

Only Erin and Ralph were left inside.

"Thank you for your comforting prayers during the Eucharist," she said. "Would you sit with me for a minute? I need a quiet time here, but I don't want to be alone."

They sat in the front pew in the silent church. The sun shone through the stained glass of the east windows, splashing the sanctuary and nave with rainbows. Several minutes passed before Erin raised her head. Tears stained her cheeks.

"Michael and I sat just here," she said patting the seat, "before he left the last time. He held my hand and told me not to worry. 'Nothing can take you from me,' he said. 'Even if I am lost, I will always be with you.' Do you believe that, Ralph?"

"I truly do," Ralph reassured her. "Michael will be with you until your dying day. Even more so with the child growing within you. God never makes anything just to be thrown away—forgotten. A love such as the one you shared with your husband is heaven-made. No one can ever take it away—not war, not man, not even death. Believe that, and face each new day with courage, for your life will go on. It must go on, for now you have a little child to lead you." Ralph paused. "That is what I believe."

She reached for his hand and squeezed it. "It seems since we met I'm always thanking you, Ralph. You have become a dear friend in such a short time. I will miss your strength when you leave here." Erin looked into Ralph's eyes. "Please promise you will write and keep in touch. I know father, too, would like to hear from you. Promise me?"

"I promise," he said lowering his eyes. The woman was in mourning, and this made him feel guilty of his growing feelings for her. If she only knew how deeply she had touched him.

The warning order was dated 0700 hrs, 27 May 40. Bewdleigh Park was a scene of hectic activity. To untrained eyes it would appear to be chaotic, but in fact, all movement was according to plan. The transport, when seen lined up in order of march, appeared a strange sight. The men jokingly referred to it as "Andy McNaughton's Travelling Circus." In the short time since their return from the aborted move to France, the 1st Canadian Division was designated as a self-contained ready force, whose role it would be to close with the enemy should they launch an attack across the Channel.

Simultaneously, events were unfolding swiftly on the beaches of Dunkirk. Masses of men and equipment streamed down to the congested beaches. News reports telephoned across the Channel portrayed the scene as one of utter confusion. In the daylight hours of the 27th of May, German fighters and dive-bombers strafed and bombed the area, blowing shattered bodies and stores high into the air. From below, men fired their small arms at the attacking aircraft. It was for the most part a futile effort.

Adjacent to the shoreline, ships of every description—from destroyers to fishing trawlers to private yachts—stood by to transport the evacuees. The morning fog provided some cover for the water-borne conveyances, and men who could wade or swim the cold Channel waters dropped their gear on the sand to scramble for the waiting vessels. Wounded men were ferried out in rowboats, or were manhandled above the shoulders of stretcher-bearers. To add to the confusion, French civilians mingled with the military, as they, too, sought freedom, while chaplains tended the dead and dying as they lay nestled in depressions above the tide line.

Time after time, the rescue fleet made return trips across the Channel. The turnabout took from eight to nine hours to complete, and this supreme effort continued until the last man was carried from the site. In all, 335,000 personnel, under constant attack, were miraculously lifted and transported back to England. It was a remarkable feat that would take its place in the annals of British military history.

England was bracing for a full-scale German invasion. Citizens who owned weapons checked their pieces. Farmers readied brush-hooks and pitchforks, and youngsters placed cricket bats beneath their beds to protect Mum against the invader while Dad was elsewhere defending his country. It was a pathetic, but determined, show of patriotism against the armed might of Hitler's forces.

Churchill's speech to the House of Commons on the eighth day of the evacuation was broadcast on the BBC throughout the land and across the seas: "We shall not flag or fail. We shall go on to the end. . . .We shall fight on the beaches, we shall fight on the landing grounds, we shall fight in the fields and the streets, we shall fight in the hills: we shall never surrender . . ."

As the crusty old "British Bulldog" growled his brave and tenacious message, people across the world were stirred, and the far-flung reaches of the Empire rallied to the cry. Men turned out at recruiting stations in even greater numbers to answer the call to arms—to face the pain and the glory.

The NCHR cavalcade proceeded north from Bewdleigh, skirting west of London through countryside towns and villages—Woking, Bagshot, Windsor, Slough, Watford, St. Albans, Dunstable, Bletchley, and finally to Towcester, where the regiment made camp on a racecourse beside the Tove River. Along the route, crowds of people waved and shouted words of encouragement to the men. The 1st Canadian Division moved into the Midlands and established temporary bivouacs near Northampton. Here it remained poised awaiting orders, ready to move at a moment's notice to confront an invading German army.

Ralph was provided with a room at the clubhouse where he could meet with individual soldiers. He kept short notes of these interviews for future reference. The information was not confidential in nature—simply an outline of the problem, and how it was dealt with. The more intimate details he committed to memory.

Each morning, the men would report for duty at the racetrack. Physical training began the day, followed by kit inspections, weapon maintenance, basic drill, and platoon instruction on a variety of topics: map reading, and the identification of enemy tanks, vehicles and aircraft. They put in a full day before retiring to their billets, where a hot cup of tea and a warm welcome awaited them.

Ralph heard a never-ending litany of praise from the soldiers for the good folks of Towcester.

"Hey, Padre, you'll never guess what the Dolmages fed me for breakfast this morning—fresh eggs, peameal bacon, and toast on the side. Had to wonder where they got the bacon from. They wanted me to have the evening meal with them, too, but I thought that would be taking too much from their food rations. I'm going to scrounge some coffee for them."

"Mr. Carter wants me to go to his pub with him tonight. Says he wants to show me off. He's got relatives in Calgary—you'd have laughed when he asked me if I might know them, being a fellow Canadian and all. Me, living two thousand miles from Alberta. They just can't imagine the distance. Thinks he's going to buy the drinks, but I have a surprise for him."

"The lady I'm billeted with is a sweetheart. She's a widow. Reminds me of my grandma. Warms my bed each night with a copper pan filled with coals, and puts a hot water bottle under the covers at the foot of the bed. Even offers to run a bath for me. Says she wished she had a son like me! I've got to get her something special. Any ideas, Padre?"

Ralph was pleased with the banter and agreed with Gramps, who chuckled and said, "Why, some of these guys never had it so good. They think they've died and gone to heaven."

The sojourn in the Midlands lasted for only twelve days. Despite the short stay, friendships were formed that would remain strong through the coming dark days, and even for years to come. Many young men found a home away from home, and would return when on leave in the months ahead.

"Andy McNaughton's Travelling Circus" had an unexpected spinoff. As the Canadians travelled the highways and byways, scores of people lined the routes with a cheering welcome. The men of the NCHR grinned and waved back. The people of Britain showered their affection on the soldiers from Canada, raising the spirits of both the civilians and the military. It was a heartening gesture in the midst of national gloom.

Colonel Morrison received his orders at brigade headquarters. The 1st Canadian Division would return to the Aldershot area, and Bewdleigh, and become a part of the 2nd British Expeditionary Force, which would include the 52nd Division and the 3rd British Division. The

CO had been given the option of a different location in which to bivouac the regiment, but adamantly refused to consider an alternative.

He told the brigadier, "We have been generously received in Bewdleigh. The men enjoy the village and have been made to feel welcome. There has been little friction between the civilian and military populations and an excellent rapport has been established, thanks in part to the good work of our padre."

"I heard he was behind that 'country show' that was staged a couple of weeks ago. I would have come had I been invited," hinted the brigadier.

"I'll remember that, sir, and if we have another production, you'll be sure to get an invitation."

"On another note, Scotty," began the brigadier changing the subject, "I'm sure your people will be well turned out for the King's Review on the eighth?"

"The NCHR is always well turned out, sir," the colonel assured him. "Remember our motto, 'Aye Ready.'"

"Get away with you, Morrison. See you at the parade."

Gramps was left to settle Ralph's kit on their return, as Ralph was anxious to see how the Gwenns were making out. He found both of them happy to see him, and Erin gladly offered to make tea. While she was gone, Ralph questioned the vicar.

"How is she doing?"

"Amazingly well," replied the vicar. "The mind can be a wonderful tool when we allow it to be. We tend to compartmentalize, and when that happens, we gradually remember only the good things and let the hurtful memories fade. It will take her time, but already I see it happening."

When Erin returned, father and daughter eagerly plied Ralph with questions about his recent activities.

Ralph laughed. "If I didn't know better, I would take you for a pair of spies!"

The vicar chortled. "Oh, come now, I know all those posters should be heeded: 'Loose lips sink ships,' and 'The Hun is listening.' It's just that we've been closeted together since you left, and you bring such a breath of fresh air into our midst. Isn't that right, Erin?"

"I'm just joking," said Ralph. "I would have thought you were on to my sense of humour by now."

Erin teased right back. "Well, you must admit, the Canadian sense of the ridiculous can be a little wry by times, but it's great to have you back, Ralph. It really is!"

"Now, it's your turn," countered Ralph, after he had given them a rundown of his recent activities. "How have the two of you been making out?"

"Dad has been behaving himself," Erin began, "but I have to keep my eye on him. He gets an idea in his head and he's hard to hold down. The doctor has been in to see him every day, and is pleased with his recovery. His medication seems to be doing its job."

"And you, Erin, how are you doing?" Ralph asked looking at her fondly. "I must say I like to see the colour back in your cheeks."

"I expect that's a bit of rouge," she said with a slight blush of pleasure. "The nights are difficult for me. As soon as I lie down, a million thoughts tumble through my head, and I lie awake half the night. When I do sleep, it's full of wild disturbing dreams, and in the morning, I feel more tired than when I went to bed. After a hot cup of tea though, things begin to look up." Erin fell quiet.

"We've had some good long talks," reported the vicar, anxious to keep the mood light. "It's better than brooding. A person must grieve in his or her own way, but grieve nonetheless. It's unhealthy if it stays all bottled up inside. I know. When my wife died, I thought that was the end for me, but with Erin's help, I saw things differently. Now, it's my turn to support her. We remember all the precious moments we shared with our loved ones, and this sure foundation allows us to go on. Life changes, and we must change with it."

"I will build a new life for my child," Erin said determinedly. "Michael would want that . . ."

"You are very brave, Erin," Ralph said with true admiration, "and fortunate to have your father to lean on. Together you will make the future happen. Wait and see!"

The vicar smiled mischievously. "What is happening with you now, Ralph . . . that is, if I may ask?"

"Well, tomorrow, His Majesty, the King, will review our division in Farnborough. I'm quite excited about it, to tell the truth. It will be my first time to see the king in person. After that, I expect the new Expeditionary Force will depart for France. It may be a long shot, but we must try and stop the German onslaught."

Erin lowered her head, and her father placed a hand on her shoulder. He turned to Ralph and said, "Our hearts go with you, my son. May the Good Lord keep you under His loving care! Shall we pray together?"

Four days later, the NCHR, with other elements of the 1st Division, joined the 2nd British Expeditionary Force en route to Plymouth. After detraining, they were marched to holding areas prior to boarding a ship. The local ladies' auxiliary made their way through the lines of troops offering hot tea and sandwiches. Their leader, Lady Nancy Astor, Member of Parliament for Plymouth, was in their midst, talking with the men and commenting on their youthfulness.

One lad, with cheeks of peach fuzz, remarked as she passed, "Oh, I'd be glad to let her mother me!"

Gramps overheard the remark and said, "I bet he would—an up and coming nipper, that one."

The embarkation call came and the troops, loaded down with their battle gear, marched to the docks, to board the SS *El Mansour*, a French transport. Members of the Royal Canadian Regiment, and several minor units of the 1st Canadian Division, joined the men of the NCHR. The ship was crowded.

The unit commanders on board requested that a voluntary divine service be held after the evening meal. Ralph was the only Protestant chaplain on board, as the RCR padre was Roman Catholic, so it was decided that a Catholic mass would be said aft, and a Protestant service forward. Ralph briefed his CO on the short order of service he planned for the occasion and asked if he would read the lesson from the New Testament.

"Thank you for asking, Padre, but it would be a fine gesture if you asked Colonel Hodson of the RCR to do the honours."

"Right, sir, I'll check with him."

Ralph proceeded to the officers' mess area where Lieutenant Colonel Vernon Hodson was chatting with his son, Major Vern Hodson, and Lieutenant George Kitching, two RCR company commanders.

The padre addressed Colonel Hodson. "May I speak with you for a moment, sir?"

"Yes, Padre, what can I do for you?"

"Would you consider reading the scripture lesson for Divine Service?"

"That would give me great pleasure. What is it that I am to read?"

"Since we are nearing battle, sir, I thought that passage on 'The whole armour of God' would be appropriate."

"Ah, yes, Ephesians 6, verses 10 through 17—one of my favourite readings. Good choice. Will you give me a nod when I'm to stand forth?"

"That I will, and thanks for accepting," said Ralph.

Immediately following the meal, soldiers began to drift either to the bow or aft of the ship, to attend their respective services. The evening was cool, but not unpleasant, and everyone gathered companionably. The padre did not robe, but appeared in his battledress wearing his clerical collar. The order of service was simple—opening prayers acknowledging the presence of the Almighty, a moment of silence for private confession, an absolution, and a prayer to commit loved ones to God's keeping. The Twenty-third Psalm was recited, followed by the reading of the lesson by Colonel Hodson. Ralph gave a few brief comments to emphasize the relevance of the scriptures in the current situation and invited all to recite the Lord's Prayer. In closing, he gave this final prayer:

"O Lord, You who in the time of trial steadfastly faced your cross and passion, help us, your weak and wavering disciples, to be firm and resolute in doing those things that lie before us. Help us to overcome difficulties and to persevere in spite of failures. When we are weary and disheartened and ready to give in, fill us with fresh courage and strength, and keep us faithful to the task before us. If we stumble or fall, be there to lift us up and guide us on our way. For you alone are the Mighty One, and You alone can guide our feet into the way of victory and peace. We ask this in Jesus' name. Amen."

Ralph closed the service with the Blessing:

"The Peace of God that passes all understanding, keep your hearts and mind in the knowledge and love of God, and His Son Jesus Christ our Lord, and the blessing of God Almighty, the Father, the Son and the Holy Spirit, be amongst you and remain with you always. Amen."

As twilight descended, the men solemnly disbursed throughout the ship. While they did not know what the morrow would hold for them, they did know that their mission was desperate and that the German war machine was in full spate, rushing irresistibly like the full moon tide across the face of Europe. It seemed that the entire free world was depending upon them—a heavy burden for any band of men. However, they were men of resolve who would do their duty, and damn the odds.

In crowded quarters they passed the night, and at dawn, the troopships entered the harbour at Brest, where men, in groups of twenty at a time, were put ashore. The height of land behind the town was used as an assembly area, and by midday, the small groups reformed as platoons and companies within their larger battalions. They marched down the slopes into the town proper and boarded railway boxcars labelled with the signs "40 men or 8 horses."

"Yipeee!" cheered the men, "we ride again."

"Look out, Hitler. Here come the farm boys riding their trusty plugs," laughed Gramps, picking up on the jest. He was sweating with effort as he struggled with the padre's kit.

Ralph and Gramps travelled with the Regimental Aid Post in a boxcar of ancient vintage, with cracks in the wall through which the wind whistled. The outside temperature was 60°F, but the air was damp and cool as it filtered through the car.

Gramps was hunched in a corner of the car, head down.

"You feeling all right, chum?" asked Ralph.

"Just a little tuckered, sir, by all the hurry-up and go. Seems the old lungs can't take the slugging any more."

The MO hooked a nod at Ralph.

"Cigarette, Ralph?" offered Sandy.

"Thanks, Sandy, I will." He pulled a Sweet Cap from the package. A lighter snapped, and the padre drew on the flickering flame.

"I'm afraid your lad's not long for infantry duty," said the doctor nodding toward the batman.

"I think you're right. He'd have a difficult time keeping up in a running battle."

"Want me to downgrade his medical category?"

"I'd hate to lose him. He's damn good at what he does," said Ralph.

"I know that, but we'll have to keep an eye on him. He needs to get in better shape. I'll talk with him," promised Sandy.

The train puffed its way across the pastoral countryside of Brittany, passing scattered farms, vineyards and small communities. Occasionally, it would stop at a station along the way, and the engineer would alight to determine the situation up the line. Progress was cautious, and speed was varied accordingly. The line was taking them in the direction of Paris through small cities like Rennes, but at Laval they changed direction to head southwest toward Chateaubriant. In the late afternoon, short of the town, the engineer halted the train. The main roadway parallelling the tracks was clogged with people on the move, men hauling carts, and women and children dragging small wagons. The troops leapt from the boxcars to stretch their legs.

"Poor buggers," muttered the men as they as witnessed for the first time an exodus of displaced people escaping their worst nightmares. Many of those on the road had experienced a similar dislocation twenty-five years earlier when the Kaiser's armies had swept into France. Their faces wore a haunted, hopeless look as they trudged along the roadway.

Several miles down the line explosions rent the air in the direction of Chateaubriant. Plumes of smoke puffed into the sky above the town.

"The Germans are bombing the railway yards. We must pull back!" screamed the engineer from his cab. The engine's wheels squealed as the train was reversed and soldiers piled back on board. It was early evening, and the growing darkness would provide some cover if the Luftwaffe decided to search for targets along the rail lines. The fleeing train reached Laval late at night, where more boxcars bearing British and French soldiers were added to it. It was ordered back for a return to Brest. The men of the NCHR wondered in the way unblooded troops sometimes do—will we ever stand and fight?

Somewhere between the coast and Rennes, in the pre-dawn darkness, the train came to a sudden jerking halt. A few soldiers awoke from their restless sleep to peer outside. Nothing stirred. Gradually, even the sound of escaping steam from the engine ceased. An officer from one of the RCR companies wandered forward to talk with the engineer, but found that the entire train crew had vanished. The officer alerted the men in the cars, and after a search, found several who had worked with the railways in Canada. One had been a fireman who quickly studied the engine cab before announcing he would drive the train to the coast.

Brest was congested with troops and civilians alike. The train slowly shunted to a stop at the entrance to the rail yards where a new French crew was found to take the troops to dockside. It would have been nearly impossible for the Canadian volunteer at the throttle to manoeuvre the rolling stock along the various tracks and switches toward the harbour front. At the docks, the troop train slowed to a stop beside rows of wine casks awaiting shipment. The soldiers recognized the cargo, and with one accord, decided to prevent the contents from falling into enemy hands—or so they rationalized. Swarming over the barrels, bungholes were breached, and the wine began to flow. A variety of containers were filched to hold the coveted red nectar. Meanwhile, officers recognizing the danger at hand ordered the casks destroyed. Groaning men were moved aside while the containers were sprayed with bullets from automatic weapons. Great plumes of the beverage flooded the docks, but some continued to be salvaged as men emptied their water bottles and filled them with wine.

One man chortled and pointed as he nudged Ralph. "That's one way of turning water into wine, eh, Padre?" In the middle of the fray, Gramps was filling two water bottles with the delectable liquid, one for himself and one for his officer.

Secured alongside one of the piers was the SS *Canterbury*. Led by the RCR, and followed by the NCHR, the soldiers boarded the familiar vessel, while other military personnel and a handful of civilians crowded on behind. In all, some two thousand souls were jammed aboard by ten o'clock on the night of June 15th. Shortly thereafter, a lone German aircraft was identified as it flew low over the harbour. In wild abandonment, troops lining the *Canterbury's* starboard side proceeded to let loose with their personal weapons. It was more effective as a release of frustration than a concerted attack upon the enemy as the plane disappeared from sight, undamaged.

The *Canterbury* sailed at first light on Sunday morning, the 16th of June, after a minesweeper had cleared the harbour entrances (the aircraft from the night before was suspected of laying mines along the shipping lane). As the hour of eleven approached, the fore and after decks were again crowded with men as they gathered for worship. Gregory Clark, a Canadian newspaperman on board, recorded the event for posterity:

"I have never witnessed a sight quite like it before. I've attended other military religious services but this one brought my mind to attention. As I gazed at the men, heads bowed in prayer, I sensed an unconscious and spontaneous sense of rededication. 'The next time we face the foe, they will feel our resolve,' they seemed to say with silent determination. Our Canadian boys are becoming a well-trained, well-led, band of brothers. Their time will come, indeed, and when it does, I'd hate to be the enemy. To that, I say, amen!"

The people of Bewdleigh welcomed the NCHR back into their midst with a display of open affection. All felt a need for closeness and mutual support in these dark hours. Everyone was well aware of the spectre overshadowing the green island called England. The country braced for a German invasion as news reports indicated an increased buildup of barges and shipping along the French coast. Aircraft reconnaissance produced aerial photographs of the massive enemy concentration poised to cross the Channel. A sense of dread descended over the people, both civilian and military, in spite of the brave words of encouragement proclaimed by Prime Minister Churchill.

Within days of the return, the earlier resolve of the 2nd British Expeditionary Force began to fade. A distinct decline in discipline was observed among the troops, and a miasma of fatalism—a momentary collapse of determination—was easily discernable. During this period of inactivity, an increasing number of men from the NCHR went absent without leave. Many began affairs with local women, some carnal only in nature, others an attempt at some kind of serious bonding. In some instances, adultery overcame decent men's sensibilities, and these liaisons generally ended in tragedy.

The padre's personal interviews escalated. He counselled as best he could, but without the will of the individual soldier, his efforts were of little help. It was as if a plague were sweeping the population. No one wanted to feel alone. No one wanted to be alone. It was as if clinging together in a physical way would make all the calamitous overshadowing go away.

Drunkenness was another symptom of the despairing times. This, in turn, led to fights in the pubs and in the streets. Military police were kept busy, and the unit police cells overflowed.

Colonel Morrison became alarmed with the sudden deterioration of discipline and good conduct. He warned his officers that they must find ways to combat the slide. Punishment for flagrant offences had to be severe in an attempt to set examples.

"Confine offenders to unit lines. Put them in the slammer. Keep them busy," he ordered. "Route marches and field training will be increased. Make them so physically exhausted that they will be less likely to get into trouble. Now, let's get a grip on this. You can bet the Germans would cheer at our apparent disarray. Just remember, they are only a few hours away, and at this very moment are preparing to invade."

Following his O Group, Morrison drew Ralph aside.

"Padre, we are experiencing a serious situation. The men appear to be losing spirit. I know they are disheartened by the fact that we have not faced the enemy—that we seem to be withdrawing every time we head for battle. But believe me, our time will come. The men must be ready. Their morale must be high," the colonel emphasized. "We must find ways to get them back on track. I need your help especially right now. If you can find ways to reverse this degrading trend, it would be greatly appreciated. Appeal to their better nature in your Padre's Sessions, and above all, pray for us all. We will need an act of God to bring us through this."

It was a demanding challenge, for Ralph found the men lethargic at best when he had them together. When he broached the reasons for their listlessness, they held back as if some kind of drug held them in its grip. He worried the problem through searching for answers. He had long conversations with the vicar.

"This is no new phenomenon," responded the older clergyman at one point. "In France twenty-plus years ago, when the men were suffering from the hell of the trenches, they would go about their duties as if in a trance. The soupy mud was so deep, and the rats at night so thick, it was no wonder they suffered from psychological trauma. Day after day, week after week, they endured enemy probes—futile charges of their own, falling shells, creeping gas, and many illnesses that arose from the filthy quagmire. It was a pitiful situation. In certain areas behind the line they would steal away on a quiet night to brothels and get drunk on cheap wine. They lived for the moment, for the next they might be dead.

"I remember the night I was wounded," he continued. "There was a house in a hollow, three or four hundred yards behind our position, occupied by a mother and her two daughters. Miraculously, the dwelling had been unscathed by the withering fire. A small orchard that had been reduced to a graveyard of tree stumps surrounded it. By all accounts, they were deemed to be a vile trio—a source of venereal disease. Somehow they managed to acquire quantities of raw red wine, for which they charged atrocious prices. Each night, a handful of men would literally slither across the muddy fields to partake in whatever 'comforts' the women had to offer. I was appalled. Oh, I told them to stay put—even threatened to charge them with deserting their posts. Deep down inside I knew I wouldn't stop them, providing only two or three slipped away at a time, for I rationalized they were reaching for a woman's touch—something they seemed to know they might never experience again. Maybe it was just lust, an escape from the horrors of reality. God only knows!" The vicar paused, deep in memory for a moment while Ralph waited patiently for the vicar to resume his story.

"Before the German attack came in, flares lit up the sky. I looked to the rear and saw four men staggering across the field in full view. They were caught in the open. Suddenly the ground around them erupted from incoming mortars. When I looked again, they were gone, blown to bits. It was one of the few images that I remember of that night, for seconds later our entire line of trenches came under artillery fire. I recall trying to rally the men even to the point of leaping up onto the parapet to encourage their attention. Several simply laid or crouched there, heads pressed forward into a wall of mud, unmoving, and let the stinking, putrid ooze flow over them. They had given up. The remainder put up a brave show and held out to the last man. The Hun was stopped.

"The next thing I knew it was morning, and someone was trying to pull me free from where I lay buried up to the neck. A woman, probably one from the house, was unable to free me. With her hands, she created small furrows to drain the muddy water that was pooling beneath my chin, then gently wiped my face with her skirt and angled my head upright to give me breathing space. She disappeared before our reserves came forward and found me. I deserved no medal for that night's work—perhaps it should have gone to the girl. My lot should have been to die with my men. Guilt plagues me to this day—haunts my dreams."

Ralph gazed thoughtfully at the vicar as they sat together in silence. A tear slipped down the older man's cheek.

"It seems somehow inevitable that each man must face his war in his own way," the vicar counselled. "You have yours to contend with, Ralph. I do not envy you. I know you will do your best for the men. They are good men—anyone can see that. Before long they will be faced with the horrific reality of death on the battlefield. Right now, they are at that point in life where they are in need of a touch of loving-kindness. The military will instill the discipline. It is their way of caring. But you must be there for them in a different way. By your example in their midst, you will build up their moral courage—yours is a ministry of presence!"

Erin entered the room.

"Would you join us for a bite of supper, Ralph?" The young woman's presence had lightened the mood considerably, and Ralph was sorely tempted to accept.

"Thank you no, Erin," he replied with genuine regret. "Your father has stimulated the shepherd in me. I must go back to the lines."

For the next several weeks, Ralph constantly visited the tent lines. As he made his way among the men he would greet them by name. Some would turn him aside for a chat, or arrange for a more serious talk in the privacy of the chaplain's office.

One morning, as Ralph was saying his morning prayers at his desk, Gramps came rushing in to alert him that there had been an accident. Ralph hurried over to the Medical Inspection Room, where Sandy was working over a soldier on a stretcher. The doctor turned as the padre entered, and seeing him, shook his head.

"Killed instantly, I expect, chest crushed and multiple head injuries. Didn't stand a chance on that motorcycle."

"What happened?"

"He was bringing the morning mail from Brigade HQ when he was sideswiped by a lorry on one of the hedgerow roads. Hardly enough room for two vehicles to pass. The truck was in the middle of the road, coming around a bend, and the motorcycle swerved to avoid the collision, but his front wheel caught a broken edge in the pavement and threw him into the side of the lorry. The dual wheels ran over him."

"Poor kid, who is he?"

"Private Frederick Krantz of B Company. He was a dispatch driver-in-training."

"Freddie Krantz?' Ralph remarked the shock jolting him involuntarily. "I know his family. They belonged to the United Church in Plevna. He's one of seven kids . . . a close family. This will hit them hard!"

Three days later, a full military funeral was held for the regiment's first casualty. The drums were muffled and draped in black, as the casket was conveyed on the shoulders of his comrades to St. Tristan's. The regiment marched behind the cortège. The solemn funeral liturgy was short, but in it, Ralph reminded the men of the green hills of the highlands, where Fred Krantz's spirit would always be found.

"Gentlemen, life is sometimes brief and full of mystery. We never know when the call will come for us. Each day is a gift from God. Live it to the full, but in doing so, be true to yourselves and your loved ones. Be the best that you can be, and remember your high calling as soldiers of the King of Kings. The Good Lord will see you through all the dark valleys, even the valley of death. Be of good faith, and be assured of the final victory."

Private Frederick Krantz was buried in a corner of the churchyard known as Soldiers' Row. A lone piper slow-marched in the background playing a dirge that echoed softly through the trees. It was a lamentation for the young soldier, and for all the soldiers who lay at rest around him.

That night Ralph pondered the letter he was writing to the Krantz family. It was the first of many that he would pen with heavy heart—a job no one envied. As he sat at his desk deep in thought wondering what he should write, Ralph's mind stole back to more peaceful days. He remembered the sparkling lakes of the highlands and the sweet smell of the pine trees as a gentle breeze stirred them. He recalled walking along an oak ridge with the dry leaves of fall rustling at his feet and the sight of an alert deer, raising its head as he approached. A tear slipped from the corner of his eye as a pang of homesickness filled him.

Slowly, the lethargy and despondency of the troops began to lift. Absenteeism became less frequent, but heavy drinking did not. It was a means to drown one's troubles, and as in the Royal Navy of yore, was deemed to be the least of two evils, providing it was kept under control. For the most part, the MPs saw to that. This, coupled with the fact that the men were busy with drills, physical training, field exercises and route marches, kept them out of trouble. They became hardened of body and swift of wit as the threat of invasion became a greater reality. The 1st Canadian Division was now a part of the British 7th Corps, whose responsibility was to confront the expected German invasion along the southeast coast of England in Sussex and Kent. The formation dug in with all units preparing defensive positions, but ready to move rapidly toward the beaches. It was a highly mobile force, and it was a time of high alert.

In July and August, great vapour trails criss-crossed the high blue by day, while British fighter squadrons engaged the enemy aloft. The battle for Britain was being waged in the air, while the soldiers of the king deployed along the southeast coast. At night, the drone of incoming German bombers was incessant. Occasionally, the night sky would light up with an explosive flare as the heavily loaded enemy bombers were hit by the tireless efforts of RAF fliers. Closer to London, anti-aircraft batteries opened up on planes that were caught in the glare of searchlights sweeping the darkness above. When hit, flaming airframes pitched earthward in a screaming death spiral.

Fire trenches were dug around the NCHR tent lines. When the air raid sirens sounded, men tumbled from their more comfortable cover to lie stretched out in these earthy pockets for protection against bomb blasts. At first many thought this was a needless caution. Then, one night, an enemy bomber that had been turned back from the skies over London dropped its payload over seemingly open countryside. The stick of bombs landed along the edge of Bewdleigh Park where the transport compound was located, causing damage to equipment and the workshop and slightly wounding one man. Thereafter, procedural orders were strictly obeyed without complaint.

Still the enemy ground forces delayed crossing the Channel as the summer wore on. It was the night of August the 2nd, Ralph's birthday, as he was returning from a visit to the vicarage following the "all clear," that he had occasion to dive into a roadside ditch. Seemingly from nowhere, the unearthly screech of flying metal passed low over his head. As he hit the ground, he saw a flaming image grazing the treetops above him as it crashed into the field beyond the road. Momentarily stunned, he watched in horror, as a man covered in flames crawled from the wreckage, followed by two more airmen amazingly unscathed. They shouted at each other, trying to determine if all had escaped the crash. As it turned out, two were missing, and one of the crew turned back toward the aircraft as one of its fuel tanks exploded. Flaming gasoline swallowed him whole.

Within minutes, armed troops crowded the scene. The first to arrive witnessed Ralph rolling one of the fliers on the ground to douse the fire consuming his body. One of the other enemy airmen had a pistol levelled at the padre.

"Drop that goddamn weapon!" screamed a sergeant, aiming his Tommy gun at the German, who immediately dropped his Luger.

The sergeant grinned, retrieving the fallen pistol. "Er . . . sorry for the language, Padre. Would you like a souvenir?"

"Thanks, Sergeant Shanks, but we'd better turn it over to the MPs."

"Right, sir, but what a great keepsake it would be," said Shanks immediately kicking himself for offering the luger in the first place.

The incident recorded the first face-to-face NCHR encounter with the enemy. Now he had a human face, a very frightened one at that. This fact lingered in the minds of those who saw the prisoners and served as a reminder that the so-called super race could be scared to death like any other mortal being.

The firestorms in London caused by the mass German bombings continued for fifty-seven straight nights. The British military saw the action as a certain prelude to the massive enemy attack across the Channel. Prime Minister Churchill announced to the nation that an armada-like force of 175,000 German troops was poised in the Channel ports. He told the people that church bells would peal a warning across the nation as soon as an enemy movement was detected. Ground troops were on a four-hour alert to move. But still Hitler's elite divisions stayed where they were.

On the night of September the 14th, the RAF gave the Luftwaffe a decisive drubbing. There were 185 enemy planes destroyed, while only twenty-five British aircraft were lost. It became a pivotal point of the war against Hitler's might. Throughout this horrific period, King George VI and Queen Elizabeth made frequent visits to the devastated areas of London. Their hearts went out to their people as they made their way through shattered streets where Londoners gathered to greet and cheer the Royals. There was an outstanding solidarity shared between the highest and the lowest of the land.

Slowly, the mass of German troops began to pull back from the French coast as their high command began to reassess their priorities. England remained on guard, but much of the tension began to dissipate. A new dawn had broken.

Fall had come to Bewdleigh Park, and with the anticipated onset of rainy weather, the decision was made to move the NCHR from its tented encampment into billets in and around the village. The troops happily received the news and eagerly moved to their new accommodations, where warm hearths and warm hearts awaited them.

Tidings of the plan reached the vicar in advance and at once he approached Colonel Morrison to allow Ralph to take up residence in the vicarage. The commanding officer thought this would be of benefit to all around, and so advised his chaplain to accept the generous offer.

At first, Ralph was pleased with the idea, as it would give him a central location from where he could best serve his men. St. Tristan's and the vicarage were in the centre of the village, and he could use the church vestry as an additional private office. As he considered the advantages he was also drawn to the realization that he would be in daily contact with Erin, and subconsciously that still concerned him. He resolved to face his problem head on and sought out the vicar.

Paul Gwenn was a wise man and had already sensed the turmoil the younger man felt where Erin was concerned. The vicar saw the way Ralph looked at Erin and knew the chaplain cared for her deeply. He also knew that Erin was fonder of Ralph than even she was prepared to admit. The older priest further sensed that guilt would play an incisive role in the developing relationship. He decided to watch carefully and only intervene if the need arose. "After all," he concluded, "they are both mature adults and, apart from temporary convention, are free to pursue their own feelings."

"Paul, your invitation to have me stay at the vicarage is very kind," Ralph began. A genuine respect and affection had developed between the two men and they were now on a first-name basis. "The central location would be an advantage for me. Many of the troops have become fond of St. Tristan's and see it as their spiritual 'home away from home.' Apart from that, I would be personally pleased to share your company. In many ways I am very much at ease and relaxed with you." He took a deep breath. "However, I must be honest with you. The more I see of Erin, the more I am attracted to her, and I must confess, this makes me feel somewhat guilty. She is only recently widowed, and I don't want to take advantage of her vulnerability. Can you advise me how to approach this?"

The vicar looked thoughtfully at the man he already considered a son. "My only advice is this—go slowly," he advised. "First become friends, and let the outcome take care of itself. If you are meant to be closer, it will happen in due course. Her wounds at the loss of Michael are still fresh, and only time will heal them. Right now," Ralph looked up, "what she needs most is a friend she can trust and lean on. I am happy to say she has found that in you, and I bless you for your kindness and support. Soon the baby will arrive, and that will fill her heart and days, carrying her in new directions. Be patient, continue to be her confidant, and wait and see . . ."

Ralph moved in and was made to feel a part of the family. Erin, now in her last weeks of pregnancy, was glowing, much to her doctor's satisfaction, for he had feared the shock of Michael's death might cause problems. She had fooled him. Her health was robust and her outlook positive.

Late one afternoon, Ralph entered the vicarage to find Erin stretched out on a settee with her feet up. Galley, the cat, was draped over her lap, purring loudly. At the sight of Ralph, he flicked his tail several times in greeting, his green eyes half closed.

"He's talking to the baby," announced Erin. "It's amusing to watch. Every once in a while the child kicks out sharply enough to get Galley's attention. There—see?" The cat jerked his head in the direction of Erin's abdomen and reached out with his paw to knead the spot that had alerted him.

Ralph laughed with her and came and sat in a chair beside her.

"You are looking absolutely radiant today, Mrs. Ross!"

"Thank you, kind sir. I feel great." Her luminous smile brought a catch to Ralph's throat.

"Is there anything I can fetch you as you recline in such regal splendour?"

"Could I persuade you to make us a cup of tea?"

"Your wish is my command, madam. I shall return shortly," Ralph called from the kitchen. "Is your father home?"

"No, but I expect him any moment."

"I'll make enough for three, then."

When he returned to the room the telephone rang and Erin made a move to answer.

"Don't get up. I'll get it." He picked up the telephone. "It's your father. He says he'll be late for tea, and for us to go ahead without him."

"I'll make us a few sandwiches," offered Erin.

"It's already done. I'll fetch them," Ralph said, passing her the tea tray.

They spent a cosy hour chatting as dusk gathered.

"We're like an old married couple," Erin commented demurely, and then, realizing what she had said, dipped her head and blushed. Ralph turned away, not wanting to embarrass her, and pretended not to hear . . . but neither one was fooled.

Then, deliberately facing her and with a gentle smile he said, "Now that's a beautiful thought!"

September was a month of intense training under the code name Exercise "Bumper." All units of the British 7th Corps, which included the 1st Canadian Division, were deployed to the southeast corner of England where, in theory, the German forces had landed in an attempt to cut off London from the rest of England. It was primarily a mounted exercise that gave the troops a tour of seven counties in that part of the country. There were enough "attack" skirmishes to allow the troops opportunity to stretch and avoid calloused butts. Soon their "tourist" days would come to an end, when the training emphasis would be placed upon physical fitness with numerous forced marches and battle drills.

In early October, Ralph met Honorary Captain R. O. "Rusty" Wilkes, a recently appointed chaplain to the Royal Canadian Regiment, bivouacked at Charlwood ten miles east of Bewdleigh. It was friendship at first sight. Rusty was a tall, rangy, athletic individual, a natural runner, who was keenly interested in track and field. He was affable and good-natured, and ready for a humorous challenge. The two men differed somewhat in personality, while at the same time having many things in common. Both were Anglican priests who had attended Wycliffe College in Toronto, although in different years. Each had begun his ministry in rugged parishes where they learned to meld into their congregations. They enjoyed a wide variety of competitive sports and were in top physical condition. The two chaplains were intelligent, always seeking ways to improve the lot of their men, and preferred to draw their men to religion rather than force it upon them. The men were typically in the middle of any camaraderie their respective messes offered, and were generally admired by their fellow officers. Both padres delighted in sharing a pint, when they weren't sipping on single malt scotch after a long day. They were fully accepted as members of their respective regiments.

Ralph and Rusty had first met at a conference called by Honorary Major H. T. Stewart, senior chaplain of the 1st Canadian Division. Stewart had taken up his appointment in the previous month, and this was his first opportunity to gather the twelve chaplains together. He was eager to learn of their activities with the field units and to find ways to enhance the padres' duties. He stressed the importance of finding ways to bolster the morale of the Canadian troops, which had become a serious problem. Also discussed was the fact that transportation was a major problem faced by many of the chaplains, particularly those who had responsibilities for several minor units. They relied heavily on limited transportation pools and basically had to "hitch" a ride. This made timings for religious services difficult. The senior chaplain promised that he would give this a high priority and would bring it before the divisional commander.

The group discussed the merits of chaplains' "talks" in the unit training cycle. Some were already developing this tool and keenly recommended it as a good way to get to know the troops. The occasion provided the chaplains with an opportunity for "bull sessions" where everything and anything was thrown into the forum for discussion. This proved valuable to those clerics who had not as yet developed a healthy rapport with their units.

The collegiality of the gathering, especially the opportunity to worship together, was a morale booster for the chaplains. It was a chance for them to relax with their peers and share concerns.

Following the conference, Rusty suggested that Ralph should join him for dinner in the RCR lines. As it was on his return route, Ralph was happy to accept. As they entered the officers' mess, Major T. Eric Snow, battalion second-in-command, met them.

"Well, Padre, how did your conference go?" he addressed Rusty.

"A good get-together. It was great seeing some of my fellow chaplains again. By the way, sir, I'd like you to meet Padre Ralph Russell of the NCHR."

"Welcome to the RCR, Padre. I trust our Rusty isn't leading you astray?"

"Thank you, sir. It may well be the other way around."

The major laughed, "Oh, oh, do I dare suggest we may have a pair of rascals here? Come join me for a drink."

The three men entered the bar area where two other officers were having an end-of-the-day libation.

"Gentlemen, I'd like you to meet a friend of Rusty's," announced Major Snow. "He's padre with our neighbouring battalion, the NCHR."

"Greetings, Padre, I'm Frank Klenavik," said a lieutenant to Ralph's right. "Just call me Klink—everyone else does." He was a wiry young man with twinkling eyes and an engaging smile.

"And I'm Strome Galloway. It's a pleasure to meet you," said a captain of medium height with a grand full moustache that curled upward. He gave the appearance of the quintessential officer, bright and immaculately turned out. "What can I offer you from the bar?"

"A beer would be fine," accepted Ralph. "I'm as thirsty as a hound pup after a good race!"

"My treat," offered the second-in-command. "How about you, Rusty? Strome? Klink?"

Rusty nodded. "Scotch and water, please!"

"Can't let that proposal pass. I'll have the same as Rusty," said Strome.

Klink grinned. "I'm fine at the moment, sir, thanks just the same."

The men spent a pleasant half hour conversing, and as others entered the mess, they were introduced to Ralph.

"You'll join us for dinner, Padre? There's a nice roast of beef on the menu," invited Major Snow.

"Thank you, sir, I will, but I must get back to the NCHR right afterwards. Who knows what's been happening over there with their shepherd away?"

Strome chuckled. "Probably the same thing as here when Rusty's on the loose. We have to keep an eye on him, as he's prone to disappear from time to time!"

"Come on, now. I can always be reached!" said the grinning RCR chaplain.

"Except when you make those little side trips that catch your fancy," piped a voice from somewhere nearby. The men in the mess laughed companionably. They were a cordial team. This confirmed Ralph's earlier impression of the RCR on their brief sojourn to France. One would tend to feel comfortable with this body of men on their flank in battle. They gave every impression of being a stalwart, efficient group. Their sense of humour was contagious, and Ralph left the mess with a lighter heart. He had enjoyed Rusty's company and the high spirits of the RCR officers.

The vicarage was strangely dark for early evening. Normally, the den and Paul's study would be aglow with soft lights, as he and Erin were avid readers. Ralph entered and called out.

"Anybody home? Erin? Paul?"

There was no answer. He went to the kitchen to put a kettle on for tea. He was amused how "English" he had become. He had rarely drunk tea back in Canada, but now he enjoyed the refreshing flavour of the hot brew. From somewhere above he heard Galley the cat call out. It was a sound he had never heard him make before—a deep, almost forlorn cry, almost frightened.

"Come, Galley, here's a treat for you."

The animal continued its plaintiff howl. Ralph decided to investigate and mounted the stairs. The clamour came from the darkened bathroom. The door was slightly ajar, and Ralph pushed it open the rest of the way, but something stopped it from swinging wide. He flicked on the light to find Erin unconscious in a heap on the floor. He bent to feel her pulse and found it thready. Galley scooted from the room, tail straight up and bristling. Gently, Ralph ran his hands over her body to check for broken bones, but only detected an abrasion on her left temple. Quickly but carefully, he lifted her in his arms and carried her to her bedroom where he laid her out on the bed. He chaffed her wrists and placed a cool cloth on her forehead. There was no sign of blood, and her swollen abdomen seemed normal. Ralph could see that the baby within was moving. Growing ever more anxious, he was about to put in a call to her doctor when her eyes fluttered open.

"What happened?"

"I have no idea," he exclaimed, relief flooding his being. "I just came in and heard Galley howling. I came up and found you unconscious on the bathroom floor."

"All I can remember is coming up the stairs . . . then nothing!"

"I'm going to call Doctor Norman. Perhaps its time for the babe to put in an appearance."

"But it's not due for another two weeks!" Erin exclaimed.

"Well, back home they say, 'the first can come any time, but the rest normally take a full nine months.' I'm not at all experienced with this sort of thing, so let me call. Where's your father?" Ralph asked from the doorway.

"He has a meeting of the vestry committee. Should be back any minute. I'll be all right now." Ralph looked doubtful. "Go ahead and call the doctor," she finally agreed.

Fortunately both mother and child were fine. "A little shook up, perhaps," said the physician after he finished examining Erin, "but otherwise all the signs are good. Don't be surprised if you go into labour at any time, Erin. A fall like that sometimes brings things on quickly. No heavy lifting, now, and I want you to get your feet up."

It seemed like everyone in Bewdliegh was waiting for something to happen. The people of England anticipated an invasion. The men of the NCHR were eager for battle. The vicar prepared for the final moment of his life. There was no question that Erin would soon deliver, and Ralph found himself in the middle of it, a long way from home.

Chapter 5

The baby was not to be rushed and chose the 11th of November, 1940, to arrive. He turned out to be a robust infant, weighing in at nine pounds three ounces, displaying a full head of fine curly black hair.

Ralph had just returned from the luncheon following the Armistice Day Regimental Drumhead Service. The vicar greeted him at the door. "It's time," he said, as he rushed past to bring the Austin around. Erin rested in a large stuffed chair. Ralph had a brief moment of concern when he tried to help her out of it, for she had settled into the deep cushion. He had to reach from behind and lift her at the armpits, until she could grasp the arms of the chair and pull herself forward. Erin saw the comedic side of the tableau and began to giggle uncontrollably.

"Steady up there, old girl," teased Ralph, "or you'll have us both rolling on the floor!"

Erin laughed the harder, and then, with a sharp cry, cradled her abdomen with both hands.

"Oh! Oh! Oh!"

"Take a deep breath," suggested Ralph, who had no idea why he suggested it. Maybe he had heard the line in a movie. Carefully, he supported her weight as she leaned back against him. Step by step, they made their way to the front door, which her father held ajar.

In minutes they reached the hospital, and Erin was taken to a birthing room where a midwife attended her. Ralph and the vicar took seats in the waiting lounge where they sat quietly for a spell, and then began to speak at the same time.

The vicar chuckled. "What a pair we are. You'd think we both were the father!"

"Ah, a father!" mused Ralph. "What a thought."

Erin had held much of his attention in the proceeding weeks, as much as his duties would allow him. He tried to amuse her and fill some of the void she felt over Michael's loss. He knew he couldn't, but tried nonetheless. She was aware of what he was doing, and loved him in a special way for it, but each time the babe moved her thoughts turned to her husband. "Oh Michael, Michael, how I wish you were here." His smiling face would appear before her and when she reached out to touch his beloved cheek, the vision would fade, and there would be Ralph. Solid Ralph. Dependable Ralph. Her friend, her protector. Sadly she would smile at him, but he knew where her mind had been. However, even that much of her attention satisfied him. Occasionally, she would reach for his hand, wanting to touch something solid—something alive—and then out of guilt, drop it, not knowing the shard of pain that cut into Ralph's heart.

An hour had passed when a nurse carrying a little bundle entered the room.

"Your grandson has arrived, Vicar!"

He took the newborn in his arms and gazed lovingly into the bright dark eyes, "Young man, you are our future." Ralph looked on enviously.

"Here, you hold him."

"Oh, I can't," said Ralph nervously stepping back.

"Nonsense, the child won't fall apart. Take him." He placed the baby in the crook of Ralph's arm. The child looked up at his new admirer, as if with seeing eyes, and squawked.

"Oh dear, am I holding him too tightly?"

"Not at all. He just wants to get going! No doubt an active one, just like his mother before him." On that note the vicar launched into his memories of Erin as a child.

"Would you like to see the mother?" The nurse had appeared again and led the men to the birthing room. All had been placed in order, and Erin smiling, appeared fully relaxed, resting against a bank of puffed-up pillows.

"My dearest girl, how good you look," said her father. "And the little one—so handsome. Michael would be proud!"

"Yes, he is a beauty, and all his parts are there too: ten fingers, ten toes and everything else that goes with a healthy baby boy. I will call him Michael Paul after his daddy and his grandfather."

Turning to Ralph she said, "And to thank you for your friendship and support through all this, I would like you as one of his godfathers." Ralph flushed with emotion. "The pleasure is mine, and God willing, I will support him whenever possible."

The early winter rains had set in, and November continued as a dull and depressing month for the troops. Physical fitness in preparation for battle had become the cause célèbre for the rifle companies, while forced route marches, with each soldier carrying his full pack and rifle, were the preferred instrument for toughening the body, especially the legs. Company vied with company, platoon with platoon, each attempting the fastest time over a prearranged circuit. Banners were presented to the winners and flown over company lines.

Ralph was in top condition. Each week he would march with a different subunit, carrying a full pack. He enjoyed the cajoling, joking, and kibitzing along the way, and he often started the marching songs that seemed somehow to lighten the load. The activity took him away from what could have been a rather sedentary life, and he found that the effort afforded him a better relationship with the troops. They came to know him as their friend, one who was concerned about their welfare and was prepared to walk in their shoes. Invariably after each outing, the men would invite him to share in more light-hearted activities. Ralph took pleasure in these parties, but always came late and left early. Often, a young soldier with a special problem would collar him. A time and place for a meeting would be arranged.

It was a nasty wet day in late November when the padre had participated in a particularly strenuous march against the clock with C Company, and the troops had invited him to attend their victory bash. They had captured the best time for ten miles at two hours and fifteen minutes. It was a regimental record. The company canteen, with a donation from the regimental fund, provided free beer and a sandwich bar to the winners. Ralph, a beer in hand, sat with several lads whom he had known from his parish days.

"Checking up on your 'black sheep'?" asked Jock MacPherson, the company commander, rubbing at his nose and chuckling.

Ralph gave him a dark look. "Missed you on the march, Major!"

Jock rarely took part in these events, as he could usually find a way to exclude himself. He turned abruptly, his face red, and joined another group.

Before the interruption, the group had been talking about the recent hunting season back home and wondering how everyone there had made out. The padre had a letter from Ernest that he had received the day before with just the kind of information they had been longing to hear. The soldiers were all ears.

"Sir!" a voice from behind him called out.

Ralph paused.

"Sir, could I see you right away?" asked a young soldier nervously pulling on his knuckles.

"Get outta here, Boggs, the Padre was just telling us about the hunt!"

"Let me finish this first," Ralph suggested, "then we can go someplace." Boggs ducked his head and moved to the side to wait.

Moments later, Ralph walked with the soldier to a quiet corner, where he invited the lad to talk. Boggs pulled a letter from his battledress tunic pocket and handed it to the padre.

"Read it, sir, perhaps you can help me. You know Margie Kokems. She wrote it." The girl, in her late teens, attended Holy Trinity, Plevna, with her family. Ralph had prepared her for confirmation.

He took the letter, a little tattered from a great deal of rereading, and perused its contents. It was brief and written in an immature hand.

> Deer Billy.
> I don't know what to say. I got pregnant. I was so lonely that I let this guy have his way with me. You don't know him. He's from the States. I was working at Birch Lodge and he was a guest. He got me drunk in his cabin and I slept with him. What'll I do? I love you. Do you still want me? Let me know, Margie.

Ralph looked at Billy. There were tears building in his eyes. He was glancing nervously around to see if anyone was watching. He didn't want to blubber in front of his mates, but he was in so much emotional pain, he was beside himself. Ralph placed a hand on his shoulder.

"I think we'd better get out of here. Meet me at St. Tristan's in twenty minutes. Go in the door at the side of the church and wait for me there."

Billy nodded.

Ralph returned to the group.

"How's Boggs?"

"He'll be all right. Just some bad news from home."

"Anybody dead?"

"No, it's personal trouble."

"Ya, I heard his girlfriend got herself pregnant!"

"Did you now? Well, keep it under your hat. No need everyone knowing about it!"

"You kiddin', Padre? Whatever happens in the highlands, everyone knows about it sooner or later!"

A truer statement was never made.

In the vestry office at St. Tristan's, Ralph listened as Boggs, head in his hands, poured his heart out, the story punctuated with shaking sobs. He and Margie had grown up together on neighbouring farms. Although the mothers were friends, the fathers were as different as day was from night. If one said white, the other would automatically choose black. They couldn't work together for long on a shared project before bickering or shouting began. It never entered their heads that they were both after the same kind of results, but reached their conclusions from different directions. However, they seemed to get some inner satisfaction from being ornery, forcing their wives to meet in private, or at a church gathering, in order to get caught up on things of mutual interest.

Billy Boggs had two years on Margie. They had attended the same school and played together there. The fathers didn't like to see them together.

"Billy, you gotta stop foolin' around with that Kokems girl. They're a no-good bunch," his father would admonish. Billy would duck his head and bite his tongue, as he knew his dad's temper. The boy feared a beating if he crossed the old man.

Margie faced similar confrontations from her father. "Girl, you keep away from that Boggs kid. I don't want to see or hear about you bein' together. If you do, I'll skin you alive," Kokems threatened his daughter.

The two children had shared the mysteries of childhood, and as young adults had more or less innocently observed the differences in their bodies by skinny-dipping in a stream that separated the two farms. The freedom from guilt continued until Margie's fifteenth birthday when she declared to Billy that she wanted to make love to him like a grown-up woman. As they were stretched out on the mossy bank after a swim, he needed no further encouragement, and from that day on, they occasionally shared their love for each other. Their knowledge of birth control was vague, and by some miracle she never became pregnant. When war broke out and Billy joined up, they made a solemn pledge to remain faithful, and when he came home, they would marry.

Now this letter! He had kept his promise. Why hadn't she kept hers? Angry and hurt, he related his story.

Ralph listened for a moment longer and then said, "Thank you for telling me, I didn't know that the two of you were so close. I guess with the feuding between your fathers, I didn't think much about it."

"We never let anyone know. It had to be that way or our dads would have killed us!"

"How do you feel about this?" asked Ralph holding up the letter.

"Wish I knew," Billy responded wistfully.

"Do you still love Margie?"

"I'll always love her."

"Do you think you can tell her that?" asked Ralph.

Billy muttered. "Don't know. Maybe! I'd find it awful hard to put into words after this."

"Why don't you try. You write her a letter, and if you want, I'll help you think it through. I like Margie, and I think she needs your help even though you feel betrayed. Take a few days to think about it, and we'll get together later."

Ralph was there for several lads who received "Dear John" letters. His compassion and empathy were well known.

The days wore on at a tedious pace. Christmas was fast approaching and the men felt the stir of homesickness coming on. They attempted to drown their low spirits in beer and liquor. Loud and rowdy behaviour was the order of the day. Fights frequently broke out over the slightest difference of opinion, and several groups went looking for trouble.

One night at the Boar and Apple, a pub on the outskirts of Bewdleigh, several lads from C Company were out on a date with some local girls. They were having a high time when a group of RAF lads from a nearby air base barged into the premises and set out to cut out the Canadians. Private Timmy O'Neil was smooching with a young lady in a corner, when a burly airman pushed him aside and grabbed the girl. She cried out with pain as he twisted her wrist. O'Neil was not a big man, but he didn't hesitate to land a sharp blow to the jaw of the intruder. In a flash, the spark ignited the entire establishment. Tables crashed and chairs flew through the air.

"You son-of-a-bitch! Take your hands off her or I'll give you another," threatened the soldier.

The airman pushed the girl aside and drove O'Neil backward, crashing him against the wall. The two fell to the floor flailing each other with smashing blows. Both men were bleeding from their noses and about their faces.

Suddenly, whistles sounded and the pub was rushed by a patrol of British MPs.

"Get the hell out of here, you meatheads," called a soldier. "We can handle these fly boys!"

The MPs waded in swinging billy sticks and cracked a few skulls before a semblance of order was gained. A phone call brought a vehicle from the NCHR, and a dozen unruly pugilists were carted away, while an ambulance arrived for O'Neil. He had lost consciousness and was bleeding from his left ear. The airman, in one last vicious blow, had kicked the soldier in the head.

An hour later, Ralph received a call from the hospital. The injured lad was in critical condition suffering from a severe concussion. The padre sat with the boy all through the night. The situation was touch and go. The doctors had done all they could for him, and said to Ralph. "Well, Padre, it's up to you now."

In the wee hours of the morning, O'Neil opened his eyes. "Hi, Padre," he said softly. "Owww, my head."

Ralph, momentarily dozing, became alert.

"Hey there, Timmy! You still trying to lick the world?" he teased. "The last time a guy at the Royal Swan got a battering. You're building a reputation for yourself in these parts."

A nurse arrived at the bedside. "That boy must have a head of iron. Any other lad would be out of it for weeks!"

"Our Canadian boys are pretty tough!" Ralph joked.

The nurse laughed and suggested the chaplain should head for his own bed.

"I'm sure things are all right now," she said. "Good night, Padre."

"See you later, Tim."

As he walked back to the vicarage, the cool night air gave him his second wind.

"I wish we could get on with this damn war," he mused to himself. "This waiting is going to be the death of us all . . . one way or another!"

In early December, 1st Brigade relieved 2nd Brigade from their defensive positions along the south coast. The line had been "dug-in" along the beaches near the resort town of Brighton, against the continued threat of a German invasion. Brighton had a lively nightlife. Dancing at The Dome and parties at Maxim's and the Star and Garter were favourite pastimes for officers, while the other ranks found excitement in the multitude of pubs scattered throughout the city. Off-duty times provided an opportunity for high living, as long as the money held out. These hours were in stark contrast to the cool pre-dawn "stand-to" with small arms and Bren guns pointed out to sea in anticipation of a German attack.

The men of the NCHR were billeted in civilian accommodation. Some were in homes, others in hotels or local boarding schools, which had been vacated because of the war. Ralph found convenient digs in one such location, and an office adjacent to the school's chapel. St. George's, a school for boys, dated from the sixteenth century and had been originally endowed by Henry VIII. Built from brick, the structure had uneven rooflines with battlements and towers, typical of the Tudor period. Great mullioned windows provided a high level of light for the interior during the day, and fireplaces scattered throughout the premises offered a modicum of heat for the cool, damp winters. Many chimney pots dotted the roof.

St. George's Chapel was a gem. The large stained-glass windows across the east end cast a rainbow of light over the chancel and nave. It offered a serene place to meditate, but when the great pipe organ came into play, the space would vibrate with the sound and send thrills up the spine of those listening.

The school's dormitories housed the men of B Company, with the officers billeted in the headmaster's residence. Lieutenant Jamie Fraser found a place here. As a boy he had been trained to play an old reed pump organ belonging to his grandmother. When he first heard the tone of the great organ, he thought he had died and gone to heaven.

A former organist of the chapel, Anthony Mudd, had permission to maintain his skills on the instrument twice weekly. He was playing a fugue in D minor when Jamie first caught the titillating sounds emanating from the house of worship. He sat mesmerized in a pew until the piece was finished, and then climbed up to the organ loft to speak with the artist who had brought the pipe organ to life. The two men became immediate friends, and Anthony offered to teach Jamie how to use the magnificent instrument, with the school's permission, of course. Jamie sought out Ralph and told him of his newfound friend and the offer that had been made.

"I'll be glad to go to bat for you," offered the chaplain, "but I'll ask a favour in return. I have just been issued a portable organ for use in the field. Would you consider playing it for outdoor services?"

"You've got a deal, Padre, and when we have services here at the school chapel, I'll be able to help out there, too!"

It was a bargain for both men. Jamie received approval to use the organ under Anthony's tutelage, and Ralph found a valuable assistant for his church services.

Homesickness struck many of the lads in December, and Ralph filled his hours with visits to the company lines, where he would be pulled into conversations with men reminiscing about Christmas celebrations back home. Sometimes he would see a boy holding back his emotions, and would take him aside for a private conversation. The men's confidence in the chaplain grew. They could talk to him, and he respected their feelings and situation.

Not everyone wanted that kind of closeness with the chaplain. A number, both young and old, considered themselves hardened men of the world. They had no intention of exposing their feelings to anyone—let alone a clergyman. They didn't need any of that church stuff. If they wanted consolation they knew where to find it in the nearest pub, or on a certain street. But even the hardest heart became home-struck on Christmas Eve. When Ralph celebrated at the midnight service, almost every man off duty filled the chapel and the hallway outside to listen to the story of the birth of Christ as it is written in the Gospels. They sang the familiar Christmas carols played by Jamie Fraser on the mighty organ. In his sermon, Ralph spoke of peace on earth and goodwill to all men.

"What a mockery war makes of these words. How deeply evil lurks in the hearts of men when they covet the well-being of others—when they become power-mad and use any means to enslave a free society.

"You may wonder if you serve a just cause. You may have difficulty rationalizing the killing in battle. Does not the sixth commandment say, 'Thou shalt not kill'? I was taught a wider interpretation of the Hebrew words to mean, 'Thou shalt not murder.'

"Life is precious and sacred. No one has the right to take another person's life in an unjust manner. But yours is a just cause. Believe this in your hearts, and you will find the strength to overcome your doubts. Our fight is against evil and it must be rooted out vigorously. The Bible is full of accounts of battles between good and evil. You have only to think of the alternative—your life, and that of your families, under the heel of an oppressor.

"I would describe war as an obscenity—a crude and filthy way for evil men to get their way. It is our job to stop it, even if the only way is to bear arms against it. Many will lose their lives. Sacrifices will occur, but we will win the victory.

"God alone knows what the next year will bring. Trust in Him, and He will see you through whatever may befall. The name Emmanuel means 'God is with us.' I believe this with every ounce of my being, and so I say 'Go with God.'"

In the silent hours of the night, the men of the NCHR made their way back to their billets. Many pondered Ralph's words in their hearts and felt their spirits lift. Others sought spirit of a different kind to alter their state of mind, to dull their loneliness and the fear they felt deep within.

The next day, the dining hall of St. George's School filled to capacity as the men came to feast on turkey, which somehow had arrived from Canada. Following tradition, the officers served the men, and the youngest member of the regiment sat at the head table proudly wearing the CO's tunic. Colonel Morrison waited on the lad as cheers rose from around the tables.

"Well, my fine fellow, you are commanding officer for the dinner," announced Morrison. "How may I serve you."

"I'd like another beer, sir!"

"Right you are, but remember, a CO has to keep his wits about him!"

"That I will, sir, and as you always say—make sure my men are looked after."

Morrison chuckled at that one and nodded to the other officers that were serving. They placed a pint in front of each man.

"Hurrah for the new CO," chanted the diners tinkling their glasses with cutlery.

Following a dessert of plum pudding, Ralph led the gathering in songs of the season, while Jamie Fraser played the little field organ. The men sang lustily, and for a while, the shadow of war faded.

Rain fell on Boxing Day, and the following day an incident occurred that disturbed Ralph. Private Sid George was put on charge for stealing. The soldier was from Ralph's former parish in Plevna—a bright, but shy, lad from an upright, country family known for their straight dealings in the community. George put in a request for a visit from the chaplain.

Ralph arrived at A Company HQ just before noon as the defaulters prepared to leave for lunch. He asked to see George and was provided with a room nearby.

Ralph spoke first. "What's this all about, Sid?"

The soldier looked downcast and said, "I've been charged with stealing, sir!"

"That's hard to believe. I've never heard of you swiping anything in your life," answered Ralph.

"And I never have," replied Sid. "So help me God."

Ralph leaned forward in his chair. "What have you been accused of taking?"

"A wristwatch, sir. They found it in my kit after a surprise inspection last night. I never seen it before in my life!" The boy was glum for he knew full well that a thief in company lines would be severely punished. The act was not to be tolerated. His proclaimed innocence fairly gushed from him. "Several guys have had things stolen in the last couple of weeks—Christmas gifts and stuff. Some think it may have been Corporal Slattery. He's been seen slinking around the lines when the guys are away, but no one's actually seen him lift anything! Honest to God, sir, it wasn't me."

"I believe you, Sid, I think I know you well enough to say that. I smell a rat here somewhere. When do you come up on CO's orders?" enquired the chaplain.

"This afternoon, sir, at three o'clock."

Ralph checked his watch. "I'll be there, and speak on your behalf. Now, you take it easy till then."

The chaplain went directly to the adjutant's office and conveyed to Captain Barnett what he had heard from Private George and vouched for the man's honesty.

Barnett, a pipe smoker, drew on his thorn-wood pipe, and nodded. "I think you may be right, Padre. There's a couple of scoundrels around with light fingers. Did George indicate who the culprit might be?"

"I'm afraid I can't answer that, as it would just be hearsay, but I'd have a couple of A Company corporals checked out if I were you. Scuttlebutt has it that one or two of them seem to have a lot of extra money these days."

"Right! Thanks, Padre. Will you attend the Orders Parade?"

"That I will. See you at three."

There were three men on charge, and Private George was the last to be paraded before the commanding officer.

Sergeant Taffy was in charge of the defaulters. "All right, George, it's your turn. Attention! By the left, quick march. One, two, one, two, one, two . . ."

George, eyes straight ahead, stood at attention in front of the CO's desk. Sergeant Taffy read the charge.

"How do you plead, Private George?" asked Morrison.

"Not guilty, sir," replied the private.

"I've heard there may be extenuating circumstances here, even though the watch was found with your kit. Can you tell me who you think may be responsible, Private George?"

"Sir, I don't know, sir!"

"The padre has spoken on your behalf, as has your platoon officer, who tells me you are an exemplary soldier. But the fact is, stolen property was found with your belongings. I look upon stealing as an unforgivable offence between soldiers under my command. How could anyone rely on a thief in the middle of battle—someone who was undependable? I will not tolerate thievery in my unit. However, given the testimony in your favour, and the fact that something 'fishy' is going on, I will put aside my final ruling until we get to the bottom of this incident. In the meantime, you are not to discuss this hearing with anyone, and as a precaution, and an example, you are confined to quarters for two weeks. Dismissed."

When the soldier had left, Colonel Morrison called an O Group of his company commanders to attend a meeting with the adjutant and the chaplain.

Morrison looked with steely eyes at the gathering. "Gentlemen, we have a developing problem within the unit. An outbreak of thievery has taken place, not only in A Company, but also in other areas, according to our battalion police. I expect you to do everything you can to root out this problem. It is bad for moral. The indications are that this is no simple theft. The person or persons responsible for the robbery are covering their tracks by planting stolen goods on innocent victims. Major Stokes, who called the snap inspection in your line last night?"

The company commander's face clouded. "It was Sergeant Haynes, sir."

"Very, well and who was with him?"

"I believe it was Corporal Slattery."

Morrison leaned forward on his desk. "How do you rate these two NCOs? Do you find them reliable? It seems to me they were pretty quick off the mark to zero in on George."

"Sergeant Haynes is a bit of a devious character, sir. It's my opinion that he achieved his rank by kowtowing to former officers. I have kept an eye on him ever since I took over A Company, but have never been able to finger him for anything. He's pretty sly. Speaking of fingering—the men call him 'Fingers' behind his back—meaning light fingers, I would guess. I suspect they don't trust him, sir," remarked Stokes.

"You don't say! And what about Slattery?" asked Morrison, intent on getting to the bottom of the matter, and quickly.

Stokes squirmed in his chair feeling uncomfortable under the intensity of the commanding officer's thoughts. "The two of them are thick as molasses. A pair to be watched more closely, I would say."

The commanding officer pushed back from his desk. "Then, do it, Major! It's the least I will expect of you, and make no mistake about it, I want this situation resolved without delay."

A close watch was placed on the two NCOs, but they sensed someone was on to them, and decided to cease their nefarious activities for the time being.

Between Christmas and New Year's, the NCHR returned to Bewdleigh, following the arrival of replacements for the south coast. New Year's celebrations took place for the troops and all messes were open to welcome 1941. A regimental dance could not be held, as there was no place large enough to accommodate everyone, but small establishments opened their doors to furnish space where the men could bring in the new year. Ralph had received invitations to them all and made his rounds with Sandy, the MO, early in the evening. Ralph had invited Erin and her father to be his guests at the officers' party to be held at Bewdleigh Hall. It was her first outing since her son's birth, and indeed, the first time she had joined a celebration of this kind since her husband's death.

Just before midnight, Squire Pride brought the merriment to a halt to announce the engagement of his daughter Julia to Lieutenant Thomas Nugent. A great cheer went up for the young couple, and Erin squeezed Ralph's arm.

"What a bright pair they make," she said wistfully. "How I wish them the very best of luck."

In the village no church bells rang in the new year. The practice had been suspended two years before as a wartime precaution. If church bells rang, it was to announce the beginning of the German invasion. However, a small bell in the Hall's clock tower marked the midnight hour and the announcement of Julia's engagement to Tom Nugent. Ralph looked into Erin's eyes, and seeing no resistance there, he took her in her arms and kissed her on the lips. She made no move to reject the moment, but instead responded ever so slightly. He held her at arm's length and gave her a brilliant smile, and she, gazing deeply into his eyes, saw his intent.

"What a wonderful man," she thought to herself, "I wonder if I dare fall in love with him?"

The vicar, observing them from a short distance away, came forward and embraced his daughter. He shook Ralph's hand and smiled with a twinkle. "May the new year bring blessings to us all, and dare I say, what a stunning couple you make standing there."

When they returned to the house, the vicar looked pale. It had been a very tiring day for him and he felt lightheaded.

"Did you take your medication, Father?" inquired Erin.

"I believe so." He paused to think, then sighed. "My memory isn't as good as it used to be. I'll check the bottle before I go to bed. Good night, my dear. Happy New Year, Ralph," and the vicar climbed the stairs, fatigue marking every step.

Ralph stirred the coals in the fireplace grate and added more fuel.

"Would you care for a nightcap, Erin?"

"Yes, I think I would enjoy a few minutes in front of the fire," she agreed slowly. "I need to unwind some after that dazzling evening at the Hall. I had almost forgotten how to relax. It was fun, wasn't it?" She curled up on the couch directly in front of the renewed blaze.

"It was a delightful evening," Ralph mused, "and everyone seemed so much at ease considering the normal tension we face these days."

Ralph sat beside her and handed her a snifter of brandy. Their fingers brushed each other. Ralph felt an electric charge surge up his arm. They exchanged glances.

"I hope you didn't mind when I kissed you at midnight?" he remarked, trying to remain calm.

"No, I think not," she paused and softly said, "It was good to be kissed like that again. I miss the intimacies I once shared with Michael. Sometimes I feel so hollow, so alone!"

They sat in silence for a moment. Ralph decided to take some courage from the brandy.

"Do you think I could fill some of that emptiness for you?" he asked quietly.

Erin took some time before replying. "You already have, Ralph!"

"I mean more than just a friend," Ralph blurted out, and he continued before she could interrupt. "I believe I have fallen in love with you, Erin.

I don't want to rush you into anything. I know it's too soon for you, but perhaps we could start slowly to develop a closer relationship? Dare I hope?" By this time, he was kneeling before her on the floor, feeling slightly silly by the image he must be presenting.

She looked long and hard into his eyes. She saw his shyness, his gentleness and his goodness. But most of all, she saw his sincerity and his unreserved devotion. The firelight flickered across his face and she reached out to touch his cheek. Quickly, he took her in his arms and held her close. No more words were spoken. They simply held each other and let their feelings mingle. When the fire died down, they reluctantly let go of each other. Ralph lightly kissed Erin goodnight, and they retired to their separate bedrooms.

Ralph couldn't sleep. His mind raced from one thought to another. He wondered if he had been too forward—too eager. He didn't want to frighten Erin with his advances, to turn her off, but she had responded to the admission of his feelings for her.

"I'll go slowly and allow time to prepare the way for us," he resolved. "Providing there is time," he groaned. "O Lord, grant us a future together," he prayed. "I love her so."

Before dawn Ralph drifted into sleep, dreaming of Erin and the highlands, and how well they went together.

The cold, dark months of January and February passed slowly. A fine rain often fell causing black ice to cover the roads, making for treacherous marches. The men of the NCHR trained at a gruelling pace in continuing preparation for battle. The men ran with full packs and scaled new and ever more challenging obstacle courses. Bellyaching became grist for the grinder. Water ran between their toes and squished in their boots, and when the boots were removed, their feet stank. Yet, they persevered, and their hardened bodies became weapons, as lethal as the rifles and small arms that rarely left their sides. Pity the poor man who was found without his personal weapon.

The frustrating wait went on, month after gruelling month, exercise after tedious exercise. Boredom weighed heavily upon most men, and many drowned their complaints in alcohol. Occasionally some went AWL only to be picked up by the Canadian provost or British MPs, returned to their units, and sent to spend time in cells. More serious cases, such as theft or rape, landed the offenders in Service Detention Barracks.

The vast majority simply played the "waiting game," and busied themselves with whatever small pleasures they could find. Many formed liaisons with English women, a number of which developed into serious relationships. Others played sports, and inter-unit competition brought some relief to pent-up feelings, while others sought to improve their education by enrolling in courses both academic and technical—some even worked toward a university degree. Cheerleading and directing in the background, the Canadian chaplains spent long hours encouraging the men in these pursuits. The padres became skilled at "pulling wires" in order to find ways to support healthy pastimes for the men they served while the YMCA supported the troops in other ways. It provided a dry canteen where the men could gather at the end of the day to shoot the breeze or write letters home. Often it provided sports equipment purchased from YMCA funds.

Ralph's time seemed to pass quickly. He kept busy from early morning until late in the evening. His sessions with the lads became a weekly event, as he tried his best to deal with their frustrations and disillusionment. At one such meeting, he used as his theme, "They also serve who only stand and wait." The men gave him a rough ride over that one, as they felt they had joined up to fight, not sit around in the damp and cold of England.

"To hell with waiting," many ranted, "for God's sake, let's get at it."

Spring of 1941 came early in April and the warmer weather was a welcome change for the training-weary troops. Although billeted in comfortable homes over the winter months, the daily routine wore on their nerves and they chafed for action. Subunit exercises began to increase in preparation for "the big one" under the command of Lieutenant General B. L. Montgomery, General Officer Commanding Southeastern Command. Once again the troops went under canvas in Bewdleigh Park, and although they missed the cosier atmosphere of their winter billets, they soon settled into the predictable routines of a tented military camp.

Ralph had a busy time around Easter. He provided marriage preparation sessions for several young couples who had been granted permission to marry. Colonel Morrison expected his chaplain to render a thorough examination of each prospective couple prior to granting consent. In many cases, Ralph had to recommend against approval. "Frivolous liaison" became the chief impediment, or information revealed that one party or the other was already married. A few men told tall tales about life in Canada to sway the heart of a girlfriend—how much wealth their families had, or what a high life they would lead back home. Some girls were even hoodwinked in believing some towns had streets paved with gold. Ralph spent long hours with prospective brides to ensure they had proper information on what to expect once in Canada, whether on a farm in the highlands, or in a city such as Toronto.

Occasionally, Ralph's counsel was rejected out of hand. He felt bad when this happened, for he could almost foresee that the relationship would fail miserably. In other instances, he shared the joy of a couple who had fallen in love and had honestly come to know each other. He happily celebrated these marriages.

Into this latter category, he included Julia Pride and Tom Nugent. The wedding took place in St. Tristan's on the Saturday following Easter Sunday with the vicar and the chaplain taking part.

Tom had chosen for his best man his close friend, Lieutenant Marty Kossowski. Marty came from the eastern side of the highlands, and his dark complexion, black hair and eyes, and heavy brows that met in the middle of his forehead proclaimed his Polish origins. The slight Asian cast to his features hinted at some Mongol blood far back in his family tree. A serious lad, with a wry sense of humour, he almost gave Tom heart failure at the wedding when he jokingly said that he'd misplaced the wedding ring.

Julia chose Erin as her matron of honour. They had been friends for many years and had been there for each other in good times and bad.

Jamie Fraser played the wedding march as the bride's party entered the church. In the lead was a petite flower girl dressed in her first long gown—pale, blue chiffon that matched her pretty eyes. Behind her came two bridesmaids dressed in darker blue, who had been school friends of Julia. Both were pretty girls, and the young bachelors in the congregation frankly ogled them.

Erin, as matron of honour, entered wearing a sky-blue gown. As she turned to enter the centre aisle, she flashed a dazzling smile toward Ralph, who stood in his place at the chancel steps. He felt his mouth go dry. To him she looked like an angel floating toward him. He firmly gripped his prayer book to still the tremor in his hand.

Behind him the vicar whispered, "Steady on, lad!"

Ralph steeled himself and looked beyond Erin to the bride and her father. The organ music swelled as they entered the narthex, and Julia, gorgeous in a full white gown of tulle silk, crowned with a veil and train—heirlooms of her mother's family—gripped her father's arm.

Emotion charged the service. Ralph's voice quavered as he tried to concentrate on what he was doing, but out of the corner of his eye, he could see a radiant Erin, holding the bridal bouquet. Her beauty had a tendency to unnerve him.

At the conclusion of the ceremony, the young officers of the NCHR provided a guard of honour outside the church entrance. They formed an arch with their swords and shouted hip-hip-hooray, as the bridal couple made their way to a waiting carriage. The carriage, drawn by white horses, circled through Bewdleigh to a cheering crowd, all eager to wish the squire's daughter well on her wedding day.

Later, in the Hall, while the music played and the wine flowed, Erin placed a hand in the crook of Ralph's arm, and drew him out to the balcony. She tried to hide an impish smile, as she scolded him for being so emotional during the ceremony.

"How could I help myself?" he pleaded. "All I could see was you."

She reached up on tiptoe and kissed his cheek.

"There," she said, "that will do until I can get you alone later."

As the days passed, Erin and Ralph grew closer. They sat together in the garden talking or in front of the fireplace on a rainy evening. Occasionally, Ralph would hold her in his arms, and she would touch his face or squeeze his hand. They would kiss goodnight, and as time went on, they tended to linger over this ritual.

The months of waiting—and waiting, and waiting—for the soldiers passed ever so slowly. Training routines grew monotonous, so the Canadian padres stepped up their efforts to provide constructive activities for the men. The educational programs they had initiated proved to be a great success. In the NCHR alone, 250 men were enrolled in correspondence courses, or had been accepted into nearby trade schools. Another handful of high achievers did exceptionally well with their university-level studies. In due course, this training co-ordination was passed to the Canadian Legion Educational Services at Division HQ. However, a great deal of credit for the men's success was attributed to the many officers, who in off-duty hours assisted the soldier-students with their studies.

Meanwhile, the padre's duties in the areas of welfare and counselling increased proportionately. The old adage concerning "idle hands" became self-evident. Several times a week, Ralph would be called by the provost to visit men in cells. Boredom often led some men into trouble, and when they complained to military policemen, they were told, "Don't talk to us about it. Take it to the padre!"

A year passed and still no action.

In May of 1942, General Montgomery held Exercise "Tiger" that proved to be a gruelling contest during the unmercifully hot weather. The aim was to give his troops experience in near-battle conditions. For weeks, the men marched at night and attacked at first light. What sleep the soldiers got was often in a farmer's field during the heat of the day. In their travels they covered more than 140 miles, which kept the quartermasters and unit shoemakers busy providing yeoman service for the repair or the replacing of footwear.

In battle formation, the men walked in single file on each side of the road, with five yards separating each man in a rifle section. This spread the regiment out considerably. Ralph spent time with each subunit and accomplished this by "changing over" between breaks. He was in peak physical condition, and enjoyed banter with the troops along the way. The men were always aware of his cheerful presence.

This was not the case for Major Jock MacPherson. He personally disliked this type of training and constantly grumbled about the need for the company commander's involvement. Invariably, he would seek ways of excusing himself from this duty.

On one spring day, he was unhappily leading his company in an advance formation along a country road. His legs began to cramp, which was not surprising considering his poor physical shape. Ahead, he spotted a small village, and he called his company second-in-command forward.

"Captain Rhodes, fall in beside me. I want you to take over when we get to the village. I just remembered a report I have to finish for Colonel Morrison. I'll catch the local bus back."

"Yes, sir," answered Rhodes with a knowing smirk.

MacPherson slipped into the village pub, where he enjoyed a dram while waiting for transport back to Bewdleigh.

The company pressed on, but did not fail to notice where their commander went. Mumbles of discontent rumbled down the files.

"You there! Boggs—O'Neil, stop that chatter. You miserable clods," shouted Sergeant Major Peter Anderson. "If you think rank has its privileges, now you know."

Captain Rhodes appeared to glare at the sergeant major, but with a wry smile said gruffly, "As you were Sergeant Major!"

It was hard training, but when the exercise was over every man realized his conditioning had improved considerably. The general was pleased and made this known during his inspections. He complimented the Canadians and singled out the Royal Canadian Regiment for special recognition. He noted they had perfected their patrolling skills, and performed superbly against "enemy" positions at the critical stages of the "battle."

It came as a surprise in August, when the NCHR was informed that elements of the 2nd Canadian Division had landed at Dieppe, in France. As rumours spread that this was the beginning of the "big show," the men of the 1st Division were downhearted, for they felt they should have been the first to go. Then, on the following day, came the news that it was a raid only—and a disastrous one, at that. Without the earlier promised support from British naval and air forces, the Canadians had faced withering fire from well-located German positions in and along the cliffs that overlooked the port. They had done their best, but had never stood a chance against the entrenched enemy.

The chaplain of the RHLI, Padre John Foote, elected to stay behind to help the wounded. As the bloody battle raged along the beaches, he time and again hefted injured men to his broad shoulders and carried them to landing craft lying to off shore, before being captured himself. Many observed his heroic efforts that led to the award of the Victoria Cross.

As summer turned into fall, a new training aid was added to the obstacle course in Bewdleigh Park. The high wooden walls that had been used for scaling practice were now draped with scrambling nets made of heavy rope netting.

Soldiers observing this installation wondered about its purpose, until one bright lad said, "I bet those are used for disembarking a ship!" He was right. In addition, drills were organized to scale small local cliffs, and all personnel were required to move at the double during duty hours. There were no exceptions, other than those who were excused for medical reasons. Major MacPherson acquired a distinct limp and reported to the MO.

"What's the problem, Major?" asked Sandy.

"Oh, it's this trick knee that keeps going out from time to time."

The doctor examined the joint, and looking MacPherson directly in the eye said, "I agree. It's tricky all right, but I think you'll manage."

There were many rumours in the company lines.

"I bet we're heading for Norway," remarked Johnny MacDonald from C Company to his buddy Joe Brash. "Look, when you put together what the new training's all about, what do you come up with?"

His theory seemed to be reinforced when orders were posted for a move to Inverary on the west coast of Scotland. In late November, the NCHR packed bag and baggage, and shipped north by troop train to Duke's Camp in Argylshire. It was an area of rugged, bleak mountains, made even more desolate by the dark days of early winter, and the rain or slushy snow that swept in from the Atlantic.

With little time to settle in, the companies were moved from the relative comfort of Nissen huts to the barren training areas. Here the troops engaged in serious mountain-climbing drills, utilizing the skills they had been practising in early autumn by climbing ropes that snaked up high cliffs until they disappeared into low-lying cloud. This activity required endurance and sturdy upper-body strength and lasted for three days. It was followed by a battalion-sized exercise, which included landings from the sea.

The NCHR was formed into four large companies that provided realistic combat training for the regiment. The four rifle companies absorbed HQ Company with its various odds and sods—supernumerary to the unit's wartime establishment. Ralph was placed with B Company HQ section where he entered into the spirit of the operation.

The company commander, Major Andy Ayers, briefed him. "Padre, you stay close to my signaller, and be prepared to make yourself useful in the event you may be needed in a 'no duff' situation. This terrain is bloody dangerous, and a serious accident could occur at any time. This will be as close as you get to the real thing until you actually come under fire."

The naval landing craft took the men some distance out from the coastline. The water was choppy and many became seasick. The boats hovered for an hour off shore before the order was given to land. They dashed toward the shoreline, and when they were a short distance from the beach, the ramps splashed down and the troops were disgorged at the tide line. Some dropped short and the men plunged into waist-deep, icy water, while others hit close in and ran ankle deep onto *terra firma.*

Seasick and wet, the men went forward to scale the cliffs with grappling hooks. Several of these didn't take hold and tumbled back, a threat to those gathered below.

Ralph huddled against the base of the precipice beside Private Ulf Gunter, the OC's signaller. The battalion communications net was buzzing with various confusing reports going forward to those controlling the exercise. The umpires were obviously not happy with efforts thus far, and transmitted their displeasure on their own radio frequency.

"All set? Then let's get up there," Major Ayers urged.

The men began to scale the rocks, while Ralph followed Gunter. The surface was slippery and difficult to scale, but with determination, the men inched their way upward, until at last they stood several hundred feet above the beach.

An umpire tapped Major Ayers' shoulder. "Sir, you're dead. Next in command take over."

Lieutenant Jamie Fraser was summoned to the location.

"You're in command now, Lieutenant Fraser. Do you know your objective?"

"I do," he replied.

"All right, so what are your first orders? By the way, your signaller was killed, too." The umpire inclined his head toward Ralph. "Choose the padre to take his place."

Ralph overheard this and his face dropped. "But I'm not trained for radio procedures. I'll only cause confusion."

"Trained or not, Padre, I guess the job is yours," said the new OC. "Right! Everyone up and at 'em—that point on the left. Let's go."

Without hesitation the men responded to the new leader.

Jamie grinned. "Padre, raise the CO and let him know what's happened. His call sign is 'Niner.' Keep it short. He'll understand the situation. You can take a voice procedure course later."

A half hour later, B Company reached their objective. Ralph was flushed from the effort and slouched down in the wet grass, drained of energy.

"Hope that was all right, Jamie."

"You did fine, Padre. Now you'll be prepared should the real thing happen!"

That evening, as Ralph wandered through the lines, the lads joked with him over his stint as a signaller. It was all in good humour, and the padre enjoyed the repartee.

"Better watch out, Dusty," he chuckled, "or I'll get your job one of these days." Dusty Lane was the commanding officer's signaller.

"That'll be the day, sir! Not till you get the patter down right, at least," he chortled back.

The training in Scotland lasted for twelve days. The exercises were gruelling, but every man learned new skills. Spirits and morale soared briefly for the troops as they anticipated action was near at hand. However, the men learned that they were returning to Bewdleigh Park. They had fully expected a sea journey to the fjords of Norway.

In the village of Bewdleigh preparations for Christmas began. Even with the food shortage, housewives busily prepared whatever goodies their meagre rations allowed. Many had put little bits by for months in anticipation of the holidays.

"We'll prepare a feast, scanty though it may be," they declared, "and forget about the war and rationing for a few days."

The vicarage kitchen was a scene of joyful planning. A parcel had arrived from Ralph's parents in Canada, which included sugar, tinned butter, preserved fruit, chocolate bars, and hard, bright, Christmas rock candy. Ralph received socks and gloves, and a carton of cigarettes, plus a can of pipe tobacco with the vicar's name on it. Wrapped in red tissue paper was a small teddy bear for wee Michael Paul, now two years old. Two pairs of silk stockings had been placed in the package for Erin, who made as if to swoon when Ralph placed them in her hands.

"Oh, Ralph! Bless your mother. How thoughtful of her to send us all this food and these gifts—such a surprise. Now I'll be able to bake a Christmas cake, too!"

"I don't think you'll have to. Here's something else from home." He produced a ten-by-ten-inch tin container in which his mother had baked a fruitcake. "Wait till you taste this," he said with a great grin lighting his face. "Her Christmas cakes are famous in our house—to add to the flavour, she splashes them with rum."

The vicar, sniffing, leaned over the delicacy and smacked his lips. "Oh, my!" he said with a twinkle in his eye, "your parents are more than generous. How will we ever be able to thank them?"

"Their thanks will be in our enjoyment of the gifts. I know them!"

"I'll get a letter away to them right away," the older man affirmed.

"Oh, dear, where will I start? With all these ingredients I'll be able to make all kinds of sweets," said Erin.

"Well, just you sit down for a minute. I have one more gift to add to the holiday spirit—no pun intended. Here's a bottle of fine, single malt whisky I found before leaving Scotland. It's a miracle it made it here at all. It could have been consumed on our way back, but thanks to a gallon of medical rum and Sandy, it was spared. Sure pays to be on the good side of the MO!"

"Well, the Lord bless us," cried the vicar. "This really will be an old-fashioned Christmas celebration."

"Then let's get started," suggested Ralph, fetching three glasses and opening the bottle. "If we are careful, we can have a glass every other night until Christmas Eve. Perhaps the mess can supply us with a bottle of wine for our Christmas dinner."

"Oh, no, that will be my treat," vowed the vicar. "You see, I have a few vintage wines put away for special occasions, and I think this is going to be one of them."

Later that evening, Erin and Ralph sat in the den before a cheery fire that cast dancing shadows on the wall behind them.

"The fire feels good," she said.

"Yes, it does. The nights are getting so chilly."

"You might put your arm around me," she suggested. "Maybe that will keep the cold at bay, do you think?"

"You don't have to ask me twice," he said sliding closer on the old leather couch. His arm circled her shoulders and drew her into the hollow of his shoulder.

"That's nice," she said. Neither spoke for a while.

"Erin," Ralph began with obvious reluctance. He was loath to spoil the mood, but what he had to say was important. "I have a feeling that things will begin to heat up in the next few months. All the signs are there, and the rumours are rampant—what with Tom Nugent and a senior NCO being sent to North Africa for battle experience."

She stirred in his arms. He could smell the natural sweet scent of her hair.

"I'm not surprised. It's only been a matter of time," she commented.

Ralph took a deep breath. "I want to talk about us."

He felt her tense slightly, and then relax. Ralph took that as a sign to continue.

"You know how much I love you. I would like us to think about marriage." Fearful that he had said too much, he added, "Is it still too soon to talk about this?"

There was a reflective pause, and then she said, "No, I don't think so. It's been two-and-a-half years since I lost Michael. He'll always be a part of me, you know that, but I have grieved long enough. There is a hollowness inside of me that needs to be filled. I don't want to be a widow the rest of my life, and there is my son to consider. Soon he will need a father to look out for him. So, if your intentions are honourable, sir, I would entertain a proposal of marriage. Is that too forward of me?" she asked smiling up into his eyes.

Ralph beamed at her remarks, then turned her about in his arms so that he could smother her with kisses.

"Oh, my darling, you have answered my fondest wish," he murmured between kisses. "Let's set the date right now! What do you think?"

Erin, returning his kisses with equal enthusiasm, replied, "I say . . . the sooner the better. Let's talk with Father."

"Right," Ralph agreed, "but not tonight. We have other things to do right now." His embrace tightened.

Erin could feel every fibre of his body, and knew how desperately he wanted her. She responded in full measure, but at the last moment, before things got beyond their control, she pushed him gently away.

"I am with you all the way, my love," she sighed and then with more resolve than she felt, "I wait eagerly for our wedding night!"

Ralph knew she was right, but still he held her in his arms until the coals of the fire dropped from the grate.

The following morning they broke the news to the vicar, who was overjoyed with their decision and suggested the 27th of December, the day after Boxing Day.

"There will be time enough to read the banns if I give them on St. Thomas Day, too! Oh, what a wonderful Christmas season it will be!" The vicar was almost beside himself. His face had a healthy gleam, and his step was light.

Ralph, as was required, spoke with Lieutenant Colonel Morrison. The commanding officer was delighted to "give his approval" and wished his padre the very best.

"I hope I get an invitation," he hinted as Ralph left his office.

"You'll be number one on the list, sir."

In the usual manner of a small community, word soon spread that the NCHR chaplain was to wed the vicar's daughter. Ralph received congratulations as he visited unit lines, then on Christmas Eve, he held an ecumenical carol service at 7 p.m. and celebrated an Anglican Eucharist at 9 p.m. On both occasions, St. Tristan's overflowed with the men of the NCHR. Each time he used the same theme for his homily.

"Well, here we are again, far from home at Christmas. I know our hearts and minds drift across the sea to be with our loved ones in Canada. These have been long months since we left our homeland shores. They have been fraught with both anticipation and frustration. No one says it hasn't been a hard go. We all want to get the show on the road. Even the people of England sense the change, from the prospect of an invasion, to a girding up for a decisive offensive against our enemies. The tide has turned. You can feel it in the air. We can't ring the Christmas church bells; nevertheless, the atmosphere is charged with the ringing of people's spirits. All can feel it! Now let us commend our righteous cause to the Almighty—to seek His blessing and strength, as we prepare for the challenges ahead.

"Tonight, as we open our hearts and souls to our Heavenly Father, let us do so with humility— the kind that was born in a manger. May the Christ child be with you!"

Later that night, at the midnight mass, Ralph assisted the vicar at the high altar. Townspeople and another sprinkling of soldiers worshipped devoutly in the hushed church. Only the vicar's voice broke the stillness of the night as he celebrated the birth of Jesus. The solemnity of the scene transfixed every person attending.

The congregation exchanged joyous Christmas greetings at the conclusion of the service and shouts of "Merry Christmas! Merry Christmas!" echoed in the nave.

Julia Nugent, now large with child, hailed Erin at the back of the church.

"So, are you ready?"

"I am! How about you? You're still going to make it?" Erin smiled.

Julia's baby was due sometime before New Year's Eve, but she was determined to stand up with Erin. It would be a quiet wedding with only a handful of close friends in attendance.

"You don't mind a small wedding?" Erin had queried Ralph earlier.

"No, not at all, and under the circumstances, I believe it most appropriate. Even at that, some old stick-in-the-muds will not approve the remarriage of a war hero's widow!"

It rained on the morning of the 27th of December. Fast moving dark clouds brought a slanting rain, sharp with ice crystals, but in contrast, all was bright and cheerful in the vicarage where the bride and her party readied themselves. Ralph had stayed in the officers' mess the night previous.

"I would like to experience some of the bride-to-be's prerogative," Erin had said. "There's still a bit of the girl left in me!"

"More than a bit," Ralph smiled. "So, I shall leave you to your superstitious 'prerogatives,' and hie myself to the mess, where my brother officers will have at me. You condemn me to a horrible fate."

"Just behave yourself," she scolded playfully. "I want you at your best tomorrow."

"Fear not," he struck a pose. "I'll drink only water!"

"I bet you will," Erin replied with only a hint of doubt in her voice. "Be careful that a splash of something else isn't added too often."

"Oh, I've learned the old trick of holding a half-filled glass in my hand," Ralph assured her. "It works most of the time."

Ralph had asked Sandy Jones to be his best man. In return, the MO promised to look after him, and had skilfully diverted an abundance of drinks offered to the bridegroom on the eve of his wedding. Although a "few splashes of something else" had been added to those drinks he did accept, Ralph arose feeling great. He watched the driving elements from the mess window and smiled.

"What's that grin all about?" asked Sandy, as he whisked some dust from the groom's tunic. Both men wore their best serge uniforms.

"I was just thinking, this is one day the rain isn't going to dampen my spirits."

"Oh, all cosy and tucked up, are you now?"

"Won't be long!"

At 1:45 p.m., the men departed for the church.

The wedding party gathered informally inside the entranceway. Erin was dressed in a pale blue, calf-length dress, with a tiny matching headdress. She wore her mother's pearls and carried a nosegay of winter flowers. The guests were seated, and the vicar waited at the chancel steps. He was misty-eyed as he thought back to his own wedding.

"Dear Lord, she looks so much like her mother."

The decision had been made that no one would give the bride away—Ralph and Erin would make their way down the aisle, preceded by Julia on Sandy's arm.

She whispered to him. "How fortuitous to be on the arm of a doctor. In my condition, we could have two memorable events today."

"Behave yourself, Julia," Sandy said, and squeezed her arm.

Jamie Fraser played softly on the organ as the party entered the nave. The vicar looked pensive as he waited at the chancel steps. He was all smiles within, as he felt this union was God-sent, and he thanked the Lord that Ralph and Erin had found each other. Their personalities and natures had meshed well from their first meeting, and Ralph had proven his worth by being there for Erin in her darkest moments.

Erin could see the tear sparkle in her father's eye, as she and Ralph stopped in front of him. She smiled, and he smiled back.

"He knows how right this is," she thought. "Thank you, Father, I love you."

The service concluded, the wedding party made their way to the back of the church, and when the doors were opened, a cheer was heard. Outside in the driving rain, a group of officers stood facing each other with swords. The honour guard was a surprise. They were invited into the vicarage, where they quickly drank a toast to the couple, and departed. The simple reception was over in an hour, and the bridal couple sped away in the Gwenns' Austin.

Erin and Ralph spent their honeymoon in a country inn deep in the New Forest—a quiet spot, away from holiday revellers. Their room was large with a huge bed fitted with a soft duvet over a comfortable feather mattress. A fireplace burned brightly, and Ralph noticed a good supply of oak logs piled on either side. It was warm and cosy in this nest, but they entertained other ideas on how to keep warm. A late dinner had been ordered, and after they had unpacked their belongings, they undressed and slipped between the sheets. For some minutes they simply embraced tightly, savouring their closeness and nakedness. They whispered words of love, but gradually, their hands began to wander, seeking secret places on the other's body.

"I really feel inept at this," Ralph whispered. "If I make you feel uncomfortable, please tell me."

"There is nothing you can do to make me feel that way," Erin responded. "I will show you the way if you need prompting, which I doubt."

Ralph nibbled her ear, and she breathed, "Ahhhh!"

The dinner hour came and went, but the newlyweds never stirred from their bed. Satiated with each other, they needed no other nourishment. They gladly lost track of time and allowed the fullness of their love to overwhelm them. Their lovemaking was mutually satisfying, and Erin, the experienced one, made sure of that, with her subtle guidance. There was no boundary for their love, and they melded into one.

"Perhaps we'll conceive a child," mused Erin, almost to herself.

"Would you mind that?" responded a sleepy Ralph.

"It would be wonderful. I had such a feeling of well-being when I was pregnant with Michael Paul." She turned to him. "Ralph, you will make a wonderful father. I just know it."

"Well then, what's holding us back?"

Chapter 6

Ralph had never known such utter bliss. His happiness knew no bounds, and he showered Erin with every attention. In a sheltered corner of the inn, late-blooming roses grew. When Ralph asked the innkeeper's wife if he could pick a rose to place on Erin's pillow, she not only cut one, but several, to make a charming bouquet for the bridal chamber.

The honeymoon drifted along for Ralph and Erin as if no one else existed in the entire world. But all good things eventually come to an end, and the day arrived when they had to leave their wedding bower. The couple thanked their hosts profusely, climbed into the Austin, and returned to Bewdleigh on the last day of the year, to face wartime realities. Julia had produced a handsome baby boy during their absence, to the delight of Tom Nugent and her parents, and, added to this celebration, Tom had received his promotion to captain.

The officers' mess was gaily decorated for New Year's Eve, and at the beginning of the party, Ralph and Erin were the centre of attention. But as the evening progressed, they found themselves alone in the middle of a crowd. They danced the night away with eyes only for each other, much to everyone's delight. No one was surprised when they left only minutes after midnight.

In the small hours of the new year, Ralph and Erin cuddled in the bedroom they now shared in the vicarage, and dreamt of a life stretching on forever. Erin awoke just before dawn, and murmured something in Ralph's ear.

He opened his eyes wide and exclaimed, "What did you say?"

"I said . . . I think I have just conceived!"

"How can you know that?"

"Call it a woman's intuition—a golden dream. Maybe I felt a quickening, I don't know. I truly believe we have started a child. Would that please you?"

"My darling, how could I not be pleased?" Ralph hugged her close to him. "You are breath of my breath, life of my life. To share a child with you would answer a prayer. It would be the next greatest thrill of my existence. It would make me whole."

"Then mark this day in your journal," she advised him, "and count nine months hence. God willing, I will give birth to your baby!"

"Wee Michael will have a brother or sister to play with," Ralph smiled with anticipation. "How wonderful for him! We'll make a fabulous family," said Ralph. "Maybe we'd better plant a few more seeds to enhance the chances of your dream coming true!"

"My love, you're a mind reader!"

The NCHR lines were abuzz. On the 5th of January, another officer and a senior NCO received temporary postings to join the 1st British Army in North Africa. Speculation ran rampant. Rumours, endemic to barrack life, spread wildly throughout the battalion. Each one was inflated significantly, and by the time it came back to the original perpetrator, he didn't even recognize it as his own.

The transfer of Captain Tom Nugent and Sergeant Major Carl Monk to the Non-Effective Transit Depot "Q" List happened overnight. As the "Q" List held people being sent back to Canada for disciplinary action, discharged for inefficiency, or for other means of disposal, they were naturally queried, "What happened to you?" or "What did you do wrong?" Since their movements were hush-hush—even Julia did not know the reason behind her husband's posting—the men had to keep silent, and soon departed leaving their fellow "non-effectives" with questions unanswered. In fact, Nugent and Monk were attached to British front-line units in North Africa to give them experience under fire and gain invaluable insights into battlefield tactics, something they would share on their return to their unit.

A great listlessness developed in all ranks as the year 1943 trudged through the winter months. Gradually, a shift in training took place, involving infantry-armoured tactics, and advance-to-contact practice runs with tanks in the lead became a routine drill. Each soldier maintained superb conditioning, while those unable to sustain high levels of physical fitness were gradually removed from regimental strength and posted to more static units. They continued to serve, but not in the capacity of a front-line soldier.

Ralph, physically strong, continued to keep up with the rifle companies. Each day he would fall in with a different section and trudge along with the men—verbally jousting with them and raising their spirits. On weekends, if the troops trained, he would gather a group of men about a tank from where he would hold a brief Sunday service. He joked that he had the toughest pulpit in the world, and that he could soon get the attention of any man that fell asleep during his sermon—as he patted the main gun affectionately.

Erin bloomed with the glow of pregnancy. She had been right. A child had been conceived, and her early months passed with a minimum of discomfort. Ralph was most protective of her and would watch her every move, ready to rush to her aid if she showed any signs of distress. She would tease him lovingly for his "mother hen" hovering.

"For goodness' sake, Ralph," she would say. "I think your soldiers need you more than I do at the moment!"

"But they're not having my baby," he would respond with a self-conscious laugh.

"Oh, you are so sweet. Really! I'm fine. If it weren't so, I promise I'd tell you."

"You promise?"

"I do. Now find something else to worry about!"

In bed at night, he would run his hands over her growing tummy to see if he could feel the baby.

"It's too early yet," she would tell him. "But I don't mind the massage. In fact it is downright pleasant. When you get finished on that side, I'll roll over and you can do the back!"

Invariably, the body rub would develop into more intimate foreplay. Their love grew steadily and the two lovers seemingly blended into one and the same person. "For this cause shall they become one flesh."

The NCHR continued to strip down for action. Several new officers replaced those who had been posted out to training units, and as more men arrived from Canada, they found themselves in holding units. The demand for officers, well grounded in current tactics, was needed to bring the recruits up to standard.

A sad parting took place between Ralph and his batman "Gramps." Now in his forties, Gramps could no longer keep up with his peers. He had developed a pot about his middle, and on marches, he was always short of breath. The MO had warned Ralph that Gramps had to lose weight and shape up, or he would have to downgrade his category. Ralph explained this to his batman, to no avail. The crunch came. Private Joe Jankowski received a posting to a static unit in London.

"Gramps, I'm sorry to see you go. You've been a tremendous help to me. I'll miss you," said Ralph.

"Sorry I couldn't keep up, sir." Gramps replied. "I hear a lad from the new draft is taking my place. Supposed to be a sharp guy—really on the ball. Hope he'll turn out well."

Private Peter Partridge, a wiry soldier in his early twenties, was Anglican by denomination and had been trained as a server in his home parish. Pete, always well turned out, had a flair for organization, and Ralph took to him immediately. Partridge was eager to please, keen to learn, and kept the padre's kit and belongings in top shape from the start.

In mid April, the regiment returned to Inverary, Scotland, for advanced combined operations training, and the new men and officers were brought up to speed. Night-assault landings were repeatedly practised to give the troops the best possible feeling to for this tactic.

One evening, after returning from a strenuous day of landing-assault training, the officers had the opportunity to welcome back Captain Tom Nugent from the "Q" List, following his stint in North Africa. He regaled his envious mates with stories of his battle experiences.

"The heat and dust of the desert was unbelievable. No wonder the locals wear scarves wrapped around their heads. I found breathing difficult and my throat was constantly parched. Within forty-eight hours, I had sore, cracked lips.

"The Krauts were on the run, but put up some pretty stiff rearguard action. They sure as hell knew what they were doing. The CO wants me to give a talk on the enemy's tactics, so I'll fill you in on this later.

"I have a feeling we may head that way soon. There's still a fair bit of cleaning up to do. The 'Desert Rats' are doing a super job, but they could do with a break." Many there would have given their eyeteeth to give the Desert Rats that break.

The men talked long into the night, fatigue forgotten, as they celebrated the return of their companion.

A feature of this period was the issue of new weapons and equipment, which sparked more rumours.

"Hot damn!" shouted Billy Boggs to his platoon mates. "Brace your feet, for here we go. Boy, is this Bren gun ever a beauty."

"What do you think of the new anti-tank weapons?" asked Joe Brash. "PIATS, there're calling them—for Projectiles, Infantry, Anti-tank."

"Yeah, they're neat," answered Pete Dolan, "an' the anti-tank platoon has new six- and seventeen-pounder guns to break in as well. All our transport is being waterproofed, and I heard a fellow in QM stores say a shipment of tropical clothing has arrived. Where do you suppose we're going? Africa is almost cleaned up. You don't suppose we're going there to keep house after the Brits are finished do you? That'd be the pits!"

"Nah!" scoffed Boggs. "It's our turn to kick ass!"

As the training began to wind down, the men were lined up and received their monthly pay. In the evening, a handful of A Company men spread a grey blanket on the floor of the barrack room and entered into a serious crap game, where one soldier, Private Buzz Benett, ended up with a fistful of money. At midnight, he stashed his winnings in the bottom of his kit bag and fell into a happy sleep. Eyes had watched where he had hidden his take.

Corporal Slattery woke Sergeant Haynes in the NCO's room and told him what he had seen. Haynes roused and grinned. "I think it's time to add to our poke. Everything's been quiet for the last while—what do you think?"

"Let's do it," replied Slattery. "There's a pile of cash there. It'll set us up pretty good when we add it to our poke back at Bewdleigh."

"When they head up the mountain in the morning for the last trip, I'll go with them," said Haynes, his beady eyes glittering with greed. "I'll order you to stay behind to return some platoon things to the QM stores. Then, you can grab the money, put it in a box, and mail it to me in Bewdleigh. How's that for a foolproof plan?"

"You think the mail trick will work?" asked the corporal.

Haynes nodded afirmatively. "Damn right, it will. The Royal Mail'll get rid of the money so we don't have to worry about it. Can you think of a better plan?"

"You're the brains, partner," agreed Slattery. "I'm with you."

In the morning, Bennet ran his hand down into his kit bag to feel for the money. The touch of it gave him a shiver, for he knew exactly how he was going to spend it. He had a girl in Bewdleigh who was playing hard to get into the sack, but now he had the means to coax her. He snapped a padlock through the top of the bag and went happily to breakfast with his chums.

Slattery finished the QM detail by eleven o'clock and returned stealthily to the Nissen hut. He watched carefully as he walked casually to the barrack. All was quiet, but as he was about to enter the building, the padre came around a corner.

"Morning, Corporal, you not on training today?" asked Ralph.

"No, sir—had some stores to return."

"Right! Have a good day, then," and Ralph continued on his way without a backward glance. In his mind, however, he became suspicious of Slattery, and wondered what he should do about it.

Meanwhile, Slattery broke into Bennett's kit bag, removed the money and a signet ring that he slipped into his battledress tunic pocket. He placed the money in a cigar box, wrapped it with paper cut from a brown bag, and proceeded to the mailroom to post the parcel south.

"How much for stamps to Bewdleigh?" he asked.

"What's in it?" enquired the postal clerk.

Slattery was alarmed at the question. "Oh, just some letters and news clippings I want to save. My kit's full, and this box is kinda awkward."

"I'll have to show it to the censor!" replied the clerk.

"What for? It's only going within the U.K.!" stuttered Slattery.

"Don't matter. New security orders are to check everything."

"Give it back, then, I'll find room for it," said the corporal.

The parcel was returned, and as Slattery was leaving the mailroom, a burly British military policeman brought him up short. "What d'ye got there, me lad?" he asked pointing to the box.

"Just some stuff I wanted to mail but decided against it at the last minute."

The policeman cocked his head, "That right, mate! Well, then, let's have a look at it."

Slattery pulled away as if to run, and the MP clamped an arm around his neck. "No you don't, chum. Yer comin' wif me."

In the military police block, Slattery was searched and placed in a cell. The contents of his pockets included the signate ring with the initial "B" engraved on it. A Company HQ was informed of the detainment, and Lieutenant Tom Nugent, Company 2IC, along with the padre, responded to the call. The parcel was opened and the money revealed. Ralph saw the ring on the desk and identified it as belonging to Private Bennet. Slattery was summarily arrested and soon "spilled his guts," not wanting to take all the blame himself. The MPs collared Sergeant Haynes in the training area and arrested him on the spot. In due course, the two NCOs were tried, found guilty, broken to privates, and sent to a service detention barracks for six months. The petty theft scam ended much to the relief of the CO and men of the NCHR.

Haynes' last words, as he was trundled off to jail, were, "It was that goddam padre sticking his big f---ing nose into other ranks' affairs. He's no bloody right to be around the barrack blocks. Someday, I'll get him for that!"

There was no question in Ralph's mind that the show would begin soon. Little scuttlebutt passed in the officers' mess, except for odd comments on preparations, but all signs indicated action ahead. Speculation was discouraged, and a blanket of secrecy was imposed. Ralph found himself, along with his batman Pete, scheduled for a five-day special leave at the end of May.

Ralph called Erin in Bewdleigh and suggested that she join him in Scotland for his leave. She had an elderly aunt who resided in Ayr, less than twenty miles from the NCHR concentration area. Ralph had visited her in mid April and had enjoyed the octogenarian's spirited company. As he departed, she had extended an invitation to drop in any time.

"I always have a bottle of medicinal whisky that needs replacing from time to time—in case it should go bad!" Aunt Maggie had chuckled, a tiny slip of a woman with twinkling bright eyes. She had suggested that Erin should come and stay with her for a few days, and promptly wrote her niece with an open invitation.

Erin expressed a concern over wee Michael. She didn't want to leave him for any length of time.

"Maybe you should come down instead," she suggested to Ralph over the phone.

"I've only five days, my love, and that would mean I would be travelling two of them. Perhaps Michael could stay with Julia? He loves being with her, and she's so good with him."

"Let me think on it. Call me tomorrow."

Erin ran the idea past Julia, and her friend expressed delight with the chance to look after Michael.

"Your father can drop in and see him—so he won't feel too homesick. I know it would work fine!"

The arrangements fell into place, and Erin took the train to Ayr via Glasgow. She arrived at her aunt's the day before Ralph's leave began. She hadn't seen Maggie in several years and was surprised to find her in such robust health.

"Och, what a wonderful man you have found," Aunt Maggie greeted Erin. "If I were a few years younger, I'd have given you a run, my girl." The elderly woman was a great sport with an engaging sense of humour.

"Oh Auntie, it's so good to see you again!" Erin exclaimed as she hugged Maggie. "You're right. Ralph is special. He was so kind to me when Michael was killed. It was such a dark time for me with a child on the way. Thank God for father and Ralph, I don't know how I would have made out without them."

"I'm glad you found him, my dear," Maggie squeezed Erin's hand. "I know what it's like, to live alone. My Henry has been dead twenty-six years. One barely exists when one loses a mate. But in one way, I was lucky not to have had a child to raise alone, but in another way, I've had a hole in my life. Now, enough of this morbid talk—tell me about your father. I trust his health is holding?"

"I'm a little worried about him—his heart, you know, but he never stops. It's the Gwenn passion for 'getting on with it.'"

"Och, yes, like his father before him—absolutely indomitable. What a family! Let me fetch some tea. You look as if you could use a cup. When is the bairn due?"

"Late September—around the twenty-ninth."

"You are absolutely glowing. How lovely for you."

The two women had a wonderful visit all evening and retired early in anticipation of Ralph's arrival the following morning.

Over breakfast, Aunt Maggie remarked with a twinkle in her eyes, "You will want to be alone with your man. I have made arrangements to stay with friends for a few days in Prestwick. They will pick me up later this afternoon."

"Oh, Auntie, you don't have to do that!" Erin protested, guilty that she had somehow forced the elderly woman from her home.

"It's already done," Aunt Maggie replied firmly. "Besides, my friends have been after me for some time to come visit them." She paused, then began again. "I remember in the last war, before Henry went to the front, my cousin Jane did exactly the same favour for me. It was the last time we were together, and I've treasured those last days all this time. Och, goodness, I hope you don't think I'm suggesting . . ."

"Of course not, Auntie." Erin quickly assured her.

A knock at the front door brought both women out of their chairs simultaneously.

"If that's Ralph, he's been up before the birds," exclaimed Erin brightly, as she dashed for the hallway.

Ralph entered laden with bundles that he hastily dropped to take Erin into his arms.

"Ahhh, sweetheart!" he exclaimed, as he covered her face with kisses.

"Easy there, my fine laddie, or you'll squeeze the wee one out too soon!" squealed Erin, all the while hugging him fiercly in return

"Sorry!" Ralph replied, immediately guilty at the thought of maybe hurting her "I keep forgetting you're in the sixth month—but you look so grand, and slim to boot!"

"Surprising what a well-designed dress can do for an expectant mother!" Erin laughed.

Ralph picked up his parcels, placing them on the hall table, and went to greet Aunt Maggie. He gave her a great bear hug and lifted her off her feet.

"Now take care with me too, young man, remember I'm just a frail old lady in her eighties! You'll crack my ribs," she said, poking his.

"You don't look a day over sixty!" he teased.

"Get away with you, my lad. Sure and you have a little Irish blarney in you!"

Ralph opened the parcels, which contained foodstuffs that he had scrounged from the mess—canned Canadian bacon, butter, sugar, some powdered milk, and several other items hard to come by in the civilian community.

"I told our sergeant cook I required these in lieu of my rations. I said I was going to visit a beautiful old lady who couldn't possibly feed me on her ration card. Naturally, he gave me a grin and a funny look. He even had the nerve to ask me the age of this 'little old lady.'"

Aunt Maggie laughed heartily. "Bring him by sometime, and let him find out for himself."

At three in the afternoon, an ancient Daimler, driven by a chauffeur, drew up outside the house. Ralph assisted the aunt into the auto, and he and Erin waved farewell as the vehicle chugged off down the street.

"Alone at last!" sighed Erin once inside the front door. She hugged Ralph around the waist and laid her head on his chest.

"Don't forget I'm six months' pregnant, too!" he said as a teasing response.

"Come this way, mister, I'll show you what a woman six months' pregnant can do."

In the chill of the poorly heated house, they quickly slipped under the covers in their bed. Aunt Maggie, a frugal Scot, dressed in warm woollens rather than spend needless shillings on expensive coal.

"I'll keep you warm, my love," Ralph promised as they snuggled into an embrace, her back tight against him. "Tell me though, can we make love without harm to the babe?"

"Of course we can. We just have to adjust our positions as necessary, and take it slow and easy—the way we like best!"

The couple spent the rest of the day in bed and made love leisurely and often, feasting on the pleasures they shared. At the back of their minds they knew that this might be the last time they would be together for a long time. Ralph had told her, without detail, of the preparations underway, but they didn't dwell on the subject. Instead, they looked to the future. He shared with her every aspect of life in Canada that he could think of, from weather to the kind of home they would live in, with central heating and modern conveniences.

Despite Ralph's rosy tales of the future, Erin could not dispel the shadow of doubt in the back of her mind. At unexpected moments, the memory of Michael's death would surface. She would pray to God that Ralph would return to her alive. Holding her in his arms, he would sense her mood and hug her tightly.

"While I'm away, don't dwell on morbid thoughts," he urged her. "Live each day as it comes, and know that I am with you always—in a sunbeam, or a breath of warm air against your face. I'll see your beautiful black tresses spread across the pillow, and watch, as your beautiful blue eyes open sleepily in the early morning. I will thank God for what we have shared, and ask Him to keep you in his care until I return. And I will return. Count on it!"

On their last night together, they located a restaurant overlooking the harbour that Ralph had been told about—an intimate, family establishment that seated only a dozen people. The menu offered one dish, a hearty lamb stew with vegetables, and from the cellar below, the restaurateur produced a bottle of fine wine.

"Not many of these left," he said. "But by the looks of you, I know you will appreciate it. Enjoy!"

It was the 3rd of May when Ralph placed Erin on the train heading south. Both gazed deeply into the other's eyes and embraced warmly before she entered the carriage. She dropped the window and bent out to share one last kiss with him. He waved goodbye as the train pulled from the station. Both held back the tears.

Ralph returned to find the NCHR lines astir. Final preparations for the shipment of men and materiel to some unknown destination were in full swing. All unit vehicles received a waterproofing, indicating that the first encounter with the enemy would be a seaborne assault.

The officers exchanged small talk in the mess. Much of it centred on the issue of tropical kit and speculation that placed the destination anywhere from the Mediterranean to the jungles of Burma. The air was electric as everyone waited for the spark to set it off. It came on the night of June 12th. The warning order stated that departure would take place the following day.

The morning dawned with a chill in the air and broken skies overhead. The weather was a teasing mix of slanting rain and sudden bursts of sunlight. Tenders flitted across the green wind-whipped waters, shuttling 27,000 men with 30,000 tons of stores to the ninety-two ships waiting at anchor in the port of Gourock. Disappointingly, the convoy swung at anchor for two more weeks in the Firth of Clyde, and from time to time a single troopship would slip down toward the Atlantic to disgorge its troops onto a barren shore to practise another assault exercise. This helped to curb their jittery energy. On one occasion, the men of the NCHR scrambled ashore on the island of Arran. Here they made a circuitous route march, which allowed them to burn off some pent-up frustrations. Finally, on the 28th of June, late in the evening, the convoy upped anchor and silently, in total blackout mode, passed north of Ireland into the vast Atlantic.

The troopship that transported the NCHR was a converted liner. In earlier service it had carried 700 passengers and a cargo of some 390,000 pounds from Europe to ports in the western Pacific. Configured for military traffic, she held 3,500 troops and a crew of 340. Internally, her cabins had been stripped and the portholes welded shut, and large messing areas were created for the men. At night, hammocks for sleeping hung over the long wooden dining tables.

The officers fared better, with four individuals to a large cabin. The liner's ornate lounge became their mess—a gracious and commodious place to relax in. It, and the dining salon, survived the gutting made necessary to accommodate large numbers of troops.

Ralph wended his way between decks daily to visit his "flock." He was, by this time, well known and accepted by the men, and he handled the sensitive role with ease. Often, he would sit with a group of lads "shooting the bull," or offer to join in a game of euchre.

"I'll be your partner, Padre. We'll whip the pants off these guys," a soldier suggested.

"Let's do it, Alf," said Ralph sitting in, and the game began.

Several hands later the points stood in favour of the champs—six to two.

"Over to you Padre, it's your deal."

The cards were shuffled and dealt. Three players passed on the chance to make trump.

"I make it hearts and go alone," said Ralph.

Alf blinked. "Go for it, Padre!"

"Your lead, Billy!"

"Right! Bet I got you here, sir!"

"Don't call me 'sir' down here. It makes me nervous," said Ralph with a wide grin. "I answer to 'Padre' just fine."

Chuckles resounded all around, as the soldiers knew him for what he stood. They knew he would speak out against blasphemy, but would tolerate a broad latitude of language while in their midst. Occasionally, things would begin to get out of hand, and Ralph would simply get up and move on to another group. The offender would bear the chagrin felt by his mates.

Billy Boggs had led the ace of spades. Ralph trumped with the ten of hearts, then announced, "I think I have all the rest." He laid his hand down disclosing the two bowers, the ace, and the king of hearts.

"Yahoo," shouted Alf, "way to go!"

The score was tied. In the next round of play, they euchred the champs, and in the last hand, Alf and Ralph took all the tricks to win the match.

"Told you we could take 'em, Padre. Good show!"

Ralph enjoyed other card games. With the officers he played poker and thoroughly enjoyed games of penny-ante. He studied his messmates to determine whether their skill was the result of brash bluffing, or perhaps indecision and hesitancy. He wondered if these traits would be detected in the battles ahead.

The convoy steamed south on calm seas. Mornings were devoted to lectures, calisthenics, and care of weapons. During the afternoons, many soldiers took advantage of the sun to stretch out on deck. Most evenings, Ralph would go off alone to stand wistfully at the rail, watching the colourful sun splash down in the west and think of Erin and his family in Canada. He was sailing farther still from the highlands of home, not to mention his new family in England. Spring had arrived in both lands, with new life emerging daily. He could visualize Ernest planting his tender garden plants, and in Bewdleigh, the vicar loosening the soil around his roses.

The commanding officer, Lieutenant Colonel Scot Morrison, opened his sealed orders on Dominion Day, their third day at sea. He assembled the officers and senior NCOs in the officers' mess for a briefing, where he announced that Operation "HUSKY" would unfold on the beaches of Sicily beginning on the morning of July 10th. Before him on the table were piled the maps and instructions for the landing.

"I want you to be aware that you are an integral part of a mighty armada of ships. In the next few days, a total of two thousand, five hundred ships will rendezvous off the south coast of Sicily. It is the mightiest invasion force ever assembled in the history of mankind, and you will become part of the famous 8th Army under the command of General Montgomery. The Canadian 1st Division will be on the army's left flank, and immediately to our western boundary, will be the Americans under the command of General George Patton.

"I want you to study these maps carefully. Take note of the environs near your objectives. Read and reread your instructions. Share this information with every man under your command down to the last private soldier.

"We are a highly trained organization, and I expect every man to be capable of taking over the job above him, should the situation arise.

"I am proud of you. In the last three years, you have faced the most frustrating conditions and tackled difficult training schedules. Your men are superior, hardened soldiers, soon to face their baptism of fire. You have taught them well, and I have no doubt that their performance will be carried out with the utmost proficiency.

"Gather your people and share with them our battle plan. I'll come around to your groups and answer any questions that may arise. But before we disperse, I would ask the Padre to lead us in prayer, for only with the help of Almighty God will our great enterprise succeed."

Ralph stepped before the assembly.

"Gentlemen, our cause is a noble one, for we stand for the rights and freedoms of mankind. We stand between the peace-loving peoples of the world and an evil force that would enslave us all. A perilous time lies ahead and many will pay the supreme sacrifice, but we will, in time, defeat the enemy.

"Let us pray." Ralph paused to give everyone a chance to bow their heads. "Lord, in the days ahead we will encounter the enemy. He is a determined foe and will do everything in his power to stop us. Our determination is greater and our cause is just, for we do battle with an evil power and You are our strength. Give us strong hearts and a clear vision. When one of us falls, lift him up into Your keeping. Now we are ready, 'Aye Ready,' as our motto claims. With Your banners before us, we cannot fail. Amen."

A great feeling of excitement gripped the troops as the battle plans were laid before them. Each man learned what was expected of him and what he had to do.

Ralph listened to the orientation given by Andy Ayers, OC, B Company, who would spearhead the attack.

"Our first objective," Ayers began, "is to take out a battery of heavy guns that lie inland roughly one mile from the beach. You will face machine-gun and small-arms fire on the approach. Stretches of barbed wire will have to be breached. Enemy mortars will bracket the area.

"You have become accustomed to battle noise during your training. Do not let this deter you. You can be scared later. Instead, press on toward your goal and be prepared for the unexpected—such is the nature of a battle. It can be disconcerting and confusing—all hell breaks loose. Keep cool. Stick to the plan, but be prepared to adjust if the situation calls for it.

"I want each platoon and section leader to commit our battle plan to memory. Run over it with your men until it's coming out your ears—then do it again. In the event of heavy casualties, or some other quirk of battle, every soldier must be prepared to act on his own initiative, even to the point of taking command of a situation if his leader is no longer available.

"You've proved yourselves time and time again under difficult training conditions. You're in top shape physically, and I trust, mentally. You are the best. Let's get 'em!"

Three days of intense planning passed. On the Sunday, the troops gathered on the forward deck for a church service under bright blue skies. The seas were calm and the sun warm, and a thousand or more men stood or sat if they could find room. Ralph organized a pickup choir to lead the hymns, while the pipe band accompanied Jamie Fraser on the field organ.

The service started with the singing of "O God Our Help in Ages Past." The men sang so loudly that they drowned out the musicians. The troops on one ship nearby crowded its rail and echoed the hymn across the water.

In the prayers, Ralph entrusted the invasion forces to the keeping of the Almighty, and from the *Book of Common Prayer* he read the collect for the fourth Sunday after Trinity.

"O God, the protector of all that trust in thee, without whom nothing is strong, nothing is holy: Increase and multiply upon us thy mercy; that, thou being our ruler and guide, we may so pass through things temporal, that we finally lose not the things eternal: Grant this, O heavenly Father, for Jesus Christ's sake our Lord. Amen."

Ralph's sermon summarized Christ's sacrifice on the cross to save mankind and alluded to the statement that no greater gift could a man give than to lay down his life for his friends.

He concluded with these words: "I do not want this to be seen as a morbid thought. You know, and I know, that some of us will fall in battle. It is to be expected. You think, and I think, it won't happen to us as individuals. I pray that this may be so. But God's will be done. If I fall or if you fall, be sure in your heart that you will be lifted up to the bosom of the Almighty. Jesus said, 'I will be with you till the end of time.' Go with God!"

The final hymn also echoed across the waters as lusty voices swelled in the singing of "Onward Christian Soldiers." The worshippers then dispersed to various parts of the ship with their private thoughts. Most had been uplifted, but some were not sure. They had lived their lives by their own lights, and had little faith in a loving God. It was their time to wrestle with what was to come. To a man, they knew that their padre was there as a friend any time they needed his counsel.

More ships joined the convoy as they neared their destination. They came from every direction—North Africa, Canada, the United States and Great Britain. Naval vessels, large and small, were dispersed among the troop ships and freighters. It was beyond doubt a mighty invasion force.

The day before the invasion was to take place, a force six sirocco blew in from North Africa, churning the waters of the Mediterranean Sea into gigantic white-capped swells. The vast convoy bobbed like corks in a storm, and it became doubtful that landings would take place the following day.

At 1000 hours, Ralph held his last communion service before the troops were due to go ashore. Several hundred jammed the lounge, while others waited in the passageways to receive the sacrament. In the pitch and yaw of the ship, Ralph had difficulty keeping his balance, and several times he sent Pete, who was acting as a server, for more bread and wine. Finally, after four hours, the last man was served and Ralph, near exhaustion, gratefully found a place to sit. More than a thousand men had received their communion. Thinking back over the service, Ralph was under no illusion that all the participants were ardent worshippers. A number would see the sacrament as a sort of insurance policy. Ralph knew that even a cynic could possess a seed of faith.

Ralph thought in a prayerful moment. "All I need to do is water it and tend the sprout with loving care."

The storm increased in strength as day turned into night, which added to the speculation that the landings would be cancelled for the morrow. The thunderous waves meant it would be a near-impossible task for the landing craft to approach the beach. Meanwhile the wind howled and screamed through the ship's rigging, and anything not tied down went careening across the decks, including small packs, gas masks and steel helmets. However, at 2145 hours, confirmation of the assault was received in stunned silence. No one could believe it possible to proceed under such conditions.

Colonel Morrison called his officers and senior NCOs together for a meeting at 2200 hours. He spoke briefly, assuring everyone that he had the utmost confidence in the men of the NCHR.

"We are a superbly trained band of brothers," he affirmed. "We will watch out for each other as best we can, but we must press on to our objectives at all costs. The people of the world will remember this event for years to come as the opening round in the rescue of Europe from the Boche.

"Be ever mindful of the fact that peace lies on the other side of war. We will not obtain it until we go through the fire first. Many will die, both soldiers and civilians. That's the ugly fact of war. Regardless we must forge ahead to rid the world of an evil empire. We do this for king and country, for our families at home, and for the regiment. With God's help, we shall succeed. You know what you have to do, but before we dismiss, I invite our padre to pray for us."

Ralph stood. "Gentlemen, you know me well. I am a simple, practical priest. I have given my best for our regimental family, and now I must face the reality of ministering to my flock in battle. I dread the task before me, and I sincerely ask for your help and guidance. I call upon God our Father to be with us every step of the way.

"Lord God, mighty in battle, look down upon your humble servants who prepare to engage the forces of evil. You know our cause is just. Give us strength of purpose and a clear determination to see our goal through to the end. If we fall in combat, lift us up to be with your legions on High. If wounded, help us to regain our strength to fight the oppressor another day. We ask this in Your Son's name. Amen." All stood silently before Ralph resumed.

"O Eternal Lord God, who has united us as brothers in the fellowship of arms, enable us to be worthy of those who have served in this regiment before us, and grant us a willing spirit to fulfill whatever tasks may be laid upon us, that when our work on Earth is over, we may find our rest in your eternal service; through Jesus Christ our Lord. Amen.

"Gentlemen, let us say the Lord's Prayer—Our Father who art in heaven . . ." A feeling of renewed confidence flowed through the room as the men recited the words of the familiar prayer.

It was now time for Ralph to send them to meet their fates. "May the Lord bless us and keep us. May He always hold us in the hollow of His hand. May He lift up the light of His countenance upon us and give us peace, now and forevermore. Amen."

The storm began to abate as the midnight hour approached, and many men saw it as a sign that God was indeed with them. The men made ready below as they checked their own equipment and that of the man next to him. Voices hummed as the excitement began to build. Most were naturally on edge going into battle for the first time, experiencing a mixture of doubt, fear and elation. They believed the discipline they shared would galvanize their actions as a fighting unit. Afraid, yet not afraid, they encouraged each other with humour and small talk. Some experienced periods of reflective silence when thoughts of home and loved ones came flooding into their consciousness. Others appeared outright cheerful, but their laughter and jokes sounded somewhat hollow.

Ralph stood by the rail as the moon dropped below the distant horizon. The wind suddenly dropped, although a residual swell still rolled in, and at 0030 hours, the troopship dropped anchor off the Sicilian shore. The roar of steel links paying out felt eerie and unexpected. The chaplain sensed a chill run up his spine.

The time had come to launch the first assault boats. Men crawled down the side of the ship like ants into the waiting craft. Ralph went in with HQ Company. When his turn came to make his way down the scrambling nets, he felt that strange jolting tingle in the pit of his stomach, a feeling similar to the one a man gets looking down from a high height—a sensation centred in the scrotum.

Judging his distance, Ralph dropped to the deck of the landing craft and moved into a crouched position, well forward beside his batman. Strain filled the air as the LCA moved away from the mothership, and the sound of rushing water gurgled against the hull as the engines churned a different tune. Occasionaly, as shells were lobbed from distant shore batteries, geysers would erupt nearby. These efforts by the enemy seemed half-hearted and ineffective.

With a jar, the LCA ramp struck the sand a few feet from the beach, and the men dashed ashore through ankle-deep water, weapons at the ready. Desultory enemy gunfire landed around them and it became evident that the Italian 206th Coastal Division had no stomach for a fight. Ralph was so pumped that he felt immediate disappointment. He had been ready for the worst, but soon he experienced relief, and gave thanks that there would be minimal casualties.

Major Andy Ayers' B Company crossed the beach first. Its objective was an Italian shore battery, one-and-a-half miles inland. However, the Canadians met two unexpected surprises. First, the six-foot-high vineyards they had expected had been drastically cut back to two feet. These could have provided some tactical cover from enemy fire. Second, the barbed wire they encountered was only eighteen to thirty inches high. Most of the troops easily leapt across it. So, after successfully engaging light enemy small-arms and machine-gun fire from dug-in defenders, Ayers' men quickly took possession of the heavy gun emplacements, and each breechblock was blown to render them useless. It was 1000 hours when Ralph caught up to B Company HQ and Ayers.

"How did it go, Major?"

"No problem at all, certainly not what we expected. Company Sergeant Major Godfrey was wounded slightly when he lobbed a grenade at a machine-gun nest. Didn't slow him down much. Got out his own shell dressing and wrapped it around his arm. He's over there—just behind that bunker with two other lads who got hit. A stretcher-bearer is attending them. They're in fairly good spirits, but I'm sure they'd like to see you, Padre.

"Thanks, Andy, I'll do that."

In the shadow of the bunker, Ralph found the three wounded men lying on stretchers. The CSM sat up at the chaplain's approach.

"Well, Sergeant Major, looks like you have the honour of being our first casualty; that is, if one could call it an honour."

"Just a scratch, sir. Hardly dented this old hide."

CSM Godfrey was known to be a tough old nut. He was a tall, barrel-chested man with a spiked mustache that he kept waxed. He took great pleasure in "chewing out" soldiers with misdemeanours, and it was almost comic when he cornered a culprit. He would make the man stand starkly at attention, then proceed to get in his face and scream soldierly obscenities at the delinquent until the soldier practically died of embarrassment. Now, this big bear of a man was almost mortified at being placed under the care of the medical attendant.

"Don't know why I have to stay here," he grumbled. "Should be out with the fighting troops."

"But you are, Sergeant Major," replied Ralph. "They're just on the other side of the bunker."

"Not the same, Padre," Godfrey scowled. "Might as well be on the other side of the bloody moon. Have to stay back till the MO checks me out. Damn it! Sorry, sir," he apologized automatically.

Ralph grinned and leaned over to whisper in the man's ear. "Don't fret, Jack, you'll be with the other guys pronto. The MO's not far behind." Ralph turned to the two privates. "Hey, fellows, how are you doing? Would you like a fag?"

"Thanks, Padre. That would be great," answered Private Rodney Dawson. "I got pinked in the leg, but no bones broken, thank God. Lots of blood, though. Got scared when I saw it pumping out. Stopped now."

"How about you, Schmitty?" Private Willy Schmitt looked pale. He took the offered cigarette between his fingers, but didn't light it. He was stripped to the waist, and a wide bandage was wrapped around his midsection.

"Scared shitless, Padre! When I saw my guts, I thought I'd really bought it."

"He'll be fine, sir," offered the stretcher-bearer. "Had a bit of intestine pop out, but we got it cleaned up and tucked back in. He's off to the RAP as soon as a carrier gets here." The Bren-gun carrier was a versatile vehicle, both as a fighting platform for the light machine gun and as a troop carrier. In this action, it was being employed as an ambulance.

"Well that's good news, then, Willy. Cheer up, everything's going to be fine."

Ralph made his way back to where Ayers was sitting, smoking a cigarette. The man was examining a cut on his knee.

"What happened there?" asked Ralph.

"Nicked it on one of those damned strands of wire. More blood than anything—no problem!"

"Sure?"

"Absolutely. Do you want to see where our next objective lies?" asked Ayers changing the subject. "See that low hill to the left about five hundred yards out? That's our forward point. I'm going there right now. Come along if you're not busy. You'll be back in half an hour."

"Hey, that'd be great. I'll let HQ Company know where I am—just in case."

Within minutes the two men made their way across low-lying ground to the rise of land where the point platoon of B Company was lightly dug in. A Company held ground further to the left.

"How do things look?" Ayers asked of the platoon commander, Lieutenant Gerald Bickerton. The subaltern was a stocky, intelligent man with alert brown eyes. He led his men with confidence.

Pointing, Bickerton replied, "Looks like the enemy are well dug in on that high ground a hundred yards north of the T-junction. They appear to be about company-size with three MG42s positioned in stone breastworks covering the southern approaches."

"Any sign of the RCR on our right flank?"

"Yes, sir, they're in their forming-up-place beyond that rise."

"Right. Check your watch. The RCR attack on the airfield goes forward in forty minutes. Our objective is to secure the T-junction. That'll prevent enemy reinforcements from using the road from the west. Padre, you'd better move back to HQ Company now."

"Lord be with you, Gerry!" said Ralph as he turned to leave.

"He always is, Padre. Thanks for coming forward."

The attack went in as planned with the RCR sweeping toward the airfield and the NCHR supporting the Royal's left flank. Ralph, using binoculars, watched with Colonel Morrison from the top of a feature where the battalion command post had been set up. Artillery and mortars softened up the enemy positions. The operation was a "set-piece attack," where the artillery program controlled the advance. The infantry followed a few hundred yards behind the wall of bursting artillery shells, and the barrage let up every few minutes to allow the steady movement of troops forward.

Meanwhile, the NCHR's two forward companies, A and B, attacked their target and laid down a furious crossfire against the enemy machine-gun emplacements. They, in turn, returned heavy fire. B Company, advancing across an open area, was ordered to ground while Lieutenant Bickerton called for close artillery support. Within moments, the ground erupted around the enemy positions as the twenty-five-pounder shells spewed earth high into the air. When the barrage let up, the Italian defenders raised several white flags. They had had enough. In all, sixty prisoners were captured and sent in a column back toward the beach where they joined several hundred others that had surrendered in the first few hours of the invasion. As yet, no German troops had been encountered.

Dusk descended on Day One. The units of the 1st Canadian Division consolidated their positions and prepared to bed down for the night, securing their perimeters with sentries. The men, travelling inland, were covered in a white powdery dust that seemed to find its way into every crack and cavity of the body. Someone joked that his chum looked like Buckwheat—the little Negro boy in the movie *Our Gang*, after a bag of flower had been poured over his head. The men washed up as best they could, ate a cold meal from rations they had carried with them, and sacked out. The adrenaline rush of the day had left them wired, but sleep soon came and they rested their tired bodies.

Ralph, now *in situ* at the RAP, talked with the walking wounded. The more serious casualties had been evacuated to a ship offshore to be hospitalized. The NCHR had four men killed and eleven who had sustained varying degrees of wounds.

"How are you doing, Padre?" inquired the MO. "You look a little beat! Bet you could stand a shot of medicinal rum."

"Not yet, Sandy, maybe a little later. Let me finish checking the guys here, first," he said. "Some are still pretty shaky."

"Right! I'm going for a good scrub and get some food. I'm feeling a little gant."

"See you later—maybe before I hit the sack. I've got to think about the burials tomorrow and jot some notes down for letters home to the families. That's going to be hard—I don't look forward to it, nor the burials."

"Don't envy you that part. Call me when you're ready."

"Thanks, Sandy."

Ralph spent the next hour with the wounded, offering to write a note home for the disabled and helping to compose letters for the men who were not sure what to write.

"I believe it's best to tell them you're going to be great," Ralph would often advise. "Just receiving a letter in your own hand will cheer them up."

Finally, the padre found a quiet moment of his own to reflect upon the events of the day.

"Thank God, we suffered few casualties," he mused to himself. "Some probably think us lucky. Perhaps they're right, except for those poor lads who lie outside wrapped up in their gas capes. In the morning we'll lay them to rest in this dusty white soil. Lord, how my heart goes out to them, and the families they leave behind. Now I'd better write some letters."

Dear Mr. and Mrs. Thomas

It is with deep regret that I pen these words to you concerning your son's death.

I want you to know that George did not suffer. He was killed instantly while bravely advancing upon an enemy position. His platoon sergeant told me your boy was one of the best men in the regiment. He worked hard to improve his skills as a rifleman and never shrunk from his duty.

I was talking with him on the troopship that brought us here. I saw him as a bright and cheerful lad. He talked of his family back home and wondered how his dad was making out fishing those nice trout in Lucky Lake. He missed their jaunts together.

He will be buried beside three of his comrades who also paid the supreme sacrifice. I will write you later with more details. I promise you, he will not be forgotten.

Sincerely and sadly yours,
Ralph Russell, NCHR Chaplain

It was after midnight when Ralph finished his letters to the families of the dead. He also dropped a note to Erin, as he promised to write a few lines daily and incorporate them into a weekly letter. He passed a hand wearily across his forehead and rubbed the grit from his eyes. He was about to stretch out on his cot when Sandy spoke to him.

"Thought you were going to drop by for a tot?"

"Hey, how come you're still up and about?"

"Had some rounds to make at midnight. Now, here's something to help you sleep, my friend." The MO passed Ralph a beaker half filled with the dark, medical rum issue.

"I don't think I need it," Ralph replied. "I'm half drunk with exhaustion right now."

"Doctor's orders!"

"Right, Bones!" Ralph replied throwing back the rum with a grimace. "Too tired to argue, anyway."

"Try and get some sleep, Ralph. We've another busy day tomorrow, and this is just the start. It'll get worse when we bump the Germans. Our baptism of fire may turn out to be our easiest battle. God only knows what lies ahead!"

Ralph dreamt of wild and confusing action. Shells burst overhead and the chatter of machine guns rattled in his ears. He heard a cry and saw a Plevna man fall. It was a lad from his parish, but the face kept changing. He strained to identify him, but something kept blocking his view. Ralph woke in a panic. He had somehow twisted his blanket over his head and tore at it to free himself. Sweat soaked his pillow and his body felt clammy. He had to urinate, and as he dashed for the outside, he felt nauseous from the burning taste of rum in his throat. He threw up and felt better. The cool breeze felt good on his face. He looked toward the front where the NCHR forward companies had dug in for the night.

"Grant them a little sleep, Lord. They'll be moving at first light," he prayed.

All was quiet. The 48th Highlanders silently passed through the NCHR lines to take up new positions to the northwest. The line of advance was already moving forward.

It was first light when Partridge awoke Ralph.

"Here's a cup of tea for you, sir!"

"Thanks, lad, just what I need."

Ralph sipped the hot brew, and gradually began to focus on the day ahead.

"Just so you know, sir," Partridge began as he readied Ralph's shaving gear, "the officer from the Graves Registration Commission has arrived at HQ Company."

"Right!" Ralph replied, splashing water on his face. "Check with the pioneer platoon to make sure everything is on track for the committals. I imagine they dug the graves last night."

Ralph slipped into his clothing and wondered how he could ever be objective in the immediate duty that lay ahead. He had become attached to those men who now lay dead. They were like family to him. But now he must don his clerical garb and deal with the facts without the distortion of personal feelings. As he said to Sandy the night before, it would not be easy.

"I must trust in the Lord to see me through," he said to himself, "otherwise I'll be of no use to the living. Jesus, be with me, for without You I am nothing. Give me a calm spirit, I pray."

At 0700 hours, Ralph joined the burial party at the temporary gravesite where the brigade dead were gathered for internment in a field near the beach. Only a handful of mourners gathered, as the NCHR had already moved forward. With all heads bowed, the chaplain read the burial office. It was brief, and in conclusion Ralph said, "These are our brothers that we lay to rest. They are now in God's keeping. May the Almighty have mercy upon them! They will not be forgotten. Amen."

Day Two of the invasion saw the 1st Canadian Division advance, expanding its bridgehead toward the town of Rosolini. It was Sunday, but Sunday routine was replaced with a rapid tactical movement forward. There was no time for a service with even small groups of men. The only religious rite Ralph performed that day was the burial of the dead. Meanwhile, Italian forces surrendered en masse, and except for the odd skirmish, there was little resistance. At one point, a tank regiment was used as troop transports and the men of the NCHR rode on the outer skins of the steel monsters. However, they raised such a cloud of dust that every man on board almost suffocated. It was a dubious method of conveyance. Frequently, the troops dismounted and brushed off their clothing, only to fill the air with clouds of dust. The men then rinsed their mouths with water, spitting out grey streams of gritty fluid, and for a change of pace, marched forward on foot. The sun, riding high, poured down a blistering heat, and rivulets of sweat ran down their dusty faces, creating muddy streaks. The trek became a nightmare of discomfort, but through it all, the Canadian sense of humour won the day. One wag was even heard to shout: "I hear we have a new title, 'The Ghost Brigade.'"

That's exactly what they looked like—"boogie men" riding their white chargers.

Colonel Morrison had a tight timetable, and he pushed his men hard. The first night was spent several miles past the town of Rosolini, which the 48th Highlanders had occupied earlier in the day. In the long grass on either side of the roadway, the men ate from compo rations before slipping under their gas capes for a well-deserved rest. The ground was hard, but the men didn't seem to notice, for they fell asleep immediately.

Ralph and his batman followed some distance behind the rifle companies. At Sandy's suggestion, they were mounted in one of the RAP's 15-cwt trucks. He deemed it a good place for the padre in the event that casualties from the next push were sent back.

"You can be of real service to me, Ralph," the MO had said. "When the wounded start coming in, we can get pretty busy all of a sudden. You'd have your own duties, of course, but in lulls you could supervise the stretcher-bearers, hold up plasma bottles, or handle a number of other things in an emergency. I know you want to be up near the companies, and no doubt from time to time you will be, but seriously, your best place to serve would be right here in the RAP."

Ralph thought Sandy was probably right, but he wanted flexibility, to go where he thought his presence was most needed. He made this clear to the MO, and they reached a loose agreement. On the advance to contact, Ralph planned to move forward with the men, choosing a different company each day. In rest periods, he would visit company lines. Above all, he didn't want to hinder or get in the way of the fighting troops. If invited forward, that would be a different kind of situation, but when the fighting started, he would drop back to the RAP to assist in any way he could and be in a position to go forward with the stretcher-bears to retrieve the wounded.

Partridge moved Ralph's kit in beside the doctor's personal gear. Private Rudy Corelli, the MO's batman, welcomed the company, and soon he and Partridge had everything organized. Corelli's family had emigrated from Italy to Canada after the First War, so he spoke the language fluently and acted as the MO's interpreter when wounded prisoners were brought to the RAP. He also served as a go-between with the local population. Corelli, a skilled scrounger, soon had Partridge working with him to provide their officers with the little extras that made life at the front more tolerable.

"Where in heaven's name did you get those fresh eggs?" the MO asked.

Corelli grinned. "Made a deal with the farmer's wife where we bivouacked last night. Gave her a couple of bars of hand soap for the dozen."

Not to be outdone, Partridge produced a loaf of Italian bread for toasting.

"She had a yen for some canned fruit, too!" he said.

"Now you two stay out of trouble. No stealing! Is that clear? Barter is one thing, but theft will not be tolerated. Understood?" demanded Ralph. "These peasants are poor. They survive on next to nothing."

"Right! Sir!" both men responded in unison. "We hear you—loud and clear."

The mail arrived and Ralph received several letters—one from his parents, one from Ernest and one from Erin.

His mother wrote in part:

> The papers are full of news of the invasion of Sicily. It appears you are sweeping swiftly through the country but we know it can't be that easy. Dad has had to deliver bad news to two families already, and at a recent deanery meeting, the other clergy indicate they are similarly engaged.
>
> We pray for you and your men constantly. Please be careful and keep safe and remember to dress properly. You know how easily you catch cold if you sweat and forget to put on dry undershirts.

His father added to the letter:

> Let's hope this war is over quickly now that our troops are commited to battle. I find it hard delivering those "I'm sorry to inform you" telegrams. The families seem to go into denial when their boys are so far away. There is no closure for them except when a letter arrives from the unit chaplain. This helps a lot. I

don't envy your job in that department, although I wish I could be there with you.

Ernest had scrawled a few words in pencil on a scrap of paper:

Hot as Hades here but not as hot as your way, I bet. The haying is pretty well done except for the low land down by Turtle Creek where I cut the marsh hay. The black flies were thick this season. We've had some bad thunderstorms that dumped a fair bit of water. Left a lot of puddles where the flies and mosquitos thrive.

Fishin' has been good—some nice black bass, but don't worry, I'm throwing the big ones back for you when you get back.

Erin's letter, an armed forces fold-up type, was as tightly written as was possible in the meagre space provided:

My darling, how I miss you. There is never a moment in the day that you are not in my thoughts. Sometime I just seem to drift off into a dream world where the two of us are alone in the other's arms. That day can't return fast enough for me.

All is well with the babe within. You'd have an armful if you were to hug me now. Doctor says all is progressing normally. Wee Michael seems to be in a growth spurt at the moment. He's always asking after you and wants me to show him on the map where you are. He keeps asking, "Will Daddy be home soon?"

Father is holding up as well as can be expected. He keeps forgetting things and this bothers him. He rarely shows his frustration, but I see it in many little ways.

Tom must be very busy, as he hasn't written often to Julia. I share those parts of your newsy letters that are not personal. Give Tom a bit of a nudge, please—even if he just has time for a few lines.

Erin's correspondance was always positive, but Ralph could read between the lines when something was bothering her. He sought Tom out in A Company lines.

"Hi there, Tom."

"Padre! How's everything with you?" Nugent stood leaning over his desk. He had a worried look on his face.

"Oh, I manage to keep up as best I can," said Ralph. "You seem to be up to your ears. Is everything all right?"

"I just had a letter from Julia," he replied with a frown. "She's not very happy about something—doesn't say what. I hope all's well back there."

"I had a letter from Erin today, and she didn't give any indication of sickness. Maybe she's concerned about you."

"Why do you say that, Padre?" Tom asked.

"Well, in passing, Erin mentioned that Julia hadn't heard from you in weeks."

"Haven't had time to write anyone. Major Stokes is quite the taskmaster and you know the pressure we've been under—if we're not in the thick of it, there's always after-action reports and checking up on the men. Rarely have time to put my head down," explained Nugent.

"I think it would be a good idea to make time, Tom. Got to put on a brave face for the home front, you know—helps their morale. Remember, Julia's special. She needs you to reach out to her."

"You're right, of course," Tom sighed. "Damn, I should have thought of that myself. Thanks for the heads-up. I'll get a note off right away."

The Canadians advanced rapidly with little resistance. Pockets of Italian soldiers were encountered along the way, and immediately surrendered and were then escorted under light guard to the rear. Occasionally, stragglers would fall into line when they saw the route taken by their compatriots.

For three days the NCHR rolled forward, on tanks, trucks, carriers—whatever became available under a blistering sun, and the pale skins the men had acquired in England soon began to burn a brilliant red. Their passing threw up clouds of white dust from the chalky soil, and nothing escaped a coating from the free-floating particles. If one took a drink, it contaminated the water. If a man blew his nose, the nasal mucous came out black. It was everywhere.

At night, men rolled up in their oilskin gas capes at the most convenient spot on the side of the road. There was no time for adequate sleep, and an order to move off might come at any time. Lack of rest and grimy bodies made the gruelling conditions worse, but the men pushed on. A few beefed loudly, but they were the usual ones who always complained. Mostly, men grinned at the complainer, and got on with it. The arduous training in England was paying off. The twenty- and thirty-mile marches that Montgomery had insisted upon were proving invaluable, and the men's physical condition carried them through the first gruelling days—their feet had hardened to perfection. This healthy state made their fatigue endurable.

The push forward went swiftly, but caution was still observed, for the enemy could be encountered at any time, and a foolhardy advance could prove disastrous if the troops were caught in an ambush.

Ralph was marching with the lead platoon of A Company when the pointman signalled an alert. Low bushes and thickets crowded the verge of the road. On a second hand signal, the troops moved into the ditches on either side.

"What's up?" whispered Sergeant Judd Taffy.

"I heard something there on the left, about twenty yards," came the answer.

"Bennet, Duffy, up the hill. Check it out."

Several moments passed before Bennet slipped back down the slope. "It's a bunch of civilians, Sergeant."

"Corporal Amodeo, call out to them in Italian. Let them know we won't hurt them."

"*Noi siamo amici,*" called the corporal.

In a startling rush, men, women and children poured onto the road, shouting wildly and cheering, "*Viva Inglese.*" They were peasants dressed in threadbare clothing; they looked half-starved. Fear haunted their eyes as they warily approached the Canadians. But, when they sensed they were not going to be harmed, they began to embrace and kiss the soldiers.

The troops shared rations with the peasants and found chocolate bars for the children. But the company commander's arrival brought the brief encounter to an end with a sharp order to advance.

That night, the NCHR bivouacked in a field beneath a high range of hills. Before dawn the order came to hold fast, as the roads ahead were jammed with military traffic. A surge of relief swept the lines, as the men finally had an opportunity to rest. Field kitchens dished out hot meals with fresh rations—the first time since the landings.

"Cup of tea, sir?" asked Partridge.

"Love one," replied Ralph as he stretched his weary body. "Hand me my writing kit, would you please?"

Partridge passed the zipped-up secretary to Ralph. "Going to write the missus, sir?"

"That's my plan. When did you write home last?"

"On the ship, sir. Not much time to drop a line since."

"You're right there, son. But I'm sure your family would like to hear from you now that they know of our landing in Sicily."

Ralph wrote Erin:

My darling,

I hope you have received my first letter by now. The postal people told us that the mail would be sent quickly from the ship after we landed. I'm not sure how much I can tell you as everyone is aware of the censors' ability to cut out anything that may appear forbidden to them.

I want you to know that I am fine. My physical condition makes all the difference, thanks to Monty's insistent call for fitness. So far, we've really been rolling along dusty roads that roil up and tend to fill the lungs. But, we push on knowing the faster we get the job done, the sooner we'll be home to our loved ones. And I do love you so much. I miss our times together. I miss wee Michael and your dad. How is he by the way? How are you? Is our baby behaving while Daddy is away?

At the moment we are having our first real rest since coming ashore. I hope to have a service for the men tomorrow even though it's not Sunday. It's a matter of catch-as-catch-can. It will be a voluntary. Perhaps I'll hold one or two in company lines. I don't expect many to turn out, as the boys are tired. But I'll be there for those who want to worship. I might be surprised, as a lot of the lads have become a little more introspective since engaging the enemy.

It's time for the evening meal, so I'll sign off for now and finish the letter tomorrow. After supper I want to stroll through D Company lines before I turn in. I like to dream of you. It helps make sense out of this terrible war.

Here I am, back again, twenty-four hours later. It has been an eventful day. Early this morning, word came through that General Montgomery was coming to visit. So my church services went on hold.

The whole brigade gathered at a central spot to hear the General. Before he spoke, however, he greeted the officers separately, and told them he especially wanted the Canadians with him in this action.

He said, "I was very impressed with you chaps right from the start. I remember well the work you did on that grand exercise we had back in England. I know in the days ahead you will remain stalwart."

Then he came to where I was standing and saw that I was a chaplain. He leaned close and said—if you can believe it—"You know, Padre, I'd rather have my chaplains with me in battle than my artillery."

Quite a remark coming from that famous soldier. When he spoke to the troops, he soon had them in the palm of his hand. He's quite a hero to them, and I'm sure they'd follow him to hell and back. When he left they cheered him off. Tired though they were, his visit sure gave rise to great spirits. Bless him. Mail is to go out soon so I'll say goodbye for now, my love.

Keep cheerful for me. Hugs and kisses in abundance,

All my love, Ralph.

P.S. I spoke with Tom. He's a pretty tired lad. Julia should get a letter soon.

Before first light the next morning, refreshed with a second wind and the flavour of Sicilian soil embedded in their tastebuds, the men of the NCHR strapped on their web gear, mounted trucks and headed out for battle. They were entering high country and the narrow roads edged steeply upward. In places, they passed vertical drops that descended hundreds of feet into the gorges below. The ever-present dust swirling up from the transport wheels soon coated them, and some men wrapped their towels about their heads for protection. However, shortly after dawn broke, the column came to a grinding halt. Orders came to de-bus and spread out on either side of the road.

Suddenly, streaking over a ridge ahead, three German fighters began to strafe the transport. Fortunately, the troops were not on board, as several trucks burst into flames. It all happened quickly, and no one had time to return fire.

"Get ready for them to come at us again," called an officer up the line. "Load your weapons!"

They waited for the fighters to swing back, but they didn't return. Then, the mount-up call was given, and the men climbed aboard the undamaged vehicles. One soldier slipped while clambering up, and his rifle went off. Luckily, no one was hurt. It turned out to be a sobering lesson to the others—be sure your weapon is cleared when not engaging an enemy. The sergeant majors used the incident to jump into action at the next break. The air was blue, but when asked the final question, "DO YOU UNDERSTAND?" everyone did.

On July 16th, the NCHR pushed forward without making contact with German forces, but an interesting encounter occurred when elements of the American 45th Division crossed the Canadian boundary line. They were fully mobile in jeeps and light trucks and had moved east one valley too far.

A few digs were traded.

"Hey, Yanks, forget yer compasses? This ain't the unmarked Canada–U.S. border, ya know!"

"Just thought we'd slip north to see if you Canucks still had snow."

"Don't see any skis with you."

"No, but we got our fishin' poles . . ."

Following the banter, the Americans veered to their left and disappeared in billows of dust.

The day had been tiring. Most of the advance had taken place on foot over rough terrain, crossing gullies and working through patches of cactus and scruff brush, snagging clothing and scratching legs bared due to heat. The troops expected to bump the enemy at any moment, as intelligence reports indicated they were scattered throughout the area. The high alert strained their eyes as they watched for movement, their ears tuned for sounds that would reveal an enemy position. Shortly after dark, the order came to halt overnight in a protected orchard below some rugged high features. It didn't take long for the men to find places to spread their gas capes and bed down.

Relatively refreshed after several hours' sleep, the NCHR began to move again at noon the next day, behind the Hastings and Prince Edward Regiment, nicknamed the Hasty Ps. The RCR took the rear position. In the town of San Michele, at 1400 hours, everything became bogged down. Some imminent action ahead brought the 1st Brigade to a full stop.

The order to "stretch out, but stay close" was given, and while the men found shady spots or a friendly wine shop, Ralph made his way to the rear, chatting up the troops. As he came to the NCHR's last vehicle, he glanced at the lead carrier of the unit following and saw a fellow chaplain, Rusty Wilkes, talking with an officer.

"Rusty!"

"Ralph, you old sun-of-a-gun!"

The two men embraced, slapping each other on the back, raising great puffs of dust.

"How the heck are you doing, Rusty? Are you staying out of trouble?" asked Ralph coughing.

"Trying to, but that's kind of hard when you have a bunch like this to shepherd around!" replied Wilkes, waving away the dust and gesturing toward the RCR.

Strome Galloway, OC B Company, was standing by the carrier and quipped right back with a grin. "You can always find our padre. If there's trouble around he'll be right in the middle of it—one way or another."

Rusty and Ralph chuckled at the remark.

"And speaking of getting into trouble, Rusty, tell your friend what happened to Sam Lerner yesterday," prompted Strome.

"Oh yeah, what a deal that was. You remember Sam Lerner, don't you?" asked Rusty.

Ralph nodded.

"He's our QM now, and he was in the rear at the ration point picking up supplies. As he headed back to battalion lines, he made a wrong turn in Caltagirone. His vehicle passed a sentry who didn't challenge him. Sam said he damn near turned the vehicle around to give the soldier a blast, but just then he saw a tank off to the side. Sam thought it looked different somehow, and then recognized it as a German tank. Suddenly, it dawned on him that their 60 cwt vehicle had crossed into enemy lines. In haste, they turned around and shot past the slack sentry at full speed. No shots were fired, and more by luck than good management, they got back to our position. You'd have to hear him tell it to get the full effect of the story. That's one he'll never forget!"

The two chaplains had a brief visit comparing notes. Then, with a fond farewell, they turned and resumed their duties visiting their unit packets.

Late in the afternoon, things began to move again and 1st Brigade entered the deserted town of Piazza Armerina. It lay in shambles from heavy bombing. Here, the RCR moved forward to become the point battalion, and at nightfall, the advance began again. The RCR pushed through the town of Valguarnera and on toward Leonforte, but their goal wasn't reached.

On the afternoon of July 18th, the RCR engaged the enemy, elements of the Hermann Göring Division, in a fierce battle. When the attack was over, three RCR men lay dead and several were wounded. Later, under cover of darkness, the NCHR passed through the RCR lines. Ralph met Rusty Wilkes and had a quick exchange. Rusty told his friend that he had been caught up in the middle of a firefight and had acted as a runner to seek resupply for the attacking companies. He played down his part in this action, but in due course, the full story came out detailing the gallant role he had played under direct enemy fire. For this, he was later awarded the Military Cross.

At 0300 hours, the NCHR bumped a German delaying force. A group of half-tracks, backed up by three Tiger tanks, had deployed around a narrow gap in the road. Enemy soldiers had dug in on the knolls on either side of the track, and the tanks hunkered, flank down, further up the way. When the initial firing began, the NCHR companies left their vehicles and went to ground. Colonel Morrison quickly gathered his company commanders together in an O Group. Major Jock MacPherson of C Company was leading when the shooting started and gave Morrison a preliminary intelligence report on the situation. The CO determined that a left flanking movement by A Company would hit the enemy positions, B Company would assault from the right, and C Company would advance to the front when the other two companies were in place. "D Company will be in reserve directly behind C. Doctor, I want you to set up your RAP in the gully between C and D. Padre, you locate at the RAP. Gentlemen, I mark the time at 0330," observed Morrison. "Synchronize your watches. You have half an hour to get into position. We kick off at 0400 hours. They will expect our attack at first light, so an early start may give us a momentary advantage. All right, let's do it."

The attack commenced at exactly 0400 with minimal surprise. The German troops immediately returned a hail of fire. Enemy *Spandaus*, directly in front of C Company, laid down interlocking arcs of fire, and flares lit the sky overhead. Crossfire from A and B Companies picked out the muzzle flashes from the entrenched enemy, as C dashed forward with weapons blazing. NCHR mortar platoon dropped rounds onto the knolls on either side of the roadway, and the Germans responded in kind. The air was filled with explosions, and small-arms fire zinged in every direction.

The three Panzers began to move forward along the road, firing their 88mm guns as they came. Corporal McNutty, with Privates Brash and Dolan assisting him, fired a PIAT round at the lead tank, striking the

Tiger's track, and causing the massive machine to slew to the left. Seconds later, McNutty fired a second projectile, which hit the tank where the turret joined the main body. There was a burst of flame, the hatch flew open, and two men, engulfed in fire, tumbled over the side. The roadway was blocked, and the remaining two tanks backed off to find cover behind one of the knolls. Using the dead ground the ditch offered, McNutty and party slithered forward in an attempt to engage the retreating enemy tanks. Suddenly, there was a horrific explosion. The three Canadians had triggered a mine at the side of the road and were blown to bits.

Meantime, A Company circled behind the enemy positions attacking them from the rear. At this point, the German troops rushed to their vehicles, and with the support of their remaining tanks, retreated down the road toward Leonforte.

Dawn broke on the battle scene. A Tiger tank smouldered between the knolls. Wisps of smoke rose from where the Germans had been dug in. A small fire burned in the long, dry grass nearby.

Ralph went forward with the stretcher-bearers to pick up their fallen comrades. Five men were killed and seven wounded, two critically.

"We must push on," Morrison told the after-action O Group. "Padre, you remain behind until the dead are buried. In this heat, the bodies will soon start decomposing. You will mark the grave locations and catch us up when you can."

Members of the pioneer platoon scooped shallow graves out of the rocky soil, and the stretcher-bearers gently laid the four men wrapped in their gas capes into the rough-hewn ground. The pioneers placed a wooden cross at the head of each grave.

"Remove headdress," ordered Sergeant Brad Muchmore, of the pioneer platoon.

Ralph said, "Let us bow our heads.

"Good Lord, we lay to rest four brave men at this battle scene who gave their lives without counting the cost. Accept them into Your eternal keeping for they are sheep of Your flock. Forasmuch as it has pleased Almighty God of His great mercy to take unto Himself the souls of our brothers here departed, we commit their bodies to the ground. Earth to earth, ashes to ashes, dust to dust; in sure and certain hope of the resurrection to eternal life, through our Lord Jesus Christ; who shall change our corruptible body, that it may be like unto His glorious body, according to the mighty working, whereby He is able to subdue all things unto himself. Amen."

A piper, one of the stretcher-bearers, his bagpipe at the ready, began to play. The notes of "Amazing Grace" wafted across the barren hillside followed by a mournful, yet ethereal lament, "The Flowers of the Forest." The sun blazed overhead as the men stood solemnly with heads bent, its rays seeming to reflect a halo on the newly printed crosses. Following the fiery hell of battle, the land was returning to its primitive setting, where hot breezes swept down from the heights, gathering up swirls of dust over the freshly turned earth. This was no Flanders where poppies grew—just an arid, sun-scorched Sicilian field that had suddenly, with the sacrifice of the men from a Canadian highland, become consecrated ground.

In a few months, the sweet taste of things new had turned into throat-parching dust—from birth to death. It was a cycle that would only intensify as Ralph followed his men over the war-torn countryside. Each day the spectre of death might replace the joy of living. Only a sure and certain hope in the Almighty would see him through.

Chapter 7

As the shallow graves were left behind, Ralph slipped into a melancholy mood in the captured German staff car. With him were the driver, Partridge, and Pipe Major Farley. The remaining members of the burial party followed a short distance behind in a Bren-gun carrier. The padre pondered over the kind of letters he would have to write to the families. He had great concern over the one to Mrs. Joe Brash, who attended Trinity Church, Plevna, in his former parish. She was a frail woman who had been widowed three years before. Joe Jr. was her only son. He made these letters of condolence a priority, but needed quiet time to compose them.

He wondered if one could become hardened to this finality. "These are my boys," he mused, "some of them, like Joe, are from my parish." He felt anguish, but knew he had to work through the feelings, or he would become a liability to the men he served. Reason and emotion wrestled within him.

"We are battling an evil enemy. If we don't, who will? What does the Commandment 'Thou shalt not kill' really mean? How can one justify the taking of another man's life? Soldiers are taught that their very existence is predicated upon the need to kill the enemy." Ralph sqirmed in his seat, thinking. "This whole question places the Christian between a rock and a hard place. I must try to resolve this dilemma, or go crazy."

Precisely at that moment, three German soldiers leapt onto the road from behind a large boulder. The first man raised his hand to halt the vehicle, no doubt recognizing it as one of his own.

The driver slammed on the brakes. In that second, the German soldiers realized their error and immediately raised their weapons to bear. The pipe major, sitting behind the padre, opened fire with his Thompson machine gun, firing directly over the top of Ralph's head. All three Germans fell to the ground, their guns flying uselessly through the air to land with a clatter at the side of the road.

Ralph shook his head, dazed, his ears ringing. The others vaulted from the car with their weapons cocked and aimed at the area from where the enemy had descended. There was no movement anywhere. The three men were dead—their blood spilling over the road's surface, their faces contorted in death.

Ralph was stunned.

"It's kill or be killed, Padre," observed Farley, "simple as that. A nasty business, but God help us, someone has to do it!"

Within moments the carrier arrived at the scene. The remainder of the burial party gathered around the bodies.

"You two lads, up the bank a few yards and keep watch," ordered Farley. "The rest of you get your trenching tools out. Looks like we have another burial, eh, Padre?"

Ralph nodded. At the side of the road, one hundred yards further on, he found a flat shelf and marked the proposed grave locations on his topographical map. Personal identification was taken from each of the three bodies, which Ralph would pass to the Graves Registration Officer. The graves in the rocky ground were of necessity shallow, and took only a few minutes to scrape out.

"We can't hang around here too long, Padre, or we might get more unwanted visitors," reminded Farley.

"You're right, Pipey," said Ralph, and taking out his prayer book, he turned to the burial service. Looking it over, he shook his head thinking, "I've just said these prayers over our own men, and now it's the enemy's turn. What a strange, convoluted world we live in. As Pipey just said, 'God help us.'"

The brief committal completed, the two vehicles moved off. A mile up the road a lone aircraft descended toward them and was identified as an American Kittyhawk. It swooped low—passing overhead, then banked sharply left, and began a second pass.

"I don't like the look of this," called Farley. "Let's get out of this 'Gerry' car, and head for cover." He hand-signalled the carrier, and the driver swung onto the verge, with men bailing over the sides. Wisely so, for at that moment the fighter sent a burst of machine-gun fire into the two vehicles. The German staff car burst into flames, as rounds from the Kittyhawk tore into it. The fighter passed overhead once more, but seeming satisfied with his strike, the pilot flew off.

"War has its strange twists and turns," mused Ralph. "First we bury our dead—then theirs. Next we are attacked by one of our own aircraft. What's next?" Ralph wrestled with this as he and the others surveyed the damage. The staff car was destroyed, but the carrier survived. Half the party climbed on board, while the remainder followed on foot.

It took an hour for the party to reach the rear of the NCHR column. The regiment eventually deployed at the outskirts of a small village on the banks of the Dittaino River where the Mortar Platoon was launching bombs into the built-up area. Three German Mark IV tanks occupied the central square, supported by infantry, estimated at company strength, taking up positions in the houses.

Colonel Morrison had issued orders for B Company to put in a frontal attack, while A and D flanked the village to cut off any enemy escape route. C Company, in reserve, would take up position behind B.

Ralph made his way to the RAP where he informed the MO of his recent exploits.

"Now there's a good reason to wear your tin hat, my friend," said Sandy.

"Wouldn't be without it. Sling it right over my heart." Many times Ralph had been admonished to wear his helmet, but preferred his beret, as the heavy headgear gave him a headache.

Shells from artillery support that Morrison ordered up whined overhead and landed in the centre of the village. Two of the enemy tanks were immobilized, while the third retreated in the opposite direction.

A PIAT team from D Company had circled the hamlet to cover the one exit road before taking up a position behind a low stone wall. As the lumbering Mark IV made its way in reverse toward them, a projectile was fired, only to bounce harmlessly off the armoured skin. The turret began to swivel right bringing its main 75mm gun in the direction of the two Canadians.

"Make sure the damn thing is armed this time," Corporal Mickey McQuire, shouldering the weapon, called out, as his teammate loaded the second bomb.

"Fer sure—this time, fire away."

There was an explosion as the bomb hit the tank's track. This was followed a split second later by the tank's answering round, which hit a building behind the two soldiers.

"Get down. Tight to the wall," shouted the corporal.

"Don't have to tell me twice," responded Private John Gunsinger, squeezing tight to the base of the stone structure.

An even greater explosion rented the air, as an artillery shell hit the armoured monster. The ammunition inside the tank ignited, blowing the turret thirty feet into the air.

An enemy MG 45 began to spray the low-lying wall. This weapon was known as "the cheese-cutter" by the Canadian troops. It was a medium machine gun, fast firing and deadly. The PIAT team was pinned down.

Within minutes, a rifle platoon from A Company attacked from the opposite side of the road. House-to-house fighting raged for forty-five minutes, until the last of the German infantry was killed or captured.

Later in the village square, Colonel Morrison held an O Group and received the after-battle report. The engagement had lasted for one hour. Seven NCHR men from B Company had been killed and three wounded. Five dead Germans were found on the objective, with ten others wounded by shellfire. Fourteen surrendered. Three enemy tanks were "brewed up."

"Well done, lads," remarked Morrison. "Take time to get something to eat, then we'll head out again at 1400 hours with B leading, followed by A and D, and C taking the rear. We should reach our stop line by 1800 hours, unless we get held up again. Major MacPherson, I want a scouting patrol out ahead now. Report back in one hour. Doctor, stay behind. That's all."

The Orders Group dispersed, and Morrison turned to the MO. "You said two of the three wounded were hurt badly. How bad?"

"Sergeant Christy was hit in the upper chest by a sniper and suffers from a sucking chest wound," Sandy began. "The top of his left lung was punctured. I've stopped the bleeding, and he is on his way to the Casualty Clearing Station. The CCS is five miles to the rear. Private Cameron took some shrapnel in the lower abdomen. He's in serious condition with bowel damage. I've cleaned him up the best I can, here. The CCS has been alerted, and will be able to do a better job there, unless they ship him directly to the General Hospital. Our third man down, Private Cobb, received an arm wound breaking the humerus. He's splinted up, and is heading down with the others."

"Thanks, Doctor." The CO cocked his head to one side. "The lads really appreciate your skills. I know I do. The NCHR is proud to have you as one of us! I hear the Padre had some fun before he got back."

"Yes, he was a little shaken up by it all—his first time under the gun, you might say. Pipey let loose with his Tommy gun, right over Ralph's head. It rattled him for a while. The Krauts were only twenty-five feet away. It sure gave our chaplain something to think about, but he's fine. He's worked through the initial shock. He calls it his personal baptism of fire!"

Morrison nodded. "Good to hear he's all right. I'll catch up with him later."

The regiment went to ground that night in an apple orchard, some distance beyond the north bank of the Dittaino River. The green fruit hung heavily on the branches; however, this didn't stop the men from sampling a few apples from the uppermost branches, where the apples were closer to being ripe.

"Hey, these are pretty good if you sprinkle a little salt on them," said Private Ed Burrows.

"You may think so, buddy, but I think you're asking for the shits!"

"Naw! We used to eat 'em back home at this stage. You know what they say, 'An apple a day keeps the doctor away!'"

"Well, it's your bunghole that'll need plugging, not mine!"

Ralph smiled as he listened to the banter and thought how resilient these young men were. One minute they're in a firefight for their lives, the next lying on their backs in the middle of an orchard munching on green apples. It was the dog days of summer back home as the padre thought of Ernest fishing for bass in Rock Lake.

"I wonder just how many Rock Lakes there are anyway?" puzzled Ralph, as his mind drifted back to the high ridge country that divided the Ottawa Valley from Lake Ontario. "It seems every township has two or three of them. Why, in the old parish there are three alone—one with speckled trout, one with bass, and the third with yellow pickerel, however they got in there. Bit of a mystery. Normally they like shallow water with muddy bottoms."

"Hey, you seem lost in some pleasant thought," remarked Sandy, as he came up to the padre leaning against one of the apple trees.

Ralph grinned "Oh, just back home doin' some fishin'. Was it that evident?"

"By the way you looked, you had a good one on the line!"

"I sure miss it. What I wouldn't give to dip a line right about now. At this time of evening, the lunker bass are coming up to feed. You ever do much fishing, Sandy?"

Sandy grinned. "Not like you. We used to go for mudcats in the spring using a ball of worms. You ever do that?"

"Sure did. Those little fellows were so delicious out of cold water. Neat how you could skin 'em out in one motion," Ralph reflected. "A mess of them would taste pretty good right about now."

"That's for sure," responded Sandy. "They'd be gourmet compared to the canned junk we're getting these days in the compo rations! I often wonder who dreams up these hard-ration packs."

Ralph chuckled. "Some contractor back home who's probably making a fortune, and splitting it with a politician!"

"Oh, so we're into politics now, are we?" prompted the doctor.

"I think not. Let's go back to thinking of something a little more positive—like fishing!"

"Right! Why spoil such a beautiful evening?"

"I'd like to think of it as the end of another perfect day—but like politics, that's not to be entertained. I've got some difficult letters to write. See you later."

Colonel Morrison called an O Group for 0600 hours the following morning, and gave his instructions. The men of the NCHR had had a good night's sleep for a change. They would need it, as the CO announced that the regiment would move out into the steep hills to the north at 0700 hours.

The 1st Brigade's primary objective was the town of Assoro, located five miles distant on the highest feature in the area. The Germans commanded ideal defensive positions, perfect for observing the adjacent countryside. The NCHR would advance to the left of the wildly winding road into Assoro, proceeding along the goat and sheep tracks clinging to the sides of the steep hills. They were not daunted by the narrow trails, as many of them had cut their teeth on the equally difficult terrain of their highland home, following deer and game runways. Only this time the game they hounded was a cautious, vigilant enemy with weapons that could shoot back.

The open side hills reflected the oppressive heat. The men moved in disciplined silence, watching their footing to avoid sending loose gravel over the steep sides, a noise that would alert any enemy outpost. Ralph chose this day to move forward with B Company, which was on the point of advance. Ayers requested that he travel with the Company HQ element, and not with the lead platoon as the padre wanted, for there was every expectation of encountering stiff enemy resistance along the way.

On one of the trails, they encountered a spring where animals quenched their thirst. A tiny excavation had been dug into the rock-hard ground to provide a basin capable of holding water, where goats and sheep could submerge their muzzles for a refreshing intake. As the men passed, they seemed to genuflect over the water and splashed their scorched faces with the cooling fluid.

Andy Ayers laughed. "Now, if MacPherson could see this, he'd really crow, and swear the regiment had all converted to the 'True Faith'!"

"I bet some of the men might even consider it, if they thought they could escape from this hellish heat," replied Ralph with a grin.

Ayers laughed again. "Said like an Irishman! Are you sure there's no popish blood in your veins?"

Ralph twinkled. "Well now, to tell you the truth . . ."

Shots rang out ahead, and the men leading crouched against the rocky ledge. A runner came back along the line.

"Sir, Mr. Fraser says there's a machine-gun nest up ahead. It's positioned in a walled-up gully overlooking the main road. I don't think we can outflank it, unless we backtrack. There are several buildings behind it—maybe a small farm—probably being used as digs for the enemy. There may be other posts nearby. We're unable to see around the bend. The lieutenant wants a couple of mortar rounds dropped that way."

"I'll call some up. Give me the reference points," demanded Ayers, unrolling his map. The co-ordinates were passed by radio to the rear platoon, where the mortars were being carried. "Tell Mr. Fraser to charge as soon as the bombs hit."

Turning to Ralph, Ayers ordered, "Padre, get your damned helmet on. We may get a shower of falling stones when the mortar rounds hit."

Within moments Ayers' prediction became true. Exploding bombs shattered the sullen silence, followed by small-arms fire, as the lead platoon swung into action. The line moved forward at a fast pace. As Ralph rounded a bend in the trail, he saw that the machine-gun emplacement had taken a direct hit, and the farm cottage was in flames. Enemy soldiers poured from the outbuildings behind the house. Fraser's men engaged them.

"Looks like that solved that problem," remarked Ralph to Ayers. But at that moment, a screaming figure stumbled from the cottage. It was a man wailing at the top of his lungs, holding a small child. The little girl hung limply over the outstretched arms and blood streamed from two stumps of legs shattered above the knees. There was no sound from the youngster. The man rushed forward and dropped the wee thing at Ayers' feet.

The major's face paled. He stood stunned, gazing down at the crumpled, lifeless form.

"My God! My God!" he sobbed as he took in the unspeakable sight before him. He turned to Ralph and tried to speak, but only strangled noises came from his throat. A soldier ran up and covered the small body with a burlap bag.

"Come away, Andy," said Ralph gently, leading the man to a spot where he could sit him down. Although in shock, Ayers' disciplined mind soon clicked in, but not before a volley of shots was heard higher in the gully. Enemy soldiers had found a naturally fortified position beneath an overhang of rock, and decided to take a stand. The cavity in the hill reminded Ralph of a rotten tooth.

Ayers, once again in control, took in the situation and ordered four PIAT bombs to be launched into the rockface above the Germans. As the projectiles struck the decayed formation, it gave way with a roar, and tons of rock and rubble cascaded over the entrenched enemy, burying them and crushing them to death. When the dust cleared arms and legs protruded from the debris. No sign of life was seen or heard.

The men of the NCHR passed through, glancing at the macabre scene, storing it as a photograph in their memories. For Andy Ayers, the imprint would be indelible.

The Hasty Ps took Assoro, perched on the top of the highest height of land in the area. The strategy used to capture the town was brilliant. Under cover of darkness, they scaled the cliffs behind the town, taking the enemy by complete surprise. The Germans, however, had dug in along the serpentine road that led up to the town, where they vigorously fought a losing battle.

The NCHR bypassed Assoro, using the valley to the west, and advanced toward Leonforte. The RCR engaged the enemy on the right, starting huge grass fires that swept with great speed across the low ground and swiftly up the sides of the surrounding hills. It became a hellish inferno that added to the already oppressive heat. The troops, near exhaustion under the scalding sun, continued to bump small pockets of enemy. Brief firefights ensued, but the 1st Brigade pressed on. Leonforte fell to the 2nd Brigade the same day, and orders were received that the NCHR were to lie up for a day before tackling their next objective. They had fought without pause for three days, with courage and determination against exhausting heat, an impossible terrain, with little rest, and against a resolute foe. The troops were weak from fatigue.

The regiment fanned out in a sheltered valley on the north side of Highway 121. A small stream had survived the arid summer conditions and offered several dammed-up swimming holes. The men, some fully clothed, gleefully splashed into the pools. It was a heaven-sent oasis.

Ralph wandered along the banks chatting with groups of men luxuriating in riled-up water. Raucous laughter filled the air, as the soldiers jumped up and down and splashed each other.

"Come on in, Padre. The water's fine!"

"Hey! Join us. There's lots of room!" shouted a man from a crowded hole.

Ralph waved and threw back one-liners to the delight of the rollicking men. They looked so very young to him. The skin of their bodies was milky white, except where it had been exposed to the blistering sun. Their faces, arms and legs below the knees were almost black, as was a deep V of brown at the top of the chest. They were like a bunch of students playing hooky from school, kicking up their heels in the local swimming hole.

Ralph and Sandy's patch of ground was under a gnarled old olive tree that seemed ageless. Partridge and Corelli had erected a makeshift tent for two out of some old canvas they had scrounged. They had placed their officers' gas capes beneath the cover and added a rolled blanket to each spot. In the blankets, they placed a bottle of local wine that they had "found" when the regiment passed through the last small village.

"Are you going for a dip?" asked the doctor, as Ralph approached their shelter.

"I think I'll wait for the water to settle a while. It's stirred up pretty good at the moment."

"Fine idea," responded Sandy. "But first come and see the set-up the lads have made for us!"

"What have they been up to now? I just saw them whooping it up in the stream down yonder."

"Not that they needed a bath."

"No more than we do. I know I smell like something the cat dragged in." Ralph raised his arm to show the sweat stain on his bush shirt. He felt grubby and there were gritty lines on his face where he had been squinting.

"Well, sit for a spell and wet your whistle with a cup of wine," offered Sandy, producing the bottle from his blanket.

The batmen had fashioned stools from olive tree rounds and placed a rough board between two others to fashion a little table.

Doctor and padre found comfortable positions, admiring at a glance Partridge and Corelli's ingenuity, and peacefully sipped wine from tin cups.

"You seem to be in a very reflective mood, Ralph."

"I was just thinking about Andy Ayers. For a moment, I thought he was going to lose it, when that child was dropped at his feet. It was a pretty traumatic experience. He said afterward that it was like a child of his own having the life ripped out of her. Good thing the firefight came when it did—seemed to snap him out of it in a hurry. But, I have no doubt it will be one of the ghosts that will haunt him for the rest of his life.

"I remember later in the day, as we rested inside some ruins where moted beams of sunlight slanted along a crack line in the wall, he said, 'There are times when I see the outlines of the faces of men I have killed in battle. They are vague and ghost-like, dark visages with no definable features. They are never clear, like my own men who have fallen. If I blink my eyes suddenly, a face flashes before me—never a dead face—but one with smiles etched with eager anticipation. More often, though, in dream-drenched sleep, they march along with me, singing a lusty song as we head down the road to another battle. In the ditches, and strewn at roadside, are the bodies of the German dead, many of whom were raised in Christian homes, had families or girlfriends. We passed them by almost heedlessly, for after all, they are the enemy dead. Yet for a moment, time would stand still, and I would feel a shiver in my bones. But to see the lifeless body of a child—that's a far different thing!"

"Now you know why they say, 'War is hell,'" said Sandy.

"Believe it," nodded Ralph. "War is the ultimate obscenity. It is a plague on the human race. How do we avoid it? Some argue that diplomacy is the only alternative to conflict, but diplomacy requires compromise, and how long can that go on? When does compromise become surrender to an abhorrent situation? Is the only answer left armed conflict?" A tinge of evangelism crept into Ralph's voice. "Evil, in the classical sense, is rebellion against all that is good."

"Wow!" exclaimed Sandy. "You're really into it today, my friend. However, if you find the answers, let me know! Right now, all I want to struggle with is this bottle of nectar. I'm too damned tired to be a philosopher at this point—just want to float for a spell."

Ralph sighed, his earlier passion beginning to drain from him. "You're right, Sandy, now's not the time to get into it. But one of these days, doctor, we're going to have a real wrestle with the subject."

"If you say so, pal. Right now, drink up, then we'll go for a swim."

Toward evening, Ralph dug out his writing secretary and wrote a letter to Erin. Their baby was due sometime within the next month. He wanted to support her with encouraging thoughts, but each time he went to pen the words, a vision of the dead child passed before his eyes.

"I guess Andy's not the only one who will be haunted by that mind-searing event," he thought.

Finally, he was able to collect himself enough to write a few light lines and described the swimming hole beside their bivouac.

> My darling,
>
> It has been a few busy days since I last wrote to you, but right now we are camped beside a delightful stream, where the men are able to get into the water and splash around. It reminds me of a place I used to go to when I was a youngster. It was a creek that us kids would dam up to create swimming holes. The guys would skinny-dip there and have a ball.
>
> Sandy and I have just had our turn in the pool beside our "hootchie." It was refreshing to be able to submerge in water and get the pores cleaned out after some dusty travelling.
>
> Our batmen surprised us with an ingenious campsite and some "interesting" vino they had come by. It was pleasant to relax for a while with Sandy and sip the nectar of the gods. We had a great talk about life in general. I wish you could have been here to share it—both the wine and the talk. But then, if you were here, we would send Sandy elsewhere.
>
> You would have difficulty recognizing me at this point, with the dark tan on my face and chest. My face looks a little funny with the white lines radiating from my eyes, where one sqints in the intense sunlight.

You are always in my thoughts, and as I sit here, pen in hand, I wonder how you are feeling, knowing that in a few weeks our baby will be born. How I wish I could be beside you. How I wish . . . but then, as my mother used to say, "If wishes were horses, then beggars would ride!"

My love is with you always. Keep chipper, as your dad would say.

Ralph.

Next, he took time to answer a letter from Ernest, and said how much he wished he could go fishing with him, knowing the bass would be biting madly at this time in July. He asked to be remembered to the folks at Trinity Church, and to assure them he was looking after their boys as best he could.

Night fell and the sky was filled with stars. It was peaceful all around them. The men of the NCHR were grateful for a time of rest and took full advantage of the respite, knowing that with the coming day they would be on the move again. Two weeks had passed since the landings, and in that time they had proved their abilities as soldiers. They had successfully fought battles. They had spilled blood, their own and the enemy's. News had come that the Sicilian Campaign would soon draw to a close, perhaps within a couple of weeks. Only a few pockets of enemy troops remained between Nissoria and the strait of Messina, where the crossing would be made onto the Italian mainland. The men's spirits ran high. Soon the first major objective in the Allies' plan to retake Europe would be theirs. Soon.

As it turned out, the Canadians faced a determined foe on the march toward the coast. It took two more weeks to end the German presence in Sicily, involving bloody fighting between Nissoria and Agira. The RCR were hit heavily and lost a number of their men, including their commanding officer, who fell from mortaring and heavy machine-gun fire. They pushed right up to within sight of Agira, only to be pulled back during a confused period where communications had failed.

Then, it was 2nd Brigade's turn. Led by the Princess Patricia Canadian Light Infantry, followed by the Seaforth Highlanders of Canada and the Edmonton Regiment, they rebuffed stiff German counterattacks and eventually drove the enemy before them in wild disarray. Agira fell on July 28th.

On the 1st of August, the NCHR entered their final engagement before the fall of Sicily. That morning, from a start line one mile short of the town of Regalbuto, the regiment put in its attack. In the low hills west of the town, the Germans had dug in a strong defensive line. Their heavy machine-gun posts were positioned to provide maximum killing ground. Tiger tanks were hull down, in protective embankments, their 88mm guns pointed squarely down range in the direction of the Canadian advance. It was intended to be an impregnable wall, until the Canadian Divisional artillery accurately laid down a dense barrage along the enemy line.

When the rain of Canadian steel ended, C Company led the attack for the NCHR with A Company on their left flank. Both companies were met with withering resistance from the enemy infantry, who had emerged from their dug-in positions. Jock MacPherson's lead platoon was caught in the open and fell before deadly German small-arms and mortar fire. The remaining platoons went to ground. MacPherson, in an attempt to regroup his men, sustained severe wounds and was dragged into a pocket of ground, where fearless stretcher-bearers, ignoring the intense action about them, gathered the wounded.

A breathless runner burst into the battalion command post and collapsed in the entranceway. It took a few moments before he could relay his message.

"Sir, C Company has been hit hard. Major MacPherson and his signaller are badly wounded. Three others in their HQ section killed outright. They took a direct hit from a mortar. There's no radio communications up there. I was sent to get stretcher-bearers, pronto!"

"Right," snapped the CO. "Captain Murray, put a call in to the MO, have the doctor get a medical team ready to go forward. I'll send the runner over to guide them, when he's got his wind back."

Ralph was at the RAP when the message was passed.

"Lord help us," muttered the doctor.

"What's the matter Sandy?"

"C Company has taken the brunt of the attack. They need stretcher-bearers. I've already sent mine to bring the wounded from A Company. I've no one to send."

Ralph thought for a second. "There's a driver outside. I'll take him with me, and we'll do what we can. I'll find a couple more lads up front to help."

"Your call, Padre. Be careful, it's heating up out there!"

Several minutes later the runner arrived from Battalion HQ.

"How close can we get a jeep to the wounded?" Ralph asked.

"About three hundred yards, sir. A rough track snakes up from there through a gully. They're bringing the wounded to a depression at the top end. Trouble is, the Krauts were bracketing the area with more rounds as I came down. There's a lot of shit flying, ah, sorry, sir!"

"I've been in shit before. Let's get going!"

The guide led Ralph and the driver to the small, protected gully behind C Company's position. There was a momentary lull in the battle as they made their way to the top of the ravine, where the wounded were gathered. Corporal Robert Gagnon, a company stretcher-bearer, was rendering first aid to a wounded man who had been just brought in.

"Looks like they've been hit pretty bad," said Ralph as he took in the situation.

"Yeah, real hard," muttered Gagnon with a field dressing between his lips.

Ralph watched feeling helpless. "What can I do?"

"Spend a moment with the wounded. Major MacPherson's in a bad way."

"Right," said Ralph as he made his way to the depression where MacPherson lay.

"Sorry to find you this way, Jock. How are you doing?"

The major was deathly pale. Dressings covered most of his face, his neck, and his upper chest. His hair was matted with blood that still oozed from beneath the bandages. He could see with one eye, and his mouth was slack. He glanced at Ralph.

"Thank God you're here, Padre." Macpherson's voice was strained. "I was afraid I'd bought it without last rites! I know you're not my priest, but would you prepare me? I know we've had our differences, but for the love of God, do me this favour!"

"Of course I will," Ralph assured the man. "But don't give up yet. We're going to get you back. You wait and see!"

MacPherson moaned as Ralph gave him the rites that he had requested. It was not the first time he had performed this act. He and the only Roman Catholic chaplain in the brigade, Father Barker, had agreed to do this for each other, when one of them was absent from the scene of battle.

Ralph then turned to the other wounded and also spoke reassuringly to them. Then, he went over to the dead, made the sign of the cross on each man's forehead, and said a brief prayer. He instructed the others to cover the bodies with gas capes. It was a grisly scene. Several men had been blown to pieces, their body parts gathered and placed on a stretcher—hands, feet, legs and arms.

"These are my boys," Ralph kept saying to himself. "I will remember them as they were: youthful, smiling faces full of fun and laughter. They have paid the supreme sacrifice, Lord, accept them into Your keeping."

"We'll have to see what belongs to who," a battle-hardened soldier said to Ralph. "Better get your fingerprint kit out, Padre!"

"Not now, not yet. We have to get the wounded back to the RAP first. Come along, now. We'll leave the dead here in the gully until the fighting is finished, then we'll come back with a burial party. I've noted the grid reference. Let's move it!"

Macpherson groaned on his stretcher. Ralph, holding the rear handles, tried to reassure the major. "Hang in there, Jock. Just think, if I didn't have you to tussle with, I'd have a pretty quiet war!"

Within moments, the enemy artillery shells began to fall around them. The earth shook.

Scattered thoughts chased each other through Ralph's mind, as the recovery party, in spite of horrendous explosions, kept low and crawled across the rocky terrain toward the waiting jeep ambulances. There was no cover available.

Ralph's mind contiued to swirl with the din. "Strange how hardened one gets after a while. It lasts as long as the sounds of battle are raging. The brain is somehow dulled to feeling with shells flying overhead and exploding nearby."

He realized that only in the penetrating silence that follows action, did the senses seem to awaken to the reality of the carnage. Only then did it hit you, that a few short days ago you had shared a glass of wine with the man lying there, a death mask now contorting his face. Oh, the depravity of war. Ralph hated the stupidity and immorality of it all. The task at hand was terrifying, but he persevered in spite of the howling in his guts and in his head.

The rescuers reached the low ground where the ambulances waited. "Load quickly now, lads," Ralph urged. "MacPherson's passed out from loss of blood; Johnson and the others are pretty desperate, too!"

The MO, covered in blood from his surgeries, stood waiting at the entrance to the RAP as B Company's wounded arrived. Ralph tumbled from the jeep ambulance and briefed the doctor on the casualties.

"Jock seems to be in a bad way. Two others have been tagged with sucking chest wounds—the remainder have varying degrees of wounds, but I fear Private Johnson is not going to make it."

"I'll check him first, as Sergeant Mulligan preps the major," announced the MO.

It was a quick examination, and Sandy nodded to Ralph. "You're right, my friend, nothing more we can do for him, except an injection of morphine. He's in your department, now."

Johnson's stretcher was laid in a tent outside the RAP, where those not expected to live were placed. The boy was from Plevna, and Ralph knew his family well.

"How are you feeling, Jimmy?" asked Ralph, wiping the sweat from the soldier's eyes.

"Terrible! Can't feel my legs! Cramps in my stomach!"

Ralph looked bleak. "I'll get some more morphine for you."

"No, don't leave me, Padre," said Johnson weakly, trying to rise up. "I think I'm a goner."

The chaplain gently laid the soldier back. "Just take it easy, son. Is there anything I can do for you?"

"Will you write to my mom? Will you tell her what happened? Tell her I miss her—and Dad."

"That I will, Jimmy."

"I wish I had been a better son. I gave them a pretty hard time when I was in high school." The boy coughed up blood and whispered. "Didn't study . . . got in with a bad bunch . . . raised hell!" Mucous and blood dribbled from the corner of his mouth.

Ralph bent closer. "They knew you had a good heart, Jim. You just had to get some things out of your system."

"Oh, God, I hurt," wheezed the soldier.

Ralph continued. "I remember talking with them just before I joined the regiment. You had already signed up. They said, 'Look after Jimmy for us. He may be a little wild, but we love him. Deep down, he's a good boy."

"Jesus, Jesus, Jesus . . . help me. Oh, oh, oh . . ."

"I know, son, give me your hand. Now, hang on while we pray. You don't have to say anything. Just let's us be together with the Good Lord."

The two men held hands together for some minutes until Ralph felt the boy's hand go slack. The chaplain looked into the glazed eyes and drew the lids down.

Ralph's throat constricted. "Sleep well, Jim. You fought the good fight. I'll tell your folks I was with you right to the end."

Later, when the battle line moved on, and new forward positions were dug in, Ralph led the burial party back to the gully where B Company's dead lay. Each body was wrapped in a gas cape. The ones with missing body parts were placed to the side, while attempts were made to match pieces with owners. It was such a ghastly task. Shallow graves were dug, and the bodies were lowered into the dusty, etched-out ground. Ralph offered prayers and a piper played a lament. The camera in Ralph's mind clicked, and the scene was indelibly engraved in his memory—a moment to be remembered forever. Ralph consoled himself with the words his father had spoken to him several years before, when, as a young priest, he had first dealt with death and the finality it brought to a family. His father had said, "Death is a fleeting thing, my son. It's simply a chapter in the larger life a man will live in the presence of his Creator."

The following morning, Sandy announced, "Word has just come back from the Field Ambulance that Jock MacPherson is going to make it. He'll be out of action for a while, but every indication is that he will live to fight again."

"Glad to hear it," replied Ralph. "I'd really miss the old bugger, otherwise!"

"I gather the two of you resolved a few differences?"

"There's times when personal stances go by the board. Jock is a devout Catholic. I tried to fulfill the wish of a dying man. Theology had nothing to do with it. It was something between Jock, the Good Lord and me, and I was only a vessel."

"If you say so. I was just talking with the CO. He's going to put your name up for a Military Cross for that job you did yesterday," said Sandy. "How you missed being wounded yourself is a miracle. Only two of you came out of it unscathed."

Ralph blushed and ducked his head. He believed he had only done what had to be done, and had taken little thought for his own well-being. This fuss was embarrassing him.

"There were stretcher-bearers out there that deserve recognition much more than I do," he said.

"There's no question of their valour," said the doctor, "but that's their job. You, on the other hand, are a full-time noncombatant. You're not supposed to be in the middle of a firefight. The driver who took you, and assisted with the recovery of the wounded, will have his name Mentioned in Dispatches."

"You know darn well I have to be with my boys. How else can I minister to them?"

"You can be with them after the battle, you know. After all, if you're killed or wounded, you won't be much use to them. Right?" admonished Sandy.

"Don't give me a hard time, Doctor. I've got to do what I've got to do!"

The MO looked at his friend with admiration, shook his head, and said no more.

The NCHR was ordered to the rear as 1st Brigade reserve battalion on 2 August, and, as it happened, it was Ralph's birthday. It was not celebrated except for a "good night noggin" with Sandy, who toasted Ralph's health and speculated, "I wonder where you will be next year at this time?"

To which Ralph responded, "Probably still in the midst of a bloody war!"

On the 7th, the entire 1st Canadian Division was placed in reserve. The Sicilian campaign was drawing swiftly to an end. Finally, the troops would have a string of days to relax, repair, and mend.

The morning of the 8th of August dawned brightly, heralding another hot day. The NCHR turned out early for a regimental church service. It was a parade, and yet it was not a parade. It was a Service of Remembrance. Even the halt and the lame appeared front and centre from Sandy's RAP group. The pipes marched each company into their position in a hollow square, before the newly constructed flagpole in front of HQ Company location. A dais had been built beneath the flag.

The squeezebox of a field organ had been brought forward from rear echelon, and Jamie Fraser, supported by the pipe band, played familiar hymns, and the men sang with great gusto. Ralph conducted the prayers and gave a short homily on "Sacrifice," reminding his congregation that "Jesus laid down his life that we might live."

Deep feelings reflected on the faces of the worshippers when Colonel Morrison read the names of those who had fallen since the landings on Sicily, eight weeks previously. He spoke briefly of the sacrifice these men had made and how proud he was to serve in a regiment of gallant soldiers. The pipe band played the lament, "Flowers of the Forest." A bugler sounded the "Last Post." Two minutes of silence were observed, followed by the "Arouse."

Before he turned the service back to Ralph to give the Blessing, Scot Morrison called out, "Are we ready?"

And the men answered with the regimental motto, "Aye, Ready!"

Later that afternoon, as Ralph composed a letter to Erin, he reflected on his feelings for her. He leaned back, as his thoughts drifted back to happier times. He could conjure up Erin's face simply by remembering her laughter and the lilt of her voice, with its soft Irish inflections, bequeathed to her by her mother. His wife had that creamy skin and clear complexion so often found in English women. He always pictured her with her shiny black hair unbound, curling down over her bare shoulders, her sparkling blue eyes flashing her love for him. She was his goddess, his Venus.

In the letter, he shared with her what he could, ever mindful of the possibility of censorship, and tried to keep everything light, but was fully aware that she had the ability to read between the lines. She was now late into her eighth month, and her waist would be expanding accordingly. He remembered when she was expecting young Michael, so he had a pretty good idea of how she would look.

He wrote:

> I suppose you would be quite an armful at the moment. How I would love to TRY to get my arms around you. Ah, but that is silly humour. You are right beside me now! You are very real. You must feel my love in return as it fills in the distance between us.
>
> At the moment we are bivouacked in the centre of a lemon orchard. There are new blossoms on some of the trees. I guess the lemon tree does that—bears some fruit and blossoms at the same time. The smell is heady, pungent and sweet. Someday, I will find a lemon orchard in bloom for you, where we can camp under the fragrant trees and inhale the glorious scent. But, the best bouquet for me will always be the scent of your skin.

Ralph wrote two more letters that day—one to his parents, and one to Ernest. He kept this correspondence on the buoyant side, too. His father and mother would be at their cottage on Mazinaw Lake, so he sent their letter to Cloyne Post Office, General Delivery. His dad liked to putter around the log structure in an attempt to make the old cabin a little easier to manage. There was no electricity or running water. The toilet facility was an outhouse, one hundred feet behind the cabin. A trapper, before the First World War, had staked the lot and built the cabin on it. Later, he sold it to Ralph's father, who upgraded it into a family cottage. It was a place the whole family loved, and in a real way, they called it home, for an Anglican clergyman's family was always housed in a rectory belonging to the church.

Ralph wrote:

> Did you get the sand-point down for the new well? That will be some change from dipping water from the end of the dock. I know Mom will be pleased as punch to have a fresh, cool water supply at hand outside her kitchen door. I wish I were there to make a leaping jump off the end of the dock. It's pretty dry and dusty where we are, and a swim would be heaven!

Ralph knew Ernest would be weeding his garden plot, and looking for the first set of tomatoes. If it were hot, he would be drawing water from his spring to sprinkle around the base of his plants. It was a labour of love, and he produced some fantastic vegetables. He always took a ribbon at the local fall fair.

Ralph penned to Ernest:

> How is the new crop coming? In your last letter, you said early July was really dry. I bet the trail from the spring is well-worn by now, and I hope the groundhogs aren't invading your garden. What a nuisance to have to deal with!
>
> The NCHR is camped in a lemon orchard as I write. You wouldn't believe the scent their blossoms produce. It's really refreshing. We are camped here for a few days, and we hope the Sicilian campaign is almost over. Time will tell. Oh, how glad I will be when the whole shebang is over! Who ever first said 'War is Hell' sure knew what he was talking about. It is!

The next day, Ralph had a visitor. His friend Rusty Wilkes, the RCR padre, wheeled into the NCHR lines in an Italian Army Volkswagen that the brigade RC padre had somehow procured.

"We're holding a brigade sports meet in a couple of weeks, and I wonder if you would give me a hand. I think it will give the men a break from chewing up the enemy."

"Sounds like fun! I'd be glad to help out."

"Would you oversee the boxing?" Rusty asked Ralph. "I know you've made a bit of a name for yourself in the ring. I'll judge the tug-o-war. We'll divide up all the track and field events."

"I'll be happy to referee in the ring," Ralph replied. "I'm getting too old to be a contender. Besides, all these young lads are tough as nails. They'd probably knock my block off!"

"Hi, there, Rusty," called out Sandy as he sauntered toward them from across the grove.

"Well, how's the doctor bearing up these days?"

"Fine, now that we've had a bit of a rest. I was just sampling a new cache of vino. Would the two of you join me?"

"Now that I think of it, that trip down the road has made me a little thirsty."

"Follow me!" said Sandy and headed toward the space he and Ralph momentarily called home. Partridge and Corelli saw them coming and had a pretty good idea what was up. They produced some "real" glasses from their "travelling box" of goodies and laid them out on a makeshift table under the blossoming fruit tree.

"Wow! Dig that scent," remarked Rusty as he sat down. "Our lines are in an orange grove. It's nice, but not as fragrant as here."

Sandy laughed. "Try this for an equally delicious taste treat." Then nodding toward the batmen, he said, "I don't know where those two scalawags do their shopping, but they've hit a fine vintage this time."

"Rusty tells me we're going to hold a brigade sports meet," said Ralph. "You're pretty good with the javelin, Doc! Do you think you'll enter?"

"The only thing I want to toss at the moment is this delicious fruit of the vine," replied Sandy. "That's about the speed of my competition. Down the hatch!"

The men laughed as they saluted each other with their glasses.

The meet was touted as the Sicilian Campaign Sports Meet and was held on the 23rd of August, near the town of Militello. The first heats took place early in the morning, with a siesta in the afternoon. The final events were held in the evening, as the air cooled down, relatively speaking, after the intense heat of the day. The friendly rivalry between the units of the brigade sometimes reached a fever pitch, as one-upmanship and unit pride were strongly stimulated. The competition was keen throughout, but was most evident in the boxing matches.

Ralph was scrupulously fair in refereeing the matches, but deep inside cheered madly when one of the NCHR's team was hailed as victor in the heavyweight bout.

It turned out to be a healthy outing for the men of the brigade. Old friends had the opportunity to visit, while others made new ones. A lot of laughter was heard, and many stories were exchanged, both serious and on the lighter side.

Following the meet, a letter from General Montgomery was read:

> The campaign in Sicily is over. We landed on the island on 10 July. By 20 July, together with our American Allies, we had driven the enemy into the northeast corner of the island.
>
> On 30 July I told you we would drive the Germans out of Sicily.
>
> By 17 August, the Germans had been driven out, and the Allied Armies, American and British, were in possession of the whole island.
>
> In February last the Italian overseas empire had ceased to exist.
>
> Today, 17 August, we have captured our first slice of the Italian home country. In these tremendous events, you, the soldiers of the Eighth Army, have played a very notable part. By your splendid fighting qualities, and devotion to duty, you have helped change the whole course of the war.
>
> It is difficult to find the words to tell you my true feelings. Since I assumed command of the Eighth Army in August of 1942—exactly one year ago—you have given me your confidence, and you have never failed to respond to all calls I have made on you.
>
> I thank you all. And I say to you:
>
> WELL DONE. WELL DONE, INDEED. TOGETHER, YOU AND I WILL SEE THIS THING THROUGH TO THE END. GOOD LUCK TO YOU ALL.
>
> Sicily—18 August 1943
> B. L. Montgomery,
> General, Eighth Army.

In this quiet period before the assault on mainland Italy, a number of things happened to affect the daily life of the regiment. First and foremost the men were ordered back to "spit and polish" routine. Webbing was to be scrubbed, brass was to be shone, company drills were held, quarter guards were mounted, and study groups were assembled to address "Lessons learned during the campaign." The sergeant majors turned their full gaze on the troops and looked for indolent or sloppy individuals in need of a tongue-lashing.

Sergeant Major Anderson: "MacDonald, why are you sauntering around like the lazy unkempt piece of baggage you used to be? You're supposed to be an old soldier now, not a new recruit just in from a holding unit."

Private MacDonald: "I was just going to the QM store to . . ."

Sergeant Major Anderson: "Well if you're going somewhere, move smartl,y and while you're at it, sharpen up your dress. LOOK AT ME WHEN I TALK TO YOU, MAN! Your boots are a disgrace. When I see you again, and I will be looking, you'd better be presentable or I'll know the reason why! Do I make myself clear?"

Private MacDonald: "Quite clear, Sergeant Major."

Another major event occurred on August 22nd, when a new draft of much needed replacements arrived—six officers and twenty-three other ranks. Individual company strengths had been depleted, not only by those lost or wounded in battle, but also from malaria and dysentery. The newcomers seemed much younger than the veterans, although the average age for both groups was nineteen. The "old soldiers" took advantage of the newcomers and gave them a rough time for some days, until the pecking order was firmly established.

The CO briefed the new officers and then introduced them to their companies. The company commanders took them in hand and instructed them in plain language: "An officer must be in control, but he must also be wise in handling his men. Get to know your men well. Do not be overly friendly, but let them know you are there for them. Do not hesitate to seek the advice of your platoon NCOs. A leader is one who makes it possible for everyone else to do his job." The new officers took this advice and soon slipped into the routine.

In the mess, the inexpensive Sicilian wine flowed freely. Each officer paid into a mess fund, and from this, extra messing items were purchased, including the wine. Normally officers would dine from their own company kitchens. Evenings in bivouac, however, began with drinks before dinner, a well-served meal of fresh rations, and a relaxing evening together. It was a time of hilarious tales, as well as the telling of real-life situations in battle. Often the "new boys" were strung along, and mercilessly teased for their gullibility.

All too soon the days of respite came to an end. As one young soldier put it, time had come to "kick butt" again. The unit vacated the rest area on the 1st of September, as the units of the 1st Canadian Division were moved to a coastal position a few miles south of the port of Messina. The order to refrain from polishing brass was received with smiles. Spit and polish routine was replaced with the careful preparation of battle kit. Bayonets were sharpened. Weapons were taken apart and reassembled in a well-oiled fashion. Personal gear was gathered and stowed in pouches and kit bags. In the various assembly areas, the Canadian troops made ready for their next adventure—crossing the Straits of Messina and landing on mainland Europe.

The Sicilian Campaign was now history. There was a total of 2,310 Canadian casualties. Forty officers and 522 other ranks lost their lives, and 124 officers and 1,540 men were wounded. Illness and other injuries took 84 more. It had been a severe campaign from beginning to end, where earlier conditioning and youthful resilience won the day. In hindsight, the men recalled the long, gruelling marches in the incredible heat, plagued by thirst, hunger and sunburn. They could still smell the acrid stench of burning grass and the unimaginable reek of dead bodies of both men and animals. Lack of sleep, constant movement and contaminated fruit and water had resulted in fatigue and dysentery, all of which contributed to the wearing down of some troops. But most of all, they remembered their fallen brothers.

Now they were rested and they looked across the straits toward their next objective. It was time to move, and in their minds, they were "Aye, Ready."

Chapter 8

The leap to the Italian mainland was preceded by a dramatic display of heavy artillery, naval bombardments, and air force bombings in the area of Reggio di Calabria. Ralph remembered that this was the same city where St. Paul landed after his shipwreck on the shores of Malta. It gave him that rather elusive feeling that comes when ancient history and modern-day events converge.

The night sky was illuminated with high explosives that reverberated across the water. It was a deadly display of firepower. The 3rd Brigade led the Canadian assault after midnight on September 3rd, and they met little resistance as the main force of the German Army had moved north in anticipation of an invasion in the Gulf of Salerno. The battle plan was for the 1st Brigade to move through the 3rd Brigade as soon as they had consolidated their positions in and around the town of Reggio. 1st Brigade's main objective was an airfield above the town.

The NCHR forming-up place was a dry riverbed some twenty-five miles south of the Sicilian town of Messina. It offered a dramatic view of the Allies' fireworks, as the vanguard of the attack went in. A short distance from where the regiment waited on the beaches, seven landing craft infantry dropped their ramps in anticipation of the next phase of the invasion. It was not until late afternoon that the order to move was given, and the NCHR was embarked.

Ralph boarded the fourth LCI and was invited to view the crossing from the vessel's small bridge. The sea was dead calm, and the sun sparkled off the gleaming blue surface. The Italian mainland could be seen seventeen miles in the distance. Mountains, mainly brown in colour, rose abruptly to a height of three thousand feet inland.

The naval rating at the wheel pointed to Reggio. "Sir, that's where we will land—at the southeast side of the town. We've been advised that there should be little or no resistance. The Hun has hightailed it north."

Ralph raised his binoculars and swept the distant shore. Here and there, he saw clouds of smoke where fires still burned from the high explosives that had raked the area hours before.

The smooth crossing lasted two hours. The seven LCIs reached the shore simultaneously and disgorged their human cargo. Troops dashed across the open beach, over a roadway, and waited at report line Red for the command to advance. The unit met no enemy fire and moved onward at a quick pace, ever watchful for German machine-gun pockets or dug-in infantry. The NCHR crossed open fields toward their objective at the east end of the airport runway and found that the Royal 22nd Regiment, of the 3rd Brigade had taken the airfield. The "Van Doos," as they were known, had taken the landing strip with little opposition from the enemy.

Light fighting continued through the month of September, as the 1st Canadian Division made its way from the toe of Italy across to the heel, thence northward along the Gulf of Taranto to Rotondella. The Canadians then turned inland, capturing the town of Potenza on the 20th of September, and continued forward to Foggia after touching the Adriatic coast. Resistance was sporadic and concentrated in small rearguard pockets where dirty little fights occurred, but the Canadians were not to be deterred. The Germans engineers systematically blew bridges and destroyed rail lines as they retreated north.

Foggia fell on the 27th of September, and after a ten-day rest, the 1st Canadian Brigade moved forward. The NCHR was ordered to dig in on the side of the town where Highway No. 7 headed west. The position on the outskirts of town made it readily accessible to the troops. A few men slipped away in an attempt to find some nightlife, but were soon routed back to their lines by regimental police.

In the early evening of the 30th of September, Ralph gathered some men together for an impromptu Eucharist in the chapel of an old monastery. The ancient ruins were open to the sky, but the place seemed to contain an air of special reverence. Rain had fallen in the morning, and the grass floor gave off a sweet bouquet. Quiet inhabited the place, except for a family of birds that had taken up residence in a niche above a collapsed arch.

Partridge erected a small table where Ralph laid out his communion ware. The soldiers stood in a semicircle around the makeshift altar. They were a weary lot, but they stood relaxed and shared in the responses of the Holy Office. Their faces were in repose, and the light of faith was reflected in their eyes. Many of them were thinking of home and their families gathered in their little churches across a particular highland ridge in Eastern Ontario.

One soldier had said to Ralph, just prior to the opening sentences, that he felt closest to his wife and children when he took his communion. "It's as if they were right here beside me—as if I could reach out my hand and lay it on my daughter's head."

"I feel the same," added another. "There's that part of me that is never very far from them. I guess that's what you'd call spiritual togetherness, eh, Padre?"

"Remember the words of Jesus when he said," Ralph replied, "'Where two or three are gathered together I will be there in the midst of them.' I'm sure that not only means we few who are here, but also our loved ones who pray for us at home. It's the strongest of bonds, don't you think? I know, as I celebrate the Communion Service, that I enfold my family in my prayers. It is a precious moment for me, too."

It was at this precise time in the village of Bewdleigh that Ralph's daughter decided to make her appearance. Erin counted the minutes between contractions. Julia was on her way to care for Michael, who was looking forward to spending a few days with the Pride family.

Julia knocked on the door and entered the vicarage. "Hello, Erin," she called.

"I'm in the kitchen preparing Father's lunch. Can I get you anything?"

"You come and sit down, let me do that. Are you ready to go?" asked Julia.

"Right-o! Not quite time yet, but soon."

"How many minutes apart?" asked an anxious Julia. "Are you down to five yet?"

Erin bent over clutching her abdomen. "Oh! Oh! The water just broke."

"All right, my girl, off we go! Where is your father?"

"He's over at the church," gasped Erin.

Julia headed for the door. "Rest there for a second, and I'll fetch him to look after Michael, while I whisk you to the hospital."

"Yes, get him, but he might want to take me," Erin responded, as she dabbed at the birth fluids with a towel.

"We'll see! You get ready. I'll be right back," called Julia as she rushed out.

She met the vicar as he was coming from the church. "It's time, Vicar. Your new grandchild is on the way. I can take Erin in, if you wish."

"No, that's fine. I want to be there for the birth. You take Michael."

"I will. We'd better hurry, now, Vicar!"

The little girl was born at 5:47 p.m. on the 29th of September, weighing eight pounds, three onces. She was named Miriam, a name Erin and Ralph had earlier agreed upon. The little one squealed, until the nurse laid her against Erin's breast.

"She is so beautiful," declared Erin. "How her father will adore her!"

News of the birth reached Ralph the evening before the forward elements of the NCHR were to enter their most difficult battle to date—the advance to the Triolo River.

Dawn broke cold and damp on the 1st of October. The advance guard moved out, the 4th Princess Louise Dragoon Guards leading. The Calgary Tank Regiment followed with the Royal Canadian Regiment as infantry support. The NCHR took the reserve position at the rear of the mainguard.

At 0830 hours, the lead tanks came under fierce small-arms fire, as they approached the hilltop village of Motta. They could only approach by a winding switchback road that offered no cover. One tank broke through into the town, only to be "brewed up" on entrance. The advance was halted, while a more careful forward reconnaissance was made. Finally, B Company of the RCR, under the command of recently promoted Major Strome Galloway, was ordered into the fray. He sent two platoons into the attack, with support from a squadron of tanks, and co-ordinated artillery barrage on the town. The infantry came under withering fire from both flanks and was pinned down. The RCR faced the crack German 1st Parachute Division, which was well dug-in—vowing not to surrender. It soon became evident to the RCR that B Company was not strong enough to take the objective. Darkness fell, and the lead platoons were reinforced by A Company of the same regiment.

The NCHR was ordered forward and given the task of making a right flanking movement around the town, with instructions to secure a bridge across a tributary of the Triolo River, a few miles west of Motta. This objective, when taken, would cut off an enemy withdrawal. In the dead of night, A and D Companies made their move over rolling ground that was difficult to traverse. Much energy was expended crossing the muddy low ground, as wet clay stuck to the men's boots in clumps. By first light, the two companies were near to collapse. They pushed on, and suddenly A Company found themselves stranded in the middle of a minefield. They realized that with the coming light they were fully exposed to enemy machine guns firing from either sides of the vale and were extremely vulnerable to mortar bombs now falling about them. The situation soon became chaotic, as men fell where they stood. D Company attempted to come to A Company's relief, only to find themselves pinned to the ground by a large force of entrenched German infantry. A clever trap had been sprung on the Canadians giving them no chance for reprieve.

The RCR, meanwhile, entered the town of Motta under heavy fire and sustained casualties. At 2330 hours, a torrential rain began to fall, putting a stop to the street fighting. The Germans pulled out under cover of the weather and took up previously well-prepared delaying positions on three hills one-half a mile from the town, a short distance from where the NCHR lead companies were floundering.

At first light, two RCR companies attempted to break through to relieve the NCHR men, but were forced to withdraw under an intense German artillery barrage. A section of Canadian tanks from the CTR were destroyed. The hellish conflict raged all day, and when night fell, the deadlock continued.

Throughout the day, Ralph had located himself with C Company, under Captain Dusty Rhodes' command, several hundred yards behind D Company's support position. Ralph could hear the desperate radio communications between the forward companies and Battalion HQ. Canadian Artillery came into play during the morning, but was unable to break the enemy's hold. Aerial bombardment was considered, but never initiated, as the lines between friend and foe were unclear.

Late in the afternoon, Ralph overheard a radio call from Tom Nugent in A Company.

"Major Stokes has been killed, and I am taking over. Those still living have scraped out shallow, muddy slit trenches that are gradually filling with water. Some of the wounded have been gathered into shell craters. We're in pretty bad shape. I took a hit to my left leg. We're out of drinking water. Can we get relief after nightfall?"

"Hold in there. We'll do our best," answered the battle adjutant.

Darkness fell, but the fire persisted in bursts. The enemy sent up flares and swept the exposed areas with machine-gun fire.

"My God, it's like trying to breach the gates of Hell," said Rhodes, as a patrol that he sent forward was hit hard.

The radio set rattled a partially garbled message in the clear.

"C Company, this is Sunray. Do you read me?"

"You're breaking up, sir, but send your message."

"Can you get stretcher-bearers forward to retrieve A Company's wounded?"

"There's a party on the way, but it's still hot out there. Those German paratroopers are firing at anything that moves."

"Right! Do your best. Is the padre up there with you?"

"That he is, sir; he's leading the SBs into A Company's position."

"The hell, you say!"

"What was that, sir?"

"I said, what's he trying to do? Get himself killed?"

"He's got a plan, sir. He's mounted a Red Cross pennant on a stick and plans to hold it up if his party comes under fire."

"My God, he must be crazy. Order him back."

"I think it's too late, sir, they've gone beyond our perimeter."

Rhodes checked his watch, as Ralph, with nine men, crawled forward on their stomachs dragging stretchers. There was a lull in the action. Ten minutes later, at 2120 hours, a German flare lit the sky, and shots rang out. Rhodes saw Ralph rise up with the Red Cross pennant over his head. The shooting stopped. Nine other figures rose from the ground carrying stretchers to follow their leader across the killing field. Another enemy flare turned night into dim day. The rescue party continued forward, until they reached the wounded, loaded them on stretchers, and turned back. This time a Canadian flare gave light to the field. Three times the party returned to pick up the casualties, and on every trip, each side alternately flooded the area with light. It was a miracle in progress, and the audacity, the sheer bravery of the incident, was engraved on the minds of friend and foe alike.

The recovery party began its fourth sortie across the open ground, but had only moved a few feet past C Company's perimeter, when the whir of German 88 shells filled the night. Ralph and the men with him flattened themselves against the soggy earth. As they crawled back, the night was once again filled with deadly fire. The unbelievable lull in the fighting had only lasted for an hour, but in that time, fifteen seriously wounded men had been saved from certain death. A couple more hours of exposure and wounds unattended to would have led to their demise.

In response to the enemy guns, the Canadian Artillery sent shell after shell into the German positions. The Gunners' forward observation officer had relayed to his batteries precise co-ordinates, and their accuracy finally broke the enemy's stranglehold. B and C Companies of the NCHR moved forward to relieve A and D. In the morning light, the tanks of the PLDG and the CTR, supported by RCR infantry, swept the entire area clear of enemy resistance.

Ralph worked in the RAP assisting Sandy with the wounded. Private Smitts, a lad who had fought with vigour right from the landings at Pachino, was curled up in the fetal position.

"What is Smitts' problem?" Sandy asked his medical sergeant.

"No visible wounds. Looks like he's shell-shocked. They found him crouched in a slit trench after the battle. Didn't seem to be able to move," responded Mulligan after examining the man.

Sandy nodded. "Perhaps you could reach him, Padre?"

"I'll try."

Ralph began talking quietly to the soldier. There was little response. The man was shaking and uttering unintelligible sounds. He had freckles across his nose and looked more like thirteen than twenty-one.

"You'll be all right, son," said Ralph. "Just try to take it easy. The morphine will soon take effect."

"I'm a damn coward," muttered the man, his eyes tightly shut. He was shaking uncontrollably.

"What makes you think that?" asked Ralph, placing a comforting hand on the soldier's shoulder. "You've done your part all along the way. I've heard your sergeant say more than once, that he could always trust Smitts to get the job done."

"B-b-but I froze. Couldn't move for fright." Smitts shook Ralph's hand from his shoulder.

"There's nothing wrong with being scared. Anyone tell you he's not scared from time to time isn't being truthful. In fact, being scared is a very healthy thing, if you let it be. You can make it work for you."

"You ever been afraid, Padre?" asked the voice, a little stronger this time.

Encouraged, Ralph responded. "If you had to wash my underwear, you'd know the answer to that one, my friend. But I'm being foolish. Of course I've been frightened—a good many times. God only knows we're in a frightening business! But we're in it together, and together, we'll see it through. Take it easy. Everything's going to be all right."

Colonel Morrison entered the RAP, his face showing displeasure. He confronted his chaplain. "I don't know whether to have you court-martialled for what you did last night, or recommend you for another citation! Where did you dream up that hare-brained scheme? You could have gotten all those men, and yourself, killed on the spot."

"I felt sure it would work, sir. Good soldiers—even enemy ones—know what the Red Cross stands for, and I believe that the German parachute unit is made up of the best. I think I was proven right, even though at the end, some Nazi officer probably ordered the shelling."

The commanding officer could no longer glare. A hint of a smile cracked the corner of his lips. "Now, I've got to write the damn thing up. Sometimes you're a real burden to me, Padre!" He turned to the MO. "How are the wounded coming along, Doctor?"

"I'm afraid we've lost quite a few. A Company has fourteen killed and thirty wounded. D Company is better off—eleven killed and seventeen wounded. There would have been a lot more lost if it hadn't been for Padre Russell's initiative."

"You're right, Doctor." Morrison turned to Ralph. "We'll done, my friend. Just don't get yourself killed!"

Later in the morning, Ralph returned to the small vale where much of the action had taken place the night before. He accompanied the pioneer platoon whose job it was to dig the graves. A grisly sight presented itself. Bodies were strewn everywhere across the bloodied ground. It was as if a giant hand had crushed the men who had dared enter this glen. They lay at grotesque angles, some with missing body parts, others curled up on the ground, as if they had simply fallen asleep.

"Padre, we've selected a spot on a gradual slope where the rainwater can drain away from the graves," said Bradley Muchmore, the pioneer platoon sergeant. "Will you check it out to see if it's suitable?"

"It looks good," Ralph observed. "I'll mark the grid reference in my field-message pad. We'll bring the dead from D Company's position and lay the lads here together. I'll let the MO know of our plan, and he can send the remains of those who died at the RAP. In all, we'll have twenty-five graves."

When the party laid the last body, wrapped in a gas cape, to rest, it was late afternoon. White wooden crosses, each inscribed with name of the fallen, were placed at the heads of the graves. A piper played his lament in the background, as Ralph read the burial office.

Solemnly, the pioneers picked up their tools and loaded them onto a waiting vehicle. Ralph and Partridge remained behind as the others departed the site.

"How many have we lost now, Padre?" asked Partridge.

"I've honestly lost count. I'd have to check my records for totals—too many, I fear. This was our worst loss, yet."

Ralph walked down the line of graves once more—remembering. There were several lads from his old parish whose families he knew well, and he could imagine their reaction to the news. "No different than most families," he thought, "only these are really close to home. They'll be the hardest letters to write."

Ominously, the sound of battle began to rage again to the west. It was time to return to the living.

The Canadian front moved forward toward Campobasso, the town that was reported to be the HQ of Field Marshal Kesselring, overall commander of the German forces in the area. The Germans planned to stall the advancing force, and then rapidly withdraw to the next high ground where they would once again form a line of resistance.

Wet fall weather had set in. The driving rain turned the low ground into water-soaked quagmires, and it was difficult slogging for the Canadian Division as they pushed westward toward Campobasso. It took two weeks to advance twenty-five miles, and on the 13th of October, 1st Brigade stood before the ancient town of 17,000 people. A thirteenth-century citadel dominated the provincial capital, rising to a height of 350 feet.

The initial assault on the town became the task of the RCR, with the NCHR poised to pass through, once positions were consolidated. The attack began at 0530 hours, and by nightfall, the entire 1st Brigade occupied Campobasso. There was little resistance.

Signs of serious fatigue began to show on Ralph's face. He had a deep chest cold that persisted. Sandy watched him closely for several days before confronting his friend.

"Hey, Ralph, you look as if you need some down time. You look all in!"

Ralph suppressed a cough. "Oh, it's just the weather, I guess."

Sandy reached for his stethoscope. "I think it's more than that. Let me listen to your chest."

"Didn't get much sleep last night. It was my time to ride the nightmare again—ghoulish scenes bombarded me. I kept wrapping a lad in a gas cape for burial, and he was screaming at me, 'Don't bury me! Don't bury me!' When I frantically untied the shroud, there was only a poor grey lifeless lad lying there. I would turn away then, but before I could move, there were more bodies around me all crying, 'Don't bury me!' I awoke in a cold sweat . . . Can't seem to get warm these days. With all the rain, my clothes seem wet all the time."

The doctor looked Ralph in the eye. "How long have these dreams been going on?"

"Since Motta—that was a depressing time for me, burying those twenty-five brave young lads."

"I'm going to give you some medication to help you sleep. I think you're exhausted. We'll talk again in the morning."

"I don't need any pills."

"You're going to take them, 'cause that's what the doctor's ordered. Either that . . . or I'll have to speak with the CO."

Ralph gave Sandy a dark look. "You wouldn't do that, would you?"

"You're damn right I would. If you're not going to look after yourself, someone has to!"

Ralph took the medication and slept soundly for the first time in weeks.

In the morning, the doctor sat beside the padre's cot. "I think it's time we had a long talk. I've noticed you've been going downhill recently. Normally, you're walking around with a big grin, cheering up everyone you meet, and often it's your sense of humour that carries an otherwise bad day. Lately you're going about like a dark cloud. What's it all about?"

Wearily, Ralph slipped his legs over the side of his cot. "I guess since our show at Motta, I've been doing a lot of thinking. There are times when I feel so helpless. For instance, I was talking with Wally Stokes, OC of A Company the day before the battle, and he was saying to me, 'Padre, I've got the feeling my number is up! Something's going to happen real soon.' And I said to him, 'Oh, come on, Wally, we all have those kinds of premonitions.' He said to me, 'Yeah, you're right, but say a little prayer for me anyway, will you?' I said I would, but nevertheless the ghosts of war drag at my heels, and cause me some painful reflection."

Sandy jerked his head. "Ah, the portent of things to come! It's an interesting phenomenon. It gives me the heebee-geebees, especially when a man is dead serious. One can't make light of it—superstition or not—the feeling is real, and deserves respect. Poor old Stokes, God rest his soul."

Ralph nodded back. Sandy continued. "You're well aware that the work of the chaplain is primarily spiritual. You pray for the men as they enter battle, then, when it's over, much of your time is consumed in dealing with their death—the burials, the letters home, the loss of comrades and the battle-weary. Some of these youngsters were kids in your former parish. So, you get a double jolt. It's a terrible task, but you have handled it better than most, I suspect. You have to let go of them, Ralph—it's the only way you can survive. I've learned that only too well as I try to resuscitate some poor kid with his lungs half blown away. Do you follow me?"

"I'm with you, Doc. In other words, I'd better get a grip on things!"

"Right you are. I wonder if I'm preaching to the converted when I say sometimes the pulling up of one's bootstraps could use a little bit of divine intervention. Bring it to the attention of the Man upstairs. After all, He's your Boss! Forgive me, I'm being somewhat facetious."

"Not at all. I respect your opinions, but like all sinners, I sometimes forget to do the most obvious. Thanks, Sandy! I think I need to be by myself for a while. At least we're up for a few days' stand-down. That'll give me time for reflection, and get rested up."

The farmhouse had thick, rock walls, plastered with a mixture of straw and clay and finished with whitewash. A low, fieldstone wall surrounding a courtyard was covered with mounds of trailing vines, still bearing a few late-blooming flowers. The original foundations dated back two thousand years to Roman times and the dawn of Christianity. The house, or *casa,* as it was called, had been spared from damage and was now being used as Battalion HQ, while the farm family occupied one of the outbuildings. Ralph selected a grassy area surrounded by flowerbeds as the ideal location to celebrate his Eucharist. The silver leaves of the olive trees rustled in a gentle breeze. A variety of late-blooming flowers held their heads high seeking the sun. The sky turned a bluish-grey as the sun drifted downward over the valley. A row of cypress trees cast long shadows across the buildings.

Late in the afternoon, Ralph erected a six-foot folding table and covered it with communion linen on which he laid out the Eucharistic vessels. Jamie Fraser pumped on the field organ. The instrument had become a little wheezy with the punishment it had taken bouncing over the rough roads, yet the music was recognizable and wafted down the slope to the valley below, where the regiment was bivouacked. After weeks of steady advance to contact and running fights, the NCHR had helped push the Germans higher into the mountains. Now, for a few days they were enjoying respite in this green and pleasant place.

Ralph could see a number of men climbing the gentle slope toward his location. They had cleaned up and put on fresh battledress; it was standard operating procedure for the troops to turn out with "spit and polish" as soon as they were out of the line. Sergeant majors looked for it, and commanding officers demanded it. It was part of the good order and discipline expected of soldiers.

Ralph studied their faces as they came closer. Some were kidding around and laughing, while others approached more soberly, deep in their own private thoughts. How he respected and admired these brave men. He was proud to be their chaplain. He had seen their feet of clay, but he had also witnessed their dedication and loyalty, elevated to the highest level, when they faced a determined foe.

Ralph addressed the gathering. "Thank you for joining me for this time of worship. We'll have a short divine service, followed by an Anglican Eucharist. All are more than welcome to take their communion. Those who do not wish to stay may depart during the second hymn."

Ralph was a thoroughly ecumenical priest. Although he might not agree with the many shades of religious expression that he encountered, he was at least willing to try to understand other Christian doctrines. He saw all the men of the NCHR as members of his "extended flock." Not that he would proselytize—that suggestion was abhorrent to him. He accepted the men for who they were and saw them all as God's children, from whatever background they came, Christian or otherwise. Within the regiment, he was their padre, their spiritual leader—except for a handful of bigots who were self-proclaimed atheists. But Ralph would reach out to even these, if he found them in need. The padre possessed simple, but firm, beliefs.

His communion services were open to all faiths. There were occasions when several members of the Jewish faith would attend his services, knowing full well that the padre served God in the Judeo-Christian tradition. They would quietly recite their Hebrew prayers as they shared in the larger worshipping community. Whenever it was possible to locate clergymen of other denominations, Ralph would do so to provide services for devout men of that particular church body. The men knew this and respected him for his wider concerns.

Ralph was a good preacher. His sermons were short and to the point. The text he chose for this service was on the dimensions of God's love for his people. It was taken from Paul's Epistle to the Ephesians: "That you may have the power to understand how broad and long, how high and deep, is Christ's love."

Ralph began:

"In the table that is set before us here in this garden we see the love of Christ displayed.

"It is a very broad table. The Gospel tells us how Jesus moved among all sorts and conditions of men and women. Rough fishermen, city lawyers, down-and-outs, young and old, rich and poor, Pharisees and soldiers, men and women. He didn't go around carefully selecting his acquaintances like a 'redneck' rejecting those 'who are not our kind.' He welcomed each individual as a member of God's great family on earth. This is His table and there is no social class system found here. King and commoner kneel as one.

"It is a very broad table, yes, and a very long table. It is a table set before us this morning, but it stretches back through the years for each one of us. For some it is a little white clapboard country church like the one in Plevna perched on a hill among the pines where some of you took your first communion. For others it may be a larger church in a town like Perth, or a cathedral like St.. George's, Kingston. Others find it at a bedside where a family gathers near a dying loved one. Yes, it is a table as long as our memories and much longer than that, stretching back through the centuries to the Upper Room where Jesus first broke the bread and passed the cup of wine saying, 'Take this, in remembrance of me.'

"Truly it is a broad table, and a long table, but it is also a very deep table. For many of us our Christianity is very shallow. We talk about fellowship, but how much of this happens outside the door of our churches back home? A handshake here, a nod there. How different was Jesus' love for his fellow man. It was so all encompassing that he went to the cross for you and me.

"There is a marble sculpture somewhere here in Italy, I am told, of Mary Magdalene. You know how she is usually portrayed as a beautiful young woman. The sculpture I refer to takes a different view of her. Instead of picturing her as the ravishing young girl, the victim of her own beauty and the lusts of men, it shows her as a disease-ridden old whore. And yet the artist has skilfully imprinted on her face the dawning of recognition, that even in the depths to which she has fallen, Jesus still loves her. The table of the Lord is the depth to which Christ's love will go for me and for you.

"A broad table, certainly, and a long one, too, but a very deep table. And finally, this table to which we are invited is a very high table. This is good symbolism because it reminds us that even beyond death a heavenly banquet is laid for us. Now as the bread and wine is offered to you—take, eat, in repentance and faith and join yourself to Him who is your shepherd who walks with you every time you enter the valley of death. That you may better understand what is the breadth, and length, and the depth, and the height of His Table of Love. Amen."

Everyone stayed until the end. Each man, in his turn, accepted the thin wafer of unleavened bread and sipped from the chalice. Each face seemed to soften a little and take on a less cynical look. For that moment at least, a peaceful serenity settled over the battle-weary soldiers.

In the evening, the officers gathered in their mess. They stood around in twos and threes with drinks in their hands, chatting about recent events. The CO took Sandy aside and enquired specifically about Ralph.

"Our padre seems somewhat down these days, Doctor, is there something in particular I should know about?"

"Nothing he won't be able to handle, sir, a bit of chest infection, is all. He's tired like the rest of us."

"I think you should know, Sandy, that if it weren't for the stingy policy on the awarding of decorations in this division, I would try to get Ralph a bar to his MC. He went far and beyond the call of duty for the way in which he handled that situation near Motta, but I know it wouldn't be approved. God only knows how many of our men deserve awards and have been refused. They are a valiant breed. They watch over their comrades with little regard for themselves. I am honoured to be their commanding officer."

"Truly, sir, Ralph doesn't concern himself over decorations for himself. Believe me, he's very shy in even discussing his MC. He says that the stretcher-bearers who helped him in that situation deserve just as much recognition as he received."

"He's right, of course, Sandy. Your medical support teams, the stretcher-bearers from the companies, are the very best. I wish we could do more to acknowledge this."

Later, in their tent, Sandy communicated the gist of the conversation.

Ralph listened as he stared up at the canvas roof. "Those were generous words of the CO. But you know, and I know, we are not out here to win medals. We're here to do a job and get as many home as possible. That should be our focus."

The rest period lasted for three days, time enough to "make and mend." The brigade's mobile laundry and bath unit provided an opportunity for the NCHR to have a thorough cleanup. The men lined up gleefully for showers and were put through the stalls a platoon at a time. Clothing was laundered, and new kit was issued where needed, especially in the footwear department. It was a rare treat, for in days on the move, there was little chance for proper hygienic procedures, or clothing changes. For a short time at least, the men would be well scrubbed and feel like proper human beings.

Partridge and Corelli were kept busy taking care of Ralph and Sandy's needs. They took pride in finding the best of creature comforts available, and usually had a supply of quite palatable wine at hand—sometimes downright delicious.

"Where did you find that vino, Corelli?" asked Sandy as he smacked his lips.

The batman's face broke into a huge grin. "You know that farmhouse where the padre had his service? Well, the little old grandmother who lives there with her family gave me three jugs and told me to see that the nice 'Father' had some for his supper. I told her I looked after the doctor, and she said 'give him some too!' Well, Partridge and I sampled it . . . just to be sure it was good. And it is!"

"So, I guess the padre and I get two bottles and you guys get one?"

"Ya, it's kinda like that . . . but we had to be sure it wasn't sour, right?"

"Of course, and we're glad to share a drop with you lads," said Ralph. "You take good care of us!"

The two batmen did their best to do just that—take care of their two officers, even after fall had turned to winter, and the seemingly non-stop rain made every gully and creek a deluge of raging water. Partridge and Corelli took every precaution to keep their charges and their belongings dry. This was not an easy task. Care had to be taken to avoid areas where ditches overflowed, especially near towns or villages where open sewers slopped out into the countryside. These shallow defiles, falling away to lower ground, were catch-basins for a summer's worth of human waste and garbage, and the winter rains swept the foul-smelling filth away on the crest of the spate.

The two men had learned this lesson the hard way, for on one occasion, when the first heavy downpours came, they had set up their officers' tent on a lush grassy surface at the bottom of a ravine. Soon, water laden with waste from a small village higher in the hills was gushing down the gorge. The tent acted as a straining device for capturing the fouled liquid, and everything inside became a stinking mess. Fortunately, personal gear had not arrived from the rear echelon when this disaster struck, but nevertheless, the two lads became the brunt of jokes from their peers and became known as the "honey catchers."

October, wet and dreary, rolled into an equally damp and cold November. Minor operational roles had units of the 1st Canadian Division challenging enemy pockets in the Daunia Mountains and the high Abruzzi Range. The men of the NCHR were encouraged by the buzz that they would be in Rome by Christmas. It was dirty slogging, but the advance continued to progress slowly. On the 1st of December, the 1st Division was pulled back to the Foggia Plain and moved along the Adriatic coast in the direction of Ortona, where it replaced the battered British 78th Infantry Division. The latter had sustained heavy casualties in a grim battle against the entrenched Germans, who were ordered to hold their positions unto the death.

Ralph travelled with Sandy in his jeep. The chaplain was wrapped in his greatcoat with a blanket around his shoulders. He had a rasping cough and looked haggard.

"Your condition isn't improving, my friend. Sorry I can't do more to help!" said the MO.

"I'll be all right. Seems the cold's right in my bones today . . . just want to sleep."

Sandy nodded. "Know the feeling. Settle back and rest."

"Right, Doc! How does anyone rest with you driving . . . trying to dodge every pothole?"

The MO grinned. "At least you haven't lost your sense of humour, yet."

"I'm trying," said Ralph, as he pulled the blanket over his head.

As the NCHR passed through the British lines in the middle of a foggy night, a British voice was heard in the blackness.

"Blimey, if it ain't the Canadians!"

There was a pause.

Then another Brit piped up. "'Ow did ya leave our wives back 'ome?"

Again, a pregnant pause.
Then a distinctively Canadian voice replied.
"Satisfied!"

On the 1st of December, the NCHR took up positions overlooking a village on the Moro River. Orders came down from brigade to send a reconnaissance party across the river to identify the enemy units and to try to determine their strength. Colonel Morrison convened his O Group and laid out a plan for the mission. The intelligence officer, Lieutenant Bill Murray, would cross into enemy territory with one of his men, the cool-headed, German-speaking Private Joe Mertz. Murray had some Italian, enough to make casual conversation, but an anti-fascist Italian schoolteacher, Marcello Rossi, had volunteered to assist the Canadians. He agreed to guide the recce party across the river, and during the daylight hours would wander through the village gathering information.

Twenty-four hours later, Ralph was in the battalion command post when the men returned from their patrol. They gave a concise intelligence report that was quickly relayed to brigade. Later, over a cup of medicinal rum, Bill Murray told the larger story.

"The night was pitch-black when we made our move. We covered our faces with camouflage grease, and pushed the inflatable boat out into the fast-moving water; our Thompson machine guns were slung over our shoulders. We found it necessary to make our way upstream, as the current was strong, and then, on the other side, we hid the boat beneath some overhanging branches. Our first objective was a house not far from the river's edge. Rossi, who knew the family that dwelt there, had selected it as a safe place to hole up and use as a base. We planned to spend a full day on the enemy side to gather as much information as possible—determining German troop positions and manning numbers." Murray grinned, "You might say the mission was dangerous—with capture a real possibility, but by this time, it was just another recce job that had to be done. We knew that getting back might be 'fun.' If all went well, we would give three blinks with a flashlight on the following midnight, and this would signal the guys on our side to cover us if things went wrong.

"When we got to the other side of the river, we were carried several hundred yards downstream from our selected landing point, as the current was stronger than anticipated. We soon found our bearings, as Rossi knew the ground well. Within ten minutes, we reached the house, but no one answered the door, so we forced our way in to find the Quattrocchi family huddled in a back room. After a few minutes, Rossi made it clear that we were not there to hurt them, but needed their assistance. Once assured, they did their best to supply us with information and told us we could observe the Germans from an upper room. The Krauts relieved their night watch at 0500 hours and we would be able to identify from the window where their defensive positions were dug in." Murray paused to light a cigarette.

"We took turns sleeping for the next four hours in the room upstairs, and at 0445 hours, we began to watch from the window. Precisely at 0450 hours, two squads of soldiers formed up in front of a three-storey building directly behind the house and were marched off in opposite directions to various posts facing the river.

"At 0730 hours, the man of the house told Rossi that he had to go to work, as the Germans kept strict track of village men at their place of employment in an army supply depot. If one didn't report on time, a patrol would be sent to the man's house to find out the reason why. He indicated he would return at 1800 hours, and at that time might have more information for us. We had to trust him, as we didn't want any German soldiers checking out the house. Around 0900, Rossi left the house to wander the village. Mertz and I continued to observe movement from the upper room, and identified a number of unit badges belonging to the German 65th Infantry Division. They appeared to be sharp, well-disciplined soldiers.

"At 1100 hours, we were startled to hear a pounding on the front door. Both of us cocked our weapons and took up positions in opposite corners of the room. The housewife opened the door, and according to Mertz, a gruff German voice demanded food. The woman said there was none in the house, but the soldier didn't believe her, pushed past her, and strode toward the kitchen, his cobbled boots scraping the floor. There was a banging of cupboard doors and a crash of dishes, as the man searched for food below." Murray was poured another tot of rum.

"After a brief silence, we heard him begin to clump up the stairs. We levelled our guns at the bedroom door, then, to our surprise, another voice called out in German. 'Herman, come next door, we've found fresh bread.' The soldier turned on the steps and left the house. It was a close call.

"At noon, we broke out the dry rations we had brought, as we hadn't eaten since the night before. We had a couple of extra ration packs, so I called the lady of the house upstairs and gave them to her for her family. I told her to be sure to carefully discard the wrappings in the event the Germans came back.

"It was mid afternoon when we saw Rossi stopped by two men in Gestapo uniforms. He was heading our way. It must have been a desperate moment for him, for they checked his papers and searched him on the spot. He looked in our direction and pointed to the house. That gave us a real start. Rossi and the two Germans then walked toward us. I said to Mertz, 'Wonder if he's informed on us?' We braced ourselves for a confrontation, determined to take them down should we be discovered." Murray blew a smoke ring into the air above his head.

"The Gestapo knocked on the door, and when the housewife answered, they pointed to Rossi and asked her if the schoolteacher boarded here. She said that he did—satisfied, the Germans left. When Rossi joined us, he shared the intelligence he had gathered. He had made his way to a schoolhouse on the outskirts of the village and talked with the local schoolmaster, whom he knew well. Together, they were able to piece together the general disposition of the German forces in the area. Three battalions of the 65th Infantry Division were firmly entrenched in the immediate area, and on farmlands outside of the village, a tank battalion of the 90th Panzer Grenadiers was concealed under haystacks. I marked their location on my field map and roughed in as nearly as possible the enemy defensive lines." Murray glanced around the gathering of officers, satisfied with his recounting of the patrol thus far.

"It was 1815 hours when Quattrocchi returned from work. He informed us that a new area of the supply depot had been allocated for armoured parts and equipment. He concluded that these supplies were being pre-positioned in advance for a larger presence of Panzer units.

"The evening seemed to drag on damned slowly. Finally, at 2330 hours, Mertz, Rossi and I crawled to the riverbank where the inflatable boat was hidden. We were only a few feet away from the shore when a flare lit the sky overhead. We froze flat to the ground. Darkness fell again. I flashed the signal light three times. A German Spandau opened fire, and its bullets sprayed the area near us, searching out movement. There was an immediate response from the opposite shore, where a blanket of covering fire was returned by our troops.

"We slithered over the bank and into the boat as fast as we could. By the time we were on the river, a salvo of German mortar shells showered plumes of water about us. Things got pretty hot, and believe me, we made the water fly with our paddles. Thank God the distance was short. We were all relieved to climb the bank and pass through our own lines." Murray closed his eyes, savouring the recollection.

Ralph shook his head with amazement. "That was quite an experience! Good to see you back. Well, it's sack time for me. You guys have a good one, too; it might be our last chance before the big push."

The main advance didn't take place for another five days, and in that time, the rain never ceased. Any concerted movement of heavy equipment, such as artillery and tanks, became impossible along the muddy roadways, so the troops holed up in a variety of buildings—houses, shacks, storage sheds, barns, a schoolhouse, even a railway repair shop. The temperatures hovered around thirty-five degrees Fahrenheit and it was an effort to keep dry and warm. Sandy noted that many men were coming down with head colds and sore throats, so he obtained permission from the CO to allocate a ration of medicinal rum to all ranks.

Ralph coughed, his chest congested, as he pushed open a barn door to discover that two platoons of D Company had found protection against the elements in the old farm building. The rum ration had just arrived, and the men were eagerly testing its beneficial properties.

"Hey, Padre, if you don't drink hard stuff, I'll be glad to take it off your hands!" offered Private Ed Burrows.

"What makes you think he'd give it to you, Burrows? As one of the old boys of his parish, I think I'd stand a better chance," said Private Joe Martin.

Ralph chuckled. "You think so, do you Joe! I think your mom would give me what for if I offered her son a shot of alcohol."

The men nearby roared with laughter.

"At least they haven't lost their sense of humour," thought Ralph, as he visited among them. The barn was fairly comfortable, as barns go. It was dry and an abundance of hay filled the mow—some of it liberally spread around the main floor. However, the air reeked with the smell of manure. In one corner, Sergeant Bill Shanks was playing cards with three others. Loud cheers—or jeers—would erupt after each hand.

Ralph wandered over. "Sounds like a close game."

"We got 'em over a barrel this time, Padre. One more hand and we'll take the rubber," crowed Shanks. He was a burly lad with biceps like hams, and the men in his platoon considered him to be the best senior NCO in the regiment. He took good care of his "boys" and had seen them through some bitter fighting—only two had been slightly wounded. He was their "good luck piece."

Ralph addressed the sergeant. "You'll be interested to know your dad hunted with Ernest this fall."

Shanks led a card. "Yep, he wrote to tell me he planned to. I wonder how they made out."

"I expect a letter from Ernest one of these days with all the details," replied Ralph. "I'll let you know when I do."

Shanks bobbed his head. "That would be great, Padre, thanks."

The chaplain moved from one group to another, shooting the breeze. He spotted Private Ken Hartman reading a book by the dim light of an old lantern.

"Good book, Ken?"

"Not bad, Padre. It's Shakespeare's *Henry V*—one of the books required for my Grade 13 Literature exam. I'll write it when I get home."

"As I recall, you were doing well in your studies before we left England. Good for you in keeping up with them," said Ralph, lingering.

The soldier grinned. "I brought a couple of novels with me. I really treasure them. They let me escape every once in a while, although this Henry guy was a pretty tough soldier!"

"That he was. Do you like Shakespeare?" asked Ralph, seriously.

"Found him a little difficult at the start, but when you get into the language, I find him interesting. I'd like to write someday. I've even started to keep a diary. Maybe I can put together something after the war on our experiences. I've sketched out a lot of character profiles of the guys in the regiment. I've even described you, sir; someday I'll let you read it."

"Thanks, Ken, that would be great."

The mail arrived, and Ralph took his three letters to the room where he and Sandy had found shelter. The rain spattered against the windowpane as he held an envelope up to the light. The first letter he opened was from Erin. It was full of news of the baby and how she was growing—in her first two months she had gained two pounds.

> Miriam is such an adorable child, placid in nature, and sleeps most of the night. Father has a hard time keeping his hands off her. She is the apple of his eye. He sits by her cradle and rocks it whether she's awake or not. He chatters away at her, and she, in turn, is beginning to make noises that he swears is an answer to his conversation. I do hope he lives to see her grow into childhood. Sometimes I wonder, for he has become quite frail,

> and his memory has started to lapse. A couple of Sundays ago, he forgot where he was in his sermon and simply left the pulpit believing he had finished. I worry about him, and his doctor says there is nothing further he can do. He is bright and cheerful other days and eagerly sorts out his pastoral duties.
>
> Julia Nugent was hoping Tom would be returned to England after being wounded. She has just received a letter from the Canadian General Field Hospital in Sicily saying that he will soon be returning to the regiment. You soldiers! Don't you ever get enough? Oh, I know. If it were up to you, you'd all be on the next ship back. My darling, I miss you so much. Sorry for my blathering, as my mother would say.

The rest of her letter was filled with small talk, a way of sharing her day-to-day life with him.

Next, Ralph opened a letter from his parents. Winter in Ontario had set in with heavy amounts of snow falling in November. His dad was busy visiting in his parish. He was determined to keep in touch with those families who had men serving abroad. He had written:

> Sometimes, I get the feeling that my visits aren't as welcome as I would like them to be. You can tell by the look on people's faces when I come to the door. That 'O-God-no-look,' expecting bad news. Unfortunately, I've had to deliver a few of those, too. It's so difficult for them to deal with the death of their loved one. There's no body to grieve over, nothing tangible to lay to rest. My heart goes out to them. I am so grateful that you and your fellow padres write letters to the families as quickly as possible. That is such a comfort to them. We had a visit from Ernest not long ago, and he told of a letter you had written to a mother in your old parish. He said she carried the letter to church the next Sunday and had the rector read it to the congregation. At the end of the service, she was heard to say. 'Now I know my son has been laid to rest with love.' I don't envy you the job of writing such letters, but they are so important.

The last letter was from Ernest, and it was full of information on the recent deer hunt. He wrote:

> Snow came early this year, and made for great trackin'. I was followin' a nice buck at the end of Oak Ridge, where the runway crosses the hay marsh toward the bear's den. You know the one I mean, eh? The dogs had gone on a run to the north out of hearing, so I picks up this here track, where the big lad had side-stepped the hounds. He took me on a dandy stroll through that cedar swamp on the east end of Dog Lake. Got wet up to my knees. Every once in a while, I could see in the snow where he would stop, turn around in my direction, and listen for me. Aha! I thought to myself, I see what you're up to. So, I held to the right of his track, snapped a couple of dead cedar branches to entice him to go toward the main runway, so his nose was into the wind. Fred Gorr was on that rocky point above the deep gully where that runway crosses over the hill toward the Brules. Sure enough, up out of the cedars the buck trotted. Fred waited 'til it was half way up where our trail to the other watches crosses the gully and dropped him there. He was a beauty. Sixteen points, plus a whole lot of tiny spikes. I vow he would weigh in at 250 pounds, but by the time we dragged him to the boat landing on McClintock, you would swear he was 500 pounds. We sure do miss you younger guys. Some of us are getting too old for dragging deer a couple of miles.

Ralph smiled to himself. Ernest, even at his age, could drag that deer himself over the snow. He had proved this many times, when he had been hunting on his own. He wasn't a big man, but he was wiry, and used the lay of the land to his advantage—a born woodsman and hunter.

On the 7th of December, the big push came. A letter that General Montgomery had sent to the 8th Army a few days before was read to the troops. In it, he had indicated that "we will now hit the Germans a colossal crack." It was a typical Monty call to arms, and the men responded to the words with a grin.

"I guess he means by that we'll kick some German ass!" remarked one soldier.

The enemy had different ideas. They were well dug in and had no intention of giving way. They meant to hold the line—or die trying. For two weeks, the Canadians attacked and were counter-attacked. Little ground was gained. Ortona was the Canadian objective, and the RCR led.

It suffered extremely heavy losses and was reduced to a fighting force of eighteen officers and 159 men, but still they battled on, as did all units, but the carnage was appalling. On Christmas Eve, in the midst of a heavy downpour, reinforcements arrived for them.

The NCHR was ordered into a flanking movement on Ortona with D Company in the lead, but they were no sooner off the start line, when German 88s opened up. The line of advance faltered, and many men fell dead or wounded. C Company, following in their wake, struggled through the sucking mud, until they were forced to ground and had to dig into the slop.

The enemy began a scathing traverse of machine-gun fire across the rain-swept terrain hoping for a response, looking for a target for their heavy artillery. The night was almost totally black, except when a new moon peeked through the thick clouds. It was the kind of night that gives a man goose bumps—staring into the darkness with his ears alert for the slightest sound. This was the kind of moment that the soldier feels most frightened, when his imagination goes into overdrive. He might feel cold or hot. If he were cold, he would let his fear warm him. If hot, he would touch his bare hand to the slimy, cold earth about him. Only when the heavily laden clouds began to break was a balance struck, with the penetrating stillness that often occurs just before the first round is fired. It was an eerie time waiting for the initial move.

In C Company, the men looked intently over the soggy landscape, where the intense rain ran down the slopes in muddy rivulets. A chilly wind whipped the low shrubbery, making it dance and rattle erratically. A sudden calmness came over the men, as the clouds finally parted, and they saw a line of German soldiers advancing toward them. The Canadian soldiers had faced their fears and demons, and now it was time to engage the enemy. The sense of panic left behind, they fought with determination and brought into play all the skills they had learned since landing on enemy-held ground. Once again, it was time to do or die!

The RAP was set up under a bridge for protection against the enemy artillery fire. Only a direct hit would render the medical team useless. The location was six hundred yards behind D and C Companies' embattled positions, and within minutes stretcher-bearers were hauling casualties back to the site.

Ralph was now accustomed to the metallic smell of blood, vomit and emptied bowels. He witnessed the shattered bones, the gaping, sucking chest wounds, spilled intestines and organs. It was the hardest thing he had ever dealt with in his life—the broken bodies of the men he knew by name.

The wounded were screened as they were trundled into the RAP. The most urgent, whose lives might be saved, were seen first by the MO, lesser casualties waited their turn. The dead were set apart. The dying were given shots of morphine.

Sandy approached Ralph and recognized the agony his friend felt.

"Look at me, Ralph," the doctor spoke sternly. "At the moment, I can only see the sucking chest wounds—the scorched flesh, the mangled arm, or what used to be an arm. I have to concentrate on the wounds, not on the person. That's your job, Padre. It's over to you, when I'm finished with them. You have to hold their hand, look into their eyes—I can't. When they come around, you'll be there to comfort them, to try and tell them what's happened, try to answer their questions—even if you can't. Try to be upbeat, hopeful, even when you're sure they're going to die! Sorry, my friend, but that's the way it is."

Ralph acknowledged the doctor's terse comments with a nod and thought, "Dear Lord, there's not much I can do for them. I feel so inadequate. Please God, give me strength to let them know that at least I'm there for them."

A voice called out.

"Is that you, Padre?" The pale face of Private Johnny Gunsinger looked up at Ralph.

Ralph turned in that direction. "Yes, I'm here."

"Am I hit bad? They say I'll be all right, but I know you'll tell me the truth," pleaded the soldier.

"You took a bullet under your left shoulder. Luckily it passed right through. The MO says it's a clean wound. You'll be fine, Johnny," said Ralph brightly, hoping to bring some cheer to the normally jolly lad.

Gunsinger sighed. "What do you hear from home, sir? Everything all right in Plevna? How did the hunt go? Have you heard from Ernest yet?" The soldier lived on the farm next to Ernest's.

Ralph smiled. "Yes, I had a letter from him two days ago. My old gang got three nice bucks. He says the deer were plentiful. His old dog Boots watered two of them in McClintock Lake—just west of the narrows on that sandy point that runs out from the north shore. You know the place?"

"I sure do. My dad likes to watch there, too. He goes up Sand Lake by canoe, through the creek joining McClintock, and either watches there at the narrows, or on the point."

A deep moan from behind caused Ralph to turn.

"Who's that?" asked Johnny.

Ralph looked. "It's Joe Brash. Corporal Brooks, the MA, is with him now."

"Is he going to make it?"

"I can't tell. Just concentrate on yourself right now—Joe's in good hands. How are you feeling?"

"Pretty groggy . . . kinda numb."

"That's good. The morphine has kicked in. You'll be all right. Hang in there. I'll be nearby if you need anything. Right now I want to see how Joey's doing."

"Thanks, Padre. Thanks for being here. Perhaps you can tell me more about the hunt later?"

"Right! That I will," Ralph promised as he turned to leave.

The MO worked at his gruesome task at the operating station. "What do we have here?"

"Sucking chest wound, sir. Blood pressure forty over zero," answered his assistant, Corporal Art Jakes.

Sandy surveyed his patient whose vital signs were dropping rapidly.

"We're going to have to massage the heart. Prepare to open."

The medical team worked quickly, but to no avail.

"He's gone, sir!" advised the medical assistant, working as an anaesthetist.

Momentarily, Sandy looked crestfallen. He stiffened, then turned to his sergeant who was functioning as a triage nurse, prioritizing the wounded.

Sandy wiped his brow with a gauze patch. "Where are we at?"

"That's it for now, sir. It makes twelve dead and three seriously wounded. We'll have to get them off to the Field Ambulance, pronto."

The MO walked over to where Ralph was quietly talking to the wounded. The doctor watched his friend for a moment, nodded at him, then turned and left the canvas-covered operating theatre. Ralph followed.

"How are you doing, Padre? How's that chest?"

There was no answer. Ralph stood with head bowed, obviously overcome with emotion.

"I keep telling you, you've got to let those feelings out, Ralph. You can't keep them bottled up inside, or you'll go whacky. I know. They pounded that into me in my intern days." He placed his arm around the chaplain's shoulder and felt him sigh. "Come on, my friend, let it out, and draw a deep breath. Another jeep ambulance has just arrived. Our work is far from being over this day!"

Ralph had learned to work through long hours deprived of sleep, but now, with a deep cold, he felt rotten. The battle sounds and incoming wounded kept him going, if not totally alert. He sensed his body floating above it all, yet completely immersed in everything happening around him and began to experience a sense of lucid detachment. Deep inside was a well of pain, a sense of almost abandonment.

He prayed. "Dear God, don't leave me!"

Time seemed to stop as Ralph experienced one of those strange moments when something unforgettable happens. An event that makes an indelible mark on a person's soul and brands him for life—a golden instant in time that always seems to belong to someone else. Like the vision of St. Paul on the road to Damascus, Ralph saw his bishop before him, as he admonished him at the time of his ordination. "Always have before you in your remembrance, how great a treasure is committed to your charge. Your people are the sheep of Christ, which he bought with his death, and for whom he shed his blood. See that you never cease your labour, your care, and your diligence, until you have done everything you can, for that is your duty."

Suddenly, Ralph knew something had touched him within. It was time to begin a new chapter. He experienced a higher maturity, born of sacrifice in the battle, against all that was evil. He realized that much of his recent depression was the result of his own insecurity—and self-pity. Sandy was right. By the help of God, he would pull himself up by his own bootstraps and renew his commitment to his suffering flock. "Come on, Padre, I need your help over here," he heard Sandy call.

Ralph turned, and with a lighter footstep, he called out, "I'll be right there."

As General Volkes, the divisional commander, would later say quite rightly, "Everything before Ortona was a picnic."

The battle for Ortona raged into January 1944 and then bogged down as the harsh winter weather superimposed its might upon the muddy fields, freezing them solid. The confrontation with the enemy took on the appearance of World War I—scenes like the trenches in Flanders, like Passchendaele. Two lines of earth-torn slit trenches parallelled each other—one German, one Canadian—across farmers' fields and blasted vineyards. In between was no-man's land, stark and shell-pocked. Canadian patrols penetrated enemy-held ground. The Germans seemed content to hide in their holes and peck away at any intrusions.

The stalemate afforded the Canadian troops an occasional relaxed moment. Ortona was a fortress, and located therein were messes and wet canteens where the men could find a breather. Good food, clean beds, and bathing facilities were eagerly sought out, but better still was the town of San Vito, where a forty-eight-hour pass could be enjoyed out of the range of enemy guns.

Ralph spent much of his out-of-the-line time writing letters, responding to family and friends that had sent mail and parcels to him. He tried to be upbeat, but this did not always come across, for his physical weariness and ailing health dragged him down. In one letter to Erin he wrote:

> I've had a bit of a cold recently. It seems to come and go, but it doesn't slow me down too much. Sandy pumps the cough syrup into me and that seems to help a lot.

His comments to his parents were:

> The winter climate over here is pretty damp. People get colds easy enough, but we seem to plug on just the same. We get no pampering!

He was a little more specific when he wrote Ernest.

> I recall your talks about the health of the troops in the trenches in the First War. I would suggest it's not much better where we are right now. The weather is lousy and everyone seems to come down with colds and chest infections. I've had one that has lasted for weeks. I feel tired all the time.

In the lines, a sort of foolish cheerfulness rippled through the waiting men, whenever they realized a break was coming, away from the line. The high from the adrenaline rush often experienced in a forward area subsided, and the men were simply glad to be alive and unwounded. They larked about, slapping each other on the back and joking. It was a form of release. Once in town, the canteens and brothels did a roaring business. (Ortona was no different than any other seaport with its red light district.)

Many soldiers automatically took the line of least resistance to satisfy their baser instincts. They feared they might not get another chance.

On a dreary, heavily overcast day in mid January, Ralph went to the front to visit troops hunkered down on a reverse slope. In the daylight hours, the men pulled back from their firing pits. Only lookouts would be left on top. The less exposed area did not shield them from enemy mortars or artillery fire, but it gave them cover from the enfilade of small arms and machine-gun fire that occasionally swept the line.

It was a Sunday morning and Ralph was delivering the sacrament to D Company's location. He would meet with little groups of four or five men at a time, read a couple of prayers and distribute the elements. As he approached the platoon HQ position, the air suddenly filled with the sound of incoming *nebelwerfers*, a type of mortar used by the Germans and called "Moaning Minnies" by the Allied troops. The explosive charge was not only deadly, but psychologically unnerving.

As Ralph was pulled to cover into the platoon commander's slit trench, the ground erupting behind him, a blast of shrapnel pierced his left arm and back. He was thrown face down into the dugout, and blood soaked through his ripped tunic. The force of the blast stunned the other men in the hole, and it took a moment for them to assess the situation. The company MA made a quick evaluation and called for an ambulance to come forward to evacuate the chaplain. Lieutenant Marty Kossowski retrieved the communion kit Ralph carried in a small pack and placed it on the stretcher between his feet. Then, the stretcher-bearers carried Ralph to the waiting vehicle.

"How is he?" asked Corporal Mickey Maguire.

"Unconscious, but still breathing. Looks pretty bad, though!"

Back at the RAP, Sandy had been alerted and was prepared when the jeep arrived. Ralph was lifted onto the surgical platform beneath the RAP canvas. Max Mulligan, the medical sergeant, cut what remained of the battledress tunic from the padre's back. Using tweezers, Sandy was able to remove most of the tattered shirt and undershirt. Some of the material had been blown right into the wound and had to be removed by probing. The shrapnel created a ghastly wound—much skin and some soft tissue on the upper left torso was gone, but on initial examination, the doctor found no large holes entering the chest cavity. There were minor abrasions at the back of the skull, where tufts of hair were missing, and the left humerus was shattered.

The MO stood back momentarily from his scrutiny. "We might be lucky. Looks like the fragments hit a glancing blow. He must have been pulled half way into the trench when the bomb exploded. Watch the vital signs. I don't want to go in unless we have reason to believe there's internal trauma. Cover the back with sulfa and pray we can keep infection away. Immobilize the left arm."

"Ambulance is on its way, sir!" reported a medical clerk.

Sandy slipped off his blood-spattered operating gown. "Good! I'll go with him as far as No. 5 Field Ambulance. Hang in there, Padre, we're all praying for you for a change."

Colonel Morrison approached the RAP. "May I come in?"

"Of course, sir. We're just cleaning him up."

"Pretty bad?"

"I'm cautiously hopeful after preliminary examination. He's still unconscious. We're keeping close check on his vital signs, but so far, they are within an acceptable range. I'm about to give him a sedative to keep him quiet for the trip to No. 5."

"Sandy?" the sound was barely audible.

The doctor bent closer to his patient. "Hey there, my friend. How do you feel?"

"Kind of numb. What happened?"

"You were out doing your communion rounds and got in the way of a 'Moaning Minnie.'" Do you recall anything?"

"Not a thing. Was anyone else hurt?"

"No, in fact, it was one of those weird things that sometimes happens in war. One day a guy like you walks through fire, and the next, you get caught by a random shot."

"Hi there, Padre."

Ralph recognized Colonel Morrison's voice.

"Hello, sir. Sorry about this! I guess I've really let you down."

Morrison wagged his head. "Nonsense! The important thing is you're going to pull through this. Right, Doctor?"

"By the sound of him, he's already on the way to recovery—let us down, indeed! Now, let's get you back to where they can patch you up properly. I've run out of thread!" said Sandy. "I'd like to go with him as far as the Field Ambulance and come right back—if that's all right with you, sir?

"By all means, Doctor, but don't dally. We may need you back here," said the CO.

"I'll be back in half an hour."

As Ralph was carried from the RAP to the box ambulance, Private Jim Clark, a stretcher-bearer and a member of the pipe band, pumped his pipes and played "Amazing Grace." It had been a relatively quiet day in the NCHR lines, and several soldiers had heard of the padre's wounds. They gathered near the medical tent to learn how badly he had been wounded. In soft tones that soldiers rarely use, they began to sing the words,

> Through many dangers, toils and snares.
> I have already come;
> 'Tis grace that brought me safe thus far,
> And grace will lead me home.

Ralph whispered to Sandy, "Tell them I'll be back!"

Chapter 9

The jeep ambulance trundled its way over the rough, half-frozen, rutted road. Inside the box, Sandy watched carefully as Ralph was knocked about. He had been secured to the stretcher face down with straps about his buttocks to prevent him from rolling off. The MO tapped on the window of the cab. "Slow down a bit or you'll make things worse." The driver nodded.

It took an hour to reach the 5th Field Ambulance with the attached No. 2 Canadian Field Surgical Unit. The medical staff was waiting to receive their patient and immediately carried him into an enclosed area to be examined by a surgeon.

Sandy advised the doctor on the circumstances of the casualty, the type of projectile causing the damage, the amount of morphine that had been administered, and the general medical condition of the patient prior to the trauma.

The surgeon quickly went to work cleansing the area of the wound and noted that there was no sign of infection.

He nodded his approval, and turning to Sandy he said, "You fellows did a good job up front. Things look good externally . . . one small perforation to the chest cavity, possibly nicking the lung . . . no sign of serious pneumothorax or tension pneumothorax. Breathing is not laboured. Vital signs are all within range. We'll administer a booster tetanus shot. I want to cleanse the wound again. I see some minor foreign bodies that have worked their way to the surface, probably fragments of cloth . . . absence of metal particles. That's a hopeful sign. Want to scrub and observe?"

"Yes, I do," answered Sandy. "This guy is kinda special!"

The procedure took an hour. A small incision was made into the chest cavity. A hemothorax would determine if there was any internal bleeding. Fortunately, the accumulation was minor and seepage appeared to have stopped. With further examination a small metal fragment was found. It had not damaged any blood vessels or vital tissue.

"This is a very lucky individual," remarked the surgeon as he closed the surgical opening. "It would appear that the damage is mainly to the soft tissue and skin. He will require extensive skin grafting. Looks like he's just won himself a ticket back to England!"

"There'll be some cheering back at the NCHR when they get the news he's going to be fine," said Sandy. "They hold their padre in high esteem. He was clearly a soldier's padre or, I should say, is."

"Padre, you say? Well the Good Lord was surely with him this time. We'll keep him overnight and move him off to the General Hospital down at Andria. It's a long haul, but I think we can safely move him. He'll be comfortable with an additional shot of morphine. They can X-ray the chest to determine if I have missed something."

Ralph was pretty groggy when Sandy said goodbye, but coherent enough to remind his friend that he would make every effort to return to his unit.

Looking hopeful, Ralph said, "I trust that's not stretching it. If I understand your medical jargon well enough I should be able to come back—even if it takes a few months. You can be sure I'll try my damnedest. Tell the lads that for me, promise?"

"Sure I will, Ralph. They'll be looking for you. God bless," said Sandy, waving as he departed, feeling an emptiness. He would miss this man. He was like a brother.

It was a tiring journey for Ralph. The main roads were reasonably smooth except for certain stretches that bore the scars of war. It was a misty day and the tires of the box ambulance buzzed along the macadamized highway spraying the rainwater in arcs. The monotony of the sound tended to lull him into a restless sleep. The ambulance attendant also nodded off in one corner, jerking awake with a guilty start whenever the vehicle hit a rough spot. Occasionally, he would take Ralph's blood pressure, and at the three-hour point of the trip, he administered a shot of morphine. Travelling on his stomach for hours was uncomfortable, but Ralph took it in stride. Erin was much in his thoughts. He wished he had thought to ask Sandy to contact her father in order to lessen the worry she would experience when news arrived of his wounds. This would no doubt dredge up a new batch of nightmares for her.

It took four hours to reach No. 1 Canadian General Hospital in Andria, and they arrived just past noon. Orderlies placed Ralph on a gurney and conveyed him to a bay in the emergency room, where the duty doctor examined him, applied fresh dressings to his back, and forwarded him to a ward. It contained twelve beds, seven of which were occupied with other casualties. Ralph was eased into a corner bed with a screen drawn around it. In short order, a group of doctors arrived to give him a thorough examination. They shared observations, then departed to determine an appropriate course of treatment.

Next to arrive at the bedside was the hospital matron—a short, but sturdy woman. Ralph grinned inwardly, thinking she had the frame of a Honey tank. It was a small, armoured vehicle that was sometimes used as a troop carrier or as an ambulance, retrieving casualties from the front line. In his half stupor, he resolved to call her "Honey," which caused him to smile for real, as at that moment she was anything but sweet. Organized and efficient, she went about her task briskly. She had two nursing sisters in tow, one the senior ward nurse and the second a young woman who had recently arrived from Canada. Their voices were music to Ralph ears. The matron, Miss Handey, had an East Coast accent; the ward nurse, Sister Monique Lapointe, was French Canadian; and the youngest woman, Sister Amy Corsey, had the distinct colloquialisms of the Ottawa Valley.

"How are you feeling, Padre? Comfortable?" asked the matron. It seemed more of a command than a solicitous question.

"A little tired," Ralph replied.

"You'll be fine. We'll see to that. Sister Monique, you'll ensure the padre gets his proper rest." No question—a command this time. "Sister Amy will tend to your creature comforts."

"Whatever that means," thought Ralph.

"Is there anything you need at the moment?" asked the matron.

"I wonder if I could speak to the hospital chaplain?"

"Yes, of course, I will tell Padre McConnell you wish to see him."

"Would that be Archie McConnell, by any chance?"

"I believe that is his Christian name."

"Wonderful, he's an old friend. He had a parish not far from me before the war. It will be good to see him."

"Well, you rest for a while. You must be tired after that trip down."

"Thank you, Matron."

The nurses departed and Ralph drifted off into a dream-filled sleep. In it he saw Matron Handey pulling up to the hospital entrance astride a Honey tank. She was smoking a corncob pipe and issuing orders to a phalanx of nurses and orderlies lined up to receive her. Little Sister Amy was crying and the matron jumped at her.

"What's wrong with you, girl?" she screeched. "Have you never seen blood before?"

Ralph could see himself being carried on a stretcher from the tank in through the doors.

"Don't drop him," screamed the matron.

Ralph could feel himself falling into a vortex. He gripped the side of the stretcher that seemed to have become a boat. He was lying in the bottom of it on his stomach with his hands grasping for the gunnels. The boat was rocking in the waves and he heard his father call his name.

"Ralph, Ralph, me lad, wake up! You're havin' a bad dream."

The voice was that of Archie McConnell. He was gently squeezing Ralph's hand.

Ralph shook off his daze and looked into the face of his old friend. Archie was an Irishman, tall and erect. Brilliant blue eyes shone from a face laced with laugh lines. His brown wavy hair gave him a boyish look. He had come to Canada after studying theology at Trinity College, Dublin, in the mid-twenties and he, too, had begun his ministry in the highland parish. But prior to the war, Archie had been Rector of Stirling.

"Sorry to hear about all this, me boy," he said in a lilting voice, indicating Ralph's dressings. "The hospital CO has described the wound to me. He says you were pretty lucky—mainly soft tissue and skin damage. The bones in your left arm have been pinned and will mend in due course. They want to be sure you are stabilized before sending you back to England. The skin grafting will require major treatment in the U.K."

Ralph sighed. "I'm going back to England, but what about my lads? Can't they patch me up here?"

"Ah sure an' they can't here. The reconstruction will require a specialist's touch and rehabilitation. Don't worry about your boyos. They'll have a man in there before you know it. There're several new chaplains in the holding unit waiting for assignment. Sure I wish it were me, but they be tellin' me I'm getting a little long in the tooth for duty up front."

"Archie, I need your help." Ralph explained his wish to contact Erin so as to relieve her of worry. He told his friend of her first husband's death in 1940 and how he thought she would be beside herself. He was concerned that the situation might also put additional strain on her ailing father.

"Faith an' don't let it bother you a minute longer. I'll get a message off to our senior chaplain in London right away . . . have him call the Rector of Bewdleigh and assure him you are coming along just fine. Your wife will have news of this by morning," assured Archie. "I'll also advise them that you will be on your way back to them very soon, all being well. 'Tis the only thing that would delay your return—infection that is. So listen to the matron, me foine laddie. Oh, I know she seems like an old battleaxe, but underneath that hard exterior there's nothing but a heart of gold, sure an' begorra —only the best for 'her' patients."

Ralph told Archie of his first impression of her and how he had dubbed her after a Honey tank. Both men had a good laugh over this, and Archie promised not to tell her of the nickname until after Ralph was on his way.

"She will pull a face when I first tell her, but afterward it will no doubt become one of her best stories. She has some dandies to tell, and when she does, that stone face of hers cracks all to pieces. She's really a remarkable woman."

Ralph had difficulty adjusting to his situation, particularly in the area of toilet training. At first, he suffered the indignities of having to be cleaned up after a bowel movement. Pretty little Sister Amy, being the junior nurse, was assigned this task, and Ralph was needlessly embarrassed by her ministrations. Voiding was no problem, as he was hooked up with a catheter. Several days passed, and gradually Ralph began to accept the routine.

Before long, he was making conversation with the wounded soldiers around him. He listened to their stories and could relate directly to their experiences. His good humour brightened their days, and soon the ward began to stir with something close to gaiety. The nursing sisters would come rushing in when they first heard the occasional gales of laughter coming from the once oppressively quiet room. Soon, they too wanted in on the jokes and funny stories. Patients in wheelchairs heard the fun and made their way down the hall to join in.

One day the matron came in to scold Ralph.

"Padre, I'm going to have to put you in solitary confinement. Every time you get this high-spirited entertainment going, one or more of my patients goes into a spasm. You're supposed to be a priest, so conduct yourself accordingly."

She made these remarks in a voice loud enough that every man in the ward overheard and broke out into uncontrollable giggles. She marched stiffly out of the room, looking neither left nor right, until she reached her office, where she closed the door and broke into laughter.

Archie McConnell entered the ward with a broad smile on his face and placed a telegram on Ralph's pillow. "Top o' the mornin' to you, me lad. Sure, I believe this will give you a lift."

Ralph brightened. "Read it to me, please."

"It's from the senior chaplain in London.

> "Please convey to H/Captain Ralph Russell that I have personally spoken to his wife Erin and assured her of his continuing improved condition. STOP. I did not relay the fact that he would be on his way back soon as this may have given her false hope. STOP. She indicated that her father was in reasonably good health and the children were fine. STOP. She looks forward to a letter from him. STOP."

"Oh, that is good news. I've been worried about her," said Ralph with a catch in his throat and tears in his eyes.

"I have more news for you," said Archie. "His Majesty's Hospital Ship, *Maltese Cross*, will be departing for England from Barletta in three days. The CO asked me to tell you that you will be aboard her."

There was a low moan heard in the ward.

". . . and he said you would be accompanied by most of these lads."

This brought a cheer.

Morale in the ward soared until twenty-four hours before Maltese Cross was due to depart. On the evening of the last full day, one of the seriously infected patients died. Corporal Bill Smart had been wounded by an exploding anti-personnel mine. Both of his legs had been shattered and amputated above the knees. Fragments had torn away his penis and scrotum. Deep infection had spread through his lower bowel and no medication seemed to stop the diffusion. He had been in constant agony, frequently crying out in pain. Morphine rarely contained his misery. He passed away with a mournful sigh. At his passing, the ward became unnaturally quiet. The men looked at each other with defeated glances, for they had been pulling for the man to stabilize and recover.

"Probably just as well," said one. "He'd have had a hell of a life to live if he'd survived."

"Poor bugger," responded another. "I wished he could have made it."

"Easy for you to say, chum. You've still got your balls!"

"All right, guys," said Ralph. "Let it go. How be we have a prayer for our companion. At least now he will be out of pain."

Once again the ward became quiet. The duty nurse had fetched the matron. They had pulled a sheet over the deceased man's head and stood by the bedside as Ralph offered a prayer.

The patients in the ward were awakened early. There were the usual moans and groans from the men as the nurses dispensed their morning care. The matron was in their midst on this particular day as the transfer to the hospital ship was to be carried out in an organized and correct manner and she was there to ensure that this happened.

One by one, they were taken to waiting ambulances and transferred to the dockside at Barletta, where they boarded the waiting ship. Ralph was the last to leave the ward. The matron stood at his bedside with a hint of mirth in her eyes.

"I must say, Padre, you have been an interesting patient. There were times I could have wrung your neck, but I must confess that your good humour and healthy attitude brightened the lives around you. The men come here pretty depressed as a rule, and it takes all our nursing skills to lift their spirits. But you, you come here badly wounded yourself, and in twenty-four hours you have our brave lads higher than a kite. You have a real gift with people. I just want to thank you. I'm not so sure I like the nickname you gave me—'Honey,'" she arched her eyebrows.

"Who squealed on me? Was it Archie McConnell?" asked Ralph with a blush.

"No, it wasn't our chaplain. I caught Sisters Lapointe and Corsey giggling in the mess with several other nurses and overheard the conversation about me being compared with a Honey tank. At first, I was angry, but then after thinking about it for a while, I had to smile to myself. After all, laughter is the best medicine. And that's what we're here to dispense."

Ralph smiled with her. "I didn't mean to embarrass you. I apologize for my sometimes odd sense of humour."

She laughed. "No offence taken. Just be glad I didn't order a darned good enema for you. Even padres need to be cleaned out every once in a while—especially those who have vivid imaginations, like yours!"

"Give me a hug, Honey!"

She bent over with a chuckle and ruffled his hair. "You be a good boy, and don't drive those nurses on the ship wild. Get well soon. God bless you."

"Hey, that's my line," said Ralph. "You keep up the fine work you do here, too, and may the Good Lord be always with you."

She turned and walked from the ward. Ralph grinned as he watched her quick march out into the hallway.

The hospital ship *Maltese Cross* slipped from the harbour into the Adriatic, turned south and proceeded at twenty-two knots toward the Mediterranean. She was built for speed, and peeled the water from her bow, leaving a churned-up white wake beneath her fantail. The sky above was grey with a hint of rain, and the dark sea offered a light chop from the southeast with an occasional higher swell that sent a spray flying over the forward parts. Below decks, the immaculate wards held 240 wounded men. Nursing sisters were busy meeting their patients and settling them for the voyage ahead.

Ralph had been placed in a room with three other wounded officers; one was a German captain, Eric Schmidt. He had been captured by an RCR patrol in the Ortona Salient and had been shot in the stomach, where a bullet had grazed his spine leaving him paralyzed from the waist down. He said not a word and spent his time with eyes closed or looking vacantly at the ceiling. He wore his Iron Cross.

One of the others was Major John Ferguson of the London Irish Regiment. He had lost a leg and sported hair that was literally carrot in colour. He wore a magnificent spiked mustache. His green eyes were intense and he stared with open hatred at the German officer.

The third occupant was Lieutenant Bill Rodney from the Governor General's Horse Guards. His tank had been "brewed up," during which he suffered from severe burns to his body. It was a miracle that the shy twenty-one year old had survived. He had no eyebrows or lashes and his face was badly burned under dressings that covered his face and shaved head. He rarely uttered a sound, as the flames had scorched the inside of his mouth, just as he dove from his flaming tank.

Only Ralph and John Ferguson held conversations. The latter was extremely caustic when the talk turned to the German. He referred to him as "that fanatical Nazi," pointing out his cold eyes, thin lips and grim countenance.

In the afternoon of the second day at sea, a medical orderly came around offering cigarettes. When they were offered to the German officer he politely declined with thanks, using perfect English. Ralph and John looked at each other sheepishly; they had thought the man did not speak their language.

"Well, at least you know what we think of you," blurted Ferguson. "No use hiding that fact."

The man did not seem to take offence. Once the language barrier was broken, he took more interest in the general conversation and offered a few remarks of his own.

"You know war teaches us to hate each other. That is part of its dark side. If we had met in Brighton before the storm broke, we might have been become friends. I used to go there for my summer holiday. It is such a delightful spot, ja!" Schmidt remarked.

Ferguson fumed. "It wasn't so delightful after your planes bombed it—civilian targets as well. Women and kids were blown to pieces."

"As you English say, 'war is hell.'" My family comes from Cologne. Your bombs have shattered many of our homes. My father and mother were killed in one of your raids!"

The room fell silent.

"You are addressed as Padre. I take it that you must be a chaplain," Schmidt enquired.

"Yes, I am," Ralph nodded.

"I am a Christian, also," said the German frowning with concentration. "It must be difficult for you to participate in the madness of war."

"Oh, you see it as madness, do you?" huffed Ferguson.

"Indeed it is madness, and not only I see this. Many a German soldier also feels the same as I do! But as soldiers, we follow orders, the same as you, hein! If we did not, we would be shot. Do you shoot soldiers who do not fight?"

Ralph blushed and countered. "But ours is a just war. You wage war on behalf of an evil dictator who would enslave the world; a madman who commits genocide."

"So you say. My people are just beginning to learn this. A German fights for his country. It has been our way for generations."

"You're pretty slow at learning, I'd say," interrupted Ferguson with a belligerent snort. "One would have thought your people would have caught on after 1918!"

"Perhaps we would have had we not been so oppressed by the reparations imposed upon us. Until the rise of Hitler, Germany was a defeated nation forced to be the lackeys of the Allies. We were poor, practically starving. We have always been a proud nation. People rallied to Hitler as a charismatic figure who began to lift Germany from its knees. Too late we began to see his cruel side, and by that time, Germany was riding high with a vision of a reich that would stand for a thousand years. We looked the other way at his aberrations, believing his councillors would change him in time."

"That kind of thinking doesn't let you off the hook. You're still damned by association in my mind, Christian or not," argued Ferguson.

"No, we Christians will have a lot to answer to before God. Not just for the present, but for the past as well. Satan is ingenious when it comes to corrupting a self-satisfied soul," stated Ralph.

Changing the subject, Schmidt asked Ralph, "Are you Canadian?'

Ralph was about to reply in the affirmative when he remembered his security lectures. He had already said too much and simply responded by saying, "Perhaps."

A few minutes later, without really thinking, Ralph asked the German if he were with a Panzer Division.

The man smiled shyly back, and with a bit of a twinkle, answered, "Perhaps!"

Each day Ralph felt his body healing. Although his left arm was still in a cast, he could exercise it, and his hand could grasp things that a few days earlier had been difficult to hold. His back was sensitive to the touch, but it, too, somehow felt better. His outlook was becoming brighter and he began to think of things to do to liven up the sombre atmosphere of the place.

Music seemed to be the answer. After lights-out one evening, before reaching Gibraltar, Ralph passed word that his room and the ward beyond would form a rhythm band to welcome the nurses who arrived at an early hour to waken their patients. An assembly of bedpans, trays and other objects that could raise a cacophony of noise were squirrelled beneath the sheets, and as the lights went up to greet the morn, these items were produced and soundly beaten, much to the fright of the staff. The bedlam brought the matron and a phalanx of orderlies on the run.

The matron demanded to know who had started the ruckus, and when no admission came forward, she promised that when the villain was found, he would be dealt with accordingly. However, she noted later in the day, that the general spirit of her charges had increased to the point where light chatter and soft laughter had taken the place of sighs and silence.

Ralph was pleased with his caper and began to dream up other ways to stimulate his fellow bed-ridden travellers. The next morning, the men greeted their warders with a serenade of instruments made by combs covered with paper. The nurses laughed at the rendition, and even the most grievously wounded were seen to smile. Ralph was jubilant.

It was late afternoon when the *Maltese Cross* reached the massive "Rock" in the Strait of Gibraltar that projected from the southernmost tip of the Iberian Peninsula. It had been captured by the British in 1704 and had become a commanding fortress guarding the entrance to the Mediterranean Sea. The hospital ship dropped anchor and soon a flotilla of small boats were rowed alongside. Hawkers plied their offerings of fresh fruit, as they had done for centuries, and these were well received by the ambulatory on board who also made purchases for the bedridden.

Early the following morning, *Maltese Cross*, receiving clearance from the Royal Navy authorities, weighed anchor and slipped out into the Atlantic for a hasty return to England. She travelled in consort with HMS Sprite, a swift Tribal Class destroyer. There were fewer U-boats plying the seaways in early 1944, as many had been sunk at sea or destroyed in their pens by bombs, but this did not detract from the Royal Navy's vigilance. Newer, faster submarines had since come into service, and they were proving deadly to Allied shipping. The great red crosses painted against the white background of the hospital ships were a deterrent to the enemy, but not always a guarantee. As it turned out, the last leg of their passage was speedy, and early in the morning of the 12th of February, the ship entered Southampton harbour. Wisps of fog straggled across the water, revealing only a ghostly shadow of buildings on shore. This landscape was made more macabre by the bomb damage dockside, stark reminders that England was still at war.

Ambulances waited alongside and slowly the wounded and maimed were transferred. As Ralph was being carried ashore, the matron walked beside his stretcher.

"Thank you for bringing a modicum of cheerfulness to the men around you. You provided them with a tonic that our medical team could not. Oh yes, I found out it was you who started all the hijinks. Should have boxed your ears for causing that fright! Good luck on your convalescence. With your bright attitude you will do well, I'm sure. Goodbye, Padre!"

"Do you know where they are sending me?" asked Ralph.

"According to these," she said peering at his travel documents, "you are headed for the convalescent hospital at Tunbridge Wells. It's a fine old country estate that has been converted for the duration. It has a fine reputation as a burn unit and, in your case, as a skin-grafting centre."

"That's wonderful," exulted Ralph. "It's a stone's throw from Bewdleigh, where my wife is."

"I'm happy for you, then. Cheerio!"

Ralph had a hard time remembering the trip to Mayberly Manor, situated on a small stream that flowed into the River Beult; however, the day had cleared and it was late afternoon when the ambulance arrived at the sixteenth- century estate. It was a sprawling old residence belonging to the well-connected Morton family and had been converted into a hospital after Dunkirk. The first Canadians to be treated there were those evacuated from Dieppe. Staff members included several Canadian medical personnel who had come over in the early part of the war as volunteers, and this included Dr. Robert Jarvis from Toronto, a plastic surgeon. He was an older man who had been turned down for military service, but his skills were exceptional and he had no trouble being accepted in England as a civilian practitioner.

Even before he was settled, Ralph convinced a nurse that he needed to call his wife immediately on an urgent family matter. He felt no guilt over this little white lie, as the need was great within him.

"It's ringing now," said the nurse passing the telephone to Ralph, "but remember, you'll have a full medical in the morning, so don't make any plans for a visitor."

"St.. Tristan's Rectory," answered the voice he had been anxious to hear.

"Erin?"

"Ralph? IS THAT YOU? WHERE ARE YOU? ARE YOU ALL RIGHT?" she exclaimed, excitement and worry mingling in her voice.

"Yes, I'm swell. I arrived at Tunbridge Wells an hour ago. How are you?" Ralph's voice was filled with emotion.

"Wonderful, now that I have heard your voice . . . oh, Ralph . . ." Then she sobbed.

"Steady on, girl. Everything's going to be just fine. How are the children and your dad? I bet Michael and little Miriam are growing like weeds. I have missed you all so much."

Erin pleaded, "Ralph, when can I see you? I want to touch you to make sure all this is not a dream!"

"Nurse tells me I'm in for a major prodding in the morning. Come tomorrow after lunch. I'll be waiting, my darling. I need to hold you, too!"

Then no more words would come for either of them. Ralph finally broke the awkward silence that seemed to deafen them both. "I love you. See you tomorrow. I can hardly wait."

"Ralph, I love you so very much."

It was an early start. At five a.m. the patients were awakened, assisted to the toilet as required, washed, and given breakfast. Promptly at seven o'clock a team of doctors arrived at Ralph's bedside and began to examine him. A stream of medical jargon flowed over and around him and in his mind, he suspended himself over the scene. Everything seemed so impersonal, as the doctors went about their business. In fact, their concentration was so intense, Ralph thought he should make a comment, or at least groan at their hands-on examination, but he remained impassive, only wincing when the prodding became too rough.

"There we are, Padre, everything seems to be progressing favourably," remarked Doctor Jarvis gruffly. "Now, we'll plan an overall approach to your treatment."

"Do keep me informed," said Ralph, with a hint of irony in his voice.

"Harumph? Oh, believe me, we have your best interests at heart, Padre. Impatience is normal when the healing process has taken over. If all goes well you should be out of here in three or four months."

"Three or four months?" Ralph moaned.

"Yes." Dr. Jarvis looked surprised at Ralph's disappointment. "The grafting is a gradual procedure. All care must be taken to repair the damage, and we want no infection, do we? Don't worry. You'll be as good as new before you know it," said Jarvis with a professional nod.

"Will I be able to rejoin my unit?" asked Ralph rather petulantly.

"I can't answer that," replied Jarvis in a tone that implied it was really not his concern. "That would be a decision for your superiors, but we will do our part to make the necessary repairs."

Ralph realized that his ill humour was uncalled for and all of a sudden knew the reason for it. He was used to being in control. Now, that had passed into other hands, and he felt uneasy. It was a new challenge he would have to resolve.

"Thank you, Doctor, I know you will—I apologize for my testiness. I guess I'm feeling frustrated."

"Understood, my friend," acknowledged the doctor with a grunt. "We all get that way by times! I'll keep you informed as we go through the process, step by step. If you are mentally up to the program, I'm sure you'll feel better about it. Have a good day, Padre. Nurse tells me your wife will visit this afternoon. That will be the best tonic for you today. I'll see you tomorrow and will be able to outline what we plan to do."

And with that, the very efficient surgeon and his colleagues went on to their next patient.

Ralph's appetite had left him. He couldn't eat his lunch. Not that it was such a tasty offering—rather bland by Canadian standards. He was feeling somewhat uneasy and anxious about seeing Erin. How would she react to his wounds? He had seen his back in a mirror and knew how disfigured it appeared. It looked like he had taken a hundred lashes with a cat-o-nine-tails. He had no idea how he would look after the skin grafting. Would she be appalled? A thousand fearful thoughts filled his mind.

And then she was there, standing in the doorway to his room. A slow smile, eased the apprehension marking her face, her beautiful face. To Ralph, it was the face of an angel. It had not changed. It was his touchstone to reality, the vision that had brought him through all the horrors of the battlefield.

Tentatively, he raised his arms and she was immediately in them. They clutched each other fiercely, frantically, until she realized she might be hurting him and she loosened her embrace by drawing back.

"Don't let go of me," he pleaded.

"I might hurt you!"

"I feel nothing except your closeness. The scent of you fills my senses. Erin, Erin, it's so good to hold you in my arms again. Here, come closer." He took her head in his hands and crushed her lips against his. "I have missed you so much."

She stayed for an hour. The nurse had warned her not to overtire him.

"You can have thirty minutes," she had said. The time had passed unnoticed.

"Mrs. Russell, I'm afraid you must leave. I must tend to my patient."

Erin straightened. "Of course, I'm sorry. I've overstayed." She turned back to Ralph. "I'll be here tomorrow. I think father would like to see you as well. The nanny will look after the children. I've not told them you are home yet. Michael will be so excited to hear of it. Will it be all right to visit tomorrow, Sister?"

The nurse moved to the foot of the bed. "That would be fine for a short visit, but we mustn't exhaust him."

Erin left the room, and the hospital matron met her in the hallway.

"Please pace your visits, Mrs. Russell," she said rather officiously. "Your husband is still fresh from the Front. He will need time to adjust. It's not just the physical wounds we must address; he is mentally fragile at the moment, as well. In fact, he is quite edgy. It will take some time before things stabilize for him. Your presence will go a long way toward his full recovery, but we must work together. I hope you understand."

Although the nurse's tone rankled, Erin was eager to do her part. "Indeed I do, Matron. I only want to help."

The next day Erin and her father reached Mayberly Manor at 2 p.m. Ralph was sitting up against a bank of pillows sipping his tea, which he quickly placed on the bedside table when his visitors came in. Erin went immediately to the bedside to greet her husband with a kiss. Paul Gwenn made his way to the opposite side and extended his hand to his son-in-law.

"It's so good to see you, Ralph," he said, his voice not as strong as Ralph remembered it. "You look much better than I thought you would . . . lost some weight, I see. How do you feel otherwise?"

"My back's a mess," Ralph replied, noting to himself how much the older man had failed. "But they keep me medicated for the pain. It creeps up on me sometimes, but I'm used to it. You haven't changed much, Vicar," Ralph lied. "How is your health these days?"

"Oh, tolerably well. Erin keeps me on my toes." The vicar smiled at his daughter. "She's become a rather efficient pill-pusher. Good thing, too, as I seem to forget to take them. The golden years are not what they're cracked up to be, what! But enough about me! Tell me how you got wounded."

"Now, Father, let's not get into that, yet. Ralph will tell you in good time. Let's get him settled first. He'll need a little time to readjust to life away from the army."

The vicar took on a rather hurt look. "But I want to hear how he won his MC!"

"Please, Father, let's ask questions later."

"Oh, all right," he answered rather sulkily.

Erin glanced at Ralph who gave a knowing nod. He could see that the older gentlemen had become rather shaky. On closer examination, he noticed how the vicar's eyes and attention seemed to become unfocused when he was not a part of the conversation. Ralph smiled at him and placed a hand over his father-in-law's hand and squeezed. It appeared withered and the veins were pronounced.

After visiting for half an hour, a rap came at the door, and the hospital chaplain entered the room. A slight man, the Reverend Elwin McKenny was a former army chaplain who had been severely wounded at Dunkirk. He had recovered at Mayberly Manor and later was assigned hospital chaplain. His dark, deep-set eyes had a penetrating quality, but when he smiled, his face took on an almost angelic appearance that reflected his gentle spirit. He was smiling now, as he came toward the bedside, and introduced himself.

"My name is Elwin McKenny. I'm the Anglican chaplain to the hospital. I understand that you are a Canadian padre."

"Yes, I am," responded Ralph.

"I presume these are friends?" asked McKenny.

"This is my wife, Erin, and her father, the Reverend Paul Gwenn, Vicar of Bewdleigh."

"Ah yes, a lovely parish. Not far from here," remarked McKenny.

"I'm sure father would like to talk to you about it," said Erin, "wouldn't you, Father?"

"Wha-what?" stuttered the vicar, roused from his thoughts.

The hospital chaplain took the hint. "By all means. Vicar, please join me in my office for a chat and a cup of tea."

When they were gone, Erin, with tears filling her eyes, said to Ralph. "He's declined rapidly these past few months. I didn't want to mention this in my letters as you had enough to worry about while in action. The bishop has placed a new ordinand at St. Tristan's to assist Father. If the truth be known, he is really there to take over the parish. The doctor says Father is entering an early stage of dementia and must receive constant supervision. The young priest is a kind, sensitive man who is quite prepared to fill this role. You will like him."

"Oh, Erin, I'm so sorry. I could see the change in him as soon as he entered the room. He looks so frail."

"He has good days and bad days. I thought today he was feeling up, but you can see how quickly he can change. He was so excited to see you and seemed so bright on the way over."

"And now you have me to contend with as well."

"I would love to care for you both, my darling. I'm looking forward to having all my family under one roof again. The little ones love their grandfather, and he seems so at peace with them. They chatter away at him, and he sits contentedly and smiles at them. They communicate with each other in their own unique way."

"Let's hope I finish with this place quickly, then," said Ralph. "They say it will take a few months to do all the repairs that are necessary."

Erin reached for Ralph's hand. "I've spoken with Dr. Jarvis and he says you must have patience. I smiled when he said that—I know how impatient you can be sometimes."

Ralph laughed. "You know me so well for a young bride! I will have to concentrate on being good and doing what I'm told, so that I can get out of here as quickly as possible. Now, come here, woman, and hold me. They tell me you will be my best medicine."

Erin sat on the edge of the bed and they embraced.

A little later the hospital chaplain returned with Gwenn. "I think your father is getting rather listless, Mrs. Russell, perhaps he can return another day."

"Yes, we must be getting along. I don't want to overtire this man, too," she said nodding toward her husband, "or I'll have Matron to contend with again."

McKenny smiled knowingly.

"I'll only be able to come every other day, my love, as gas rationing makes things tight," said Erin.

Ralph acknowledged her statement. "We'll make every minute count," he said, and held out his arms for one last hug.

Dr. Jarvis was as good as his word. That evening, he laid out in detail the steps that would have to be followed in grafting new skin onto Ralph's back. The process would begin on the following Monday, when skin from the thigh would be removed to fit the first area to be addressed. The doctor explained, in layman's terms, that the reconstruction would be like piecing together a patchwork quilt—one piece at a time, working from the outside toward the centre. It was a delicate operation that could only be done in gradual steps, and the duration of the procedure would be determined by the speed of the healing process and the absence of complications, such as infection.

"Other than your wounds, you are in top physical condition. You should heal quickly," predicted Jarvis. "Heed the nurse's instructions, and all should go well."

"I will try to be the perfect patient, especially if it means I will be discharged at an early date. You can count on that."

"I plan to, and if you don't, I will sick Matron on you," said Jarvis with a mischievous twinkle in his eye.

Ralph crossed off each day as it passed on the calendar and kept procedural notes in his diary. The grafting was painful. He was left with a burning sensation as each section of skin was removed for grafting to his raw back. The first three grafts took well, but when the fourth was applied, infection set in, and Ralph found himself in a strange world of hallucinations. A fierce battle raged around him with all the sounds of battle echoing in his head. Men screamed, and wild winged beasts entered the fray, devouring the wounded that Ralph was desperately trying to save. It was a scene from hell, and he could feel the fires hot on his skin. Erin reached for him, but their fingers never quite touched. She would fade in and out of the picture, always close, yet far away. The fighting became grim, and he thought he was losing it, but he continued to struggle, clinging to a thread of hope.

The delirium lasted five days. Erin stayed by his side, and when he cried out her name, she would bathe his head with cool cloths and whisper softly in his ear. "There, there, my love, I am here. No one is going to take you from me." Her message seemed to reach him in his delerium and his terrors eased.

When the high fever passed, Doctor Jarvis took her aside and said, "We very nearly lost him. The bout has left him weak and we won't be able to proceed for several weeks. You have been his mainstay, of this, I have no doubt."

Slowly, Ralph began to respond. For awhile, he continued to slip in and out of lucidity, or simply fall asleep in mid sentence. Then, he would ask where he was, or wonder where Erin had been. Why had she left him? He would accuse her of not caring, and he would rant at the ghostly images that occasionally passed between them. He was living in a confused world between nightmare and reality. But each day Ralph improved. A week after his temperature returned to normal, he was almost his former self and began to laugh and make funny little jokes. He told Erin some of the escapades and terrors he had experienced in battle, which had a cathartic effect on him. For her part, she told him of her worries and fears while he was away. Things she had not wanted to put in letters for fear of upsetting him, like the minor childhood sicknesses afflicting the children and her father's turn for the worse. They were back together again in mind and spirit. He became more relaxed, and the distance that had separated them was gone.

The Wednesday following Easter, on April the 28th, a great excitement rippled through Mayberly Manor, for it was the day that George VI was to visit the hospital. When word came down, it was assumed that this visit was to be one of those semi-casual events that he and Queen Elizabeth often took upon themselves—brief calls to hospitals and institutions where the wounded were brought from the battlefields. The queen showed special interest in Canadians and would spend extra time talking with them. These moments were held in deep regard by those visited and would become a highlight in their lives for years to come. They would tell their children and grandchildren of the day when the king and queen came to call on them. The event was a tremendous boost to morale.

On the day in question, Mayberly Manor was spotlessly clean. Senior staff were on hand to greet the royal couple and their escort made up of political and military dignities. It was a grand entrance for something that was supposed to be spontaneous. His Majesty wore military uniform and the queen glowed in a yellow garden party dress. The matching hat sported an elegant white egret feather. She was a beautiful and gracious lady.

The royal party stopped at each bedside. The king spoke very little; the queen, on the other hand, chatted freely with her bedridden subjects, and her radiant smile seemed to brighten every corner.

When the royal couple came to Ralph's room, a high-ranking officer, equerry to the king, came forward and handed a small box to the monarch. King George approached the bed and extended his right hand to Ralph.

"I am very p-p-pleased to meet you, Padre. I've been told wonderful stories of your g-g-gallantry with your regiment in Sicily and Italy. It is my p-p-pleasure to award you the Military Cross. Colonel, would you read the citation so all present may h-h-hear of his bravery upon the field of battle."

The colonel, so addressed, unfolded a document and read from it.

THE MILITARY CROSS
Canadian Chaplain Services—
the Honorary Captain Ralph Russell

On August 1, 1943, near the town of Regalbuto, the North Country Highland Regiment met strong enemy opposition and suffered very heavy casualties in an initial attempt to drive the enemy from the town. During the early stage of the action, Hon. Captain Ralph Russell, the battalion's chaplain, was carrying out routine duties at the Regimental Aid Post. It soon became apparent that numerous, helplessly wounded were lying between lines exposed to fire from ememy tanks, mortars and machine-guns. Realizing this situation, Hon. Captain Russell showed superb initiative, and with no thought for his own personal safety, elected to enter the deadly area in an attempt to save the lives of the wounded. By his cheerful and fearless conduct, he managed to organize several bearing parties and led them time and time again into the danger area, then despatching them to a sheltered gully where a jeep ambulance conveyed the wounded back to the RAP. Hon. Captain Russell's utter contempt for danger showed moral leadership of the highest character and undoubtedly his action saved many lives, and inspired the stretcher-bearers to do their utmost to carry out his instructions.

Erin watched the presentation with tears on her cheeks. The vicar stood staunchly at attention and seemed very much aware of the situation. He proudly wore his own Military Cross. The king noticed this, and engaged him in a discussion following the formal proceedings. Paul Gwenn was able to modestly recount his own experience that had lead to his decoration. Meanwhile, the queen took Erin's hand.

"You must be very proud of your husband. His efforts were truly heroic. These Canadian boys hold such a special place in my heart—they are exceptional soldiers. Their contribution to the war effort has made the difference. I want to visit Canada again when the war is over. Will I see you there?"

"It would be my honour," said Erin, curtsying before the Queen. For sometime, Ralph's wife had been contemplating the changes that would happen when the war was over. She had no doubt she would accompany her husband to Canada, but the Queen's comment had suddenly brought this future event into focus. If her father were still with them, he would no doubt join them, too. It was time that she and Ralph had a serious discussion about this eventuality.

When the royal party departed, Ralph replayed the afternnon's events over and over in his mind. He could hardly believe that the king himself had presented him with his decoration. Erin was a-flutter over the attention she had received from the queen, and the vicar was quite himself again, at least for the moment. He sat smiling out the window as the royal couple made their way by motorcade from the hospital grounds. He raised his hand in salute. It was an occasion to be remembered.

In late May, Doctor Jarvis announced the last graft was successfully in place and Ralph's back was healing well.

"Harumph . . . I'll release you to your family in two weeks' time. You'll only have to return here periodically for a check up. How does that sound to you?"

"Marvellous! What wonderful news! Wait till Erin hears this."

On her next visit, Erin brought with her several letters from Canada, one from Ernest and three from his parents, which only added to Ralph's joy. They all contained cheerful and encouraging messages. In the first one, his parents said how delighted they were with the news of his steady recovery. They had been in shock after receiving word by telegram that he had been wounded. His mother went on to say that they were preparing to open the cottage:

> You know your father! As soon as the ice is out, he wants to get up there before the blackflies and mosquitoes hatch. Besides, I like it, too, in early spring. The air is so fresh and you can smell the leaves bursting out!

In another, she said:

> Your dad has the garden worked up here at home and the potatoes are in. It was a hard winter, but we rejoice now that spring is here. The daffodils and tulips are brightening up the yard and we've had our first feed of asparagus.

In the last letter she said:

> The cottage is open and wintered well. There was the usual amount of dead flies to clean up, but no sign of mice, thank goodness. I hope we've finally found all the places they could get in. Your dad caught some lake trout. They were close to the surface, as the water is still very cold.

Ernest's letter was full of "spring things," too. There had been a good run of sap in April and he had boiled it down to a total of eighteen gallons of syrup:

> As soon as the ice was out I went speckled-trout fishing with Fred Gorr. We walked in to Little Round Lake and I fished from that flat rock on the north side and caught a nice mess—the biggest was close to three pounds. Were they ever good fried up in butter—even their tails were delicious. You know, the way I crisp them up?

Erin could tell from Ralph's face that the letters made him a little homesick. Perhaps this was a good time to bring up the subject of moving to Canada.

"I have been thinking about the time when we will go to Canada," she began, the thought creasing her forehead.

Ralph's head jerked up.

"It must be lovely to have four distinct seasons. I'm anxious to see the brilliant colours of autumn and snow at Christmas. Spring sounds lovely, too! I can't imagine swimming in fresh warm water . . . and the tales you tell of skinny-dipping in the late evening. Oh, my! I wonder if I'll be too shy to try that?"

Ralph grinned. "Once you try it, you'll never have any doubts again. It's like bathing in velvet. It gives a person a physical sense of freedom—quite an aphrodisiac, too!" he grinned.

"Now, you are sounding fit. Wait till I get you home," she teased.

They were young and eager to share life to its fullest once again. War wounds, for both of them, were healing nicely.

The 6th of June was a day full of excitement. Ralph was released from hospital and the Allies launched their invasion across the English Channel. Wave after wave of aircraft crossed overhead as Erin drove her husband home to Bewdleigh. There was a great deal of military transport on the road as well, hauling supplies and equipment toward the coastal ports. Frenzied anticipation permeated the air, affecting both armed forces as well as civilians. At last, the big push was on. Radio broadcasts filled the airways with news of the crossing, and the degree of enemy resistance experienced. It augured to be a stiff fight, but an immediate toehold had been established with the Canadians pushing inland from Juno beach.

Bewdleigh was a welcome sight for Ralph. Great hedges of rhododendrons were in full bloom, and flowers of all descriptions painted the countryside a myriad of colours. It was hard to believe a mighty battle was in full spate across the Channel.

Paul Gwenn met his son-in-law at the vicarage door. He seemed a little confused by Ralph's presence. Once, he called him Michael, and Erin had to gently correct him.

"Father, Ralph is home from the convalescent hospital. Isn't it grand to have him back again? His back is healing nicely."

"Oh dear, was he hurt?"

"Yes," she said, "he was wounded in Italy. You remember?"

"Of course, I remember. How could I forget? One never forgets a war wound. I recall being hit in France in the First War . . . almost buried alive!"

Erin and Ralph exchanged knowing glances.

"Father, if you put the tea on, I will get Ralph settled in our bedroom. He will have to rest for awhile, but we can have tea upstairs."

The older clergyman toddled toward the kitchen as Erin assisted Ralph up the stairs. She helped him lay on the bed and then went for his suitcase. On her way back, she checked in the kitchen to find her father seated at the table staring vacantly out the window toward the garden.

"I think it's going to rain!" he said.

The kettle had not been set on the stove.

"I'll make some tea, Father. It will be ready in a few minutes. You go up and see Ralph and I'll bring it up."

"Ralph? Ralph is upstairs?"

"Yes, Father, you go ahead up and have a little visit while I get things ready."

Erin watched him leave, sadly realizing that his mind was slipping badly. She prepared the tea and carried it on a tray to her bedroom. She entered to find Ralph sleeping and no sign of her father. She went to his room to find him sitting in a chair.

"I'll bring you your tea, Father."

"Thank you very much. That would be nice."

It was obvious that he had forgotten about Ralph. Erin realized that these two men, who meant the world to her, would need constant attention. Her husband would continue to improve, thank God, but her father would not. Both realizations brought tears to her eyes.

The Reverend Stuart de Clerk was a short, stocky, friendly young man, with dark brown hair and hazel eyes that always seemed to sparkle with intelligence and mirth. He arrived at the vicarage two days after Ralph had returned and was greeted at the door by Erin.

"Father de Clerk, good to see you. Come in."

"Good afternoon, Erin. How are your patients?"

"Ralph is doing well, but I fear Father is slipping. I doubt if he will be much help in the parish anymore."

"Well, I will make sure he is always welcome to take part in any of the services," answered the young priest.

"That's most kind of you . . . come see my two fine men." She escorted him into the den where Paul and Ralph were chatting comfortably.

"Ralph, I would like you to meet Stuart de Clerk. He has joined our parish ministry."

"Lovely to meet you at last," said Ralph extending a hand in greeting. "I've heard a lot of nice things about you,"

"My pleasure, Father Russell."

"Let's be friends from the start . . . call me Ralph."

The two young clerics hit it off immediately. Companionably, they joined in lively conversations that included the vicar at every turn. The older man seemed content to listen to his young colleagues.

"I'll soon be able to help out with the services," proclaimed Ralph, "once I get my balance."

"That would be welcomed, but I believe you should take things easy for a bit longer. You've been through a lot and it'll take time for everything to mend."

"You're right," said Erin, "but he's a hard one to keep down. But I can be a stern nurse when I need to be, and I'll not let him do anything until he is absolutely able." She grinned at Ralph, who hung his head with mock acquiescence.

Father de Clerk leaned against the mantle. "The news from the Invasion Front continues to improve. The Allies are pushing deeper into

France, but the Boche are putting up a stiff fight in the British and American sectors."

"I know just how fierce they can be when they decide to make a stand," observed Ralph. "The 6th of June will be an important date to remember, but the world must not forget the 10th of July, 1943, when the underbelly of Europe was torn open. It pulled a lot of German troops into Italy, considerably weakening Hitler's might in central Europe." Ralph grimaced in remembrance.

"You're right, of course," agreed Stuart. "But the focus has shifted to the European heartland, and that's where all the publicity will centre. I've no doubt that your boys will soon finish up the Italian campaign and head north for the final *coup de grâce*."

The three men fought their wars, while Erin listened in the background, giving thanks that her men were now out of it.

"I wanted to become a chaplain as soon as I was ordained," said Stuart, "but I was not allowed. A clergyman had to have a minimum of two years in a parish before he could join up. Then, it was discovered I had a heart murmur, and that precluded any thought of military service. So here I am, a bystander." Ralph noticed the touch of envy in de Clerk's voice.

"Good men are needed at home as well," said Ralph. "There's a lot of work to do here, looking after families. Then, there's the task of informing them of death and casualties. Not at all an enviable position."

It was late afternoon when de Clerk finally bade Ralph, Erin and the vicar farewell. It had been a satisfying visit for him. He liked Ralph's frankness and willingness to share his experiences.

The children had grown. Michael was now a vigorous three-and-a-half-year-old. He was a precocious child, forever finding something interesting to challenge. Invariably, he would end up in trouble and would have to be rescued. He and Ralph were soon inseparable. Little Miriam, who had recently learned to walk, enjoyed ambling between her father and mother, chattering away like a magpie in a language all her own. In the evening, she would curl up on Ralph's lap for a cuddle before bed. It was a time of bliss for Ralph—getting to know Michael again and falling in love with his precious little daughter.

His cup runneth over one evening, when he was able to make love to Erin for the first time since his return. It was, of necessity, a very gentle love-making, but they handled it well. Each was sensitive to the other's needs, and both were fully satisfied afterward when they lay side by side in the great feather bed. Before he fell asleep, Ralph gave thanks again for his deliverance from death's door. His last days in Italy were a blur, but his thoughts were never very far from the boys of the NCHR. As he drifted off he prayed, "God willing, I shall be with them again."

Chapter 10

It was the first of August 1944, the day before Ralph's thirty-second birthday, that word came down from London for him to report to the office of the Principal Canadian Chaplain Protestant Overseas. The grafts on his back had taken well, and he was quite comfortable in his skin except for the occasional burning sensation when he overstretched. He was careful not to overdo it, as he was eager to return to his regiment. It was not to be. In London, he reported to Honorary Colonel C. G. Hepburn, Principal Chaplain Protestant, a gallant old soldier who had served in the Great War and was well experienced in the ways of the military.

"Welcome back, Ralph. I've been looking forward to seeing you again," greeted Hepburn. "Glad to see you on your feet and looking healthy."

"It's good to be back, sir, and ready to rejoin the regiment."

"That's very commendable, but I'm afraid it will not happen. As you may suspect, your replacement is doing a good job, and the NCHR have taken him under their wing, thanks to your influence, I'm sure!"

Ralph's face fell. "But I need to get back to my lads."

"Sorry, my friend, that's not possible. You have been seriously wounded, and the medical authorities have designated you unfit for active duty at this time. So, for now, you will be tasked with special duties. The British Chaplain General has requested me to provide a chaplain recently from the battlefields to instruct at The Royal Army Chaplain's School, Bagshot Park. There, all newly inducted chaplains of the Allied Forces staging in England will be briefed and educated on the role of the chaplain under battle conditions. I am sending you. Your experiences will add a positive and realistic dimension to this training. It is of vital importance that our new padres be given first-hand information before they join the front-line units."

"But sir, I'm sure I could get medical clearance. I'm told I'm fit as a fiddle." When the colonel's expression didn't change, Ralph changed tack. "If I can't get the NCHR, is there another Canadian unit that can use an old hand?"

"I wish I could grant your request, and I do know where your heart lies . . . but for the time being, I am sending you as our liaison with the Brit Chap Gen. You will report for duty at Bagshot Park on the fifteenth. I'm told there is accommodation for a married man and his family there. That should be a perk to entice you." said Hepburn. "Plus, I have another surprise for you."

Hepburn took from his desk a pair of crowns and passed them to Ralph. "As of the first of August you are now Honorary Major Russell. Congratulations!"

Ralph was momentarily dumbstruck. "Thank you, sir. I am honoured. I don't know what to say."

The principal chaplain smiled. "Then say nothing. You deserve the promotion."

Despite his promotion to major, Ralph departed the principal chaplain's office in a depressed state. He felt guilty being away from his regiment for so long. Did they feel he had deserted them? Did they miss him? They were his military family, and he certainly missed *them*. He knew they were in the thick of things again, and he wondered who had been killed or wounded.

Morbid thoughts, Ralph concluded, as he mounted a double-decker bus and headed to catch a train for the short run to Bewdleigh. Giving himself a mental shake, he wondered if Erin would be interested in a move to Bagshot Park. Her father had been poorly of late, and Ralph doubted if she would want to leave him.

It was teatime when Ralph arrived at the vicarage, and the doctor's auto was parked outside. Concerned, Ralph entered the house and called Erin's name.

She came down the staircase looking worried. "Father has taken a turn for the worse. The doctor fears he may not survive this attack. He says there is nothing more he can do, only keep him sedated and free of pain."

"I am so sorry, my dear. Is there anything I can do?"

"The nanny is taking care of the children. Would you stay with me?" Erin began to cry. "I fear I'm going to lose him. Oh, Ralph . . . hold me tight." Her sobs came from deep within. "I need to feel the reality of you!"

"Erin, you had better come up," called the doctor.

They climbed the stairs together and entered the vicar's room. He was gasping for air and his face was scarlet. He tried to speak her name, but only a hoarse wheeze came from his mouth. Erin knelt beside the bed with Ralph standing by her side, his hand on her shoulder. The vicar rolled his eyes toward them and gave the slightest smile. In a strangled voice, he spoke his final words: "Love each other."

The muffled funeral bell tolled from St. Tristan's as the body of its late vicar passed from the narthex outdoors to the cemetery that surrounded the parish church. The cortege wound through the ancient markers to a plot beneath a giant oak tree whose branches swept out like guardian arms. Ralph had arranged for a trumpeter from a nearby military camp to sound the "Last Post" for the old veteran. Erin, dressed in black, with the children by her side, wept silently as Ralph read the sentences of committal. Then, from the foot of the grave, he made his way to his family and held them in his arms. They were all enclosed within the shelter of his surplice, alone but not alone, as the entire congregation gathered around them to offer final condolences.

In the vicarage following the funeral reception, Father Stuart de Clerk took Erin aside. "I want you to feel free to stay in this house as long as you want. As you know, I am a bachelor, and am happily ensconced in a private suite at the Widow Rutledge's comfortable home. Take your time to sort things out. If you need it, there will be lots of storage space available in the vicarage."

"Thank you, Father Stuart, that is most kind of you. But Ralph has been offered a residence in Bagshot Park, and we will be moving there as soon as I can gather things together. But I will take up your offer to store some items of personal furniture and a few steamer trunks. I hope to bring these to Canada after the war." And with that statement, her life took on a new direction. In her mind she heard the echoes of Ruth from the Old Testament, "Wither you go I shall go and your people will be my people."

In mid August, Ralph reported for duty at his new posting in Bagshot Park. The park had been a royal hunting lodge for many generations, a favourite estate of the Stuart kings, but the stately red brick residence had been rebuilt by Queen Victoria in the late nineteenth century for her son, Prince Arthur, the Duke of Connaught, who lived there until his death in 1942. In early 1944, the Royal Army Chaplain School received royal consent to occupy the buildings.

As he entered the long avenue leading up to the school, he took in every aspect of the impressive house and grounds. He parked the vicar's old car and entered the main entrance, where he was greeted by a sentry who inspected his orders and directed him toward an office bearing the name of the director, Colonel Thomas Tiffton. He gave his name to the colonel's secretary, a dour woman of indistinct age, impeccably dressed in a dun-coloured tweed suit. She asked him to be seated while she knocked on the door of the inner office. In less than a minute, a lanky, hawk-nosed man with deep-set eyes came out, extending his hand in welcome. His thick hair was greased and combed straight back. Ralph thought he looked a bit like a porcupine.

"Russell, how good of you to be prompt. Glad to welcome you aboard."

Ralph thought it rather strange to be greeted with a naval salutation.

"How was your trip up from Bewdleigh? Do you have your family with you? I did know your father-in-law." Tiffton spoke in short sharp sentences. "Grand old chap. Sorry to hear of his sudden demise. Come along now, and I'll show you about."

Before Ralph had a chance to answer any of the colonel's rapid questions, he was whisked away on a lightning tour of the establishment, starting with the officer's mess lounge and bar, followed by the dining room, the lecture rooms and the students' quarters.

"You and your wife will occupy a suite in the east wing. Grand view of a sunrise whenever the sun decides to show its self. Ha! Ha! Not often in this climate, eh, what?"

After the cursory whirlwind tour, the two men returned to the director's office.

"So, what are your impressions so far?" asked Tiffton with a hawkish smile. He had a habit of nodding his head when he asked questions, as if always expecting a positive answer.

"It's a marvellous setting—certainly 'royal' could be applied to the décor and the estate. I'll bring my family up on the weekend, if that would suit."

"By all means. It will be ready for your arrival. Now, please feel free to wander about. I have the usual pile of paperwork to sort through before luncheon. We'll meet in the lounge at noon and I will introduce you to the others of the cadre."

Ralph strolled through the majestic grounds. Great oak and beech groves interspersed with meadows of green grass and wild flowers stretched into the distance. Deer, in groups of two or three, grazed along the banks of a small lake, where ducks dipped and dived in the clear water. A pair of royal swans floated on the glassy surface. Ralph knew instinctively that young Michael would thrive here in this pastoral paradise.

Precisely at high noon, he entered the lounge where several men stood about chatting and savouring a glass of sherry. Tiffton spotted Ralph as he came through the doors and walked over to him, nodding and smiling broadly.

"Russell, come meet our staff and the other chaps in your cadre. Gentlemen, this is our newest faculty member, Major Ralph Russell, a Canadian chaplain. He has seen service in our recent scuffles in Sicily and Italy. A short time ago King George invested him with the Military Cross, citing Russell's bravery on the field of battle. He will no doubt add a remarkable dimension to our presentations to the new chaplains. The new draft will arrive on Monday."

Each man came forward to welcome Ralph to the school. In his cadre, there were two British chaplains: Major Peter Rebbeck, a tall spit-and-polish type from the Gloucestershire Regiment, and Captain Tom Foreman, a diminutive but wiry man from the Royal Tank Regiment. The third chaplain, Captain Philip Ratcliffe, was from Australia. He was a robust man of medium build, with a shock of unruly red hair that spiked into a rooster tail at the crown of his head. A seemingly endless smile stretched across his ruddy face. "Brother colonials," thought Ralph, who took to the man immediately.

Over a working lunch, served on a glistening oak table set with silver plate and candelabra, the men discussed the course syllabus. Organization and administration would be under the tutelage of Colonel Tiffton, battlefield casualties and treatment of the wounded would be delivered by the Area Medical Officer who had seen duty in North Africa with Monty's Desert Rats, while instruction in the fields of infantry, artillery and armoured structure and tactics would be delivered by the appropriate specialists. The battlefield chaplains' personal testimony would form the heart of the program.

The men worked through the afternoon to flesh out the framework of the three-week training program. In a friendly, but pronounced way, the colonial and British chaplains naturally paired off.

Later that evening, when Ralph arrived home, he was full of news to share with Erin. She noted that he had become quite excited about his new role and relationships. He told her about his first meeting with Tiffton and described him as a rather eccentric individual who was obviously good at what he did. Erin laughed at his impressions of the three members of the chaplain's cadre.

"I can just see our two rather correct English chaps trying to gang up on the colonials," she said with a twinkle in her eye.

"Oh, I think we'll hold our own with our pompous English cousins. It will be interesting to see how our individual presentations will compare. I'm looking forward to it!"

"That's obvious," she remarked. "I haven't seen you this excited since you came home. It does my heart good to see it. I was worried you were going to be depressed about not being able to return to the NCHR."

"Well, you know where I would be, if I had my choice. At the moment that's not an option, so I must concentrate on what's next best. I want to contribute something of value to the new chaplains going into battle. Now, are you ready for the move?"

"Aye, ready, Major!"

The family move to Bagshot Park went without a hitch. Really all they had to take with them were their personal belongings, as the suite was furnished as it had been in the Duke of Connaught's time. The most difficult part of the transit came when Erin closed the door on the vicarage and realized that this was no longer her home. She rested her hand against the door and nodded her head as if in prayer, as Ralph led the two children to the car. As she came down the walk, Ralph saw a tear slip down her face as she bravely tried to smile in his direction.

"I guess I should be thankful that Father's passing was peaceful. I miss him dreadfully," Erin turned and looked back, "and this place has been such a wonderful home."

"I know, my love," said Ralph as he took her in his arms, "but you have so many treasured memories to take with you."

Erin tried again to put on a brave smile. "And so, we begin a new chapter in our lives!"

The children, especially Michael, were quite excited as they drove into the Park. The boy chattered away like a magpie when he saw a deer grazing at the side of the lane.

"Look, Mummy, see the deer. Is it a boy or a girl deer?"

"A boy deer has antlers, Michael," said Ralph.

"What are antlers?" he chirped.

"They are like bones that grow out of the top of a boy deer's head. You've seen them before. Remember?"

"But they look funny. What's that cloth on them?"

"That's called velvet. Each year the boy deer loses his antlers in winter. He rubs them against small trees or branches until they drop. Then, when spring comes again, he grows new ones that are covered in velvet to protect them as they grow. At this time of year, the horns harden, and the buck, as the boy deer is known, begins to rub the velvet off until the antlers are shiny. This makes him look good to the girl deer and . . ."

"All right you great Canadian hunter, let the biological lecture end there for now. He's still a baby," cautioned Erin.

"Not a baby," pronounced Michael. "When we get to Canada, Daddy's going to take me hunting. Aren't you, Daddy?"

"There are many things we'll do together in Canada. We'll go fishing and camping and swimming . . ."

"I want to go there, now!" shouted Michael.

Ralph turned to Erin and smiled. "Let's hope now comes sooner, rather than later."

There were sixteen chaplains of various denominations assigned to the course, averaging thirty years of age. All were reinforcements, eager and excited with the prospect of joining a combat arms unit of their own. Six of the men were from the U.K., four from Canada, two from Australia, one from New Zealand, and three from the U.S., especially invited to share in the Allied experience. They were a lively group—full of high spirits—but serious, when it came to appreciating what was being presented to them.

The first week concentrated on military structures and procedures. It was a time to form the men into a group and assess their strengths and weakness, particularly in military knowledge. On the Friday, Ralph drew the first lecture on the "Chaplain in Battle." He tried to steel himself for the presentation, for he knew it would be an emotionally draining experience. He gave the talk in the main hall to both students and school staff. It was a command performance.

Ralph began with the Canadian Chaplain's Prayer:

"Almighty and everlasting God, who by thy Holy Spirit didst preside over the first gathering of the Apostles at Jerusalem, and hast promised to be with thy Church always even unto the end of the world: vouchsafe, we beseech thee, to be with us who are Chaplains to the Armed Forces of our Country. Grant unto us thy gracious presence and blessing. Deliver us from all error, pride and prejudice; enlighten us with thy wisdom, and so order all our doing that thy kingdom may be advanced.

"Make us considerate of those whom thou hast entrusted unto us, and faithful to the duties laid upon us by our country. Let our uniform remind us daily of the tradition of our Service. Grant us thy Grace that we may lead many to thee, and that we may touch many lives by the life we lead, the deeds we do and the words we say.

"Guide us with the light of truth and keep before us the life of him by whose example and help we trust to obtain the answer to our prayers, Jesus Christ our Lord. Amen."

His lecture plan was to share with his audience some of his background, starting with his first parish, and the fact that a number of the men of his regiment came from there. He spoke of his difficulty in persuading his bishop to release him to become a military chaplain, and how he eventually succeeded in joining the NCHR. He described the days when the volunteer force trained for overseas service, eventually arriving in England, and quickly covered the frustrations all ranks experienced in the "waiting years," and how eagerly the young men sought to engage the enemy, destroy them, and return to home and family.

He then went on to characterize the role of the chaplain in battle.

"When I review the life of the chaplain in battle, I sometimes compare it to looking through a kaleidoscope. When you first put it to your eye, everything is bright and rosy. You enter an exciting new world where you are about to change things for the better. You are optimistic and zealous to get on with the task ahead. Like the young men around you, you are enthusiastic to make a go of it.

"In these seminal days, you get to know the people around you as best you can. You will find the men of your regiment a brash and sassy lot, full of barley and beans, chafing for a good fight. They will see you, and many will wonder why you are there. Sometimes, you will wonder why yourself. You will begin to question your motives for putting on the uniform. But as you watch, absorb and inquire, the wheel turns and new images form, new colourful events take place. The men around you become trained to kill an enemy he sees as an evil beast, not as another human being—an enemy who treads on women and children, men who will kill you, if you do not kill them first. You see your young men change before your very eyes, and you, as a chaplain, begin to change, too! You lose your naïveté. The reality of what you are about to face hits home, and gradually a new kind of thought process takes over. Now you are just beginning to face the ugliness of war.

"In all this, the chaplain's faith teaches him to focus on God's light. By doing so, he finds strength for service in this world of the fighting soldier, where the emphasis is placed on destruction. Then the tumblers fall again, and the scene changes. The chaplain is in the midst of a battle. He is a non-combatant. Where does he go? What does he do? He wants to help, but fears he will get in the way. So, he takes another step toward a more profound maturity, when he realizes that his is a *ministry of presence* in this hellish turn of events.

"He normally positions himself with the medical team, but he could also find himself at the front facing the hot flying metal of death alongside the soldier in his slit trench. The soldier looks at him and seems to say, 'What are you doing here, Padre?' And the chaplain answers, 'I am here because you are here.' The soldier looks at him and nods.

"In the Unit Aid Station, the wounded boy looks at the chaplain and asks, 'Am I going to die?' And the padre answers, 'Hang in there son, you're going to be all right.' Is this a lie? Sometimes, but the chaplain tries to calm the lad and give him hope for the future—whatever that may be. With a sigh the soldier looks into the chaplain's eyes and breathes, 'Thanks for being here, Padre.' *The ministry of presence.*

"You see in this example the importance of getting to know the men. You do not 'buddy' with them, but you do your best to touch their lives. This takes time. It certainly doesn't happen overnight. It will seem like an impossible task when you first arrive at a new unit, especially if you are in action. You must work at it, slowly but surely. You will find opportunities to share a significant moment . . . engage in a comradely spirit. You will not win them all, but you will establish yourself as their chaplain . . . someone they will come to trust. Always be sincere. The men can spot a phony a mile away. Walk amoung them as a man of God. Never let them down, for your example helps to keep them going when their darkest hour comes upon them. Dare to achieve moral clarity and an abiding hope, even though you may feel swallowed up by the fires of hell.

"Again and again the wheel turns—new actions, new events—and the chaplain responds to the changing situations. Time and time again, he questions his own faith. Doubts strike him like bullets. He finds himself shaking with the stark reality of war about him—shattered bodies, broken minds—and over and above it all, the mindlessness of war . . . the ultimate insult to thinking man . . . the sheer hell of it all. Then, looking more closely, he views again the light at the end of the tunnel. Is God speaking to me, he asks? What is the meaning of all this? For a moment he stops thinking this through, as another voice has called out to him. A wounded soldier is dying, and the chaplain turns from his self-questioning to lay a hand on the boy's brow, 'Go with God, my son!'

"There will be times when you look into dead eyes and want to scream, 'God where are you?' The scene may appear godforsaken, but never doubt His presence. You are uniquely consecrated to serve—even to the very end. Serve your men with pride and confidence. They will see it and respond."

Ralph paused.

"Gentlemen, if you think for one moment that you are about to embark on some wonderful adventure—think again. What you are about to face will mark you forever. You are about to grow up in one hell of a hurry. Your faith, seen by the men, will see both them and you through the worst of it. Your ministry of presence will truly give them the opportunity to become valiant soldiers of Christ.

"When the kaleidoscope finally drops from your eye, you will see more clearly than you have ever done before. Your vision will be enhanced to the degree that your men will see, through your example, a new and better world for future generations. If you can achieve that, by your ministry of presence, then your role as a chaplain will be largely fulfilled.

"Your faith will be your compass. Let me conclude with an incident that happened to me back home in Canada. My first parish was located in a rugged, forested area. Deer were plentiful there and were harvested by the local men as a winter meat supply. I was invited to join them, and I enjoyed their comradeship. At one point, I was asked to take my turn as 'dogger.' This meant going into a section of the woods to chase the deer out to the men on watches. I had never done this, and I was apprehensive about entering a completely unknown area. My companion, an old woodsman called Ernest, instructed me on the use of a compass.

"He described the lay of the land and said, 'If you find yourself lost or turned around, rely on this instrument. There may be times when you may not believe the direction in which it is pointing—but never doubt it. You might call that an act of faith.

"I have never forgotten his plain guidance, and when all was said and done, it was the application of his simple philosophy that saw me through my most difficult times. You, too, will have to face hardships ahead. Let your faith be your compass."

Ralph's stint at the Chaplains' School lasted for six months. In many ways it was an idyllic time. His duties were not onerous, and his little family thrived in its peaceful setting. He enjoyed working with his fellow chaplains and never tired of instilling battlefield skills in new-entry chaplains. A firm bond was established between Ralph and Philip Ratcliffe, and the latter found a warm welcome in the Russells' suite. He romped and played with the children, all the while missing his own family back in New Zealand.

However, deep in his heart, Ralph's thoughts were with the NCHR. He followed their progress through Italy and learned that, soon, his old regiment would be crossing to the south of France to begin the march northward in pursuit of the retreating Germans. It was time for Ralph to lobby for a return to action. However, he received the same response from Hepburn as before. There were now ample chaplains for the front-line units. Ralph knew this, for he had trained many of them. Nevertheless, he was insistent. Finally the principal chaplain brought him into London as a staff chaplain.

"Now I can keep a closer eye on you, Ralph. There are a number of administrative units about the city that require the attention of a chaplain. Whether you realize it or not," Hepburn pointed out, "they are also working to end this war."

"I know you are right, sir, but you know where I truly belong."

The principal chaplain smiled. "Indeed I do, so why don't you get on with the job? By the way, I have been informed that your family can remain in residence at Bagshot Park for the time being. The trade-off for that is that you will be required to present the odd lecture to refresher courses at the school. It is a short commute—only fifteen miles from the city centre. So, off with you now, and get yourself organized."

Erin was pleased to remain at Bagshot Park, where she and the children were happy and comfortable. Ralph quickly worked out a timetable, and found that he, with no unexpected delays, could be in his cubbyhole of an office in Trafalgar Square within thirty minutes.

London had suffered imense war damage, but its inhabitants were indefatigable. The cleanup of bomb damage was ongoing, and most thoroughfares were kept free of debris, allowing passage for emergency vehicles and public transport alike.

Ralph's workday was at the disposal of the principal chaplain, but most often he went about the city visiting various subunits of the Canadian military. His ministry of presence took on a different, more mundane meaning. Here he found uniformed Canadian men and women working in offices. They greeted him on his rounds, but gave the impression that they couldn't care less if they saw him or not. They chatted about news from "home" or trivial events in their lives. Many had contracted intimate relationships with Londoners and some of these came to Ralph's attention when trouble arose, especially when one of the parties was already married with their spouse out of the country or back in Canada. Ralph had little patience with this type problem and often said to a soldier thus caught up: "Why don't you apply for a transfer to the front? I'm sure your dilemma would disappear in a hurry!"

The first of May dawned fair and was made even more delightful when he saw Sandy Jones waiting for him in his office. He was still the NCHR medical officer, but he, with several others, had been called to England for consultation on new equipment for field units.

"What are you doing here?" exclaimed Ralph after giving his old friend a slap-on-the-back and a bear hug.

"Well, they just couldn't run the war over here without me." Sandy grinned broadly. "We are having a serious look at some new equipment that has just arrived from Canada and the Senior Staff wants the opinion of us 'field types' before sending it across the Channel. I'll be here for a week. The conference will last for two days, so I'll have some time to put in before I head back. Do you suppose you could give me the grand tour?"

Ralph was elated. "That would be wonderful. I'll get us a car and driver to cart us around. You'll have to stay with Erin and me at Bagshot Park for part of the time. I want to hear everything that's gone on since I left the gang in Italy."

"Well, there's lots to tell. There's only a handful of originals left. In fact, you'd never know the regiment as far as faces are concerned. Those officers who were there when you left are either on new postings in the division or have been promoted to serve in new units where battle-hardened veterans are needed." Sandy leaned forward in his chair.

"You'll be happy to hear that Andy Ayers has been promoted and will command the regiment in June. Jamie Fraser, your old organist, has been promoted to major and will shortly take command of A Company, while Tom Nugent will take over B Company. He got his majority last month. Pretty well all the rest have either moved on or 'bought it' one way or another. Many were wounded, including Gerry Bickerton, or killed—Jim Brown, in a resupply misadventure, and Marty Kossowski, on a night patrol in February. The subalterns are all new, as are many ORs. However, when the Old Guard heard I was coming to England, they asked me to pass their regards to you, 'Tell him we'll meet again some day—and that's fer sure!'"

When Sandy was not occupied with medical meetings, Ralph showed him the sights of London, both good and bad. The doctor was amazed. "I can't get over how these people get on with their lives. If it weren't for the colossal bomb damage, you'd never know these people were in a fight for their lives. Talk about pluck!"

Ralph nodded. "They're a brave lot, no doubt about it. Look at that elderly lady over there . . . head held high, strutting along like a woman half her age. And that old chap on the park bench, chewing on the stem of his pipe . . . no tobacco, but sucking on it just the same!"

In the evenings, Sandy stayed with the Russells. After meeting Erin again, he told Ralph that he had married a true gem. "I think I could easily fall in love with her myself," he said with a twinkle. "Does she have a sister by any chance?"

Michael and Miriam were soon all over him, and he was delighted with their attention. "I can hardly wait until this damn war is over and I can get on with my life. I want a family and a peaceful little practice somewhere—a country doctor would be right up my alley."

"I think you have to find a wife first, Sandy!"

"Oh, there's a young lady back home I've had my eye on. She was only eighteen when I came overseas and since has become a nurse." Sandy paused with a faraway look in his eye. "We'd make a great team!"

"How come I've never heard about her before?" asked Ralph.

Returning to the present Sandy brightened. "I guess I never thought I'd have a chance with her, but now she's started to write and things look promising."

"Hey, that's great news. If you need someone to tie the knot," Ralph offered, "You know who to ask."

"If it comes about, you'll be the first to know!"

The week passed quickly, and all too soon it was time for Sandy to leave. He went into London on the morning of the eighth with Ralph, but was unable to leave for three more days—as Victory in Europe was triumphantly announced. The Germans had surrendered unconditionally and the city erupted in joyeous celebrations. Every street overflowed with masses of people. Church bells pealed nonstop. Ralph and Sandy found themselves caught up in the crowds filling Trafalgar Square, the Mall, and Whitehall. Although massive, it was for the most part a well-disciplined multitude that gathered to celebrate the end of the British Empire's finest hour.

Civilians and servicemen and women alike sang and cheered, waving Union Jacks and the Stars and Stripes high above their heads. A few undaunted taxi drivers attempted to thread their way at a snail's pace through the mobs. In every direction, smiling and laughing people thronged into the streets. People on rooftops were hugging and kissing, waving their flags and hats, while sending streamers down upon the gatherings below.

Some went to extremes. Beside the statue of Charles I, a young woman, hardly out of her teens, removed her underpanties and hoisted her skirt above her waist, gyrating and showing off her private parts. However, she scampered away and was soon lost in the howling crowd.

Ralph and Sandy were swept along under Admiralty Arch and down the Mall, until they managed to climb the steps by Carleton House where they eventually ended up at the Haymarket Club, a preserve for Canadian officers on leave. The club was packed with fellow countrymen celebrating, vying to buy each other drinks.

As Ralph made his way to the bar, a loud and hearty voice hailed him, and when he turned to see who had called out, he spotted his old friend, Padre Rusty Wilkes from the RCR.

"Who's that sober sawbones trailing along behind you?" Rusty shouted. "Come this way, we've found a table in the corner. Strome Galloway is protecting it with his life."

Ralph laughed, "Why Rusty, you old scalawag. I thought you had left for home already. I heard you were nominated to run in the Ontario provincial election. Do the people for Kenora–Rainy River know what they might be letting themselves in for? Those Progressive Conservative Party members must be shy of good men back home to call you out!"

"Jealousy will get you nowhere, Ralph. Get over here and let me shake your hand. You, too, Sandy!"

With drinks held high, they made their way across the crowded room to where Strome was arguing loudly with a Patricia officer who was attempting to make away with one of the chairs.

"Get your hairy hands off that piece of furniture. It has been posted to the RCR," he bellowed. Strome was known to raise his voice when the occasion merited it.

Before the stakes were raised any higher, the three friends arrived at the table and the party began in earnest.

Ralph told Rusty about the near-naked nymph they had seen earlier. Wilkes replied. "Hell, that's nothing, I've seen worse than that," and the stories began.

At the next table, another group roared in a vain attempt to keep their conversation above the noise of the crowd. Ralph noticed an officer wearing collar badges in the shape of a kangaroo. Taking him for an Australian, he slapped him on the back, and welcomed him as a fellow colonial to the "Canadian Officers' Club." In reaction, the officer advised Ralph that he was not only a fellow Canadian, but the commanding officer of a newly formed unit of armoured personnel carriers, originally given the code name "Kangaroos." The name stuck and the CO was proudly displaying the newly designed regimental badges on his lapel for the first time.

A little later the four men left the club and made their way down Whitehall. They were just in time to see Prime Minister Winston Churchill and two of his cabinet ministers on the balcony of a government building, far above the crowd. Churchill spoke briefly, ending his remarks with "Advance Britannia!" The masses screamed their voices hoarse. Then, a bugler from the Brigade of Guards appeared, and as a ceremonial gesture sounded the high shrill notes of the "Cease Fire." Europe's war was over.

The foursome continued along the Mall toward Buckingham Palace. The day had gone quickly, and evening was descending on a city that was about to light up again after six years of blackouts. The song, "I'm Going to Get Lit Up When the Lights Go On Again," was heard from many groups in varying degrees of inebriation. Indeed, many of them were already "lit up."

In the park along the Mall, there were eager lovers, oblivious to the multitude around them, moaning and groaning, throwing caution to the wind.

"See what I mean about not seeing anything yet?" said Rusty.

At the gates of Buckingham Palace, the four companions joined with the crowd in singing, "God Save the King," "Rule Britannia," and "Land of Hope and Glory." Soon the lights came on and a chant went up from thousands of throats, "We want the king! We want the king! We want the king!"

The palace's balcony doors opened, and their majesties came out accompanied by the two princesses, Elizabeth in her khaki ATS uniform and Margaret Rose. The king and queen acknowledged the cheering masses standing as far as one could see. The royal party withdrew, but was called back several times by the chant, "We want the king!"

There was no question that celebrations would outlast the night, but Ralph explained to the others that he wanted to get home and share some of this momentous day with Erin. Although ruing his departure, they understood, and bade him a fond farewell as they headed back to the Haymarket Club.

It had been a great day—for saint and sinner alike.

Unbelievably, the trains were still running, although not necessarily on time. Ralph arrived home about nine o'clock to find the children abed sleeping and Erin with a bottle of champagne on ice awaiting his return.

"Well, I hope you are still able to help me celebrate, too!" Erin beamed. "By the way, thank you for the phone call . . . I would have worried had I not known you were in such good hands!"

Ralph reached for his wife. "That I was, love. Now let's you and me celebrate the rest of the night together in each other's arms!"

The war was over and the celebrations were continued. Soldiers, sailors and airmen were beginning to talk about returning home—some more eagerly than others.

Within a month, Ralph received orders for his repatriation. He was given duty as the ship's conducting chaplain aboard the *Aquitania,* a grand old ship of the Cunard Line that had served in both world wars in several capacities: as hospital ship, troop ship, and transport for war brides. She displaced 45,647 tons and stretched 910 feet in length. It came as a bonus that he could bring his family at the same time. Many of the war brides and children had to wait months before they could obtain transportation to Canada, their men having preceded them.

A system of rotation was devised on a point basis that allowed those who had been over the longest to return first, the wounded receiving top priority. In July, the *Aquitania* docked in Southampton, embarking troops and war brides with children for passage to Halifax. Her former luxury appointments had been stripped away to accommodate a maximum number, every nook and cranny used to provide sleeping space. The cabins were crowded with tiered bunks; troops were quartered below decks, while the women and children were given the relatively more comfortable lodgings on the higher decks. Every means was employed to keep the men and the women separate. It was taboo to mix.

Stuart de Clerk, the Vicar of St. Tristan's, drove Ralph and his family to Southampton. He promised to send Erin's heavy belongings at a later date when shipping space became available. It was an emotional departure for her. She was leaving her homeland in exchange for life in Canada, but she had no regrets. It was the tug of memories that held her fast at quayside. Her husband put his arms around her and pressed his face to hers.

"We will return someday, never fear, but now a new chapter begins in our lives, and we will face it together."

He turned her toward the gangway. Her tears ceased as she said goodbye to Stuart.

Nearby, a tearful separation was taking place. Thomas Smith, the greengrocer in Bewdleigh, was saying farewell to his twenty-one-year-old daughter, Irene. She had married Private Joe Brash of the NCHR days prior to the regiment's departure for Sicily. Joe had been wounded in Italy and had returned to Canada earlier in the year. It was a particularly difficult parting for father and daughter, as Smith's wife had passed away three months before.

"Promise to write me regularly, Irene." The normally gruff man had tears in his eyes as he hugged his daughter in a tight embrace.

"I will, Daddy, every day. You write, too."

"I will. I will!"

"Look, Irene, there's Mrs. Russell over there, the padre's wife. She must be going too!"

The Smiths had attended St. Tristan's, and the vicar and his family shopped at his store. Irene waved and Erin responded by walking over to where the pair stood.

"You must be coming with us, too, Irene. It will be nice to travel together. We can keep each other company," offered Erin, kindly.

"That would be grand, Mrs. Russell," declared Mr. Smith. "You'll take care of my girl, won't you?"

"Of course I will, Mr. Smith. You can count on me. Now, I must get aboard. I see my husband is having a difficult time with the children.

Michael is absolutely beside himself. Irene, when you get settled, come see me."

Irene responded, "I will and thank you. Daddy will feel better knowing I'm with someone he knows."

Erin rejoined Ralph and took her wildly excited children in each hand and proceeded up the gangway.

Michael was all eyes as he took everything in. His mind was like a sponge, and he fired questions at Ralph concerning the ship and its workings. Miriam was quiet. She sensed her mother's mood and didn't know quite what to make of it.

"Mummy sad?" she asked.

"I will be fine," Erin replied. "It's just that we are going far away."

"It's all right, Mummy, I'll be with you."

"That's right, darling, as long as we are all together, everything will be grand. Look how excited Mikey is! I bet he'll keep Daddy busy with his questions."

At the moment, this was not to be, for Ralph turned to his duties as soon as he boarded the ship. He was immediately caught up in counselling war brides who seemed unable to manage their new circumstances. Many were exhausted trying to control fractious children. The Red Cross escorts in attendance were few in numbers and overburdened with work—and this was just the beginning. The medical staff on board cared for the sick and disabled, but they, too, had their hands full, as many women and children felt unsettled as soon as they came aboard, a psychological prelude to seasickness. There were four women to each cabin, two of whom had babies. The childless women took the two top bunks, and a mother with her child occupied the lower area. Each cabin had a toilet. As the passengers began to settle in, those women that were not ill-disposed pitched in to help alleviate the discomfort of the others, Erin among them.

She had spoken first to Ralph expressing her concern.

"But you have your own little ones to contend with," he replied.

"That's no problem. Irene Brash has attached herself to us and already the children adore her. She's prepared to act as a nanny for them."

"You could become heavily involved. Are you sure you want to do this?" asked Ralph.

"I think I can be of assistance, and I would dearly like to help."

"I'll talk with the Red Cross staff. Maybe you could help them for a few hours each day."

It was arranged, and Erin was welcomed to the group. She shortly found her niche as a caring listener for despondent women. Once a day, she would wander through the decks, and when she found someone looking overwhelmed, she would find a way to sound her out.

The deck space sometimes became fetid alleyways with the smell of vomit and dirty diapers. Portholes had been welded shut for wartime passages and the air circulation on board was minimal. Mothers rinsed the diapers as best they could and hung them wherever they found a spot suitable. It was a challenge for the best of stomachs, and many women floundered helplessly in the stench of it all. The cabin crew also did their best to clean things up, but this became a daunting task. It was a depressing scene, and Erin expressed her views, not only to the Red Cross team, who were well aware of the situation, but also to Ralph, who was powerless to assist. He spoke to the captain, but that only brought additional pressure on the crew members, who were undermanned for such onerous duties. Erin's "couple of hours a day" soon became eight or ten.

"Not much of a holiday for you, old girl," said Ralph one evening as they slipped into their bunk, tired beyond belief.

"At least we are halfway across. I am weary, but feel like I have contributed something to those who don't have a hubby to snuggle up to at night," she sighed as she fell soundly asleep.

The meals aboard ship were a revelation to the passengers. For the first time in years they ate white bread and fruit. One of them took two buns below to a friend who was unable to eat, just so she could admire them.

For the most part the crossing was over calm waters, and spirits began to lift as they neared Canada. Most talk centred on their expectations. Many, however would be disappointed when they learned reality paled somewhat in comparison to the rosy pictures their husbands had painted. In fact, a few of the women thought the streets of Toronto and Winnipeg were paved with gold. Some had been told of the large, prosperous farms their husbands had left, only to find later that many of them were rocky scrub land, marginally farmable at best. A number would experience outhouses for the first time and no electricity or running water in the dwelling. For the city girls this would come as a real shock. But at the moment, there was great excitement and most of these women, who had been deprived of so much, would later face the conditions with the grit and fortitude that had seen them through the war.

On the eleventh day at sea, the coastline of Canada appeared on the horizon. Outer decks were crowded to capacity for the first view. Again, excitement escalated, and very few retired early as the ship neared the shore. The *Aquitania* arrived at Pier 21 in Halifax harbour in the wee hours of the morning, and the dining areas were quickly crowded for breakfast with people anxious to disembark. In only a few cases were passengers expecting to be met at dockside; others lined up to board nearby trains that would carry the majority to distant locations in Canada. Most had no concept of the country's vastness, and one girl, travelling to British Columbia, was stunned to learn that her journey would take another five days.

"Why," she proclaimed, "we can go the entire length of England and Scotland in one day—and that's a long way!"

It was a grey, overcast day in Nova Scotia. Halifax harbour was misty and drab-looking with naval ships in wartime dress adding to the gloom. Ralph had found a semi-sheltered location for Erin and the children to watch the shipside activities. The Russells would be one of the last families to disembark, as Ralph's duties kept him on board until the final passenger was put ashore.

Michael was excitedly taking in all the hustle and bustle along the quay. He danced and clapped his hands, pointing this way and that, as the ant-like movement criss-crossed below him. Across the harbour, a tug sounded its whistle as it edged an American destroyer into the outer harbour in preparation for a sea voyage. Michael ran to the rail and waved wildly at the sailors strung out along the warship's deck. Erin was wistful as she rocked Miriam in her arms. The child was becoming listless after so many days of confinement.

"It will be so good to get ashore where we can really stretch our legs," said Erin, as Ralph joined them in late afternoon.

"I'll second that motion," he replied. "In fact, we'll be leaving the ship shortly. The Movements people are arranging a hotel room for us and we will catch the westbound train in the morning."

"You must be tired, darling. It's been a long haul for you this last while, especially with all those calls at night!"

Ralph answered. "Ah, the twenty-four-seven life of a duty chaplain. One gets used to it. Actually, it's pretty tame compared to some of the days and nights in battle."

"Thank God those days are behind you. Soon you'll have to get used to being a civilian again. Will you find that a rough patch?" she asked.

"Time will tell." Ralph paused. "I have hesitated to tell you that the principal chaplain wants to know if I would be interested in staying in the service after the war. I wanted to give it a lot of thought before broaching the subject with you. What do you think?"

Erin gave him a sideways glance. "You'll have to give me more information before I can answer that one. What would your duties be in a peacetime army?"

Ralph grinned and said, "That's a good question. I'm to report to Ottawa after my disembarkation leave for a full briefing, then we can make our decision. But first, I want to get you home to meet my parents. They are dying to meet you, and no doubt eager to spoil the children. And wait till you meet Ernest . . ."

For Ralph and his family, the conflict was over. His journey into war had lasted four years and nine months. How the world had changed. How he had changed. And he stepped ashore with many mixed feelings—both happy to be back in Canada and sad to leave so many comrades buried abroad. He saw the light of excitement in Erin's eyes and watched as the children skipped ahead. The dark days were past. Now, was a time for new beginnings.

Author's Note

While many characters in this novel are fictitious, the events and circumstances are real. During World War II, 465 Protestant chaplains served in the Canadian Armed Forces; nine of these were killed in action and many others were wounded—several taken as prisoners of war. Eighty-six chaplains were granted military awards and honours ranging from the highest recognition, the Victoria Cross, down through the various medals conferred. Commanders at all levels recognized the role of the chaplain as indispensable, most notably, Field Marshall Montgomery, who did in fact say,"I'd rather have my chaplains with me in battle, rather than my artillery."

I owe a great deal of thanks to the several readers who were kind enough to scan the manuscript as the chapters were written. In particular, I recognize Colonel Strome Galloway, The Royal Canadian Regiment (RCR), Sometime Colonel of the Regiment, for his contribution in keeping the story within the historical fact. Many of the battle scenes in the novel were developed from his own experiences in Sicily and Italy, as well as his descriptions of events that he witnessed in London on VE Day. Unfortunately, he did not live to see *In This Sign* published.

My appreciation also goes out to Brigadier General Gerry Peddle, former Chaplain General to the Canadian Forces, and Major Bruce Sweet for their input from the chaplaincy perspective. My daughter Darlene Blakeley, an editor in her own right, gave me many insights into the use of correct grammar and punctuation, and Susan Code McDougall, senior editor at General Store Publishing House, worked patiently in the preparation of the final draft. Many others contributed in helpful ways, especially my wife Wineita as my first line reader and Colonel Michael Barr who supplied me with references from his library. The Canadian Chaplain Service Badge and the Chaplain's Motto are used courtesy of the Canadian Department of National Defence.